MW01064346

Legend of the Coltstone Keep

Legend of the Coltstone Keep

Lisa J. Lusby

Copyright © 2011 by Lisa J. Lusby.

Library of Congress Control Number: 2010918844
ISBN: Hardcover 978-1-4568-3654-2
Softcover 978-1-4568-3653-5
Ebook 978-1-4568-3655-9

All rights reserved. No part of this book may be reproduced or transmitted in any form or by any means, electronic or mechanical, including photocopying, recording, or by any information storage and retrieval system, without permission in writing from the copyright owner.

This is a work of fiction. Names, characters, places and incidents either are the product of the author's imagination or are used fictitiously, and any resemblance to any actual persons, living or dead, events, or locales is entirely coincidental.

This book was printed in the United States of America.

To order additional copies of this book, contact:
Xlibris Corporation
1-888-795-4274
www.Xlibris.com
Orders@Xlibris.com
90911

CONTENTS

1. A Letter 7
2. Uncle Sidney's Estate 12
3. The Coltstone Fate 30
4. Goings and Comings 35
5. Dispossessed 51
6. Revelations 57
7. Coming to Terms 72
8. Sanctuaries and Tower Turrets 79
9. Something New . . . Something Old 86
10. An Arrow, a Gypsy, and the Ruins 100
11. Kingston College—or a Maiden in Distress 105
12. The Baron's Treasures 115
13. Of Gypsy Spells 122
14. London 127
15. The Hart Flies Home 136
16. What the Gypsy Knew 141
17. A Turning of Fate 150
18. Ships That Sail 156
19. Leticia 166
20. Guest of the House 171
21. Fairy Towers on a Hill 180
22. At the Shoals of the Gulforth 189
23. The Whole Truth 199
24. Announcing the Banns 205
25. Brigands on the Border 216
26. Under the Sword 229
27. Home Again 234
28. A Letter from the Past 245

A LETTER

Ellen Lancaster shoved a sheaf of graded term papers across the desk and slid the grade book into the drawer before leaning back in her chair with a stretch and a deep sigh. The evening was growing late, and soon, the night-class students would enliven the quiet hallway beyond the door. Outside, lampposts flickered on in the dusk beneath the tall oak trees that bordered the winding sidewalks. Ellen gazed absently through the old double-sash windowpanes, drinking in the calm quiet of early evening. The window was open just a crack, and she basked in the cool breeze laden with the scent of spring blossoms.

Springtime in Texas, she mused as she smiled whimsically. The students' minds were obviously not upon their studies. The stacks of graded papers on her desk were witness enough of that. Thoughtfully, Ellen reached across the letter holder to her cup of blackberry tea; and taking a sip of the tangy brew, she pulled a long thin cream-colored envelope from the holder. It was addressed to her from a small village half a world away. She read the letter again, considering its words and its author.

My dear niece, Ellen Lancaster, April 16, 1963

I write you after these many long years, hoping this finds you well, and still the young lady I once enjoyed common thoughts with. I have not seen you in several years, nor written in as many more. For this I hold regret.

The cold and damp of England have taken their toll of me and I write to you in extremity of poor health. It is my request that you travel here upon the completion of your semester for a final visit. There are matters of estate and family that I long to discuss with you while I am able.

Sincerely
Sidney Lancaster,
Derbyshire, England

Uncle Sidney. Tall, eccentric, and once-wealthy Uncle Sidney. A bachelor all his life, he'd never been comfortable around women, though he liked his young niece, Ellen, well enough. They both enjoyed horses and horsemanship, a topic to bridge many social difficulties. He'd made his more-than-tidy fortune in government contract manufacturing during the war. After two generations of family had happily Americanized, leaving the trappings of the old world behind, Uncle Sidney had left Texas and the West Texas land and cattle to Ellen's father and returned to England.

An elderly maiden aunt had offered him title to her estate upon her death. He had journeyed there—to England—ten years ago. He had liked the countryside's ancient landmarks, the evidence of his family's heritage there, and he had remained.

Ellen had heard from him only once since he'd left: he had sent a letter, brief, but heartfelt, upon her father's death. Now fingering this letter thoughtfully, Ellen considered her uncle and thought that it would be good to see him again: so few of their family remained. She thought of the trip, of England, of the prospect of cold, drizzly green summer days . . . Texas could be so hot and so dry in the summer.

Sliding the letter back into the envelope, she placed it in the leather satchel and slung the satchel over her shoulder as she strode from the office. As she walked to the entrance doors that were propped open in the cool of evening, several students greeted her with friendly gestures and self-conscious smiles. Ellen, a professor of Old World European history, taught a wide variety of courses and was well-known among the students. Watching the college girls sway past in their miniskirts and go-go boots, Ellen smiled. She always thought it ironic that in a society that accepted much and which had coined the phrase "anything goes," she was considered *different*.

She was tall—taller than most—angular, and simply pretty in a way that some would consider plain. She wore a brown riding skirt, boots, and a linen shirt. Her hair, glossy straight and dark brown, was pulled back from a widow's peak into a tight band . . . without a bow.

As she walked past the fountain circle gardens where the brick paths branched artistically around the front of the University's impressive Old Main building, Ellen smiled to herself. The young couples seated on benches under the trees were pretending to study or philosophize, but they were sitting too close to effectively do either.

Ellen smiled and remembered a boy back in high school, a basketball player that she had once taken a fancy to. They had dated, but he was all basketball and muscle cars; and she . . . well, she was in love with her books and her horses. She was a country girl, and she enjoyed her weekends riding the ranch pastures with her father and evenings reading Shakespeare while her mother played piano in the parlor.

And she had wanted to do other things with her life: she'd planned to go to college and have her own place and her own job. Still, there were times when she wondered how her life might have been had she chosen to stay in her home town with her high school sweetheart and to have had a family instead of a career.

She loved teaching in the university where so many eager, energetic students shared her passion for learning, but it could seem a lonely trade sometimes, especially in springtime, when the blue bonnets and Indian paintbrush were blooming in the fields under the live oak trees.

Reaching the faculty parking lot at the edge of campus, Ellen walked to her battered Chevy truck and opened its door to the accompanying screeches of the rusty old hinges. She grimaced: it always sounded as if the old thing was complaining. Throwing her leather satchel across to the passenger side she slid in behind the wheel, banged the door shut, cranked the window down, and thumped the lock down with her elbow . . . the door latch was worn and prone to opening without warning.

At the outskirts of town, she turned from the pavement onto a half mile of dirt road that led to the small farmstead that was her home: the white framed house nestling in a cluster of trees surrounded by gardens and backed by a barn and horse paddock.

Ellen was the only child of a late marriage, had grown up on a ranch in West Texas, and loved her private space. She loved her vegetable garden in the sunny space just beyond the live oak trees, her rosebushes from her mom's garden growing beside the porch, her peach orchard just out behind the house. And she enjoyed her cup of tea in the old porch rocker every evening, though that was invariably when she thought about her family most and the quiet memories made her both happy and lonely.

Her mother had died five years ago at the age of seventy, and after her mother's death, her dad had sold the ranch and come to live here with her. They had enjoyed two delightful years of comfortable companionship before he had fallen ill. He'd died almost a year ago, in the cool of the early March rains, and she still missed him terribly.

Ellen parked the truck in the gravel drive that ended beside the picket fence, and walked up the brick path to the front porch. Throwing the leather satchel onto the seat of the old porch rocker, she walked out to the barn as the last glow of sunset settled in rose and teal on the horizon. The tall sorrel in his open stall whinnied when he heard the rattle of the barn door latch and dipped his head over the stall door to watch Ellen stride down the stable run with his feed bucket in her hand. Dumping the bran mash into the sorrel's trough, Ellen smiled and stroked the sleek neck as he flicked his ears toward her and munched the grain. Tomorrow was Saturday; and they would ride the tracts through the fields beside the city golf course, take a lunch, and enjoy the blue bonnets beside the river.

Ellen stacked hay into the sorrel's manger and stood a moment in the quiet, companionable warmth of the barn before she walked back to the house and entered its dusky quietness.

She propped the satchel on the small oak table in the kitchen, pulled a pot of leftover roast and gravy from the refrigerator, and set it on the stove to warm. Roast, potatoes, and gravy with cooked carrots—it was a meal her dad had always liked, and her mom had cooked it often.

She remembered how they used to walk hand in hand along the dirt track from the hay field to the old ranch house in the cool of summer evenings. They would sit in the old porch rockers after lunch on hot summer days and watch chickens peck around in the yard and dust devils wander across the dry pastures. They always rode together at roundup and they sang when they worked together in the kitchen.

She shook her head bemusedly, thinking that it couldn't be just chance that brought people together like that, and she doubted it would ever happen for her. She laughed to herself as she set the plate of left-overs on the table and thought to herself that most of the men her age seemed very much like the popular skirts: short and double knit, (more so in thought than in stature.)

Double knit, polyester, and plastic, Ellen mused. *A whole new world might be built of it, and, while it might not rot, in her opinion it would never compare to the beautiful wood and leather of the past ages.* Sitting at the old oak table, Ellen pulled a pen and piece of paper from her satchel and penned a letter, warmly polite, to her uncle. She would travel to England that May and stay with him until early June.

Sealing the letter in an envelope, Ellen sat for a moment in thought. She would board the sorrel at a stable in Austin. The elderly neighbor whose property joined hers would watch over her place and water the young plants in her garden. She was not teaching during the summer term, so arrangements to be absent for a month could be made easily. England, she thought with anticipation, would be a nice diversion, a mild adventure, a break from her everyday life, and she speculated that she could return with new energy and enthusiasm for the fall term.

UNCLE SIDNEY'S ESTATE

Stepping down to the station platform as the train's brakes steamed and hissed, Ellen looked at the scene around her with quiet pleasure. She had arrived in London's Gatwick Airport the day before and, although the bustle of the foreign city was intriguing and its architecture and antiquity of great interest, she much preferred the placid English countryside with its soft rolling hills of green, the quiet folk, and the humble streets of the small villages.

Briarwick was a typical township of old stone shops and cottages. Its two cobblestone streets met at a crossroads at its center, and the few cars in sight were interspersed with pony carts and bicycles. People on foot carried cloth-draped market baskets and were often tailed by a faithful dog.

Ellen's breathe smoked in the cool, crisp air as she stretched and sighed deeply, still feeling weary from the transatlantic time change. Buttoning her coat against the chill damp air, she glanced at the ragged clouds and wondered if the sun ever shone warm at these latitudes. Her travel case was accompanied by only one other on the baggage cart just wheeled from the train, and she surmised that few travelers stopped here in Briarwick, and that the tourists most often came by car.

Watching the bicycle and pedestrian traffic, Ellen wondered how she was to travel from the depot to her uncle's home and was therefore relieved and surprised when an elderly man of shy demeanor and pleasant smile stopped at her elbow.

"Are you Ms. Ellen Lancaster?" he asked, hat in hand. His accent was a thick Yorkshire brogue, and his sidelong glance was disarming. , "Thought ye might be," he continued at her nod of assent. "Old Darvin up to the manor said you'd be arriving today and would need a lift . . ."

"I would certainly appreciate one," she replied. "I didn't think about it that the town wouldn't have a taxi."

"Taxi," laughed the old man. "No, ma'am. We've no need of such like as that." Grasping her travel case, he led her to a squatty little black sedan of '40s vintage and motioned her inside.

Sitting on the scratchy horsehair seat covers, Ellen watched in amusement as the old fellow went through a complex series of gyrations to start the engine. It roared to life finally in a cloud of blue smoke and, with more noise than power, eased off down the town's main thoroughfare and out onto the country track. Ellen watched the countryside slide past with keen interest, unaware of the old man's studying gaze in the rearview mirror.

"Is Coltstone far from here, Mr . . . . ?"

"Culpepper, miss. Andis Culpepper," he supplied.

"Yes, Mr. Culpepper. Have we far to go?"

"No, miss. It's no but four miles across the barrows . . . five by the road."

Not far from the edge of the village, they passed a stone edifice of Norman architecture.

"Is that the church?" asked Ellen.

"Yes, ma'am," Andis replied.

Ellen watched as it passed by her window: a massive stone structure with two towers in the fore and tall arches above the doors. The peaked slate roof towered high above flying buttresses, and stone gargoyles scowled down from the spouts of the guttering. A dreary cemetery bounded by a stone wall, its markers tilted and moss grown, separated the church building from a parsonage that appeared only slightly younger than the church. A man she assumed to be the priest was working a plot of garden beside the grey cottage.

The countryside unfolded around them, rolling and green with fertile fields bounded by stone walls and thin tree lines, and ahead a copse of wood cloaked a knoll upon which stood what Ellen assumed was Uncle Sydney's castle—its square towers, all that could be seen above the ancient wood.

"That's the place?" asked Ellen, looking ahead through the smudged windshield.

"Yes, ma'am. Called the Garrison Keep. Older'n Moses. Built in 1340 by the Coltstones. Wonder it's still livable."

"And that's the Coltstone Keep?" she queried, looking beyond the wood to the rising ground some miles distant where a great stone edifice crowned the ridge crest, its gardens and grounds sloping down to a river and a tranquil lake.

Culpepper smiled. "Yes, ma'am. The old Coltstone Keep, yer uncle's place, and the ruins over toward Sheffield town are all that's left of the Coltstone family's estate."

"It all looks different than I expected," Ellen mused aloud. Histories in books, old photos, and drawings could never do justice to the vivid panorama of life.

Culpepper laughed. "You, Miss, look different than we expected."

To her queried look, he seemed embarrassed. "Well, you know, miss. We heard you were a big professor at some American university. Figured you'd be like so many of that crowd nowadays . . ."

Ellen laughed, thinking of the hip crowd in the streets of London. "No, never held much with that kind of thing," she answered.

"That's good, Miss. Folks round here been more than a little concerned about that."

"And how do you know so much about me?" she asked him.

"Aw, well now. Old Darvin Sutter, what works for your uncle up at the Garrison, he likes a pint now and then at the Bowl & Pitcher. He brings us all the news of how the old man, yer uncle, is getting along. Yer pardon, Miss, but in a village the size of Briarwick, your own business is yer neighbor's business. Things affects us all. You're probably not used to that where you come from . . ."

"Oh, but I am." Ellen smiled. "Out west, the land is big, but the towns are small, and everyone knows everyone else's business."

"That's good," said Culpepper. "You'll feel right at home here, then." He turned through the tall gates of a lane leading down through the forest of great trees.

Ellen appreciated his words of assurance and hoped she would feel at home here but was not so certain when the great stone fortress came into view through the trees. Grey stones, draped in ivy, rose in four great towers bounding the crenelated walls of the castle and the vast entry courtyard. As the car slowed to a stop with a squeal of worn brakes, an old man in the worn livery of a servant stepped through a small portal in the tall wooden doors of the ancient Keep.

"That's Darvin," said Culpepper as Ellen stepped from the car and gazed in awe at the castle and its ancient gardens and grounds. It all seemed a bit unkempt and run down. The gardens were overgrown, loose slates had fallen from the Great Hall roof, chimneys tilted drunkenly, and rotting wood crumbled on the lintels. But still, the whole impression of massive stone and venerable age was overwhelming.

Darvin greeted her with a slight bow and shook Culpepper's hand as he lifted Ellen's travel case. As Andis Culpepper drove away with one last backward glance, the old servant, Darvin, smiled a warm wrinkled welcome and led her into the castle Keep through the portal door.

Ellen surveyed the castle Close for a moment as Darvin ambled across its confines. She felt like she was at the bottom of a well with the walls rising high all around the enclosure—one side forming the parapet of the outer wall of the Keep, the other, the curving wall of the castle proper from which narrow windows peered down oppressively. Ellen figured the intention of the architect was to intimidate any—friend or foe—who ventured into such a vulnerable position, and the architect, she thought, had been quite successful.

Crossing the great stone pavers to the iron-bound double doors where Darvin awaited her, she stepped into the arched stone entry—again, a fortifying ingenuity as it was set five steps lower than the main castle hall, and those steps were of wood. Ornately carved and burnished smooth with wear, they yet stood witness to the harsh reality of their time. Any invader should find himself fighting his way upward, over a burning wooden pier, should he try to breach the Keep's defenses. The prospect drew a smile of grim respect from Ellen; the fears and defenses of her time, though formidable, were never so ever present as to be a fixture of the home. She felt pampered.

The main hall of the castle was a long room, arched over and shaped like a barrel. They entered at its middle, with doorways to the other wings and stairs to cellars below and towers above opening from the back wall and far ends. As castles go, Ellen was to find, this one was a small fortress of medieval design and little comfort. It had been modified and additions built by more recent occupants to make its lower story comfortable; but the cellars, towers, and upper story had been left in their original design, except where repair was necessary. Ellen felt keen to explore as Darvin led her through the Great Hall with its sparse, dusty furnishings; great fireplace; and narrow, deep-set windows. Through a door at the far end, they entered a corridor of which several doors gave hint of mysterious rooms beyond; but they had traversed its length before Darvin, setting her travel case carefully on the floor, motioned her through an open door into what Ellen surmised were the modernized quarters of the castle.

The old castle scullery had been renovated into a kitchen where the range, refrigerator, and glass front cabinets were incongruently framed in grey stone and timber. Two large rooms had been converted into libraries where towering shelves bore volumes of reference books, histories and artifacts of antiquity. The old living quarters were redesigned to form a sitting room bright with sunlight from a bank of floor-to-ceiling lead glass windows and two private rooms each joined by a water closet.

Ellen was shown into the sunlit sitting room, where her uncle awaited her with the anticipation of an elderly man: lonely, dying, and longing for that rare companionship that only comes from kinship.

Uncle Sidney rose stiffly from his chair and his smile, open and warm, was so very much like her father's. Ellen crossed the room to him; and they hugged, smiled, and laughed in greeting.

"Ellen, my dear girl!" He beamed, grasping her hand in his with a grip that belied his age. "How was your flight?"

"Fine, Uncle."

"Aw, when I crossed, it was on a steamer . . . all this newfangled stuff," he dismissed with a wave of his hand. He saw her eyeing the canister at his side and the clear thin tubing that ran from the oxygen tank to his nose, held there with a thin band.

"Funny lookin', ain't it?" He smiled.

"When you wrote . . . you mentioned you weren't doing too well," Ellen said self-consciously. "I didn't know . . ."

"Aw." He laughed. "This is nothin'. Doctors won't let me smoke my pipe anymore—now that's a poor plight."

"Uncle!" Ellen mock scolded.

"Well, why can't they let an old man have a few vices?" he rejoined.

"Because it's your vices that are killing you, Uncle," Ellen chided.

"Naw, it's not this that'll kill me," he said, motioning toward the tank. "It's not easy, but it's not what's gonna get me. It's the old ticker that's given out. They don't say it, but I know . . ."

Ellen noted the blue tinge to his face and bruised look of his hand on hers.

"Now enough of this talk," he said. "Take a seat there, and tell me all about my favorite state of America. Ten years' worth of news please."

"Where should I start?" Ellen laughed.

"Anywhere! My land, but it's good to hear a true Texas drawl again. Just keep talking!"

Ellen laughed. "I don't think half the people I've spoken to here have understood a word of what I said."

"Probably not. Too many 'yups' and 'y'alls,' but I like it. Now, tell me all that's to know—what have you been doin' lately?

And beginning just shy of ten years past and prompted by her uncle's interested queries, Ellen rambled on for over an hour about all the goings-on of the family, the ranch, and her work with the university.

"I'm proud of you," he said at last. "Yer true to yer upbringing . . . as you should be. Though I'm afraid yer as independent as a hog on ice—like all the Lancasters."

"And as adventuresome too, I hope," she quipped.

"And as resourceful," he added, nodding sagely.

"And humble," she finished as they both laughed.

"Yes, yes, we are of fine stock, for sure. Shame we're the last of them . . ."

"Yeah," sighed Ellen. "I hope we find a better end than old Rastus . . ."

Uncle Sidney joined in her mirth in remembrance of his brother's favorite mustang-bred cow pony. The canny animal had lived to be thirty years of age before he was struck by lightning in a West Texas thunderstorm and then ignominiously eaten up by the local band of coyotes.

"Yes, let us hope . . . ," agreed Uncle Sidney. "Do you still ride as you once did, Ellen?" he asked.

Ellen warmed readily to the new topic. "Of course," she quipped. "I have a great big sorrel named Jack. You'd like him. Smooth as butter and jumps like a rabbit. Third level dressage . . . or close anyway." She smiled proudly.

"Aw," sighed Uncle Sidney. "I kept some several horses in my stable until a few years ago. Couldn't ride anymore." His face dimmed sadly. "So I sold them. I lease the pastures yonder." He motioned to a sunny green space beyond the trees, and Ellen followed his gaze through the sunlit windows to the fields she could dimly see beyond the forest's gloom.

"The fields border the Coltstone Keep estates," he continued. "That old place went to the state some fifty years ago—nearly fell down before they got the notion to open it up for tourists. Lots of folk go there to gawk. They opened a riding stable several years ago—renting horses for visitors to ride on the bridle paths around the estate grounds. Quite popular, I suppose. Anyway, I let them turn some of their horses into my fields for pasturage."

He paused and looked at her, considering. "I figured you'd not be at home without a horse to ride, so I asked them to loan me one while you're here. Nice little filly . . . feisty . . . needs a bit of edge taken off. You'll make her look good."

"Oh, Uncle, I didn't even bring a helmet along."

"You don't need it."

"Or a saddle . . ."

"Got one."

And she finally accepted with a smile.

"I'll show you the stables tomorrow . . . Oh, I can make it that far," he groused at her doubtful look. "But I am tired now, and you must be too after your trip . . ." At her nod, he waved his hand toward the door. "Pick any room you want. The ones downstairs have heat and water and electricity, but make yourself at home. You're welcome to the whole place."

Ellen voiced her gratitude, but he waved it off surreptitiously. "Yer family, girl," he said. "Just act like it, and treat the place like yer own."

"All right," she said, rising. "What about dinner? Do you have a cook too?" she teased.

"Nope, had to let her go. Just keep Darvin part time—till I'm gone. I do fer myself . . ."

"Well, I'll do the cooking, then," Ellen volunteered. "And the laundry and cleaning, if you'll trust your woolens to me."

"Don't use hot," was all he said, and she knew he was quite willing to turn the work over to her.

"Well, then," she sighed and stretched, "I think I'll take a nap and freshen up. Dinner at seven?"

Uncle Sidney nodded and smiled as he leaned his head back in his chair and closed his eyes.

He looked so very worn and ill, Ellen thought as she picked her case up at the doorway and headed off up the hall to explore and find a room for herself.

After finding the kitchen, a pantry, a library, and Uncle Sidney's quarters by mistake, she at last opened a doorway into a private room that was much to her liking. The bed was a Renaissance half tester with tall springy mattresses under a layer of down comforters and wool blankets. Tall windows draped in green velvet graced the outer wall, an open fireplace dominated the inner wall, and tapestries covered most that remained.

A rose-patterned wool rug warmed the floor, and a painting of horses and hounds at the hunt hung between the great armoire and the heavy wooden door.

An adjoining room boasted a nice old claw-foot bathtub, and although the stone floor was cold, the amenities were pleasant.

Looking forward to the prospect of exploring more on the morrow, Ellen bathed and slept, then enjoyed a pleasant—though meager—meal with her uncle late in the evening. They conversed for some time until her uncle grew tired, bid her good night and stood to leave. At the door of the kitchen he paused and looked back.

"It's not haunted," he said unexpectedly.

"What?"

"The castle . . . It's not haunted. You know, so many of them are."

"Oh, Uncle . . . ," she began, mirth quick upon her lips, but she paused at his serious expression and admonishing finger.

"They are, my girl . . . and for good reason . . . Terrible things used to happen . . ."

He went off to his room mumbling; and Ellen, with a doubtful glance at his retreating back, picked up her cup of tea and walked down the dark hallway to her room. The walls were eerily cast in moon shadow, and the dim light of a single lamp seemed fragile and insignificant. Shaking off the too-keen imaginings her uncle's words had stirred, she prepared for bed, drank her tea in the chair beside the moon-drenched windows, and slid between the soft sheets to sleep soundly through the night.

After a light breakfast the next morning, her uncle insisted that they walk out through the dissipating mists to view the stables and horse yards. Eager for the fresh air, Ellen agreed, walking patiently beside him as he pulled the oxygen bottle along the path between them.

"There," he said when they reached a wooden paling; and leaning upon it, he pointed at the horses grazing in the pasture beyond. "See the black one—white socks in the back? That's her. If you want to ride, she's yours to use."

Ellen gazed in appreciation at the obviously well-bred horses of the small herd. The filly was long legged and graceful. "She's nice," Ellen said, perusing the black. "Thank you for borrowing her for me."

Uncle Sidney smiled his satisfaction. "My pleasure, gal. Love to see you ride her some . . . Now," he said, easing himself down on a stone bench near the stable wall, "go on and look over the stable. Tack room's just inside to the left. I'll wait here."

Ellen looked about the paddocks joining the thick-walled stone stable, noting the ruins of many more stone walls where carriage houses and extensive stable wings used to stand. Only one row of stalls stood in any usable repair, and these were musty and bare from long disuse. Still, the stable with its tall stone walls, open-timbered rafters, and old slate roof was an impressive structure. The center aisle was paved in stone, worn smooth with time and use, and the stalls were dirt floored and wood paneled. A single saddle and bridle hung on the rack in the large tack room and Ellen presumed it was hers to use.

Stepping from the grand empty space where not so much as a fly's buzz was heard, she joined her uncle upon the stone bench; and they sat, silently gazing at the grand beauty of the ancient place. The stone-paved lane—arched over by aged oaks and bordered by shaggy, unkempt gardens—led from the stables to the castle walls, where it skirted around the stone balustrades to the lawns in front of the Keep. The towering grey walls of the castle Keep, ivy bound and formidable, seemed unreal in their fabled antiquity.

"It's beautiful," breathed Ellen.

"I hoped you would like it," said Uncle Sidney.

Ellen twiddled a twig between her fingers. The green of English spring budding on the trees was enchanting. "Uncle," she said, "what did you find here that made you stay?" She'd always thought that he'd only been overly impressed with the grandeur of owning a medieval castle. Now she wondered.

"You don't know?" he said, somewhat troubled. "Look around you."

She did. "It's beautiful . . . ," she said cautiously.

"Beautiful, yes," he admitted. "But more, isn't it? It's . . . ancient . . . It's got roots, deep and alive." He paused, struggling to find words for his meaning. "America, Ellen, it's all young and strong and brash. It's all on the surface still. Strong and adventuresome, but—untried somehow—all cars and billboards and cinema and soda pop.

"Here . . . Ah, well. Here, there's the heart of it, deep and strong. History, Ellen, tried and tempered."

"It seems very tame," said Ellen, thinking of the West Texas she knew and its wild and often savage history.

"Tame?" scoffed Uncle Sidney, and then sobered. "Aye, it seems tame, on the outside. The English countryside—like the people—has had years to be tamed, but there's always something just under the soil. The soul, Ellen. You never really know what will happen here. So much of the past, so much vivid history . . . It can't be covered over with smooth grass and placid words—not all the time."

"You intrigue me."

"I hope I do, gal . . . I hope I do."

At the earnestness of his words, she turned an inquiring gaze to him, "Why?"

"Because I intend to give this place to you." Ignoring her stare of shocked amazement, he continued. "When I die, this estate will pass to you. I hope . . . I believe . . . you will find the same love for it that I do."

"But, Uncle!" Ellen began to protest, thinking of all she had to return to in Texas, of the countless impossibilities of time and cost and change.

Her uncle stopped her protest with an upraised hand. "We'll speak no more of it now. There's time to discuss all this later, you know . . ." He patted her knee. "You run along and explore to your heart's content while I go make myself some strong black coffee."

With a twinkle in his eye at her look of astonishment, he rose stiffly and ambled painfully up the path.

Ellen sat watching him until he was obscured from sight by a curve of the path and the boles of the trees. She looked around her with an eye of new appreciation, trying to encompass all he'd just said, and, deciding it was all too much, she decided to accept his invitation to explore all she wished and think of his weightier words later.

From the stables, she walked through the grounds and gardens, appreciative of the artfully laid walks, statuary and curbed gardens alternately sunlit and shaded in the guardianship of the grove. Entering the castle Keep by the same way that she had the day before, Ellen indulged her curiosity by exploring every corner of the Close, entry and Great Hall. Then leaving the known ground, she climbed the precarious wooden steps of the north tower to the upper reaches of the castle dusty, dank, and unused. Sparsely furnished rooms alternated with those completely barren. Artifacts of ancient times and pieces of furniture too massive to be moved from the old halls peopled the rooms in cobweb-shrouded remembrance. The attic was stuffed full of odd antiquities, a worthy collection and worth something, Ellen surmised, if a market could be found—and if, of course, there was a reason worthy of breaking up such an eclectic collection.

From the highest turret window, Ellen looked away to the north, where the tower tops and roofline of the great Coltstone Keep could be seen rising above the treetops, and further away and obscured by a misty river fog the ruins of the unfinished Coltstone Manor stood. Curious to know the history behind the great house and the reason for the unfinished ruin, she decided to ask her uncle about it or read what she could find on the subject in his library; but that afternoon, when she sat with him in the comfortably furnished room with the tapestries, wool rugs, leather wingbacks, and tall shelves of leather-bound volumes, the conversation followed another path.

"Where do you buy groceries here about, Uncle?" she'd asked.

"Tired of baloney and stale bread?" he laughed.

"Just a bit. Thought you might like some home cooking."

"How 'bout some barbecue brisket and mashed potatoes?" he queried.

"Done! Now how do I find the fixings?"

He told her about the different markets in the town and the weekly farmer's market day where she could find the freshest produce.

"What about mouse bait?" she added.

"They that thick upstairs?"

"No, more downstairs than up. But a few too many, either place."

"Leave it to a woman to come in and wreck the natural ecosystem of a place," Uncle Sidney chided.

"You sound like one of these new conservations, Uncle, but even they aren't so concerned about mice . . . ," she countered.

One hand held up in surrender, he told her where to find mouse bait—and any cleaning supplies she desired. "Ebenezer Grimmel, old gypsy fellow, keeps a shop on South Cross Street. Knows all about such things and a bit more about other things."

Ellen did not ask concerning the "other things," but enquired about transportation and was given the use of her uncle's 1959 Coupe . . . the keys left in the ignition . . . the car stored under the stable shed.

Before she left to scrounge what dinner she could from the meager stores of the pantries, her uncle motioned her to keep her seat; and closing his book and placing it on a side table, he leaned forward and pulled an envelope from his pocket.

"This," he said, "I figured might interest you."

Ellen pulled a slip of paper from the envelope and read—it was a job announcement for a professorship, requiring New World studies as well as Old World specialization in the history department at Kingston University. Looking up at her uncle inquiringly, she met his appraising glance.

"I sent an enquiry to several colleges and universities when I knew you were coming to visit. This is the only one—only vacancy—I thought you might be qualified to fill."

"But, Uncle . . . ," she began, almost exasperated. Again, he quieted her with an upraised hand.

"Just think on it. You might call them. Couldn't do any harm to ask now, would it? If you should decide to stay . . ."

"But, Uncle, I have a job—in Texas." She stopped short when she saw his troubled expression. He really did want her to stay. She realized that he had planned for her to remain here and take up the old place as her project. He seemed almost adamant about it, and she did not want to upset him with her arguments. She looked down at the paper in her hand.

"All right, Uncle. I'll call them—tomorrow—but I'm not saying I've decided to stay."

"That's fine, gal. That's fine," he said, placated for the moment "Now—how 'bout that bologna and bread?"

Smiling wanly, Ellen left the room, the envelope and paper still in her hand, and Uncle Sidney sat, watching the sunlight fade and the shadows grow long across the room. He felt tired. He hoped he could help her to see the reasons why she needed to stay. He hoped he could be certain of her decision before he left. But then, he trusted in her resourcefulness and her enthusiasm for the challenge of restoring the old place to give her success in doing so. If only she would decide to stay . . . if only . . . He was asleep when Ellen returned, carrying their dinners on a tray.

The following morning, Ellen drove her uncle's car down the drive to the narrow track to the village, remembering at the last minute to swap sides on the road, as she waved to old Darvin, who was trimming a hedge along the stone boundary wall of the estate.

Shopkeepers in town were eager to speak to her and just as eager to fill her list of goods. Her uncle and his health were humbly enquired of, and Ellen felt the genuine concern of the local population. "What happens to one affects all," Andis Culpepper had said. She knew they were all wondering if she would stay and what would happen to the Garrison Keep if she did not.

Ebenezer Grimmel was indeed an old gypsy and did indeed have all she needed to cure the household of rats, mice, spiders, and dust. He seemed amused at her requests, and she figured he was imagining her tackling the whole job herself from cellar to turret. The thought made her smile too.

"Uncle says you know a lot of things," she commented as she was gathering her parcels to leave.

He ciphered through her accent for a moment, and then appraised her with a piercing gaze. She felt oddly uncomfortable as he spoke slowly, almost absently. "If you do as I feel that you will, Miss, you will come to know much more than I."

Resisting her very American urge to make him speak plainly, Ellen only smiled, shrugged and turned to leave. And although his expression was bemused, the gypsy's eyes, following her as she carried her packages from the shop, were pinpoints of dark study.

As Ellen drove the five miles back to her uncle's estate, her thoughts lingered on the old gypsy man, and she thought that of all the many local folk she had met that day, he stood out as truly unique. But then, she admitted, she'd always thought a gypsy should be different somehow . . . odd—and mysterious. He'd do a better trade, she laughed to herself, if he were selling crystal trinkets and beads to the tourists rather than rat poison and cleaning powders to local farm wives.

After unloading her packages and parking the car back under the stable shed, Ellen put a roast on to cook and spent the afternoon cleaning the downstairs living spaces. If her uncle made no protest when she scoured through his bedroom and bathroom and if he was delighted by the gleam of the tall windows throughout, he was outspoken in praise of the dinner served him that evening.

"Ellen," he declaimed, "You could fix this old place up and run a hotel-and-restaurant setup. Don't you think?"

"What? And serve roast or barbeque brisket every night . . . I'm not that good a cook, Uncle."

"Wouldn't have to be," he said around a mouthful of beef. "Different folks every night. They'd pay well, you know. Rare chance to stay in a real medieval castle . . ."

"I don't know," Ellen hedged. "Sounds like work . . . cooking and laundry and cleaning."

Uncle Sidney shrugged, knowing better than to push the subject, but he was pleased by her next comment.

"I called today about the opening at Kingston."

"And?" he prompted.

"Oh, nothing much. I talked to the dean of the college. He was amicable enough. Said he'd send out an application and thought I might at least get an interview. But I get the feeling he's not too keen to hire outside his cronies."

"Well, girl, cast your bread on the water . . . You never know what might come back."

"Yeah. Could be soggy bread." Ellen teased, thinking that at the moment, she would not be brokenhearted if it were. She had a job and a place, back home, where there were no troubling challenges or complications. It might be mundane and sometimes boring, but it didn't have a centuries-old leaky roof or rats in the cellar.

She slept better that night just knowing the sheets were freshly washed.

The next morning, her uncle was pleased when she announced that she intended to saddle the black filly and explore the bridle paths around the Coltstone Keep and estate grounds. Enthusiastic to encourage her interest in the local area, Uncle Sidney followed her down the stable path at his torturously slow gait, arriving as she was working the filly in the paddock. His breath came in ragged wheezes that drew looks of concern from Ellen, but as he sat upon a rickety wooden manger to watch, his eyes were bright with enjoyment.

After receiving brief instructions to the nearest riding trails, Ellen bid her uncle a good morning, mounted, and rode out across the field toward the estate boundary. Watching with eyes full of envy, her uncle gazed after her until she was lost from view. It had been three years since he'd sat a horse—three very long years.

The path along the border of the Coltstone estate led Ellen and the black mare along a winding track under tall trees, through several open glades, and—at last—down along a riverbank deep in grass. Pausing to let the filly graze, Ellen surveyed the tranquil beauty of the place. The deep current flowed in an unhurried swell from below the earthen dam of the mirror-smooth lake upstream, and all was bordered by oak and rowan trees. The river above the lake curved around the knoll on which stood the great castle of the Coltstone Keep. Green lawns, gardens, and artfully arranged groves draped the slopes of the hill above the wood.

The castle was a formidable structure, ornately adorned with carved stone lintels, lead glass windows, soaring balustrades, great stone arches over heavy oak doors, and grotesque gargoyles leering down from turret, tower, and eves. All was newly refurbished—all in good repair, as only money from the state could afford, mused Ellen. She could see the corner of a parking area that was filled with the Saturday crowd of tourist's cars and touring busses.

The walls and windows of the castle seemed ever to gaze down over her as she rode the path along the river and lakeshore, crossing at last over a narrow wooden footbridge to continue up the stream. At a place where the rise of land and dense wood at last completely hid the castle from view, Ellen noticed a marker beside the trail:

"Site of the drowning of Sir David Coltstone, 1449," it read.

Ellen sat a moment, considering the deep slow waters. *Sir David must have been wearing heavy armor*, she mused, *or been a very poor swimmer.* A three-legged cat could swim out of such a hole—but then maybe the river had run differently five hundred years ago. She resolved again to read up on the history of the Coltstone family. It bothered her to know so little of the history of her surroundings. Her resolution was doubly committed when she rode into view of the ruins on the hill, far beyond the Coltstone Keep.

The stark, windowless holes stared like lidless eyes from the walls that rose upward, only to end abruptly in jagged toothy lines, the stones and mortar crumbling and fallen. The architect had obviously had an eye for the aesthetic: curved walls and banks of windows, alcoves now grass grown, and tower bases all hidden in scrub revealed an appeal to the beautiful as well as the practical and the defendable.

A brass placard on a stone pillar before the gaping doorway of the ruins shed some light on the project's demise.

"These ruins are the only known architectural project of Lord Garrett Coltstone, begun circa 1450 and incomplete upon his execution May 27, 1463."

Execution! Now there was something to find out about! thought Ellen. The whole place seemed suddenly to feel very private and forbidding, and with one last glance, Ellen turned the filly back along another path toward the Coltstone Keep and home.

She arrived back at the stable by circuitous paths later that afternoon and busied herself cleaning out a stall and sweeping out the tack room. It was late when she at last walked back to the house.

Uncle Sidney seemed so very tired and looked so very ill at dinner that thoughts and questions of the day seemed suddenly less important to Ellen. Although he fended her comments and concerns with light brevity, he could not mask the weariness of his voice or deny the labored breathing. When she offered to help him to his rooms after dinner, he lost patience.

"Go on, girl," he scolded. "I'm too old and ornery to be mother-henned! Now git." And he shooed her off with a wave of his hand.

Ellen laughed. "Not fit for heaven and too mean for hell?" teased Ellen.

"Might be. Might be," he replied, softening. "I'll know soon enough."

Leaning her elbows on the table and resting her chin in one palm, she twiddled with a three-tined fork as she watched him struggle up from his chair.

"Uncle," she said suddenly to change the subject. "Where does a body go to church around here?"

He paused and looked back at her. "You plan on goin' tomorrow?"

"Yes . . . like to."

"Well, there's only the one, and it's not much like what you're used to. But it's a church anyway."

"The one down toward the village?"

"Yeah. I've gone there, but it's been a while."

"Come with me tomorrow, then," she said casually.

He paused to consider. "You drivin'?" he asked finally.

"Well, I'm not riding with you." She laughed.

"All right, then, you smart-alecky thing. But don't go expecting me to pick out a cemetery plot," he rejoined.

"Oh no, Uncle, not a bit. But you better start payin' the preacher, or he won't say nice things over you."

"Not goin' to anyway," he scoffed with a wave of his hand, but he was smiling as he shuffled from the room.

The next morning was bright and clear as Ellen drove the car as close to the doorway as she could and helped her uncle into the seat. He was dressed in a neatly pressed—if old-fashioned—suit, and Ellen felt proud of him for making such an effort to join her.

Arriving at the old church building well before service so they could enter and find a seat before too many people arrived, Ellen led her uncle to a pew halfway up the aisle and near the wall. Once he was seated comfortably, she took the opportunity to wander the aisles briefly and peruse the elaborate windows, the tombstones engraved on the flagstones underfoot, the beautifully carved altar, and the odd alcoves and anterooms roundabout the sanctuary.

One alcove intrigued her so particularly that all through the song service, chanted prayers, and priestly rhetoric, her mind kept wandering back to it. It was a cool, dusky, and deep alcove opening out onto the vaulted sanctuary halfway along one side wall; and it held a large crypt and a surprisingly lifelike statue of a knight with cloak and shield and sword.

After the formal service was concluded and all the local folk had filed from the building—stopping to speak to Ellen and her uncle as they filed slowly past—and when only the priest was left, arranging his implements and storing them away, Ellen walked back to the alcove and stood gazing within. Only the rustling of the priest's robes and her uncle's labored breathing troubled the chilly silence.

"Lord Coltstone's tomb," said her uncle from where he sat in the pew nearby.

"I thought he was executed," said Ellen.

"Was . . . beheaded . . . for treason, they say."

"Then how did he get a tomb here and a statue? I thought . . ."

"Oh, well, they later decided he was innocent—too late to help him though." Uncle Sidney laughed sardonically, nodding his head at the statue. "Dug him up and brought him here as sort of an apology . . . though his family was all dead by then too."

"Sounds tragic."

"Yeah, suppose so . . . five hundred years ago."

Ellen looked at the dates chiseled upon the crypt: "circa 1421–May 27, 1463." Her gaze then traveled to the statue.

"Whoever carved that must have thought highly of him," she commented.

"Why do you say that?" her uncle asked with a knowing wink that she missed.

"Because nobody looks like that. It's too perfect. He must have had a stoop or a crooked nose or big ears or *something*." She gazed at the statue critically. It stood life-size on a short platform above the floor: a knight in chain mail armor draped over with a cloak, one hand resting atop a large shield engraved with the Coltstone crest, the other hand upon the hilts of a tall sword. The image was one of strength and resolve, and the visage held such haunting appeal as to seem almost alive.

"No, he could never have looked like that," she said firmly.

"I think you're overly critical of the male of the species," chided her uncle as he turned to shuffle slowly toward the door. As they walked down the aisle of the now-vacant sanctuary, he was amused to see her turn and look back.

The history of the Coltstone family and their estate was the topic of discussion over lunch that day. One question was answered after another and all in such a jumble of fact and surmise that at last, Ellen leaned back, casting her napkin on the table.

"All right, Uncle," she cried in exasperation. "Tell it from the beginning. I'm getting it all mixed up like this . . ."

He laughed. "Sure, sure. Only, let's go to the library, I've some good histories in there that you can look at . . . and the chairs are softer."

And so there, they spent the afternoon in restful companionship amid the retelling of old stories and dim histories.

THE COLTSTONE FATE

"Well, I suppose I should start," began Uncle Sidney, "with this place here. You see, it was built long about 1340. Not sure by whom, but one of the Coltstone ancestors anyway. Middle Ages, Dark Ages, you know, Black Plague and all of that. Whoever he was, he built the place for the advantage of power and defense. He must have had a lot of strength himself to survive in that time and do all he did. Some years later, the fourth of his lineage built the castle of Coltstone Keep—larger, more opulent—to reflect the family's increased power and fortune. They had achieved a noble title by that time, I believe."

Uncle Sidney had risen from his comfortable seat by the window to retrieve a book from the shelf. Opening it with a thoughtful ruffling of pages, he thumbed finally to the section he desired and laid it in Ellen's lap. "There," he said, "is the most complete written history of the family from that time until the demise of the last baron of Coltstone."

Ellen perused the pages as her uncle continued, "That would have been the Baron Maxwell Coltstone, who died in 1390, leaving the now-extensive land holdings, two castles, a vassal tribute of some fortune, and a large force of tenant farmers . . . all to his son, Andrew Garret Coltstone. There, I suppose, the famous longevity of the Coltstone men began to fail. The Baron Andrew died, in 1438, of what was probably pneumonia. He was perhaps fifty-two years old. He left all his estates and his two sons, David and Garrett, to the capable management of his wife, Lady Eleanor.

"David Coltstone was born in 1417. He married in 1442: a marriage arranged by his mother."

Following the history sketchily in the large volume, Ellen studied the small color prints, replicas of portraits in oil, of the eldest Coltstone son, David, and his wife, Leticia. She was of the wealthy house of Mansfield . . . so the book read.

David was a stout, square-built man, clear featured, with hair of golden brown. Leticia, his wife, was a full-figured woman of noble pallor and haughty expression. Ringlets of thick yellow hair fell over her shoulders mantled in pearl-beaded velvet. “Quite a pair,” murmured Ellen.

“In more ways than one, I suppose,” agreed her uncle enigmatically. “Sir David died in 1449. Thirty-two years old, he drowned in the Gulforth River that runs through their estate.”

“I saw the marker,” said Ellen, “on the trail. He must have been a poor swimmer,” she said with a questioning eye.

“So it would seem—or maybe there was foul play . . . Though if there was, the family did not want it known. He, reputedly, was hunting with three of his servants and a game keeper . . . out distancing them in the chase. They lost sight of him . . . found him in the river.” Uncle Sidney only nodded briefly at Ellen’s doubtful glance.

“Anyway, he died without an heir and left a very wealthy widow for his mother to tend to.”

“That sounds lovely,” quipped Ellen.

“Umm. Well, she knew how to handle it well enough. To keep from losing the lands and wealth Sir David’s bride had brought the family, she married the grieving widow to Lord Garrett, her youngest son.”

“Was he in favor of that?”

“Don’t suppose she asked him—or her—things being as they were back then. But it doesn’t seem to have been a happy union. If it was, it certainly was not fruitful. Lady Leticia and Lord Garrett never produced an heir for the Coltstone name and fortune.

“Lady Eleanor died in 1455 at the age of perhaps sixty years. Five years later, the now baron of Coltstone, Lord Garrett, began construction on a third castle, the ruins of which you can see up on the hill yonder.” Uncle Sidney motioned vaguely out the windows where the sun was casting long shadows under the trees.

“I’m sure all has never been told about the events of those years. It seems misfortune began to stalk Garrett . . . that, or his sins were coming home to roost. Historians say”—Uncle Sidney nodded at the book under Ellen’s hands—”that he was repeatedly called from the project to settle unrest among his vassals and pursue a band of highland brigands that troubled his herdsmen serfs.

“When the project at last got well underway, he was again called away by the summons of the king—matters at court. That was perhaps the beginning of his demise. Two years passed before he was given leave to return to his home. The project still remained a scarcely assembled collection of materials.

“Some months later, letters were intercepted—the baron of Coltstone was accused of treason. He was arrested without warning and taken to the Tower of London where he was beheaded—without trial—a letter of appeal still unfinished upon the desk in his cell.

“You make it sound quite awful,” Ellen said with dismay.

“I think, perhaps, it was—considering he was later declared innocent.”

Ellen ran her finger over the closing paragraphs of text in the chapter and gazed thoughtfully at the replicated portrait of the Baron Lord Garrett. “Plenty of court intrigue and a lot of things yet untold, it seems,” she mused.

Uncle Sidney nodded, “The letters, treasonous epistles of insurrection sent to nobles of questionable loyalties, were found to be masterful forgeries. Their origin is still unknown . . .”

“Who could have duplicated his script so well as to be convincing . . . ? And who had access to his seal?” wondered Ellen.

“Exactly,” replied Uncle Sidney, smiling. “Unless perhaps Lady Leticia . . .”

“His own wife?” exclaimed Ellen.

Her uncle shrugged. “She may have been a jealous woman, or spiteful. Perhaps she loved—or hated too much.

“It is obvious from the course of events that whoever penned the forgeries had accomplices at court . . . among the nobles there. It is conjectured that Lord Garrett had made grievous enemies of several at court through insults and insinuations made to some there. Notably, to several very influential noblewomen.”

“A bit too generous with his attentions?” smirked Ellen, eyeing the portrait that looked back arrogantly from the page.

“Too generous . . . or not generous enough,” rejoined Uncle Sidney. “Women are altogether precarious and unfounded in their sentiments. It often colors their motives.”

Ellen cast him a deprecating look.

“Truly,” he insisted, “Whether for what he *did* or what he did *not*, these found justification to malign him among his peers. Hatreds formed of jealousy are often bloody, unreasonable, and cruel.”

"But what of Lady Leticia?" Ellen persisted, "What could she have stood to gain from such duplicity? A traitor forfeits all lands and wealth to the crown . . . His family is left desolate. Why make her own husband a traitor?"

"Ah," said Uncle Sidney triumphantly. "More proof against her honorable self and more evidence for fellow conspirators in court . . . Lady Leticia was the very one to first claim the letters as fraudulent. Her appeal was promoted by a member of the royal court, an especially favored lord and advisor who would later marry Leticia after his own wife died quite unexpectedly. Leticia did not pine away in mourning," Uncle Sidney said with a wink.

"Leticia's appeal was entertained by the crown, evidence was examined, and Lord Garrett was exonerated, pardoned, given a proper burial—as you have seen."

"And Lady Leticia lives happily ever after," said Ellen dryly.

"Oh, not really. She never did have a child. Her new husband, a younger man, eventually sent her away, though he kept her inherited estates. She died in a convent . . . destitute."

"Hmm," mused Ellen, gently closing the book, "If she truly was guilty of such hateful intrigue, she got her just desserts."

"If not, she was ill-used all her life," added Uncle Sidney.

The two sat in silence for a long time in the contemplation of their separate thoughts. Finally, Ellen broke the silence.

"Don't you wish you could have been there?" she asked. "Somehow told the baron what was about to happen. I wonder how things would be around here now . . . if . . ."

Uncle Sidney scoffed lightly, "Aw, gal, no one could change all that."

"Why not?"

"Well, now think about it. Do you think Lord Garrett was a man to listen to warnings or to threats? He was wealthy, powerful . . . self-assured. He was a hunter and a soldier, and he had vassal lords at his call. His own men-at-arms were a virtually impermeable defense for a fortress such as the Coltstone Keep. If anyone had told him of his imminent destruction, I figure he would have laughed first and then flung the poor soul into a dungeon. You'd be rotting there long after he'd been beheaded, absolved, and buried himself.

"No," Uncle Sidney mused, "men like that . . . all men I suppose . . . are bound to a fate made of their own designs and affirmed in their own character."

Watching his expression change from philosophical to introspective, Ellen ribbed him out of his reverie. “Is yours, Uncle?” she asked.

“Mine what?”

“Your fate—is it so determined and so affirmed?”

“Yeah, gal. You bet it is.”

“Any regrets?”

“No, except I would like to have had a good dog for company these last few years . . .”

GOINGS AND COMINGS

Monday and Tuesday of the following week were sunny and warm. Ellen took advantage of them to ride the black filly wherever a trail offered or a road beckoned. She learned the countryside quickly and was becoming known by sight among the neighboring farmers. On market day, she rode with a basket on one arm to carry all the supplies and pantry items she purchased. The horse stood restively, tied to a tree in the market square, as Ellen visited the green grocer, a peddler, and—lastly—the old gypsy. He filled her order, regarding her with an amiable but enigmatic smile.

"How long have you lived here?" she asked to break the silence.

"Since I came here," he replied, and Ellen looked at him sharply but found no sarcasm in his face, only a thought-clouded frown. "Perhaps too long, perhaps just long enough . . . I'm not sure," he mumbled. "I think I will know soon."

He looked up suddenly as if just remembering she was there. "And you, miss," he said contemplatively, "how long before you leave us?"

"I don't know yet," she replied. She had meant to stay two weeks, maybe three, but now the dean of the College of Arts and Science at Kingston University had requested an interview with her in the first week of June. Decisions of larger portent than she liked were coming to her more quickly than she preferred. She smiled at the old gypsy. "Maybe till mid-June or so."

Nodding, the gypsy bid her good day, saying quietly, "You too will know soon, I think."

Thursday dawned cool and windy, with squalls of rain. Ellen, watching the dismal wind bluster in the trees outside the sitting-room windows, turned to her uncle with inspiration. "Let's go up to the Coltstone Keep and take the tour. We can have lunch at the Bowl & Pitcher. What do you say?"

Her uncle waivered, unresolved, while Ellen promised to drive, buy the tickets, and buy lunch—and at last, her uncle agreed to go. She brought his shoes and a coat, grabbed up an umbrella, and sprinted out to fetch the car.

The drive through the mists along the river was pleasant, with the rain drumming on the cartop and the windshield wipers thumping back and forth. Over the narrow stone bridge that arched over the river, the road to the Coltstone Keep branched from the main village road just shy of the old church. It wound through forest glades and farms until it reached the estate's diminished borders, where the trees arched over the road in ancient moss-grown boughs and the deer grazed tamely beside the embankments.

"How did the Keep fall into the possession of the state?" asked Ellen as they drove slowly along the winding road.

"A lot has happened in the world since 1463," Uncle Sidney replied. "Lady Leticia remarried to a wealthy lord. Arnold DeBruce was his name, if I remember right. Of course, he put her away not long after and kept her estates for his own."

"Ill-gotten gains—who would think any good could come of it?" mused Ellen.

"Well, now. Actually, he did quite well by it. It was his great-grandchildren that began to lose the family's fortune. It was as near as the last generation—the newly impoverished nobility I call them—refused to change and adapt after the war. Poor investments perhaps . . . I don't know for certain, but they sold off the estate a piece at a time and lost the rest to unpaid taxes."

"That's how Aunt Eunice came to own the castle she willed you, isn't it?" asked Ellen.

"Yes. Taxes," he mumbled. "They're quite high."

"How high, Uncle?" queried Ellen.

He seemed loath to answer, but at her persistence, he named a formidable sum. Ellen almost stopped the car in her astonishment. "Uncle," she exclaimed. "That's a third of what I make in a year."

He nodded but did not comment.

"How do you think I could manage that on a professor's salary—plus the repairs and upkeep? I had no idea it was so much!"

Turning to her with a searching expression and entreaty in his voice, he said, "I thought you might have something left from the sale of the ranch—after Lester died . . ."

She shook her head. "We used it all while he was sick," she said. "He never had insurance, and his treatments were expensive. Very expensive. I only finished payments on the medical bills two months ago."

Uncle Sidney looked away. "I'm sorry. I was unaware. And I have nothing monetarily to leave you. Been living off of savings for years . . ."

He looked so glum that Ellen was quick to brighten and reassure him. "Well, fear not. Maybe there are restoration grants available. Maybe low-interest loans or tax breaks . . . Maybe I'll win the Texas lottery when it's instituted." She laughed, acting much more confident than she felt. Her inheritance seemed a greater white elephant all the time, but she didn't wish to burden her uncle with any more of her doubts.

"I have an interview at Kingston, you know," she said to change the subject.

"Really now," he said, brightening.

"Yes. Sixth of June."

They spoke of the interview's possibilities and Ellen's credentials as she drove into the guest parking lot.

"I need more published articles," she said, holding the umbrella and helping him from the car. "Writings, especially more Old World specific."

Uncle Sidney stood stiffly, pausing to catch his breath painfully as he looked up at the great stone edifice rising above them. "So get writing, gal," he said. "Get writing."

Up the path in the rain, they reached the vast entry of the Keep and crossed the Close where pools of water filled the worn paving. The gargoyles spouted water from the guttering above, and the drops fell and hung like jewels on the ivy leaves vining over the walls.

Dropping the umbrella in a corner of the castle entry, they paid the tour guide and joined a group of five others who had braved the English wind and rain to view the castle and its antiquities.

Uncle Sidney had seen the old castle before and had once viewed portions which were beyond the public tour, but to Ellen's eye, it was all new and all overwhelming in its vast splendor.

Drawing rooms of grand proportion opened off the Great Hall. A great stone stairway led to upper stories where the living quarters were opulently furnished, warmed with rich wool rugs, and hung with vivid tapestries. The guide led them into a large library where shelves of ancient leather-bound volumes filled the humid air with a musty scent. High up on the walls above the shelves hung the life-sized portraits of men and women long dead.

The guide directed their attention to the paintings of the Baron Maxwell Coltstone; his son, Andrew Garrett; and daughter-in-law, Eleanor. The Lady Eleanor looked a formidable character of strong constitution for all her yellow-haired beauty. Her youngest son, Garrett, greatly resembled her, while the oldest son, square of feature and darker of color, looked more like his father.

Ellen came back from her own musings to hear the tour guide, a young man of Scottish accent, recounting briefly the history of the castle and its family. His monologue left out much of Uncle Sidney's surmising, but retained the flavor of intrigue that surrounded the death of the last baron of Coltstone and his wife's subsequent remarriage to DeBruce.

"Don't see his portrait hanging up there . . . ," queried a large, balding man with a German accent.

"No," replied the tour guide, "He had more affluent estates elsewhere. You'd be findin' his portraits there—if you could get in to see, I suppose."

"And the Lady Leticia died childless?" observed a young woman in tall boots and miniskirt.

The tour guide gave her a flirtatious wink. "Aye. But there were enough wee bairns, with the look of Coltstones about them, rollin' about the crofter's cottages to assure that the fault lay not with them."

The girl looked abashed and changed topic quickly. "Did the castle always look like this?" She gestured toward the lavish furnishings.

"Ach, no lass," laughed the guide. "In the fourteen hundreds, it would have looked much less comfortable and much more practical. It was a fortress built for display of power and for defense.

"These fine amenities were brought in during the 1800s by DeBruce's heirs. In 1910, the estate began to languish. It fell into disrepair and was acquired by Her Majesty in 1936. We opened for tourism in 1956 . . ."

Helping her uncle out to the car, Ellen drove through a slight drizzle to the Bowl & Pitcher, where they found a table beside the warm hearth in the cozy duskiness of the old pub.

"So what did you think of the Keep?" asked her uncle as he settled back with a cup of hot tea.

"Big," Ellen said. "And impressive . . . and probably very cold five centuries ago."

"And probably smelled of cabbage and tallow candles," agreed Sidney. "Amazing anyone survived long in those times." He eyed the oxygen tank beside his chair morosely.

"For all you say, Uncle, I get the feeling you would rather have lived then," surmised Ellen.

"Hmm, lived then . . . No, I think perhaps those were hard times to live in," he said, "but—probably easier to die in."

Over the next two days, Ellen watched her uncle decline remarkably. There were things she wished to ask him about the estate. There were matters she would like to have discussed; but seeing him faltering so, she kept her conversation to happier, less worrisome topics.

That next Sunday, he did not feel well enough to go to the old church to worship. His energy seemed to be waning rapidly. "Uncle," Ellen said, that morning. "I am going to call a doctor."

"No!" he said adamantly, half rising from his reclined position in an armchair near the sitting-room windows. "No doctor!" He sank back into the chair, breathless.

"But, Uncle," Ellen cajoled. "Your condition is getting worse. We should get help before . . ." Her words faltered uncertainly.

"Before what?" he laughed and fell into a violent spasm of coughing.

"Before it kills you," she said almost vehemently.

"But, my dear girl, that is exactly what it is going to do—doctor or no doctor. And I am content with that."

At her deprecating look, he repeated, "No doctor. Promise me. You know it's best."

In her heart, she knew he was right, and it was only her love for him that made her wish to prolong the inevitable. "I promise," she replied. And yet that morning, in the cool dusky tranquility of the ancient sanctuary, as she sang the old hymns and listened to the liturgies so unfamiliar to her, she watched the dust motes dancing in the multicolored light from the stained glass windows—and her thoughts were much on her uncle and her father and her mother.

It was comforting to be in a place where the dead were buried under the very floor pavers and in alcove crypts roundabout. She felt the empty stare from the stone eyes of Lord Coltstone's statue, and the entity of death and timeless eternity folded around her like an embrace of warm reassurance. She would lose her uncle soon, she knew, and she could accept it gracefully, even as he had already.

Before the close of service and its final benediction, she had determined to call home and let Texas know that she would be staying a few more weeks . . . maybe a month . . . however long it was before her uncle died. The time with him was important.

As she left the sanctuary, the priest asked after her uncle. He knew, more by her look than her reply, that he should plan for a burial soon.

It was, however, sooner than either of them had expected. When Ellen arose to the bright sunshine of that Monday morning, she was intent upon riding the black filly further downstream along the Gulforth. She breakfasted at leisure as she waited for the morning mists to rise from the fields, and fixing a bowl of cereal and toast for her uncle, she went to his room to bid him a good morning and was surprised to see him still in bed. She called to him, but he did not respond; and it was with a dull dawning of realization that she walked to his bedside and looked down at the still, pale form.

She stood there in silent reverence as tears welled in her eyes and fell in wet splashes upon the counterpane. His hand was still warm and supple and she held it and touched his cheek and said her own good-bye before she quietly left the room.

Darvin was working in the vegetable garden when Ellen called him in to sit beside his last master while she opened the dusty phone book and called the constable and the coroner. Then heating water for tea, she sat down in a kitchen chair to wait.

People arrived, questions were asked, and reports were written. And after all was satisfactorily concluded, Uncle Sidney's body was taken to coroner's small shop in the village. Ellen spent most of the morning and early afternoon making preparations for the funeral; the priest was notified, a plot selected in the cemetery, a suit of clothes taken to the coroner, eulogy written, and calls made to folk of the town.

Late that afternoon, Ellen was surprised when Darvin and his wife arrived with a shepherd's pie and cozy of tea. They sat with her in a comfortable way, making the old kitchen warm and warding off the loneliness.

"If you need help, dearie," said Darvin's wife, "cleanin' out things and such, you know—just give me a ring. I'd not mind, if it makes it easier."

Ellen thanked her earnestly. "I've not decided yet what I'll be doing with the place or his things."

"He's left it to you, then?" asked Darvin.

"Oh, yes, I suppose so," Ellen said quietly. "I've not seen his will, but he said so last week."

"That's good," said Darvin, "I'd hoped that's how it was."

Looking at the man's honest old features, she felt humbled by his trust.

"Darvin," she said hesitantly, "I know you've always served Uncle Sidney well. And I . . . well, I appreciate the companionship you were to him all these years. But I have to be honest with you. I have no money to maintain this place—probably can't pay the inheritance taxes. I certainly, well . . . I can't afford a gardener . . . ," she faltered, fearing to insult this kindly couple.

"Aw, lass, think naught of that," he comforted. "I have my pension, and it keeps me and the missus just fine."

"I'm glad of that," said Ellen. "You've planted the vegetable garden already. I hope you will feel welcome to its produce all summer and fall."

"That's right kind of ye," said Darvin's wife. "Truth is, the old man just loves to potter about in the gardens. It's what keeps him spry."

Darvin smiled at his wife. "If you don't mind, miss," he said to Ellen. "I should like to do a bit of work now and then—just to keep things tidy . . ."

"I appreciate your offer," replied Ellen. "But truly, I have no way to pay you . . ."

"Ach," laughed Darvin. "Your uncle hasn't paid me these two years."

At Ellen's look of dismay, he held his hand up reassuringly. "Didn't ask none, lass. Your uncle was a good man. I thought that much of him, you know. When his health gave over on him and he calls to me and says he can't pay me no more—have to let me go . . . Well, I quit workin' for him sure enough, and started workin' for myself—'cause I like it . . . like bein' around the old place. Grand old place. Yer uncle never asked aught of me, but what I wanted to do anyway."

Ellen smiled in understanding, knowing there was no wage worthy of such sincerity. "I'll do what I can to repay you in some way when I can," she said quietly.

"Just see the old place never falls to ruin," he sighed, casting his eyes appreciatively about at the massive stonework. Ellen wondered ruefully if she could even honor that request.

The morning of her uncle's funeral dawned rosy and warm. A small group gathered at the graveside to hear the prayer and eulogy and watch as the casket was lowered into the brown earth.

After a lunch at the parson's, Ellen spent the afternoon riding the black filly along the country paths, going high up on the hills far past the ruins of Coltstone. She would meet with a clerk in town the following day to read her uncle's will and find out exactly what his desires were for his old estate. She wondered just what liability she was inheriting.

The prospect weighed heavily on her, and she wished that she could simply fly back to Texas now, where all was plain and simple and held no frustrating challenges. But then she realized it was the challenge that intrigued her: only the fear of failure made her think to leave.

She had no idea just how great the challenges were until she sat across the desk from the precinct clerk as he read through the will. He continued without pause into a long list of legal fees and taxes.

The upshot of the story, the way Ellen deciphered it, was that the estate and all of her uncle's worldly goods were hers, as well as an account of perhaps ten thousand pounds. That sounded quite nice, except that the estate owed that much in back taxes, another eight thousand to come due in October, as well as six thousand in inheritance tax to be paid within the month.

Trying not to let despair cloud her heart, Ellen forced a smile and signed the appropriate documents where the clerk indicated. Her fingers moving mechanically while her thoughts rolled and tumbled from one fact and figure to the next. *Eighteen thousand pounds in taxes, six thousand more within the month, and that did not figure in upkeep and repair—or food,* she thought disparagingly. *A person could become enslaved to a place like this,* she mused. Such things were for barons and earls and kings, not for West Texas schoolteachers.

She drove back to the old castle disconsolate. The loose slates of the roof and crumbled walls of the garden terrace were sadly accusing as she studied the place anew with an appraising eye. Such great craftsmanship in its walls: such rich history within them. It intrigued her, made her dread the thought of forsaking its possibilities. Perhaps she was overlooking a great opportunity. "Texas thoughts," she smiled to herself.

She sat up late into the night with pencil and paper, figuring and refiguring: if she sold her place in Texas—and her truck—and the sorrel . . . if she could secure a professorship at Kingston . . .

She sighed. The profit off her farm would pay her mortgage with only three or four thousand left over. Her truck was worth less than two hundred. She could perhaps ask for a loan, but then she had no secure job here in England. To live in Texas and pay off taxes in England made no sense unless she could rent the place, and that did not appeal to her at all.

At last, in the wee hours, after the last cup of tea was cold, her pencil dull and her mind numb, she knew that unless the Kingston professorship could be made certain within two months' time, the inheritance tax and back taxes somehow made in incremental payments—which she doubted—unless she could see her way clear in those matters before mid-August, she would go home. She would return to her old mundane life. She would let the estate go to Her Majesty's acquisition, she would be debt free, and she would be less one medieval fortress. It was not a satisfying prospect, but it was good to know her mind. She slept late in the morning.

Determining to know the laws concerning deferred taxes, Ellen saddled the mare and rode into the village before noon the next day. The clerk was not encouraging. The deference of the inheritance tax was unprecedented, he said. Most heirs of such estates planned well in advance for the initial costs, and he felt her appeal not likely to find approval.

The cheery sunlight was dimming under dingy clouds when Ellen left the clerk's office. She treated herself to a leisurely dinner in a quiet corner of the Bowl & Pitcher before she rode slowly toward home.

Home, she mused. If an Englishman's home is his castle, this one was probably not to be hers for very long. Nearing the old church, Ellen reined in beneath the tall bell towers and sat gazing at the tranquil green countryside. She tethered the mare to the cemetery gatepost and walked among the grey headstones to the freshly mounded earth of her uncle's grave—fresh and dark and loamy smelling. She knelt there for a quiet moment, wishing she could have once again the benefit of her uncle's insight or her father's steady wisdom. Even her mother, she thought, would have kept a good firm perspective in such a situation. She missed them.

Walking through the lush grass between the graves, Ellen read the names and dates from the stones as she passed by. Satterfields and Maxwells and Chesters and Brocks: old names—the oldest stones worn beyond reading. At the far back of the cemetery, near the wall, was a stone sheltered under the church's great eves. "Alice Sheffield and son," it read, and 1463 was the only date engraved beneath the name. Ellen surmised that Alice must have died in childbirth and hence the common grave. She walked on with thoughts subdued.

The church doors were unlocked and opened easily, the sanctuary cool and dusky within. Hesitating momentarily, Ellen stepped inside, thinking it would be a calming respite to sit a moment in this timeless place.

All was eerily quiet within, and her footsteps on the stones seemed irreverently loud, her shadow too tall against the wall. She sat for a short time in a pew near the altar, comforted to know that these benches and these floors had been worn smooth by generations who had sought solace here. It was with better peace of mind that she stood to leave as the afternoon sunlight angling in shafts of rainbow splendor through the high windows cast spangles of splintered light across the walls and emblazoned the alcove of the Coltstone crypt with a rosy light. Ellen paused there. The glow seemed to enliven the features of the tall statue, and the effect was captivating.

Lord Garrett, Baron of Coltstone, she mused, *died twenty-seventh of May 1463.* With a jolt she realized the date was exactly five hundred years past—to the day. Five hundred years . . .

"I wish *you* were here," she mumbled absently, looking up into the cold stone face. "*You* would know what to do, I suppose." And she smiled to imagine it. What would a baron of Coltstone do in her place? Her uncle would have had a colorful answer for that, she laughed to herself, and she was turning to leave when a sudden odd shift of light caught her attention and arrested her midstride. Perhaps, she thought, it was a trick of the light from the windows high above that had made an illusion of movement in the alcove. She glanced up to the windows, then back at the alcove, and then up again, still unconvinced that this was the source of the light that she had seen. Something seemed different; something seemed very strange.

She looked closely at the statue and the smile on her face changed to wonder and surprise as before her eyes, the stone, so grey and cold, wavered and colored in watery tones of brown and gold. The hands and the features seemed to warm momentarily in the tan of flesh, and transfixed by curiosity, Ellen stepped closer, studying the wavering light on the stone features, determined to find the source of this strange phenomenon. She touched one finger tentatively to the stone cheek and was astonished that it felt warm. It did not feel like stone at all. She looked, perplexed, at the tips of her fingers and rubbed them against the cloth of her skirt as she stood on tip toe to study the strange illusion more closely. She watched the strange warmth and light play across the features and she had determined that illusion it must be, when suddenly the eyes, so close to her own, flashed open and met her gaze in cold steely blue.

Ellen stumbled backward, her face a mask of astonishment and horror, her mind fumbling between acceptance and denial. *Not enough sleep,* she told herself, *and too much stress. I'm just imagining things. It can't be real, so I should just turn away and ignore it.* But for all she admonished herself, when she tried to make her feet move, they would not obey her. Like the paralysis in a nightmare, she could not run and she could not scream. She seemed destined to stand mesmerized as the statue changed, the muted grey stone filled with color and its form to took on breathe and life. Then, as if a layer of the stone were splitting off from the face of the statue, a living form peeled away, fell forward, and sprawled out upon the worn stone pavings of floor.

Ellen stifled the cry that rose in her throat as she looked from stone to creature and back again. Shaking uncontrollably, she struggled to back away. She was certain that what had just happened could *never* happen. She knew that this simply could *not* be real and she simply would not *let* it be real. *Too much fairy-tale literature,* she thought to herself. *Just stay with the facts, Ellen. Stick to the history, don't make things up . . .* But try as she might to dismiss what she was seeing, the reality simply would not go away; and as she watched in terrified immobility, the form on the floor struggled to hands and knees as if it were very weary, paused, and then rose, stumbling to its feet. It was the knight of the stone, but he was no longer stone. And he was tall. Taller than her. He wore a linen tunic and breeches and boots, with a robe of brown, and a belt of black leather. The scabbards of both sword and dagger were empty, and Ellen wondered that she found some bizarre comfort in that fact amid this freakish *Twilight Zone* episode.

The figure looked around the sanctuary with an air of mixed recognition and surprise until his gaze fell upon Ellen and became cold and appraising. She blanched.

"You!" he said hoarsely. She scrambled backward, tripped, and fell hard on her rump.

"Thou witch," he said, advancing. "How hast thou wrought this work?" He glanced at the walls roundabout and then back at her.

"I am no witch," Ellen gasped, sliding backward until her back was against a pew.

He ignored her denial. “Indeed, thou art the very one,” he asserted, “For I have heard thy voice even as the ax was raised above me: I heard you calling me hither.”

“I did no such . . .”

“What bounty dost thou require for thy service?” he interrupted, thinking it best not to tamper with such a powerful sorceress and eyeing her garb with a wary eye. *She might be a changeling,* he thought. “Come, speak quickly, for I am in haste. There be matters I must see to forthwith.”

“Matters,” Ellen muttered, her mind racing, wishing she could deny all that was happening, wishing that what she was seeing would *go away*. She closed her eyes tightly; but when she opened them, he was still there, glaring down at her now with impatience. She stumbled as she struggled to her feet, and he was wondering if she were actually a simpleton.

“Speak quickly, witch,” he prodded. “I cannot tarry.”

“Tell me,” Ellen said slowly, finding her voice and wishing it were steadier. “What is your name?”

He looked impatient. “I am the Baron Lord Garrett of Coltstone. Dost thou not know this?”

“Just checking,” Ellen muttered. “And do you know this place?” she queried again.

“Be not insolent, witch,” he said scornfully. “I have worshiped within these walls every Lord’s day since my birth.”

“Give or take a few centuries,” Ellen muttered under her breath.

“Do not mock me.” He glared at her. “Name thy fee that I may be gone.”

Ellen thought quickly. Somehow she had to tell him—convince him—that something even more extraordinary than he thought had actually happened. “Lord Garrett,” she addressed him cautiously. “For reward, I would have you—I would ask you—to believe what I am about to tell you.” She tasted the irony as she knew she was not ready to believe any of this herself . . .

He looked at her and gave no reply.

“You see, sir, you’re not only in a different place, but a different time . . . perhaps.”

He regarded her with something like annoyance and total disbelief.

“You’re right,” Ellen said tiredly. “That sounds much too outlandish . . . even to me. But look,” she said, inspired by a new tact. “Turn around and look.”

At her gesture, he cast a glance over his shoulder and then turned, arrested by the sight before him. Eyeing the statue with a hard scrutiny, he looked from it to the crypt. He traced his fingers over his own name and the dates inscribed there.

Ellen watched with bated breath. Now he would know, but she wondered how he would react. Maybe, just maybe, in the next instant, he would disappear in a puff of smoke or swirl of mist. Maybe she would wake up from this crazy dream . . . any moment now.

When he at last turned around, she was dismayed to see not the surprise and amazement she had hoped for but a closefisted ire and angry flash of eye.

"Thou devious creature," he hissed, "Thou hast been bought by my enemy."

"What?" Ellen gasped.

"To portray my death, and have it so perceived," he growled, striding forward, "to take my lands while I yet remain—dispossessed." He grasped her by the shoulders in a cruel grip. "An uncommon vile plotting . . . Who has paid your wage?" he shouted, shaking her.

"I don't . . ."

"Who hast bought you to do thus?" he demanded. "Or is this perhaps your own plotting, witch?"

Ellen bridled, suddenly angry at being so roughly handled. "Stop calling me 'witch'!" she rejoined. "I am *not* a witch, and I am *not* responsible for whatever is happening here! Look! Look at the stones beneath your feet. Look at the dates engraved there. I could not machinate all these deaths, all these burials, and all this history . . . just for your benefit or anyone else's. You are now in 1963!" she cried.

But he refused to look at the evidence she offered and threw her backward upon the floor in disgust.

"Ow!" she cried, thinking—as she landed on her backside once again—that she was landing there far too often this day.

"Thou mayest scheme so," he sneered at her, "but my vassal lords yet owe me allegiance. My men at arms still honor my command." He grasped her by the wrist and hoisted her to her feet, "And I will see thee burn for thy craft!"

Just like Uncle said, thought Ellen. *No room in the past for a glimpse of the future.* He dragged her along the aisle to the open door. Fortuitously, just as they reached the upper step, an automobile rounded the bend of the rarely frequented road and rumbled slowly along the open stretch within view of the old church. Garrett stopped midstride in astonishment, and his grip loosened on Ellen's wrist as he stood staring at the place where the auto had disappeared.

"What new devilment is this?" he breathed.

"It's a car," said Ellen flatly, wrenching free from his grasp and backing away, ready to leap from the stair curb and run if he came at her again.

"Car." He tried the word. "Some fell beast . . . ," he began, smelling the fumes of exhaust.

"Not a beast," said Ellen. "A machine. Metal, glass, rubber . . . It burns gas . . ." She felt helpless to explain. "People ride in them."

"Them?" he said with alarm. "There be many?"

"Yes."

"I must go to the Keep with haste," he muttered to himself, feeling this a very evil day and looking a bit ill.

Ellen, glad at the prospect of being rid of him, was suddenly visited with the appalling vision of him clearing his castle of tourists and guides.

"No," she cried, suddenly grabbing his arm. She felt the hardness of muscle under her fingers before he cast her hand off disdainfully.

"Please," she said. "Come with me to my house—castle—whatever, just over yonder." She waved her hand. "We can discuss this all there . . ."

Stupid, she thought to herself. *Just let him go . . . Let him disappear. Let him star in someone else's nightmare.*

"Yonder," he mimicked scornfully. "Thou meanest the Garrison Keep, a castle my own. Is this what they have paid thee—they parted out my holdings even ere my death?"

"It's not like that," Ellen cried, exasperated.

Garrett looked at her, perplexed. He'd never met anything like her. She apparently had no fear of him. She certainly showed no due respect. Perhaps her powers made her confident, he thought, yet it was odd how she clung to her preposterous farce so tenaciously. He shrugged. He would be glad to be rid of her for now, and he would deal with her later.

Rounding upon her, he spoke with a coolness and composure more menacing than any tirade of anger. "I ride to my castle, and when I come to the Garrison Keep, I will bear a sword and my men will ride at my side. It will behoove thee not to tarry there."

Without another word, he vaulted over the stairway curbing and strode to the black filly who fidgeted at her tether at his approach. Jerking the reins from the post, he leaped to the saddle even as he wheeled and spurred her on.

"Don't you dare take my horse!" cried Ellen, but her voice was drowned by the thudding of hooves as Garrett raked his spurs over the filly's flanks, sending her flying over the open sward toward the road and the Coltstone Keep.

Ellen watched until the forest hid them from view. Then feeling shaky and tired, she sat down on the stone step with a jolt. She wondered what would happen if the police were called and they arrested this wild character who claimed to be the baron Lord Garrett of Coltstone? He had no identification, no credentials, only a crazy claim and an arrogant attitude; and she would never be able to explain this to the constable. It would be the loony bin for sure, she thought wryly, for *both* of them if she got too involved; and that would be worse than a beheading, she figured morosely, but better than burning at the stake.

Rising carefully, she walked back into the quiet sanctuary. Unreal. It was all unreal, and the quiet now so terribly quiet, the air so terribly breathless and still. Edgy as a cat, Ellen went back to the alcove. The statue and the crypt looked just the same as when she had sat there in the pew and wished . . . wished for what? For help? For someone who would know what to do about taxes, about money? *A deliverer,* she mused, *I wished for a deliverer . . . I should be more careful with my wishes.*

She sat down in the pew as her heart settled back to a more comfortable rhythm and her mind once again explored the option of denial.

"Someone must have slipped something in my tea," she told herself half seriously. "This may be England . . . But it is still 1963 . . ."

"You," she said, addressing the statue. "You are dead, and you should stay that way." She felt as if she were admonishing an errant child.

Pushing to her feet, she rubbed her backside. If she doubted what had just happened, she still had the bruises to deal with . . . and a long walk home . . . and a horse to find. Walking outside, she glanced at the ragged clouds scuttling overhead, deemed rain in the offing, and decided it was best to begin the walk home. If this was all somehow real, she still could not prevent whatever was about to happen at the Coltstone Keep. Lord Garrett would reach there soon enough at the furious pace he had set—if he didn't break his neck—and she could only hope that what he saw along the road and what he found at the Keep would convince him that she had told the truth and curb any rash actions. She shook her head to clear her thoughts, swallowed hard, and started out on the long walk to the Garrison Keep.

As Ellen strode through the dim shadows of the wood below the Keep, hoping to reach home before the rain that scented the freshening breeze could begin to fall in earnest, she tried to imagine what Garrett might do after reaching his castle. She frowned. She really didn't want to think of all that might happen there and wondered where he would go when he finally realized that things were not what he'd expected. Would he resort to the Garrison Keep as a sanctuary? Perhaps. She was his only resourceful contact here, and the Garrison Keep was the only shelter.

She resolved that she could do nothing more than wait and see, though she'd rather he just disappeared. There were enough things on her plate without this to deal with.

"Uncle, you weren't kidding," she laughed drily as rain began to drip through the trees. "One can never know what lies in the soil around here."

DISPOSSESSED

While Ellen trudged along under trees that now dripped with misty fog, Lord Coltstone rode at breakneck pace toward his castle, hoping to find everything there in some semblance of normality—or at least familiarity. His mind was troubled by all the witch had said and apprehensive that she might have spoken some truth. He was weary from days of struggle—weary in mind, weary in body, and weary in soul.

Reaching the road, he yanked the filly to a skidding stop and stared at the new wonderment before him. What had once been a rough, muddy track through the river bottom was now a smooth, continuous black paving. Dismounting, he stepped cautiously to the pavement verge, touched the smooth black tarmac carefully with his boot, and then knelt to examine this strange new thing. He found no joining, no seamed stonework—only smooth hard graveling, spread like jam over bread. He backed away, perplexed, then remounted the filly and was surprised when she crossed the road without balking.

Now he rode the filly more slowly, looking for familiar landmarks; and when he found few and those changed, he wondered if the witch's power was strong enough to change so very many things.

Crossing the river by the arched stone bridge his own grandfather had set amid the torrent, Garrett once again spurred the mare on, fearing what he would find when he reached his home. Such fear was a thing foreign to him; even at the bailiff's dock, he had not feared. But now a great dread tightened his throat at the prospect of existing in a place no longer his own, a world so familiar and yet so changed.

Upon reaching the garden, green below the towering walls, he reined the filly to a halt and stared at the scene before him. A car was rumbling up the road, bright light shining before it. It stopped beside several others in a square of paving near the castle's wall, and three people stepped from it. They were dressed oddly in breeches without tunics, and shiny bright-colored coats. These, he thought, were even more strangely attired than the witch had been.

As they walked toward the entrance of his castle, a dark drizzle began to fall, and the lamps in the parking lot flickered on. Garrett squinted; he'd seen no man light them and could see no flame of fire within them, and the light from the castle windows shone extremely bright through diamonds of glass panes he had never before seen there.

With a sinking heart, he urged the tired horse forward and, drawing rein beside a lamp, studied it closely, eyeing the glass orb within with its flameless fire. He touched the glass tentatively, but felt no heat from it. Swinging from the saddle, he tied the filly to the lamp's post and strode resolutely up the path to the Close, where once servants had bowed to meet him and where his mother and his wife should have been waiting to greet him; feast and fire should have welcomed him within . . .

A sign at the gate read "The Coltstone Keep. Entrance fee $2.50." He walked past it and into the Close, where the stones underfoot were clean swept, with no sign of horse or footmen; and a long swatch of yellow light fell across the pavers from one tall open door. He crossed the Close cautiously and stepped inside.

What had once been the large, bare guarded entry of his fortress castle was now the opulent foyer of a dwelling. No torches burned in the sconces upon the walls; the door of the guard's anteroom had been walled over, and plush wool carpet felt mushy under his boots.

The young lady behind the small ticket desk looked up at him with an air of tolerant distaste. She looked at his mud-spattered boots, outlandish garb, long hair, and several days' growth of beard. *Hippies!* she thought. *You never knew who you'd have to deal with in this job, and you have to be nice too.* A decidedly sour smell suddenly permeated the room, and she coughed and wrinkled her nose.

Garrett, for his part, did not know *what* to think of the young woman before him. She stared at him without deference, respect, or curtsy. Her dress . . . well . . . He was beginning to think that this style must be quite common somehow. But her skinny legs, bare from the hem of her plaid skirt, were indiscrete; and the thick-soled black shoes were ugly and impractical. She was thin and pallid, altogether unadorned, with long lank hair falling unkempt over her shoulders; looking thus, she reminded him of the scraggly gypsy tramps that wandered through his lands, peddling tinware. He wondered if perhaps a family of them had moved into his castle.

"Good evening, sir," she said in the trained tones of her trade. "The last tour has already started. You may join it in progress, if you like, or you may return tomorrow at 10 a.m. for our first tour of the day." Her smile did not look genuine.

"Tour?" said Garrett flatly, wondering what the word meant.

"Yes, sir," replied the receptionist. "They have just entered the third room—this way." She motioned through a door to her right with a hand from which a cheap, gaudy bracelet dangled.

With a curt nod, Garrett stepped toward the door.

"Sir?" called the girl, "That will be two dollars and fifty cents."

Pausing, Garrett looked at her uncomprehendingly.

"Your ticket, sir," the girl persisted, holding out her hand.

With an impatient look, Garrett strode past her and through the door. He had no time for beggars.

The girl looked after him, disgruntled. She did not like confrontations, and she was not paid enough to deal with weirdos like this. Looking around surreptitiously to make sure her supervisor was not watching, she shrugged, walked to the entry to hang the "Closed" sign, and locked the door against the cold and damp that was seeping in. As Garrett walked through the rooms beyond, she counted the cash box at her small desk, carried it to the safe in the back room, put on her rain coat, and left for the day. When the last tour was finished, there would be no one at the entry door to know that one visitor yet remained.

Garret strode through the door that the girl had indicated and into the Great Hall with its two massive fireplaces; but there were no trophies and shields upon the walls now, no rows of trestle tables, no torches burning bright, no musty matting of rushes upon the floor. Garrett felt as one imprisoned in a disquieting dream as he walked through the room and gazed about him, astounded. The three chandeliers of gold and crystal that hung from the carved wooden beams high overhead bathed the room in the stark light of their flameless fires. Rich wool rugs, heavy tapestries, leather wingback chairs, and heavy, ornately carved settees cushioned in red velvet were arranged throughout the room in artful groupings. Glass-fronted cabinets displayed artifacts and books and oddities—articles now of the past, once things he had used daily.

He did not linger there, but passed on to a prettily appointed sitting room which had once been his scribe's workroom and, from there, to the space that had been the open landing of the wide tower stair. It now served as a sunny garden room, where a bank of tall glass windows would sometimes shed a golden light on wicker and greenery. Today, the seeping fogs from the river had stolen their light.

The tour had moved on up the stairs, and Garrett followed the sound of their voices cautiously, curious of who they were and what they were doing in this place. At the second floor landing, the guide had led the tour quickly through a sparsely furnished drawing room and a music room and along to his favorite library, with its books and portraits and the Keep's history.

Standing out of sight behind the thick stone archway of the library door, Garrett saw the tall shelves with the familiar bindings of his record books, his own writings; and from this vantage, he could see the corner of a large portrait on the adjoining wall. He knew whose it was.

"These books," the guide was saying, "are a rare collection, beginning with these, dating from approximately 1340, to these written in 1440 by the baron of Coltstone himself . . ." The tour guide rambled on, describing the significance of the valuable collection. "This collection of poetry by Livingston, 1790 . . . ," he was saying, and Garrett felt as if the room had begun to tilt beneath his feet. He leaned his forehead against the stone, breathing heavily. "Seventeen ninety," the guide had said . . .

"You can find copies of some of these works in the visitor's gift shop near the tour entrance." The tour guide droned on.

Seventeen ninety! The words rang in Garrett's head. The present year should be 1463, and yet here was this bizarre evidence of time passing beyond him. This was his castle, his lands, but this was not now his home. Where was his wife? Where was his son? What had become of his family?

In one week, in his own time, he had lost everything; and he now wondered if this present nightmare might be his eternal punishment: to be here in this place, not miles, but *centuries* away from home; to be lord baron of Coltstone . . . lord of nothing! Although his life seemed to have been given back to him, this was not his place to live.

"The Lady Leticia remarried . . . ," the voice of the guide continued.

Remarried, thought Garrett. He had no doubt to whom. But the tour guide made no mention of his son, of his vassals, of his men at arms, his serfs—all of those who had looked to him for protection. *What had become of Alice*? he wondered with a heavy feeling of foreboding.

There were too many questions that needed answers, and he had no one here whom he could ask . . . except perhaps the witch! She had acknowledged who he was; he believed that she had called him here. And she, if anyone, he thought, would have the answers to his questions. He would go to the Garrison Keep and hunt her from there.

Backing away from the door as the tour guide led the group into "the baron's own private quarters" with ironic familiarity, Garrett slipped silently down the tower stair, stood a moment upon the landing until he felt secure that he was not watched, and then passed into the room where he had once conducted his estate's business. The corridor beyond led to the servants' quarters and workrooms, the kitchen, pantry, and scullery; and Garrett moved along it with quick stealth.

A bright light shone from the doorway of the kitchen, and Garrett paused to peer cautiously within. A man, the janitor, was seated with his back to the door, a mug in one hand and a book in the other, as he waited for the last tour to end so he could sweep up the foyer, vacuum the carpets, and go home. A small black box on the table was blaring forth the sound of voices and banging noises that hurt Garrett's ears but covered his footsteps as he slid past the doorway, past the scullery, and down a short flight of steps to regions of the castle visitors never saw and staff rarely frequented. Pushing open an unbarred wide door, Garrett stepped into the once well-stocked armory. He left the door open for light and stared at the walls roundabout with disappointment.

Only one suit of armor hung on the racks, a suit of diminutive stature made for a youth. All those worn by his men must have rusted in the field, he guessed, or fallen there and been buried with their bearers. Several swords and daggers hung displayed upon the wall. But most were cheap, gaudy replicas; and the others were old, rusty, and dull. There was yet one, however, that suited him well. It was a long broadsword, plain of make, rust pitted, nicked, and dull; yet it bore the balance and steel of a sword he had once known, and he slid it into his scabbard with satisfaction.

He eyed the daggers there but saw none he cared to have, and he turned away, thinking that he knew of another . . . one he very much desired . . . And he wondered if it yet remained in the place he had once hidden it in his own time. He turned without hesitation and walked back down the corridor until he came to a wide-arched opening and another flight of steps. The heavy wooden door at their base was weathered, its latch rusty and stiff but not locked.

He knew that neither Leticia nor his mother would ever have left this door unlocked. It had once guarded the stores of all the estate: the wines, the spices, all things not housed in barn and granaries. His mother had guarded the keys to this door closely; had hung them on a chain at her belt. Garrett thought of her now and wondered what she would have thought of his present predicament.

The cellar smelled of mice and mold and rotting wood; odd pieces of cloth and trash lay strewn about the dirty floor. At the back of the cellar, a short corridor led deeper into the gloom and ended at a broken wooden door. The latch and bolt had been pried off long ago, and the door hung crookedly on broken hinges. Garrett pushed past it, feeling his ways in the dark. He knew the heavy chests of coin would never be there; but perhaps, just perhaps, there yet remained something where no one else had thought to look.

Behind an arched pillar, Garrett felt along the wall and then grinned in satisfaction to find the stone he searched for still in place. Carefully, he pried with the tip of the sword blade until, with a dull rasping sound, the stone loosened and slid forward; and he strained to pulled it from its place and lower it carefully to the floor before looking hopefully within the dark open space revealed behind it. With bated breath, he wondered if he would find what he sought there until his groping fingers met the bulky lump of an object, and he smiled with satisfaction. It was all there: the leather bag of coins, the small casket that contained his mother's circlet of emeralds, her rings, and several precious stones. He'd never given these things to Leticia. He knew they would never have made her beautiful, but only whetted her appetite for more wealth and more power. He removed the leather bag, careful of its brittleness, and slid several gold coins from it to a pouch at his belt before placing the bag carefully back in its dark niche.

Reaching beyond the casket, his fingers found a long thin object wrapped in suede pigskin, and he drew it out into the light. The leather crumbled as he removed it, and he felt the cool blade against the palm of his hand. Even in the dusky darkness, he knew its elegant curve, the smoothness of the bone handle carved by his great-grandfather, the gleam of the blade wickedly keen. It was never meant to be his, but he was glad it was there now.

Slipping it into the scabbard at his side, he then replaced the stone, smoothing the crumbly mortar with dust from the floor before slipping away, like a haunting spirit, back down the dim corridors and out of the castle by the back scullery door. Rain was falling, cold and steady, and the last light of day was fading as he mounted the shivering mare and turned her toward the Garrison Keep in hopes of finding shelter there.

REVELATIONS

Ellen had arrived at her own door, weary and wet and sore. She hoped beyond hope that this would all make some sort of sense somehow and soon. She took a hot bath, and changed clothes, pulling on a cotton sweater and her jeans, and she told herself—half in jest—that it was best to be able to run and to wear things that didn't burn, just in case.

The kettle was set on the stove to boil as she pulled ham, cheese, lettuce, and tomato from the Frigidaire and set out mayo, mustard, and bread. Things so normal were comforting after things so strange. When the kettle sang, she decided to sit down with a hot cup of tea, heavy on the cream and honey; and she sat for some time, elbow on the table, thinking and thinking and thinking some more, while her eyes grew heavy and the tea grew cool and the window panes darkened as the rain trickled down. She must have fallen asleep when the neighing of a horse jolted her awake and pulled her to her feet.

The black filly. Ellen swallowed hard as her heart began to race. The filly had come back, and Ellen fought a sudden urge to flee, feeling it unreasonable to believe that the specter of Garrett Coltstone should be there too. The filly had simply returned home, she told herself: most horses do after running away.

Still, she hesitated. What if she *was* inside some weird time-warp ghost story? What if he really *was* outside there in the dark? She did not like reading statistics, much less being one. "Teach history," she muttered. "Don't be it." And she slid a butcher knife from the drawer and slipped it into the belt under her sweater before walking to the windows to peer outside.

Lord Garrett had reached the stables as the filly began to stumble with fatigue, and his fingers felt numb on the reins, and cold rain dripped down into his boots. Little surprised now to discover the dilapidated state of the stable, once so well kept, Garret placed the tired horse in the only furnished stall, stripped off her gear, and wiped her down with the brush and rag. He found the bran mash Ellen had left in the feed room and fed the mare and stacked the saddle in the tack room before walking to the stable's high-arched entryway to look up the path at the castle beyond.

The Garrison Keep, where once he had housed the core unit of his fighting men—it had never looked so weathered and timeworn and dowdy as it now did in its cloak of ivy. The light of three tall windows and a door shone forth in long fingers across the grass under the trees, casting eerie looming shadows in the rain. Perhaps, he thought, it was best to stay the night in the stable and accost the witch in her stronghold by daylight. It seemed a cowardly thing to do, but he felt he'd dealt with enough that day; and he was just turning away when the door opened, and a figure stood there, framed in the brilliant light. Something flickered in its hand and became a steady beam of light searching here and there among the trees as the figure stepped forth into the night.

Keeping to the shadows, Garrett slid the heavy sword from his scabbard and held it down at his side in ready double-fisted grip. If this be the witch, he told himself, then he must speak with her; but he would take no chance of her doing him some mischief.

The figure paused where the light from the doorway faded. It stood still, silently listening; and then a voice, slightly unsteady and none too loud, called out.

"Is anyone there?"

This witch, mused Garrett, was not very intimidating, even though her powers did seem great. Guardedly then, he stepped forward. The beam of light found him quickly—blindingly—and he thought he would be struck down; but before he could react, the light fell to form a circle at his feet.

Ellen, regarding him from her vantage, wondered what she should do now. She thought earnestly about running back inside, barring the door, and calling the police; but what would she report? A lunatic or a misplaced person? He looked tired—he was soaked through, and she couldn't just leave him out here . . . Or could she? Still undecided, she flicked off the flashlight.

"Put down your sword," she said as calmly as she could. "I mean you no harm."

Seeing her better with the light extinguished, Garrett eyed her mistrustfully, but slid the sword into its scabbard with a motion made smooth by habit; and Ellen decided that if he was going to act rationally, perhaps they should discuss this dilemma together before she made any decisions about what to do with him.

"Come inside, if you wish," said Ellen, backing slowly away. She felt like she was coaxing a wild dog in out of the rain. "There is food—and it's warm."

Several pensive moments later, Lord Garrett's form darkened the doorway; and he warily entered the room, glancing at its meager furnishings and then staring at her wordlessly. His sodden cloths were making dirty pools of water on the floor.

Stepping forward slowly, she pulled a chair from the table and set it near the radiator. "Here," she said, motioning him to the chair. "Sit down. It's warmest here."

The radiator chose that unfortunate moment to grumble and gurgle as only an old radiator will; and Garrett, eyeing her doubtfully, backed away, watching her like a hawk.

Ellen sighed, decided that this is going to be a very long evening, and nervously closed the kitchen door. As casually as she could, she walked to the kitchen cabinet, pulled two plates down from the rack, and placed bread on them.

"How did you find things at the Keep?" she said quietly to break the heavy silence.

Without answering her query, Garrett eyed her morosely, crossing his arms upon his breast, and asked, "What year is this?" His voice was cold and flat.

"Nineteen sixty-three. This is May 27 of 1963," said Ellen, opening the jars of mayonnaise and mustard.

"Why?" he asked wearily. "Why have you brought me here?"

Ellen sighed again, wondering how she was going to sound convincing. "I wish I could say I did it on purpose," she began. "I could claim that I did it to save you a beheading, if that would make you happy." She opened a drawer absently to look for a knife. "But I didn't. Honestly, truly . . . I did not *bring* you here. I don't think it's even possible for you to be here, and I certainly am not a witch."

"Then how have you done this?"

Remembering where the knife was, Ellen pulled it from her belt as she answered, and Garrett noted the action appreciatively.

"I really don't know. I was standing there, by your crypt, just like I'm standing here"—she waved the knife artlessly—"and I made a wish."

"A wish," Garrett said disbelievingly.

"A wish."

Ellen cut two thick slices from the ham and cast them into the frying pan "Like any silly schoolgirl throwing pennies into a fountain . . . I made a wish—and poof!" The flame flashed up under the pan on the stove as if to emphasize her words. "There you were."

She turned to find him braced against the far wall, his gaze on the enigmatic fire.

"It's only a cookstove," she said, realizing her mistake. "See, it works like this." She turned the knob back and forth to demonstrate. "You try it," she said. "There's no magic . . ."

He did not take her invitation but edged away warily, his brow furrowed in study.

"Then if thou are no witch," he said, "how hast this happened?

"I don't know," she replied earnestly. "I don't know."

"And if thou art no witch . . . then thou cannot send me back?" His voice told her that he hoped she would assure him otherwise.

"I wish that I could," she replied tiredly. "I certainly would if I could!"

He walked slowly to a chair at the table and slumped into it.

Turning back to her work, Ellen flipped the ham slices, cut tomatoes and cheese, and washed the leaves of lettuce . . . It all seemed very commonplace amid the extraordinary.

"I must go back," said Garrett suddenly. "I must! There are things I must see to. How be it if I am *dead* in that time, while I yet live in this?

"Maybe you just vanished . . . ," Ellen suggested.

"Yes, perhaps. Yet all the same, if I exist there, no longer my lands will be forfeit—my wife, my family, cast out . . ."

Ellen bit her lip, considering it not an appropriate time to amend his surmises with her own knowledge of the Coltstone history.

"And my son," he continued. "Whoever has plotted this against me will hunt him also . . ."

"Your son?" said Ellen in surprise.

"Yes, my son."

The ham, sizzling in the pan, smelled delicious; and Garrett suddenly felt terribly hungry and thirsty.

"But I thought . . . well . . . I did not know that you and Leticia had any children," said Ellen.

Garrett watched as Ellen stepped to a tall white box, opened its door, and pulled out a clear glass jar in which green things floated in a sort of brew.

"Leticia is not his mother," he said in a tone of voice that encouraged no further enquiry. He watched her pull the green things from the jar with a fork.

Placing a pickle on each plate, Ellen thought of the tour guide's words: "Many a wee bairne bearing the mark of the Coltstones, rolling about . . ." Doubtless, this man could choose an heir from among a dozen.

"Well, you needn't worry about Leticia," Ellen said casually as she picked up the two plates and carried them to the table. "She does well enough."

He looked at her in consternation, wondering if this witch would now turn fortune teller, and decided it was probably all one and the same. "Tell me why thou dost say so?" he asked.

She filled two glasses with water, and Garrett watched intently as the faucet spouted into tumblers as clear as crystal. He wondered if this were normal in 1963.

"Because," said Ellen, turning around with the glasses in her hand. "She is the very one who proves that the treasonous letters were forgeries, that you did not write them. She thereby retained your estate for herself, and then marries a fellow named DeBruce two months later."

Garrett's face darkened grimly as she spoke, and Ellen was reminded of her uncle's words that a man such as Lord Garrett of Coltstone would not take kindly to meddlesome words from a stranger. She wondered if she had insulted him or wounded some clannish pride, or did her words greave him? Perhaps he had truly loved and trusted his wife. Somehow, she had never considered that possibility.

"Lord De Bruce," he muttered. "Double-tongued blackguard." He knew Leticia coveted De Bruce's great wealth and delighted even more in his power. She had always longed to go to London, to appear in the royal court, something Garrett had never permitted her. "So De Bruce would gain my lands."

"Yes."

Ellen set the glasses on the table. "Then he sends Leticia away, three years later, to die a pauper in a convent, while his family enjoys the wealth they've gained."

"How dost thou know this?" Garrett asked again, studying her in bewilderment. "Who art thou? What art thou that thou canst prophesy so of my family?"

"I am a professor of history," she said and, at his uncomprehending stare, set her hands on her hips impatiently. "I am a teacher," she said more assertively. "I study history and lecture in history at the university."

"Ah," he said, "But women do not teach—they do not so much as study at a university . . ."

"They do now," said Ellen assertively. "I do."

He nodded slowly "And these things thou speakest of . . . Thou hast learned them there?"

"No. I read them in books, here, in the library."

"Books?"

"Yes, books of history." She thought of the volume her uncle had shown her. "Here" she said, sliding the plate toward him. "Eat this. Don't go anywhere. I'll be right back."

She looked like a fussing mother hen to Garrett as she raised a long thin admonishing finger at him, and he chose to ignore her as he studied the food on the white china plate. When she returned with the heavy book under her arm, she found the plate clean and Garrett studying the water glass, tapping it gingerly with one fingernail.

"You were hungry," she observed.

"Um. It was good."

"How long has it been since you last ate?"

"Four days," he said, looking up, "and five centuries." The twinkle of mirth in his eyes was surprising, and Ellen laughed.

"I like a man with a good sense of humor."

"And I a maid who appreciates one," he replied. "A merry heart doeth good like medicine."

She pushed the other plate across to him. "Here, eat mine. I'll fix something else later." He obliged without protest as she thumped the volume down upon the table and flipped it open to the Coltstone history.

Wiping his fingers on the binding of his cloak, he touched the thin, smooth pages, marveling at their texture. He studied the bold black print; but his brow furrowed, he squinted hard, and then looked at Ellen in disappointment.

"These words," he said. "They are must peculiar. I know not the half of their meanings."

Seeing the frustration in his face, she puzzled a moment before exclaiming, "No, but of course not! You read the Old English, like that of Chaucer's *Canterbury Tales",* and she quoted the opening lines of Chaucer's prologue with its oddly formed and archaic sounding words.

Garrett brightened to hear something he understood so readily. "Yes," he said. "That is so, but what now say these words?"

Sighing, Ellen looked over the book, upside down from where she sat across from him at the table. "This is your family history as best any now know it. You, I'm sure, could rewrite it more accurately." The words had a ring of inspiration to her even as she said them. "I will read it to you . . . but not tonight. Tomorrow. In the morning. But anyway, here are prints of the existing portraits of your grandfather, father, mother, and you." She watched his eyes follow her finger over the pages. "This is Leticia, De Bruce, and here, a note referring to another volume for a history of the DeBruce family."

Ellen saw that he was staring at the picture of the Coltstone Keep and the photo of the ruins upon the hill, and she wondered what it felt like to read one's own obituary.

"You like to build?" she asked.

"I should have finished it," he muttered.

"Well, perhaps you'll get the chance to now," Ellen said, stacking the plates and carrying them to the sink. Her comment was startling, and he watched her as she walked away, and then carefully closed the book. His head hurt. He rubbed his temples and looked up at the gleaming light fixture suspended in the center of the wood-beamed ceiling.

"How does it do this?" he asked, pointing upward when Ellen turned around inquiringly. "There is no flame . . ."

"No," she said, considering how to explain. "It's electricity."

Garrett tried the word quietly.

"It's like lightning from a summer storm—or the little sting you feel when you rub a furry coat and then touch metal."

"How is it captured?"

"It is made . . . by generators . . . and sent through wires." She pointed to the switch on the wall. "Flip that, and it goes off and on."

With hesitation, Garrett walked to the wall and studied the small square box by the door. He touched a finger to it, and the room was plunged into darkness.

"Turn it back on please," said Ellen tightly and was vastly relieved when he did.

He commenced to explore the room while she dried the day's dishes and set them in the rack.

"This?" he asked.

"Refrigerator. Keeps stuff cold."

He opened the top bin and felt the frost and frozen meat.

He turned a knob on the stove and held his hand above the heat of the flame, turning it on and off and on again. Ellen watched him surreptitiously. She thought it was like having an overgrown child in the house and figured it would get tiresome quickly.

Standing near her at the sink, he turned the handles of the tap on and off, yanking his hand back quickly from the scalding water.

"Heated," she said before he could ask, "in a tank in the cupboard."

"And this," she said, "is soap. Something you need." Taking the bar in her hands, she washed and rinsed and handed him the bar. He mimicked her movements, and dirty brown water drained down the sink.

"Do it again," she admonished, and he did.

"Well, that's some better," she observed, looking at the black rings around his fingernails. "But it will take more than that, I'm afraid." She looked up at him. "You smell like a wet sheep that's soured," she said, wrinkling her nose, "and you look a little worse."

His answer gave her a pang of remorse.

"I am sorry if I offend ye," he said with a slight, deprecating bow. " I was taken from my home without warning, and I rode three days tied to a raw-boned, stiff-gated nag. I have spent a day and night in the Tower of London, and have knelt on the greasy, blackened stones of the bailiff's docket . . . I am sorry if I do not stink of rosemary and lavender as seems to so please the gentle folk."

"That's ok," she mumbled. "I prefer the smell of leather and horse sweat actually. But I suppose it's time to do something about you."

She had been wondering exactly *what* she would do about him, and she did not like the idea of his staying in the castle. "I don't suppose you would mind staying in the stable, would you? We could fix up the old groom's quarters," she asked offhandedly. And she was considering that maybe old Darvin and his wife might be willing to take in a boarder, when Garrett's angry scowl precluded any further thoughts.

"Be it one century or another, this is *my* castle, and I will not be made to sleep in *my* stable." He growled, and Ellen decided that if it were a bluff, she did not intend to call it.

"Ah," she said. "I was afraid you'd feel something like that. Well, now," she considered, "since I don't have anywhere else to go either (and I am not moving into *my* stable), you will just have to be content in the north wing and I in the south, and keep to your own ground."

He nodded assent, and resignedly, she motioned for him to follow her down the wide corridor to the rooms that had once been her uncle's, and that she had cleaned just the day before, putting her uncle's things away.

"You can stay here," she said without looking at Garrett as she ushered him through the door. "This was my uncle's room."

"Where is thy uncle?" Garrett asked, glancing around the room.

"He won't be bothered," she hedged.

"Over here"—she motioned—"this is the bathroom, the 'water closet' as you Brits call it."

"Brits?"

"English people."

She continued the explanation of the room's fixtures, ignoring his blank look. "Here are towels and washcloths, and this is the sink." She turned the knobs "hot" and "cold." But he was not watching or listening. Instead he looked past her and reached a tentative hand to touch the reflecting glass of the mirror. Ellen laughed. "Mirror," she said. "Glass with silvering. People like to have lots of them nowadays."

"So clear," he muttered.

"Yes, sometimes too much so," said Ellen and swung the mirror on its hinges to show the cabinet behind. "Here is a toothbrush—and toothpaste. Put it on the brush like this and scrub. And *do it*—you've never had sugar like you will in 1963, and you'll want to keep your teeth.

"This is a razor—to shave." She eyed his thick beard, but he shook his head.

"I will use the scissors," he said, pointing to the pair on the shelf.

Ellen shrugged. "You'll fit in . . . And this is the bathtub . . . hot-cold, stopper for the drain. Fill it up and get in and use soap."

She was beginning feel like a preschool teacher, and Garrett thought she sounded much like the monk who had been his tutor in his early years.

"Shampoo," she was saying, holding up a bottle. "For your hair. Scrub it in—rinse it out. Rinse out the tub when you're done . . . Any questions?"

Garrett shook his head silently and followed Ellen at a distance as she walked from the room.

"There is one question I would ask," he said before Ellen could leave.

She nodded patiently.

"What is thy name? Thou hast not told me."

"Thou didst not ask," she quipped with a mock curtsy. "It is Ellen."

"Eleanor?"

"No, just Ellen. Ellen Anne Lancaster."

"Lancaster!" he exclaimed in surprise.

"Yes. Why?" She was puzzled by his expression.

"My pardon, Lady," he said, bowing slightly. "I did not know thou were of that great house."

The dim light hid her embarrassment. "Of that great house, nine or ten generations down the road and half a world removed," she amended. She ignored his puzzled expression: if he wanted to believe that she was a person to be respected and honored, why bother disillusioning him? "Now," she continued, "put your cloths and boots outside the door when you have washed, and I will clean them. There are clothes in the dresser," she said as she stepped from the room. She closed the door firmly and made her way quickly to the kitchen, where she stood for a moment, wondering what to do next, and finally she filled a pail at the sink and began mopping the dirty puddles from the kitchen floor. She knew it was not the puddles on the floor that bothered her as much as the muddle of thoughts in her mind. Cleaning one, she felt, might help sort the other.

Exploring the room quickly, Garrett examined the late Sidney Lancaster's wardrobe. Fingering the soft smooth texture of woven cottons and wools, he chose what suited him, stripped off his sodden trappings, left them in a pile outside the door—boots on top—as Ellen had requested, and sank gratefully into a bath of steaming water. He had never taken many baths in his life: baths were generally cold and drafty and overly public. Relaxing in the steaming vapors, he vowed he would change the design of the castle he was building to accommodate such as this, and then he shuddered as he wondered if he would ever regain the opportunity.

Ellen carried the smelly, wet pile of clothes to the old scullery chamber that was now the laundry, spreading the garments out upon a table, casting socks and underclothes into the machine, and examining the tunic and cloak carefully.

The tunic was made of finely woven linen, embroidered with muted colors of silk twist at the collar and cuffs; and the cloak was worsted wool, light, soft and sturdy. Its rich brown color was enhanced by threads of gold, stitched along its edges and woven into a wide border along the hem. Ellen set the washer on cold water, gentle cycle, and—hoping the garments had been washed at least once in history—poured in soap and closed the lid fatalistically.

She scrubbed the boots clean in the big laundry sink and set them to dry by the radiator while she wiped down the leather breeches—she dare not wash those—and pulled saddle soap and bootblack from a bin under the sink. The boots were polished, the breeches cleaned, the clothing dry and—thankfully—still their original size when Ellen folded them neatly and stacked them beside her uncle's chamber door. The belt, with its sword and dagger, had not, of course, been proffered. She would have felt better with them locked away in a cupboard.

She went to her room and propped a chair under the doorknob before she lay down to sleep. The steady rain was still drumming on the lead glass windowpanes, and she thought about the day and decided it was all just too ridiculous: she told herself again that things such as this did not—could not—happen.

"Well, Uncle," she muttered as she fell into fitful slumber. "If you had no ghosts in your castle before, you'd not believe the sort you have here now."

The following morning dawned clear and bright with that sparkle of fresh newness that only daybreak after a night of rain can bring and Ellen, awakening much later than she had intended, rose hastily, and pulled on her boots, jeans, and sweater only to find that all was silent in the old stone halls as she stepped quietly to the kitchen feeling like a trespasser in her own domain.

Finding no one in the library or sitting room and her uncle's chamber door still closed with the clothing stacked against it, she gave a sigh of relief and strode out into the glorious morning to feed the filly. Leading the horse into the paddock, Ellen took an extra-long time cleaning the stall, sweeping the stable run, and cleaning her saddle, knowing all the time that she was only delaying the inevitable. But when she entered the castle once more, she found all still quiet, and she ate toast and cereal in edgy peace.

She was slicing potatoes into a pan, with roast and carrots, when she felt, rather than heard, Garrett enter the room. She turned around and was startled to see him standing in the doorway.

Regarding her, Garrett wondered if she always brandished a knife so readily, and a smile played across his face. "Good morning to you, Lady Ellen," he greeted with a shallow bow.

"Good morning," she returned with a cautious nod. "I hope you slept well?"

"Like the dead . . . ," he said and Ellen wondered if he meant to be humorous as he settled into a chair at the table, expecting his breakfast. *He'd probably never had to ask for anything in his life,* she thought as she threw sliced bacon into a pan, buttered toast, and cracked eggs. Setting the plate before him with a steaming cup of cocoa beside it, she went back to her potato slicing while he ate; and she began to wonder how easy it would be to become cook, maid, servant, and scullery wench to one who expected nothing less. The thought galled her.

When Garrett tasted the brown liquid in his mug and asked what it was, she replied snappishly, "Chocolate!" and banged the lid down on the roast pan as she shoved it into the oven.

Garrett watched her speculatively. Women, he knew, could be so temperamental. "Hast thou no servants?" he asked. "No maid? No cook? Where are the people of this place—the family?"

Wiping her hands on a cup towel, Ellen leaned on the counter and regarded him. He looked better this morning: less wild, definitely cleaner. He'd trimmed his beard neat and short. The sword and dagger were in place . . .

"There are no people," she replied, deciding that it was silly to be offended by him when he simply knew no better.

"How dost thou then manage the business of thy estate?"

"I work."

"Work . . . yes . . . but you—alone . . . ?"

"I work for money, as a teacher. The university pays me to teach. I buy what I need with that money."

"What of the vassals, the serfs—how dost thou keep them subject without men at arms . . . ?"

Ellen laughed. "There are no vassals or serfs anymore. Everyone owns what they have, or they rent it outright."

Garrett was speechless, and Ellen considered whether it were possible to explain world governments in five minutes or less.

"People govern now, Lord Garrett. The power of royalty is gone. The queen is kept around for ceremonial things: christening ships, meeting the pope, keeping her kids out of trouble. England is ruled by a parliament and has a prime minister. Other countries have democracies. Few countries have dictatorships."

She stopped. There were books he could read if he truly wished to absorb five centuries' worth of social, technological, and economic change.

"Your worth to the university must be great," mused Garrett, considering the costs he well knew of such establishments.

"Not that great."

"Then . . . how dost thou manage?"

"I don't know," Ellen said simply. "I inherited this place, three—no—four days ago, from my uncle."

Garrett looked at her intently. Great houses with no inhabitants, estates with no tenant farmers to work them—it made no sense. "And thou art alone here?" he asked. "Alone?"

"Well, I was thinking of getting a dog, a Dachshund maybe," she replied to evade the question. His look made Ellen nervous, and she turned to the sink to wash up the breakfast dishes without giving him a more definitive answer. She was surprised when he carried his plate to the sink and slid it into the sudsy water.

"Here," she said. "You rinse in that side and dry them with towel while I wash." She thought her request had met resistance when she saw him hesitate, but then he stepped to the sink and looked down into the clear, scalding water; and after a moment, he began to roll up the cuffs of his sleeves.

Ellen regretted her request immediately: he was standing too near and his presence made her nervous. She did not look at him, though she thought he was looking at her; and from the corner of her eye, she saw him reach around her.

Reactively, she shoved him away and, red of face, glared at him. "Don't you even think of it, cowboy!" she spat vehemently.

"Cowboy?" he repeated uncomprehendingly, backing a step away.

"Cowboy! Ploughboy! Goatherd! Whatever you call it! Get this straight, and get it now! I am not your servant wench, your scullery maid, your farmer's daughter, or your mother's chambermaid. So don't even think about messing with me! Got that?"

"Messing with?" he muttered, raising his hands against her tirade as understanding slowly dawned on him. Regarding her flushed face, he almost smiled at her misinterpretation of his intention.

"My good Lady," he said softly, lowering his hands. "I beg pardon that I have insulted you. I have no desire to cause thee shame. I will guard thy honor as my life, if thou dost you so desire."

It was the flowery talk of chivalry, and Ellen thought it probably as transitory; but he seemed properly set back on his heels, enough to serve for the moment anyway.

"I dost so desire," she said adamantly and turned back to the dishwater, keeping a peripheral eye on him. Garrett stood a moment as he was; then cautiously, he stepped around behind her. Ellen tensed, wondering just what he was up to this time; and then he picked up the cup towel from the cabinet just beyond her and walked back to his place at the sink.

Blushing with trepidation, Ellen ducked her head and scrubbed industriously at the frying pan as Garrett pulled a plate from the rinse water, examining its shiny glaze curiously as he wiped it dry.

"I'm sorry," she said at last. "I am a little on edge."

He smiled. "You no more than I, and yet I hold to what I have said."

"Good," she said, wringing out the dish rag and pulling the stopper from the drain. "So do I."

It was a good to know.

"Now if you want, we'll go to the library, and I'll read that history I showed you last night."

Garrett nodded, placing the last plate in the rack. "I should be most curious to know its words, though I do not believe it matters greatly to me now."

"Why not?"

"History, my history, I well know," he replied. "How to return thither is what I must find."

"Don't you believe that you could find valuable answers about the things that were happening to you back then? It won't do you a lot of good if you return—if we find a way for you to—only to fall into the same trap and get beheaded again."

He thought a moment and nodded.

"Perhaps," she continued, warming to the prospect of solving the mystery and gleaning a truer knowledge of the past, "perhaps your knowledge of how things really were and the history we know of what happened after your death . . . Maybe if we put that together, you will know who was behind it all and what motivated them."

"And then," he said, "I should know what measures to take to right these wrongs."

Ellen did not like to think much about his "measures." By the dark brooding look of his face, they probably involved boiling lead or piles of dry wood . . .

"Come on," she said, motioning for him to follow and lead the way to the library.

COMING TO TERMS

Seated cross-legged in a cozy chair near the window, Ellen opened the volume of history, propping it on her knees and holding the pages from the tug of a whimsical breeze that wandered through the open sash. Garrett sat astride the piano bench like a horseman, fingering the instrument's polished wood and cautiously opening the keyboard cover as Ellen began to read:

"The first stronghold of the Gulforth River region was built circa 1340 . . ."

"Thirteen seventy," Garrett said flatly, touching a key and tilting his head to the ringing note.

Ellen looked up, intrigued. She pulled a pen and paper from the drawer of the table at her elbow and scribbled a note: "By an unknown ancestor of the Coltstone family . . ." She continued.

"Albas Blackstone." Garrett played two notes in harmony and watched her scratch down another note. He was glad to know that she was also a scribe by trade. "A man of great stature," he continued. "Black beard, bushy eyebrows."

Ellen's pen paused in its scribble. "How do you know that?" she asked incredulously.

"I don't," he grinned, finding the third note of the chord and rolling it softly under his fingers "I only jest . . . But his name was Albas Blackstone. His son's son married the Lord of Coltsfords daughter and only heir. He agreed, in doing so, to join the names—hence Coltstone."

"Thou dost not jest?" queried Ellen.

"Nay, nor do I. Thou shouldst know when I do."

"I'm beginning to figure it out," she said, making a final note. "The baron Lord Maxwell of Coltstone . . . ," she began again, and Garrett did not interrupt her this time as she read through the pages, though his tampering at the piano was mildly distracting. At first, he seemed bemused by the history; and then as the text came to the years of his own life, he sat in studied silence, frowning slightly. At the recounting of his brother's death, he rose abruptly and paced to the windows, looking beyond them through the trees. He remembered that day, and it was not five centuries old to him; and as Ellen continued, the written words brought lines of sorrow to his face and conjured grave doubts and misgivings in his mind.

At last, Ellen came to the closing paragraphs of the history: "Lady Leticia of Coltstone, wife to the late baron, remarried in August of that same year, to the lord Arnold DeBruce, Earl of Manchester . . ."

Folding his hands behind him, Garrett stood braced like a soldier at ease; his head lowered in dark study as Ellen finishing the reading, closed the book, and looked up. Standing in the window's golden glow, he appeared like his own statue: pensive, and brooding.

"I must return," he muttered. "There must be some way. I must foil this plotting."

"You think, then, that you know who is responsible for the forgeries?"

He regarded her thoughtfully. He felt he did now have some suppositions, but he did not wish to speak of them to her, not yet, not now. "My mother," he replied evasively, "would have been proud to hear our family name yet so honorably recorded, our history, so—pardonable . . ."

Ellen shrugged noncommittally. "To the lay person, perhaps it appears so."

"What meanest thou?"

"Only that there are obvious omissions in the writings, obvious to a historian or observant student."

"Such as . . . ?"

Ellen considered her words carefully, wondering how much to say, what was too bold to suggest. "When I first came here," she said, "my uncle told me the story of your family—because I asked—and because I would inherit this part of your estate . . . He pointed out several mysteries that he felt the books left unanswered."

When Garrett only regarded her silently, she continued. "For instance, who wrote the treasonous letters and why? Obviously someone who wanted you dead: someone who could pen your own hand convincingly or could coerce your scribe to write as if for you and who had access to your seal." She looked at Garrett inquiringly, but still, he gave no answer.

"My uncle wondered why, after two years of faithful service at court, no lord there rose to befriend you or spoke in your defense. The wives of several courtiers seem to have hated you intensely—according to the texts. Why? Jealousy? Insult?" He still made no reply, though a frown creased his brow. "And why, when none at court gave aid . . . why was Leticia's appeal so quickly promoted by those same lords and your pardon so unanimously approved only a month later? Leticia remarried rather quickly too—to a very powerful man . . ."

"Thy uncle was a man of suspicious mind," interrupted Garrett.

"Not suspicious—inquisitive."

"Verily," Garrett said crossly. "And what dost *thou* find lacking in these words of history?"

"Hmm," she said wondering at Garrett's reaction. "I agree with my uncle: too many stray sheep . . . But what I find very improbable . . . ," she hesitated, walking absently to the cold grate of the fireplace and looking into the grey ash, "is that your brother simply drowned." She glanced at Garrett over her shoulder to catch his reaction, but he gave none, and she resolved never to challenge him to a game of poker. "So your brother was either a very poor swimmer or wearing very heavy armor to drown in such a docile stream."

"Mightn't he?" said Garrett flatly.

"You would know," she said, facing him. "Face it, the Gulforth is not the Colorado."

"Colorado?" Garrett was nonplussed.

"Never mind," she said impatiently. "But the Gulforth River is so sluggish and tame, a man could crawl out of even its deepest holes—if he had his senses about him."

"And thou thinkest he did not?"

"My uncle seemed to think that there might have been foul play." She watched Garrett's face intently. "His belief is that the Coltstone sons were perhaps none to discreet—a bit too free in their affections—and that your brother had probably offended one too many. The histories favor that surmise."

Garrett's face colored in anger, but he voiced no denial. "What else dost thy uncle surmise?" he said a bit too softly, his mouth set in a grim line.

"When my uncle told me these things, I remember saying how interesting I thought it would be if somehow, you could have been warned—if someone had told you what was going to happen. I wondered how things might have changed and how they might have been around here now."

"And?"

"He laughed at me. He said that a man of your power and influence would laugh first and then put the poor prophet in a dungeon to rot while it all happened anyway."

Seeing a faint glimmer of mirth at last in Garrett's eyes, Ellen continued, "He said that such men—perhaps all men—are bound to a fate 'made by their own desires—affirmed by their own character.' I think, now, that he is right." Her voice held regret, and in the silence between them, Garrett thought her words through carefully.

"Your uncle was an astute man," he said at last, breaking the silence.

"Yes."

"But I do not think I will be casting you into a dungeon."

"That's good," she replied. "The doors are all rotten now anyway. They couldn't hold a house cat."

"Pity," he said. "That should be mended."

"Yes. Well, if you want to take up repairs around here, it will keep you very busy . . ." Ellen turned toward the door, but paused, still wanting to know what he thought of all she'd suggested before she let the matter drop.

"Don't you think," she said precipitously, "that Lady Leticia is very likely responsible for the letters?"

Garrett straightened and uncrossed his arms. *How typically like a woman,* he thought, *to worry a matter beyond reason.* "I believe," he said, "that such is quite possible. Indeed, thou hast given me many thoughts to ponder, and none of them are pleasant."

"If she wrote them . . . ," Ellen began, but Garrett interrupted her.

"Leticia," he said flatly, "could not write."

"Oh," said Ellen, the wind taken out of her sails. "Well, that shoots that in the foot."

"'Shoot in the foot,'" Garrett repeated. "Yes, I suppose so."

"I am planning to ride to the stable at Coltstone Keep this afternoon," she said with a resigned sigh. "They rent horses to ride. I thought I would lease something for you so you won't be stuck here and dependent on me to drive you around." She hesitated. "I hope you will be . . . discreet . . . around the locals if you go out."

"Discreet—and disaffectionate—as ever," he replied sarcastically.

"You know," said Ellen from the doorway. "The book says nothing of your having a son . . . ?"

"Nor would it," Garrett replied with a look that curbed further question, and Ellen quietly turned away.

That afternoon, when Ellen set out to ride to the Coltstone stable as she had promised, she grabbed up the satchel she had made to carry market goods in, slung it across her back, and jumped down the rickety wooden steps from the scullery. When she reached the stable, she was surprised to find Garrett in the paddock, brushing down the filly, her saddle and bridle hanging upon the palings.

"You don't need to do that," she said.

"No," he replied, "but it be a thing I like."

"*Me too*," she said as she reached to take the saddle down, but he took it from her and set it upon the filly's back, studying the cinch straps momentarily before buckling them through.

"Is this how it is goes?" he asked.

"Yes, but you could have let me," she said, grasping the bridle firmly in her hand lest he take that from her too.

"A lady does not do such things," he said quietly.

"They do now."

"Then it is a fault of this age."

"Probably so," laughed Ellen. "Still, I bet you never treated the poor peasant women of your time so nicely."

"No, nor did I ever treat one ill," he rejoined thoughtfully. "To each person, there is a place, a task, some amount of regard due. It is wise to find and keep one's place—gracefully," he said and backed away as she swung up into the saddle.

She looked down at him as she gathered the reins. "Have you always thought that way?" she asked.

"No," he replied, "only since this morning. Now go get me a horse, thou quick-tongued wench—and make him no jaded nag." He opened the gate and sent the filly through it with a slap on the rump. As Ellen posted across the field to the tree line, he returned to the stable. There was much to think about—and not enough to do, and he spent the hours of her absence by roaming the grounds of the stables, the gardens, and the grounds of the castle Keep, appraising the sad state of disrepair with concern even while admonishing himself to pay no mind to such matters. The state of the old castle was not now his to be troubled by—the roof not his to repair. He sat down on the stone bench near the stable to pick foxtail burrs from his boots and to think . . . and to think.

Too much of what Ellen had read and too much she had said had hit too close to the mark. He had suspected that someone in his household had sent those letters and that someone at court had orchestrated their interception. After all his years of faithful service, all at court had been too ready to believe the allegation of treason against him . . . all those years of faithful service . . . all those years as an advisor at court when he had never cared for such ambitions.

Leticia was the one who had always hungered for the pomp and the intrigue and the power to be found at court. She craved it and ranted at him shamelessly for not taking her with him when he was summoned to London, and Garrett thought grimly that her marriage to DeBruce must have pleased her well, to be among that noble set at last.

Perhaps Ellen was right, and Leticia *had* schemed and plotted so. There was no love between them, certainly; though he kept her well and treated her fairly, he knew that he had never trusted her—she knew that he did not.

Would she, then, have conspired to murder? And if so, who was her accomplice? His two scribes and his clerk he thought to be loyal, but money bought loyalty too often, and there were some grievances from the past that he should not have assumed resolved.

The sound of hoofbeats far off under the trees disturbed his thoughts, and he rose from his reverie to see Ellen galloping over the field, leading a large grey gelding who looked seedy and settled and stood, blowing tiredly, as Garrett took the proffered reins and eyed him critically. "Thou hast brought me *this*?" he scoffed.

"He's sound."

"Such a beast could not be otherwise," he retorted, looking into the placid eyes of the old gelding.

"Well, I couldn't have you sporting around the countryside on anything else!"

"I can see no harm in it, if better is to be had," he replied.

"You'd turn too many heads . . . And I can't afford something better," Ellen said tiredly. "Get on him and try him out. We'll go up toward the hills a bit."

It was in the dusk of evening that they returned to the Garrison Keep, and Garrett admitted it felt some better to have a horse beneath him, even if it were an old plow horse.

"Nothing better for the insides of a man than the outsides of a horse . . . ," said Ellen as she thumped plates of roast beef, potatoes, and gravy down upon the table. "Teddy Roosevelt," she added at his inquiring look. "Rough riders, 1820, America." And the questions began and continued until a comfortable good night was spoken, and Ellen once more laundered the clothes before going to her room.

She did not neglect to place the chair against the door.

SANCTUARIES AND TOWER TURRETS

Ellen was startled once again when Garrett strode into the kitchen that next morning, and when he inquired why it was that she continued to react so, she could find no better answer than that she somehow kept expecting him to vanish overnight, just as suddenly as he'd appeared.

"Try awakening to wonder which world thou art in," he returned, picking up a bowl and mimicking her preparation of cereal and milk.

"I'm off to church this morning," she said, sliding the plate of toast and jam to him. "Want to go?"

"Verily, I shouldst," he avowed.

"Well, I thought you might," she said. "And I've been thinking. We can't have you walking around claiming to be Lord Garrett, Baron of Coltstone, or they'll lock you away in a loony bin."

"Loony bin?"

"Place for crazy people, 'moonstruck . . . '"

Garrett nodded.

"I think I will introduce you as Gary Coalson, an old family friend. Sound OK?"

"Gary Coalson," he repeated. "It sounds very common."

"Yes. Well, I doubt you'll be considered that, one way or another."

He arched one eyebrow in inquiry.

"You don't look very *common*," she explained. "And something else we need to work out. I am not Church of England, and so I don't know much about this . . . But I don't think you should go to confession or anything while you're here."

He laughed outright. "No, Lady, I deem I shall not. I was absolved before my execution, and now that I am dead, I can do little to require confession."

"Oh, I'm sure you could do enough," she muttered into her teacup.

"I'll bring the car around and meet you out front," she said as she picked the car keys off the hook by the door and walked to the stable to feed the horses and crank her uncle's old sedan into life. *This is going to be a real adventure,* she thought as she walked briskly along the stable path.

Garrett had been out early, and she found the horses already munching their mash and the stables clean. He was standing on the paving in front of the great double doors of the Close when Ellen drove around the track from the stable and stopped the car with a squeal of rusty brakes.

Setting the hand brake, she got out and motioned him over. It looked like a scene from some situation comedy, Ellen thought as she watched him approach, sword and dagger, boots and all, the stone walls of his castle rising behind him . . . and a rusty old sedan sitting where a carriage should have been waiting to carry him away.

He touched the metal cautiously and looked doubtful when she opened the door. "Don't worry, I've been driving since I was ten," she said as he settled into the seat warily, eyeing the wheel and gauges suspiciously. He tensed visibly when she ground the gears and let out the clutch with a lurch. "I think I'm as nervous as you are," she muttered but saw that he smiled delightedly at the smooth-rolling speed and the trees flashing past at all of thirty miles per hour.

Wait till we take a train ride, thought Ellen, *or an airplane.* And she wondered how much of modern technology it was healthy for him to know if he ever should go home to his own time.

Garrett's presence in the old stone church caused a notable stir. As old Andis Culpepper had said, "In a town the size of Briarwick, your own business is your neighbor's business." And Andis was one of the first to greet her after service, shaking her hand with condolences for her uncle while eyeing the stranger beside her curiously.

"And who be this one, miss?" he finally asked outright to the relief of all gathered around.

"This is Mr. Gary Coalson, an old family friend," she replied, avoiding the mirth in Garrett's eyes as she answered their questions.

"Yes, my uncle knew him from years ago," hedged Ellen.

"No, he was not here for the funeral . . ."

Ellen noted that, from her angle, Garrett was juxtaposed before his own statue and that the effect was startling. She hoped no one else noticed. "He had a bit of difficulty with time and travel scheduling . . . No, he did not come by train . . . Yes, it's fortunate the weather has cleared . . ."

Ellen was vastly relieved when at last the church was empty except for the young priest who was asking Garrett if he'd be staying long and where he was from and whether he'd considered a chair in the choir. Garrett answered after Ellen's artful lead, and when at last they stepped out of the doorway and stood upon the steps, the sunlight and fresh air were a relief.

"I have never lied so much nor so shamelessly ever in my life," she muttered.

"Ah, but thou hast not lied—only omitted truth," Garrett observed.

"Yeah, and bent it all out of shape," she added dryly. "So how did it feel to sit next to your own grave?"

Garrett shrugged, and his face creased in a smile. "I feel I could begin to enjoy this," he said. "Here, I am nobody. So now, here, I can be anyone or anything I desire to be. It has never been so for me."

The words alarmed Ellen in a way she could not explain. They felt wrong, they left things undone, and she watched his face intently for a troubled moment before turning away and descending the steps. Without knowing exactly why she did so, she walked to the old cemetery gate instead of going to the parked car. She was standing beside her uncle's grave when she heard Garrett behind her. He paused briefly and then walked along the row of weathered stones nearest the church wall where the graves were not so very old to him and none were anonymous though graven names were worn away.

Striding slowly he perused the row, pausing at some, remembering, passing others, until he came to a stone that was placed at an angle and out of line like an afterthought near the wall at the end of the row. Ellen saw him stiffen as if struck before he knelt there in the grass with one hand upon the stone and the other upon the green mound beneath, his head bowed, his shoulders hunched in grief.

Ellen read the gravestone quickly. It was the one she had noticed only days before: "Alice Sheffield and son" engraved upon the granite.

"This evil," Garrett said hoarsely. "This devilry goes too far." He brushed his fingers over the lichen-covered stone. "It is as I feared, but now I know it done."

"Who were they?" Ellen asked softly, hardly daring to speak.

"My son," he said, his face a pale mask of anger and grief. "Edward Maxwell Coltstone, though they dost not honor him with my name, and Alice, his dear mother."

The road home was silent and passed quickly and Ellen knew that Garrett's thoughts no longer toyed with freedom and change. At the kitchen table, he sat with pen and paper and a calendar, charting and marking and counting, until Ellen finally surmised that he was figuring dates and times and perhaps moon phases or some such. "If I could only know," he muttered. "Be it a month or a year or another five hundred?" he hissed. "Be there an incantation, a setting, a situation? If such a magic has brought me here, then such must be able to affect my return." He rubbed his temples in frustration.

"And if you knew," she chided softly, "still, you've not learned what you must in order to change the course of events."

Looking down at the plate she'd shoved across in front of him, he admitted that she was right. She had remained silent since they had stood beside the grave. She'd asked no question, made no comment. Looking at her now, he wondered what she was thinking and was surprised that he wanted her to know the truth and believed he could trust her with it—sometime—when it was not so raw a wound on his heart.

They ate without talking, but as she cleared the dishes, Ellen pointedly stacked the papers and calendar away to the side.

"I would like," she said, "for you to tell me the history of this castle, but not from an armchair. Tell it to me room by room—as you knew it—when it was alive and full of noise and people."

The notion did not appeal to his present state of mind, but as they stood in the Close, behind the tall iron-bound doors, and he told the stories of hunting parties and the garrisoned troops and a winter siege long before his time, his heart warmed to the memories and eased in its pain.

Room by room, from Great Hall to cellars, and finally up to the attics, Garrett proved an expert guide. Ellen's pen scratched and scraped in her notebook, capturing each thought and story, each picture painted in words, until at last they came back to the long dusty attic stair all draped in spider webbing that they had climbed into the attic's dusky reaches. Ellen had begun the descent when she noticed that Garrett had crossed instead to the round alcove of the corner tower and was gazing upward at the board ceiling of the turret. Following him, she stood, watching curiously as he shoved an old wooden chest over against the wall and stood upon it, beckoning her to him with a proffered hand.

"What is it?" she asked.

"Climb up here," he said.

Doubtfully, Ellen placed her notebook on the dusty top of an old keg, wiped her hands on her skirt, took his hand, and climbed up beside him. Garrett then braced one boot on a stone that protruded from the wall and, with a mischievous grin, said, "Now climb up here."

"I don't think . . . ," Ellen began, but Garrett took her by the waist and lifted her lightly.

"Stand up," he said as he steadied her with his hand.

"Now," he directed, "reach up. Canst thou touch the ceiling?"

"Yes," she answered hesitantly, placing her hands against the rough-hewn timbers.

"Push up."

She did, and the boards above her gave way in a shower of dust and dirt.

"Push them up and slide them over," Garrett directed from below, blinking and shaking the dust from his face as Ellen lifted the boards and slid them to the side across the floor of turret above.

"Wow!" she said as she looked up through the opening at the dim space beyond. And grasping the edge of the timbers, she hoisted herself up and crouched on the turret floor.

"Now take my hand," he called from below; and lying flat on the boards, she stretched downward until he grasped her wrist and leaped up to catch the edge of the woodwork above. He pulled himself up and sat beside her, smiling with boyish glee.

"What place is this?" asked Ellen, looking at the low peak of the turret roof above them. The heavy slates of the roof were held in place with iron spikes driven into the timbers, and the timbers joining overhead were fitted and pegged with shipwright's craftsmanship. Garrett hunched low as he scrambled across the boards to a basket and pile of leather and cloth stashed against the far wall where the rafters met the ceiling.

"This," said Garrett, looking around him nostalgically "was our secret place."

Ellen looked questioningly.

"Mine and David's. We came here as boys . . . to get away from our tutors and the wardens of the practice yard when we'd gotten into some mischief." His eyes glowed with happy remembrance, though his voice was tempered with sadness. “We dreamed a lot here as boys. Dreamed and planned . . .”

The moment was his, the memories close and real; and Ellen respected that, knowing well the charm such places held. “I had a tree under a creek bank,” she said after the silence had grown long, “where the dirt was always damp and cool in summer and the wind never blew. But I had no brother, only a wise old collie dog named Sam.”

Garrett nodded, feeling slightly foolish for indulging in such maudlin emotions, and moved back toward the opening in the floor; but Ellen was not ready to leave.

“What things did you and David dream of?” she asked, tucking her skirt around her legs and hugging her knees.

“Oh, naught of great importance.”

“But what?” she urged.

Garrett thought for a moment, picking at a drip of candle wax left upon the floor by a beeswax taper five hundred years before. “We dreamed of being sea captains,” he said.

“No!” She winked.

“Yes! I was to build the ships, and David was to captain them to all the foreign lands we could dream of.”

Scooting the basket across the floor toward her, he pulled some pieces of crumbly brown leather scrap from the jumble of its dirty and mouse-chewed contents. “There,” he said, fingering them, “these were some of my plans.”

The black ink was scarcely visible, but the outlines of ribs and spares and masts were evident in the crude childish drawings. Ellen heard Garrett laugh softly; and looking up from the leather pieces, she saw he held a rotted piece of lace, the border of a lady’s kerchief.

“This was my mother’s,” he said. “We tore it playing “Lady’s favor” with it and were too afraid to tell her. She searched for it for over a month.” Taking up the scraps of hide and placing them on top of the basket, he shoved it against the wall once more, but a brittle old weaver caught and broke on the rough boards; and where it gave way, the tired old basket bulged, and a small something fell out upon the floor. It was the small tarnished bronze casting of a horse.

Garrett picked it up, fingering it in his palm, rolling it over and standing it on its sturdy legs.

“What is it, Garrett?” asked Ellen, watching the emotions play across his face.

"I lost this," he said, "Years ago. It was my great-grandfather's. He brought it back from a crusade, he said. My grandfather gave it to me when I was ten. I always wondered what had become of it."

"Did anyone else ever come here?" asked Ellen.

"No, only David and me. We stopped coming here sometime after I was fourteen and David sixteen, and we began to think of other things." He slipped the tiny horse into the pocket at his belt, slid through the opening in the floor, and jumped down to the wooden chest below, where he reached up to grasp Ellen's hands and lowered her lightly to the floor.

"You had a good childhood," she said,

"Yes," he agreed. "But 'little did my mother think, when first she cradled me, the lands I was to travel in and the death I was to die.'"

"Mary Queen of Scots said that," said Ellen.

"Many have said the same," he replied.

Ellen sat up late that night at the old typewriter in her uncle's study, typing out the notes she had written and making more and jotting down questions as they came to her mind. It was two in the morning when she finally paused for a cup of tea and fell asleep with her head upon her arms at the table. She awoke much later with a crick in her neck and wandered off to bed. Garrett had not worn his sword that day, she realized, as she propped the chair against the door. But she had seen the dagger hilt in the top of his boot. She thought the dagger was an interesting item, very beautifully made; and she decided she should ask him about it, tomorrow maybe. That would be Monday, one week before her interview at Kingston, and the reminder sent her mind wandering fruitlessly over all the difficulties besetting her inherited estate. She fell asleep recounting the taxes due and totally forgot the small stack of very dirty laundry by His Lordship's chamber door.

SOMETHING NEW . . . SOMETHING OLD

Ellen did not, in fact, remember the laundry at all until she came through the kitchen door early the next morning after feeding the horses and cleaning the stable. Stomping the dirt off her boots and closing the door, she turned to see Lord Garrett standing at the kitchen cabinet, studying the flashy print picture on a cereal box. She turned away quickly to hide her smile and cleared her throat gruffly, but Garrett was not unaware of her mirth.

"I believe thou dost not approve of this attire?" he said.

Ellen shook her head, eyeing him appraisingly. Uncle Sidney's old clothes were not in ill fit, but the effect of cotton trousers tucked into tall black boots, button-down shirt, and cardigan belted with the wide leather sword belt was simply comical.

"No," she said finally. "You can take the man out of the century but not the century out of the man."

At his look of chagrin, she laughed. "It looks fine," she said. "Uncle would be proud, but it does not suit. I will wash your things while we eat."

"Thank you," he said. He had been feeling more foolish than he liked to admit.

"We need to have some things made for you," she commented when she finally pulled the tunic and cloak from the dryer and handed them to him, "We don't know how long you'll be here, but these will be worn to a frazzle at this rate."

"Do you weave?" he asked

"No." She laughed. "And I don't have a sewing machine with me here."

"Sewing machine?" he inquired, but Ellen did not attempt an explanation.

"There is a lady in the village who sews for others. I'll call her while you go get normal looking—normal for you at least—and we will drive into the village."

Bowing slightly, Garrett exited the room; and by the time he returned, Ellen had arranged to meet with a Mrs. Betty Sayer, a widow in the village, who was more than happy to sew a set or two of clothes for Ellen's "old family friend."

"Curious questions could get sticky around here," she said to Garrett as they drove along the road to Mrs. Sayers. "Remember, you are Gary Coalson, and try not to say too much."

"Yes, my Lady," he said dryly.

Mrs. Sayer was a short wiry woman of fifty-some-odd years, of which she had been a widow for only three, and managed meagerly with a large garden, a small pension, and her sewing machine. She smiled widely at Ellen and Garrett as she beckoned them into her small sitting room, motioning them into chairs with an offer of tea which could not be refused. Indeed, finding it vastly entertaining to watch Lord Garrett ensconced in a small wingback near the fender, sharing a cup of tea with little Mrs. Sayer, Ellen was not about to refuse the invitation. She perched comfortably in an old Victorian-era settee as Mrs. Sayer eyed Garrett curiously and chatted happily . . . She entertained so rarely . . .

"Mr. Culpepper said he had made your acquaintance on Sunday, Mr. Coalson," Mrs. Sayer was saying. "He said he thought you were not from around these parts." She cast him a questioning glance.

"Ah," he replied without meeting Ellen's gaze. "I spent some little time here years ago, but it is far from my home."

Mrs. Sayer thought briefly, weighed his accent thoughtfully, and made quick assumptions as people do. "Oh, then you are from the continent?" she said, smiling cheerily. "Not Germany, I hope."

"No, not Germany," Garrett replied affably, but gave her no further encouragement on the subject. Looking him over, she decided he must be Swedish.

"And you are a friend of Ms. Lancaster's?" she asked with a sidelong glance at Ellen.

"My uncle," interjected Ellen, "knew Mr. Coalson well, by letters mainly, Mr. Coalson being an authority in matters of antiquity, a mutual interest of study to them."

"Oh!" exclaimed Mrs. Sayer, "You are a professor at the university?"

"Not presently," Garrett said, tapping the thin gold rim of the teacup. "I am more interested in research."

Ellen looked at her wristwatch; Mickey Mouse was moving along, and she set her teacup in its saucer with obvious purpose. Taking the cue, Mrs. Sayer, having already appraised Garrett's odd costume, leaned forward.

"Now then, Mr. Coalson," she said brightly. "Ms. Lancaster tells me you need a suit or two of clothes." *People do wear the oddest things these days,* she thought to herself. "I have some nice patterns for very practical suits, perhaps a gabardine in blue. I happen to have a bolt of good stuff just in."

Garrett, nonplussed, looked to Ellen for assistance.

"Actually," said Ellen, leaning forward, "what we need is two sets of clothes as nearly like these as you can make them." Seeing Mrs. Sayer's disparaging look, she continued quickly, "You see, Mr. Coalson is presently researching the durability of the design and cloth of fifteenth-century clothing. Unfortunately, his baggage did not make the transfer—lost somewhere, you know—and so he needs some things made."

Mrs. Sayer nodded, slowly accepting the outlandish tale. *People did odd things nowadays,* she thought, *one just never knew.* She looked closely at Garrett's tunic, robe, and breeches.

"Well," she said. "That should be simple enough, although I don't do such fine needlework as this." She fingered the silk stitch upon the cuff of Garrett's sleeve. "Still, I can sew what you wish quite nicely. Come with me," she said sweetly as she stood; and she led them through a hall to her tiny workroom, where her machine sat in a corner under a low window. Pins, needles, and scissors were all neatly arranged on a table alongside; and bolts of cloth were stacked from floor to ceiling on two walls of shelving.

Ellen picked out a bolt of brown cotton canvas for breeches, unbleached cotton for the tunic, and a bolt of rich midnight blue wool for the robe. Mrs. Sayer measured Garrett from head to foot and made drawings of the tunic and breeches. "Interesting cloth," she muttered, fingering the wool robe with its gold trim. And Garrett, looking at a fold of forest green twill, hazarded one more request. He asked her to sew a cloak, hooded, circular hemmed, and lined, with an inside pocket, just such as he was used to wear. Intrigued, both Ellen and Mrs. Sayer watched as he briefly sketched the lines of it on paper, and Mrs. Sayer quickly agreed to include it in her work. She tallied the bill, and Ellen was digging in her satchel for her money when she heard the clink of coin upon the wooden boards.

"Oh? What are these?" exclaimed Mrs. Sayer, leaning over to squint at the gold coins. Ellen quickly covered them with her hand and slid them off the table into her palm. "Foreign stuff," she said lightly as she laid out several paper notes in their place.

Eyeing the flimsy paper, Garrett arched one brow. "You purchase with these?"

"Yes," said Ellen wryly. "With enough of this, you can buy anything you want."

Garrett shrugged.

They were bidding farewell at the door when Mrs. Sayer took Ellen's hand in a gesture of commiseration. "And how are things up at the old place?" she asked. "Mrs. Darrow says things need lots of fixing up."

Nodding, Ellen considered how much of what she said would be at the tables of the Bowl & Pitcher by evening. Still, she thought, folks may as well know about matters that affected their community—and an American heiress was indeed quite a worrisome unknown.

"The roof hasn't fallen in yet," she replied lightly. "It's the taxes that will be my undoing."

"Aye, yes. They would be a mite steep on a place like that," commiserated Mrs. Sayer.

"Yes, a 'mite.' I've applied for a professorship at Kingston. If that comes through, well, then I'll see about a loan for the taxes. And everything will be just fine."

"Oh, I do hope so, dearie. I do hope so." She patted Ellen's hand. "I'll have yer things ready by day after tomorrow. Jacob, my neighbor's boy, can run them up to ye."

"Thank you," said Ellen as Garrett flattered the old lady with a parting bow, and they walked back to the car with that good woman's speculative gaze following after them.

Ellen slammed the car door and dropped her satchel on the console between them; then grasping Garrett's hand, she pressed the two gold coins firmly into his palm.

"I wouldn't be throwing these out on the boards anymore if I were you," she said with a sidelong glance.

Garrett looked his enquiry as he slid the coins back into the pouch upon his belt.

"They are probably worth three times more in antique value than they are for their gold, which is quite enough." She shifted the car into gear, "If you stay here much longer I'll find a place in London where you can sell them at auction or find a dealer to exchange them. You could live quite well, for a time, off of that." She thought for a moment. "Got any more?"

Garrett shrugged noncommittally.

"You could always buy yourself a castle," she said, half jesting. "I know one that might be up for sale soon."

"You spoke of taxes . . . ," he replied absently, his mind lingering on her words of how long he might be staying here.

"Yes, my uncle left lots of bills unpaid. I'm trying to figure out a way to pay up and make a go of it here, but I'm not sure if it is going to work. I have a job interview in Kingston on Monday. You can ride along if you'd like."

"Hmmm," he replied. "Yes, I'd like to see Kingston again—now." But his mind was saying that he could not stay, that he must go back, and that he must find a way soon. He must find the door, the spell, the way, whatever the magic was, before it was too late. He looked at Ellen and was convinced now that whatever had happened to bring him here, it had not been by any power or cunning of hers. Perhaps she was involved, like he, by some greater design, some intertwining magic that foreknew their actions; and maybe she had said the right words at the right time, but it could only have been by chance. He shook his head. The walls of the church loomed in the clearing ahead as they rounded the bend of the road.

"Prithee," he said, "halt ye at the kirk yard." And seeing the look on his face, Ellen complied without question.

If he were to begin a search for answers and clues, he thought, this place seemed the logical place to start. Perhaps there was some clue or some message to be found in the sanctuary alcove, something enduring over the centuries that could show him the way to reverse this spell, unless (and his heart stilled at the thought) it was truly a curse and never meant to be reversed. Perhaps he was meant to be lost—dead and alive—forever. He wondered whether his enemy could be that strong.

Ellen followed without a word as he strode up the high steps and into the sanctuary where all was pensively quiet except for the rattle and buzz of a wayward honeybee in a window sill up high. Garrett stood before the statue, studying it closely, then knelt, brushing his fingers lightly over the smooth granite base.

"What are you looking for?" Ellen asked finally as he leaned over the crypt, his face inches from its marble engravings.

"I am searching for anything . . . anything that might be a message, an incantation, a key to the magic . . ."

"That might send you home," she finished, moving forward to join him in the search.

Together, they inspected the floors and walls of the alcove, the designs in the ceiling, even the scenes in the stained-glass windows above and at either side; but they found nothing that seemed relevant to their search. At the point of admitting defeat, Ellen peered into the two-foot space between the wall and the crypt.

"What about back here?" she asked. "It's pretty tight . . . but maybe . . ." Unzipping her satchel, she dug out a key-chain flashlight and, swiping away the thick cobwebs, wedged herself down against the wall, sliding along the dusty flags behind the crypt.

"Dost thou see anything?" asked Garrett, gazing down over the top.

"Just a minute," said Ellen, wiping the griming stone with her hand. "Yes, something. It's not really an engraving, more like very shallow etching."

"What does it look like?" Garrett asked impatiently.

"It's a picture. A big deer with horns, jumping into a grove of trees. There are rays of sunlight shining down over him and behind him there's a sickle moon with a single star."

"Waxing or waning?"

"What?"

"The moon—is it waxing or waning?"

"Oh, waning . . . I think."

"May I help you?" said a dignified voice that made Ellen jump.

Garrett turned around slowly to find the young priest staring at him in puzzlement and concern.

"We were looking . . . ," began Garrett and paused uncertainly

"I've been looking for my ring . . . ," said Ellen, prying herself up out of the cramped space behind the tomb. "Never found it. You know how they roll," she said as she climbed over the top of the crypt, pulling cobwebs from her hair. Garrett lifted her down easily, and she smoothed her skirt and her composure.

The priest nodded agreeably, although his expression was still that of puzzlement. “If I find it, I will keep it for you,” he suggested; and Ellen thanked him as they walked to the door.

“See you Sunday,” she called as they got into the car, and he waved from the doorway.

“I’ll draw you a picture of the etching when we get home,” she said to Garrett as she wrestled the car into gear.

He was looking at her with a perplexed smile—her hair was a mess and netted with dirty cobwebs, dirt smudged her skirt where she had wiped her hands. “What’s so funny?” she asked, irritated.

Garrett noted her long thin fingers upon the steering wheel; there was no white line where a ring had been worn. “I have never seen you wear a ring,” he said.

“Nor do I,” she said. “Though I did have one once—my high school ring. I lost it in the sand of the arena at a dressage clinic in Las Cruces, New Mexico.”

“You are resourceful . . .”

“I feel I’m becoming a horrible liar.”

He noted the remorse in her voice and shook his head “I have not yet heard thee tell a bold lie.”

“No, but my truths are getting thinner all the time. In my family, our word is our bond. It’s a matter of honor.”

“Aye,” he replied, eyeing the signet ring upon his own hand. “In ours also.”

He was silent a moment, in thought; then with a wry smile, he said, “My mother would have liked you.”

“Your mother,” replied Ellen, laughing sarcastically, “Would have thrown me in a dungeon as soon as look at me.”

“Yes, probably,” he agreed. “But she would have liked you.”

“Why?”

“You have a quick wit, and you are resourceful.”

“Yeah, well. It’s pretty hard to be resourceful in a dungeon, I would imagine.”

Garrett thought of the letters that he had never finished written in haste in his cell in the Tower of London. “Yes,” he said. “It is difficult.

“How old are you?” he asked suddenly “You do not appear much over twenty.”

“Twenty!” she shook her head. “Credit that to the easy comforts of this modern age and add ten years, sir. I am thirty-two, thirty-three in October.”

"Thirty-two," he repeated quietly. "And never yet married?"

"Never found anyone worth having," she said flippantly, and then regretted having said it so. It was too shallow a thing to say to his honest curiosity. As she turned into the Garrison Keep gateway, she shook her head. "I grew up in West Texas," she began again.

"West Texas?" he queried.

"Yes, in the New World. I'll explain that all later. But things are very different there—it's a tough place, takes strong people. My daddy was a rancher."

"Rancher?"

"Yes, he had cattle, a herd of cattle."

"Ah . . . a drover."

"Well, after a sort." Ellen laughed. They pulled into the stable shed, and she set the hand brake. "Daddy owned ten thousand acres and leased as much more . . . a ranch . . . He worked a lot of cattle over a lot of land."

Garrett's brow furrowed as he wondered why Ellen was alone if her father was so vastly wealthy. Why was she working and her estate so poorly maintained?

"Your father must have been a man of a great fortune," he suggested.

"No," said Ellen, getting out of the car and thinking how to explain as they walked along the stable run. She stopped at the filly's stall and leaned her elbows upon the paling, rubbing the horse's neck as it nuzzled her shoulder.

Watching her, Garrett thought of Leticia, always hungry for power and for wealth, hungry for the influence those things afforded and never satisfied. "You wait for one this wealthy and this powerful?" he prodded, feeling vaguely disappointed in her.

Shaking her head, Ellen weighed her words, trying to make her thoughts plain. "You don't understand," she said at last. "It's not like here. One hundred acres of dry mesquite and cactus—it might feed one cow.

"Desert? Like the Holy Land?"

"Yes, only different. They say everything in Texas either stings, sticks, or stinks." She laughed. "I'll show you pictures of it in a book up in Uncle's study. But my dad," she said seriously, "was not rich or powerful, and that's not what made him so wonderful. It's that he could look at hot, dry, mesquite-grown grassland and see a place where he could live, where he could be his own man and raise a family. Men like that . . . Well, they don't just grow on trees."

"And this is what you search for?" Garrett asked, leaning on the fence next to her.

"Wait for, more than search," she said. "I'm not into fixing things that aren't broken." She gave the horse a final pat. "Come on, I'll show you some pictures of Texas." And together, they walked back to the castle.

In her uncle's study, Ellen pulled out an old yellowed photo album and placed it on a table before laying a clean sheet of paper out upon the desk. She sat down to draw the etching from the tomb while Garrett flipped open the album.

Most of the photos were brown tones of the late nineteenth century and the cut, edged black-and-whites of the thirties and forties and depicted the wagons and mules, long-horned cattle, and wood-frame houses with dry, dusty dirt yards of that time. Setting her simple drawing aside, Ellen stood at Garrett's shoulder, pointing to photos and naming the people and the places and explaining the way of things in the New World.

"This is my father and my uncle as boys," she said, pointing to two tow-headed boys on scrappy mustang ponies.

"This was my mom when they married. This is me." She fingered the picture of a cherubic baby in a frilly white smock.

"This was our ranch house. That fellow worked for Dad. That's roundup. That was our first Hertford bull."

The pictures brought back so many memories of so many times. Ellen smiled in happy nostalgia, unaware of Garrett's gaze upon her, thoughtful and sad. When she looked up, his gaze fell back to the page upon the table. "Is this, then, how your world, your New World, looks now?"

"Oh no!" she replied, perplexed. "Here, I have snapshots that I brought to show my uncle." She pulled the packet of photos out of a drawer in the side table near his old chair. "This," she said, laying the color photos out upon the table, "is where I live. That's my house," she said proudly of the neat little white farmhouse with the live oak trees all around. "That is the university where I work."

"And this is you?" Garrett asked, holding out a photo.

Ellen nodded. The photo was of her and the sorrel, the sleek creature in midleap over a six-foot barrier jump. The photo had been taken at a cross-country jump meet earlier that spring.

"You are a person of many talents, Lady Ellen," he said appreciatively as he placed the photo back among the others. "You have a good family, a good life. And as you say, you have nothing broken to fix, though I think you will yet find that someone who is waiting *for you*, someday."

Ellen laughed to think of someone "waiting for her." She leaned back against the desk, folded her arms, and asked impulsively, "What of you, Lord Garrett? What have you to fix? Tell me about Leticia."

"Leticia," he snorted. "Of Leticia, there in naught to tell."

"Well, then tell me about Alice . . . please. I would like to know something about her."

Garrett considered Ellen for a long moment; and he saw no guile in her face, no judgments, no mean curiosity, only a sincere desire to understand, to know the things he knew . . .

"Alice," he said softly, turning to gaze out of the window. "Alice Sheffield was the only daughter of a lord vassal to my father. She came to serve as a waiting maid to my mother in hopes that she might there meet and marry a person suitable to her family station.

"She was young and bright and pretty." Garrett thought of her golden blonde hair and eyes of sea green, and he smiled sadly. "She was all of sixteen—perhaps—and she took a fancy to the baron's youngest son.

"She was always likable—her kindness were simple, her speech without guile. She would meet us at the gates when we came in from the hunt, always with a cheerful word and a warm smile. We became fast friends, she and David and I.

Seeing a disparaging look cross Ellen's face, Garrett grimaced and shook his head adamantly. "No, there was none such as you suppose. She was not the sort to meddle with so. Alice was a cherished friend, and we guarded her like a sister.

"We continued thus for well on two years until the winter of my twentieth year when I fell ill to a great sickness. It weighed heavily upon me for a month or more and bound me bedfast. Alice stayed ever at my side to comfort and care. And what had been friendship grew, until that spring when I at last regained strength of new health, we spoke of love and of marriage.

"But my mother would not approve our vows, and my brother held with her that I should not marry so below our cast, at least not until my brother was married more auspiciously and the fortune of our family secure. We heeded their words but not our own counsels of wisdom. And by that fall, in my twenty-first year, Alice was to bear me a son. I loved him. I claimed him. I gave him my name. I would have married Alice then. I should have in spite of all—that I know now. But by then my brother was in somewhat of a difficulty, having flirted too often and too ardently with the eldest daughter of the Earl of Mansfield, which lord now expected an offer of alliance in marriage to our house.

"My mother feared that to do otherwise would anger this powerful man, and although she did not think highly of the Lady Leticia, she did not trust that my brother and I could defend the estate against such an opponent as her father. My father had been dead only three years at that time.

"And so Leticia was to marry David that year, and my desire to marry Alice was once more confounded lest such a base alliance in the family insult the new lady and her noble father. My mother advised that we should delay our vows until there was an heir of David and Leticia. And so we would wait, and so the love of passion grew a deeper root as time and distance enforced. Alice had our child to love, and I had them both to cherish and watch over.

"Did David love Leticia?" asked Ellen.

"Love?" Garrett scoffed. "Love Leticia? No. She was only a sin come home to roost, a pretty bird to be the bane of our family ever after. They came to hate before they ever learned to love. Leticia, you see, desired wealth and prestige above all else. And I suppose she saw in our family and our lands and in David's natural charisma the potential and the opportunity to acquire. And David might have succeeded in all that Leticia desired as years went by—he might have claimed a position at court, the favor of the king. He might have taken Leticia there with him as she so desired, one day. But the more she pushed and demanded, the less he gave. What love he had for her quickly changed to dislike, and what time he might have spent in pursuit of wealth and influence, he spent in the field at sport and at the hunt. He was content to govern his lands and live peaceably . . . until the day he was slain."

"So he did not drown?" cried Ellen almost triumphantly.

Garrett shook his head. "No, and yes." He slouched into a wingback by the hearth and cast his leg over the arm comfortably. "He did drown—after he fell from his horse with a cloth-yard arrow through the breadth of him."

Longing to question more, Ellen curbed herself as he continued with his narration.

"With David buried, I—and my mother too I presume—assumed that Leticia, who had never been happy in our household, would return to her father. And in this, all my hope of marrying Alice was lost."

"Lost! Why?"

"I could not now marry to one so humble in station, for the good of my family . . ."

"Your family!" said Ellen scornfully. "What of Alice? What of the love you claim you had for her?"

Garrett favored her with a scathing glance. "You," he said, "in this age of peace and plenty, cannot know how it was, when by your word and the deed of your hand was there food on your table or a long desolate winter of cold and famine for all. When the safety of all you owned and those whose lives were yours to defend depended not on some great magnanimous rule of order, but on the keen blade of the sword you held. Personal desires must be subject to duty—sacrifices made both noble and common."

Ellen watched the tension of sadness that the words brought to his face and considered that not all men would have thought as he did. Few now did. "But you married Leticia?" prompted Ellen.

"Yes. She requested it so."

"She?"

"Yes. By some Levitical law that she declared binding, even though I knew it not so, she claimed the right to wed the surviving heir. I knew that she only wished to keep hold of the wealth of the estate and the place she had established for herself in our family in hopes that upon my mother's death, she could wield that power through the perhaps more malleable younger son. My mother promoted the arrangement, loath to lose the rich dowry Leticia had brought with her, and we were married. A fell day it was too. 'Better a dinner of herbs where love is than a feast with strife.'" Garrett mused. "Leticia was the proverbial 'dripping of water.'"

"And what of Alice?" asked Ellen, imagining that lady's grief.

"She remained my mother's lady-in-waiting and was well provided for and carefully protected until my mother's death, at which time I sent her away to her father's house with our son—then a boy of eight years. I knew her father could protect them."

"From whom?"

"I did not trust Leticia. Her jealousies could be cruel.

"When Edward was fourteen, I brought him back to the Keep to continue his education with a private tutor and to train him to manage the estate as my heir. He was a fine, handsome boy with a heart like his mother's, her charity of spirit. He would have been my heir even had there been another, and I was to have named him so to my vassals and in my will this very year, his twenty-first year. But as you know, I was prevented."

"Prevented? Of course you were! And do you still think Leticia innocent of plotting against you?"

"I think her capable. I believe it probable, but by what means the letters were writ, I do not yet fathom."

The silence hung heavy in the room as Ellen thought of all he'd said. The noontide sun seemed too warm and bright to have seen the struggles of all those centuries. She closed the pages of the old photo album, thinking how simple and kind those lives seemed in contrast to the hate and duplicity Garrett's family had endured. As if reading her thoughts, he smiled at her knowingly. "Our families have one thing in common, you know."

"What?"

"They are all dead now, and the struggles are over."

"Yes," she agreed resignedly. And then seeing the humor in his eye, she brightened and said, "All but two of us anyway, and I'm not at all sure about you."

While Ellen prepared lunch, Garrett studied the drawing she had made from the tomb: the trees, the sunlight rays, the hart, the moon, and the star.

He knew that there was some message in the emblems, and he believed the message was meant for him; but try as he might, he could not find their significance. He wondered if there were more clues in the old chapel or if there were writings, old legends, or stories passed down locally that might help him find an answer. Feeling uneasy and tired, he was surprised and relieved when Ellen appeared in the study again, carrying a plate and a broadsword.

"What's this?" he asked, pointing to the sword as he picked up the sandwich.

"I want lessons," she said. "I borrowed it from the metal guy in the Great Hall."

"Lessons?"

"Yes, from an expert."

The afternoon was spent in the old practice yard by the stable. The horses shied and whinnied at the unfamiliar flash of sunlight on steel, and the ringing clash of the ancient broadswords awakened a thousand dreamy visions from the old stone walls above. Weary and sore that night, Ellen slept soundly, walking in realms of ancient stories among people who seemed now familiar; and the chair did not lean against the door.

Garrett sat long at the oak desk in the study, the drawing before him, his life behind him, and all about him a world of unknowns.

AN ARROW, A GYPSY, AND THE RUINS

In the days that followed, Ellen spent her mornings and evenings typing and writing, amassing the vast wealth of information she gleaned from Garrett's comments, his stories, his manners, and his way of doing things. She could write a book, she knew, on his knowledge of weaponry alone; volumes more could be filled from his description of fortress defenses, feudal social policy, diplomacy with vassals and serfs, and all that made his domain a feudal statehood.

And while she wrote and studied, Garrett wandered the halls and attics of the Garrison Keep and the grounds roundabout the church, the gravestone etching ever in his mind as he searched for he knew not what. Old Mr. Darvin grew accustomed to his hauntings; and the priest, who thought him an odd sort, often found him sitting silently, gazing at the statue and crypt as if he would see something beyond their grey stone.

In the afternoons, Garrett and Ellen often sparred with the swords in the practice yard, where Ellen was a quick, if not talented, student. "You are too stiff," he constantly critiqued. "You study too much and move not enough. You must move—not think. The blade will not stop while you consider." Still, he was pleased at her progress, though amused at her interest in such sport.

The days passed quickly, and Ellen realized that Garrett no longer seemed a guest at the Garrison Keep. Indeed, at times, it felt more as though she were his guest. His comic otherworldliness and congenial personality were welcome distractions to her financial concerns and her thoughts of the upcoming interview. Still, as the days passed and they were no closer to finding his way home, Ellen felt more and more certain that he really should be going back there soon. He could not stay here forever, she thought, or could he? And she told herself not to think too much in that way.

On Friday, she suggested that they take a lunch and ride up along the river to the far border of the old Coltstone estate and then return by way of the ruins. Ellen was hopeful that Garrett would tell her all he knew of the tenant farmers, their homesteads and their livelihood, and where each farmstead had been located. She packed her notebook in with the sandwiches and apples and slung the satchel across her back as they mounted the horses and set out at an easy trot.

Garrett was a horseman as only those born in an age of horses could be. His easy grace made even the old grey round up and stride out like a horse well-bred, and Ellen watched him with admiration until she told herself that she would do better to ride ahead and admire less.

The path beside the river was shaded and cool, its current placid and clear in its blue-green mossy depths. When they reached the parks and tourism sign that marked the sight of David's drowning, Garrett shook his head. "This is not the place," he said. "It was farther upstream. I will show you."

They rode on quite some distance until they entered an area of tilled ground, and Garrett reined in, perplexed. "It was here at this shoal," he said, "with the deep pool below, although there were trees here then. It was heavily wooded."

Gazing at the deep, still water of the pool below the rocky shoals, Ellen imagined the form of the man drowned there, tangled among the long, roping water weeds. "What happened?" she asked.

"I don't know," Garrett replied matter-of-factly.

"Don't know?"

"No . . . I was not there."

At her questioning gaze, he sighed, raking his fingers through his horse's mane roughly. "I had been injured that morning in the practice yard."

"By accident?"

"Of course!" he said, and then reconsidered as he rubbed the long scar that crossed from his shoulder to his elbow. "At least, I thought so then."

"And so you didn't ride with them on the hunt?"

"No." His voice was charged with remorse. He well remembered the group assembled in the Close, jesting with him at his staying behind with the women, and he remembered the solemn group that returned with his brother's body tied across his horse's back and a gypsy man bound and gagged led along behind them. The memory still brought pain

"I stayed behind," he said. "They told me he had ridden ahead of the hunt with two others. His squire had reined in to help another whose horse had stumbled. They said he was struck by an arrow as he was crossing the fords. They claimed the great gash upon his temple happened in the fall, that he was dead ere they could pull him from the water."

"Who shot him?"

"I was told that the gypsy man had fired the arrow from cover of the trees on the far bank. They had beaten him senseless, and he was unable to speak for himself. I then acted most foolishly. Losing wisdom in the heat of grief and anger, I ordered the man hung forthwith. So it was done."

Garrett looked up from the pool below and then across the field where once the trees had grown thick and tall. He swallowed hard. "I slew an innocent man. I do believe it and will never cease to regret the act."

"Why do you believe him innocent?"

He squinted in thoughtful memory. "The man had no motive. My men said they believed David had insulted the man in some way and that the deed was one of vengeance. When I rode here the following day, I found where the gypsy had camped, up over there," he pointed, "with his wife and twelve-year-old boy. They yet awaited his return." Garrett's jaw tightened as he remembered that meeting: the woman, round-eyed and frightened; her son beside her, angry and trying to be brave. "No man is so foolish as to fight when he is certain to lose and when he has all to lose and naught to gain. Perhaps he could have done so, but I do not believe it."

"Then who?"

Garrett faced her. "I slew the only man who might perhaps have known."

In the silence that lingered between them, each pursued a different road of thought. Garrett remembered how he'd brought the gypsy's wife and son back with him to the Keep, provided for them, given them a place at his table. The woman had eventually returned to her people. The boy had remained and, under Garrett's guidance, become a worthy scribe and accountant, loyal and privy to all his lord's business.

"Did Leticia bring her own retainers with her?" asked Ellen, breaking into his thought.

"Yes."

"Men-at-arms?"

"Thirty."

"Were they loyal to you?"

"They served among the others under my brother's command."

"Yes, but did you trust them?"

"Trust them? Yes," he said grimly. "Three rode with him that day."

"And who was it wounded you in the practice yard?"

Garrett shrugged, "That I could not know."

Ellen grinned sardonically, thinking she really did not need to know, and urged her horse forward past Garrett's grey as he lingered in memory and thought. She rode on to the tree line and dismounted under a broad oak. Sitting on the grass as the black filly grazed, she pulled a sandwich out of the satchel and nibbled it while she wrote in her notebook.

"What do you write now?" asked Garrett, dismounting and sitting with his back against the tree. He found her constant scribbling amusing.

"I'm writing everything you just said," she replied, handing him a sandwich and tossing an apple in his general direction.

"To what purpose?"

"I think we're on to something. Don't you?"

His appraising look was eloquent.

She ignored it and continued, tapping her pencil on the tablet. "I believe you were wounded on purpose. I think those men at arms were not so loyal—to you anyway—as you think, and I think Leticia is behind it all. She had your brother killed. She would have you dead too—before you named Edward heir. All we lack is a clue to her method, her accomplice, and proof of who wrote those letters!"

Ellen's brow furrowed as she thought hard and chewed the tip of her pencil.

Garrett only chuckled to himself at her odd manner, sitting cross-legged on the grass like any boy, writing, chewing pencils, and delving into matters not her own. He leaned his head back against the tree and closed his eyes. Women, he thought, did not change so much no matter what the century. Ellen thought he slept.

She finished her notes, ate her apple, and sat some time with elbows on knees and chin in hand, regarding the river below, the farms out upon the rolling hills, the patchwork of fields, the borders of trees. The horses munched placidly nearby, and the summer sun shone warm. *It should be a dream,* she thought, *it really must be.* Rising, she walked down to the river to look again at the clear, deep pool and was surprised to hear Garrett's step behind her. He knelt and cupped a handful of water to his mouth.

"I wouldn't drink that," she mumbled. "Might make you sick."

"I doubt it," he replied, laughing as they walked back to the horses.

"But then you might try that," said Ellen. "Perhaps if you die here, you go back there."

"So eager to get rid of me?" he chided, mounting the grey.

"No," she said, "but I probably ought to be."

After some hour's ride, they turned away from the river and rode around the base of a long hill, coming upon the old ruins from behind the great stone-retaining walls.

Ellen watched Garrett intently as he reined in to study the crumbling arch works of masonry. He saw his plans, his vision, his dream, and his work, now a creation lost in decay. He guided the grey slowly around the crumbling walls, then—tethering his mount—walked in among the leaning walls and sod-covered paving.

"Tell me about it," said Ellen softly, joining him as he stood dejectedly in what was once to have been a great sunlit hall.

"I dreamed it. I planned it. I began its building three times, but always, other matters interfered." He walked through the roofless spaces with her, pointing out each detail as if the structure stood complete. She could see it that way too as his words gave life to the hands of fairy builders and his eyes shone with the delight of creating.

"Tell me," she queried as they at last turned their backs to the ivy-bound walls. "If you could have done anything you wished in your life—how would it have been?"

Garrett gathered the grey's reins and looked back wistfully at the still-graceful arches. He sighed, "I would have had David live—long and happily—with a wife and a score of children to keep him busy, so he could be the baron and I, the younger brother.

"You'd marry Alice . . ."

"And build and design and create all the things I dreamed of."

"Ships?"

"Maybe."

"Cars and airplanes too?"

"Of course." He smirked. "Why do you laugh?"

"You are ambitious. My uncle only regretted not having a good dog."

"Your uncle," he said, gathering the reins and heading the grey toward home, "was a very fortunate man."

KINGSTON COLLEGE—OR A MAIDEN IN DISTRESS

Saturday dawned grey and weathery. Ellen was forced back to her typing, and when she wearied of that, she combed through the castle rooms, exploring their dusty corners, studying them in light of all Garrett had told her of them. In the attic, she lit a lamp and sat among the trunks and junk and dirty litter, sorting through stacks of old papers: the disarranged remains of legal transactions and correspondence from several eras. The rain beat a drumming tattoo on the slate roof, gurgled pleasantly in the stone guttering of the eves, and she could imagine the gargoyles spouting their mouthfuls of water over the walls below.

In the Great Hall, Garrett was seated at a trestle table before the massive fireplace where beeswax candles in candelabra lit the scratched and scribbled papers of his own figuring and the drawing that Ellen had made of the crypt's etchings. Of all the rooms in the castle, he felt most at ease in this space perhaps because, of all rooms in the castle, this room was least changed from what he had once known. He had begun to spend most of his time here if he must be indoors.

Several books of history and modern literature lay open at his elbow, and he perused them with avid interest; but always, his thoughts returned to the drawing. He felt that the moon phase and the companion star were the keys, though he'd never been a student of astronomy, and wondered who in this time he might find to explain matters to him.

He looked up as Ellen entered the room, sneezing and blowing her nose from the dust and mold of the old papers.

"Allergies," she explained to his look of concern. "I don't suppose people had them back then," she said of his time. "Or if they did, they called it something else and died of it."

"Yes, we died of many things," he said, amused. "Like hunger."

"Oh, I'm sorry," she said in mock dismay, seeing the time well past two o'clock on her watch. "I forgot lunch . . ."

"Yours, not mine," he added, stabbing a piece of cheese and slice of apple off a plate at his elbow with the point of his dagger.

"Explain this to me," he said, sliding a book across to her; and Ellen settled into a chair as she looked at the pages he'd opened to. An airfield, battleships, the flight deck of an aircraft carrier, the aftermath of Pearl Harbor, all smoke and fire . . . a convoy of tanks rolling past the dead of a battlefield somewhere in France, Iwo Jima, Auschwitz, WW II. Garrett watched as her eyes scanned the pages, the pictures, and then seemed to search for something beyond them.

"What is it?" he prodded. "What is this?"

"It is proof," she said, "that men do not change over centuries. Only our world grows smaller, and we become more capable of destroying it and each other."

He did not speak, and she continued uncertainly. "You see, as we progress and invent and build, it is all still mostly motivated by money and by power—even the good things. New medicines to keep us alive longer, new weapons to kill faster—both are often made by the same hands."

She paused, not knowing what more she should say. Leaning her elbow upon the table, she fixed him with an earnest stare. "These are photos of a great world war, the second one in this hundred years. We have weapons that kill thousands at one blow, bombs and bullets and poisonous gases. I do not think it wise for you to know more."

"Why thinkest thou so?"

"Because if—when—you do go back, if you should remember any of what you learn here, these things could change the course of humanity. This kind of knowledge would affect much more than just the fate of your family and estate. And that, I think, is too great a burden for any one man to bear."

Garrett read her sincerity and, feeling the wisdom of her words, closed the book carefully and slid it aside. "It is true," he said. "And I should not like to know so much. A man should have hope for his children that things will be better after him." He skewered another slice of apple.

"Now I have a question," Ellen said, leaning her chin on her palm and eyeing the dagger's intriguing design.

At Garrett's nod, she continued, "Where did you come by that knife? You didn't have it when you came here."

"No. But I knew where it was." He flipped the blade in his fingers and slid it across the table to her, hilt first. Picking it up, she studied the finely wrought damask blade, carved bone handle, bronze hilts, and haft set with a large black stone. It was wickedly beautiful.

Seeing her appreciation of it, Garrett smiled as she slid it back across the table to him. "It was my grandfather's," he said. "Made by his father and given to mine."

"And he gave it to you?" asked Ellen, wondering why David did not inherit.

"No, I stole it . . . off his corpse."

"You didn't!"

"I did," he said with a conspiratorial grin. "After he died, when the maidens and my mother laid him out upon his funeral bed, they placed his sword and this dagger at his side. I had wanted the dagger always, and he'd promised it to me. But they didn't know that. So I snuck in at night and traded this for a paring knife from the scullery."

"Good trade."

"My father perhaps would not have thought so."

"And you've carried it ever since?"

"No, never."

"Why?"

"Because that is the problem with things stolen—they can never be openly enjoyed. I never told even David. No one has ever known of it."

"Where did you keep it."

"Ah, that is like your bullets and bombs. I'm not certain that you should know—yet. Lest it change your history, or you."

"Fine, then. Keep your secret," she said, rising, "I shall go on my own quest: I go in search of lunch."

He watched her walk from the room, and then picking the blade up from the table, he balanced it over the palm of his hand. He'd told no one of this knife, all his life, yet it felt quite natural to tell her. For one instant, he felt as if he were back in his own time, his own place, and she the stranger out of place. He wondered whether he would trust her so, if such were the case.

Sunday passed quiet and grey and uneventful, and Monday morning found them driving the roads to Kingston in the cool of early morning when dew falls on the fields and mist twines among the trees. Garrett was growing more at ease with car travel and dozed, wrapped in his cloak in the passenger seat, while Ellen drove and thought and considered and thought some more. As the sun rose and the countryside came to life as they passed through it, Ellen asked herself why she would want a job *here* when she already had one—in Texas. She questioned why she would want to live *here* when she already had a home—in Texas. And she deliberated why she would struggle to keep this piece of real estate *here* when she already had one—in Texas—and *that one* didn't have a load of taxes hanging over it and a leaky, rotting roof. Why did she even want to consider doing this she asked herself. It really just didn't make much sense.

Looking over at Garrett, she saw the lines of care and worry etched at the corners of his eyes. She could not help but feel that in comparison to the difficulties he faced, her quandaries were quite frivolous. Would it really matter that much or make that big a difference to anyone whether she stayed here or not?

It would only matter to Garrett, she mused, until they found a way to somehow send him home. Was it, then, she asked herself, only a matter of her pride and her appetite for challenge that made her think of trying to make this work? She considered that thought for a moment and realized that, after all, she really did like the idea of staying here. It was all the difference of telling a story and living it. Here, somehow, she was part of a history ongoing . . . At least, it felt that way.

Garrett awakened to hear her humming.

They drove into the streets of Kingston just before ten o'clock, and Ellen parked the car in front of the university hall where her interview was to be held that hour. While Ellen pulled her satchel and a briefcase from the backseat, Garrett stepped from the car and stood on the sidewalk, gazing up and down the street. The buildings and streets had not changed much since he had last seen them, but the people and traffic were outlandish and strange.

And if he found *them* outlandish, the people passing on the street, thought Garrett looked like some king from a Gothic fairy tale surveying his realm, and most smiled and assumed he was costumed for some Shakespearian play. Noticing the stares from passing pedestrians, Ellen wondered just what she was going to do with Garrett while she attended her interview and she considered whether she could, in good conscience, turn him loose on college society. She shrugged. Why not? They, of all people, would never know—never even guess—who he was or where he had come from.

"Would you like to come with me?" she asked, pulling his attention from the passersby. "You'll have to sit outside, and it will be about an hour."

"No," he replied. "I know this town well. I should like to look around."

"Ok," she said, hurriedly handing him some paper bills. "Take these then."

He fingered the money doubtfully.

"It will buy you a hamburger or soda if you get hungry," she explained. "Meet me at the library—there"—she pointed—"when the clock tower chimes eleven, OK?"

Garrett nodded and watched bemusedly as she hurried away. He spent part of the hour wandering the streets, watching people, and looking at shop windows. Many people stopped to gawk at him, but he paid them no mind, and at half past, he strode back to the library, where a pretty miniskirted blonde coed was more than happy to help him search out astronomy in the card catalog.

When Ellen found him at a quarter to twelve, he was leaning upon a tall shelf ladder, a stack of books heaped beside him on the floor and a small paperback in his hand.

"What have you found?" she asked when he looked up.

"A book of stars and moon phases and constellations," he said, showing her the cover of the little book.

She grinned. "An almanac?"

"Yes, an 'almanac,'" he repeated. "Perhaps it will tell me how to know what moon and which star is etched on the tomb, and then perhaps I can know when we shall see that particular alignment again."

Ellen sobered. "Yes, perhaps . . . maybe so. I would have thought a book of incantations might help more."

"Yes," he agreed, eyeing the stack of books on the floor. "Unfortunately, such things are not studied seriously here."

"Let's go," she said. "I found something interesting too, but I'll tell you later. Professor Lowell has invited us to lunch, and we shouldn't be late."

They were late, anyway, though only just a little; and Professor Lowell, a short rotund man of red cheeks and a thatch of curly grey hair, was only checking his watch for the first time when they entered the door of the large private club.

Dr. Lowell was dean of the department of history and had headed the panel of professors interviewing Dr. Ellen Lancaster. Her interview had gone well. Her specialties and studies well suited their curriculum needs, and they liked her. But there were some deficits that might place other candidates above her; and it was this he wished to discuss over lamb, potatoes, and brown bread.

Introductions having been made, the maître d' led them to a table in a quiet corner, where they were seated and then fussed over by a ceremonious waiter and his flurry of napkins. When at last the food was ordered and conversation drifted to light pleasantries, Ellen found it comic to watch as Dr. Lowell spoke chiefly to her while watching Garrett appraisingly from the corner of his eye and gave short startled glances at Garrett's archaic table manners. Garrett, with quiet dignity, ignored him.

When the meal arrived, Dr. Lowell was shocked silent in midsentence when Garrett, thinking the table knife too dull, laid it aside and pulled the bone-handled dagger from his boot. Nervously, Lowell looked to Ellen, who only shook her head reassuringly, prompting him on with his conversation.

At last, over dessert, Dr. Lowell came to the point of his discourse.

"Dr. Lancaster," he said, "I believe it fair to tell you that with your experience and credentials, I should truly like to see you a member of my staff."

Ellen only nodded, wondering where this was leading and if his next words would be the qualifying "However . . ."

Leaning back in his chair, Garrett cleaned his fingernails with the dagger tip and watched between the two of them, finding such parley peculiar.

"However"—*There it was,* thought Ellen—"I must admit that I find your research publications somewhat lacking compared to other applicants."

"I have one book published on . . ."

"Yes, yes, I know," Lowell interrupted. "And many published articles, but I feel we are looking for things more specialized—writings on less commonly researched topics. Perhaps if you were to make a concerted effort in the next month, before we make our final selection, you might research and write several articles in, say, medieval cultural history or some more locally specific history. These are areas of study that you would also be required to teach. You could submit them to us before the end of the month when we will convene to make our final selection."

Ellen was silent, considering how to answer. The task he had suggested would have seemed monumental were it not for the fact that she had begun the rough drafts of several such articles in the last week while compiling her notes from conversations with Garrett, and these research drafts lay in her briefcase beside her on the floor at that moment. She knew, however, that those articles had no research foundation, no bibliography. What would she say when they asked for her reference sources? "A dead man told me"? That would scarcely get her a job. As she hesitated, Garrett slid the dagger back into his boot and leaned forward, placing his elbows upon the white tablecloth as he spoke to Dr. Lowell in a low voice that yet stopped conversations at tables nearby. Ellen watched, perplexed.

"I deem then that you wouldst hire Dr. Lancaster (he said her name as if it were foreign to him) if only she can prove that she knows more of your history than does any other?"

"History of more unique detail, I should say," rejoined Dr. Lowell, eyeing Garrett doubtfully.

"Such as how a horse was trimmed and shod in the fourteenth century?" asked Garrett.

"Something like that, yes, put in proper form of a complete article . . . rustic topic that . . ."

"Or perhaps the details of records kept by the accountant of a feudal lord?"

"Yes, exactly, though that would be a rare research find."

"She has done these already," Garrett stated flatly. "And others of such ilk, though I have thought it folly . . ."

Lowell turned to Ellen, who felt totally adrift. "Have you truly?" he asked with some incredulity.

"Yes, sir," she said as confidently as she could manage. "Although they are yet rough draft and lack sufficient documentation . . ."

"Did you bring these with you?"

"Yes."

"Well, now, this is most fortuitous!" he said enthusiastically. "Let us see them, then. It will save us time and effort. You can send bibliographies when you have got them prepared!"

Ellen opened the briefcase upon a chair beside her and thoughtfully selected several of the papers there—ones that she might most easily document from library volumes if need be. She handed them across to Dr. Lowell, with a sidelong glance at Garrett.

Thumbing through the typewritten sheets, Dr. Lowell squared them smartly on edge and thumped them down on the table under his hand.

"Well, now that's champion!" he crowed. "Thank you, Mr. Coalson, for your help." He turned to Garrett with a new appreciation. "Are you by chance interested in the research of antiquities also?" he asked, eyeing Garrett's garb more forgivingly in that light.

"I have been a student of the thirteenth-century barony for most of my life," replied Garrett with such alacrity that Ellen stifled a laugh with a fit of coughing. Both men ignored her. "Though I have delved into modern studies of late."

"Ah, I should like to discuss your studies, Mr. Coalson." (*They might be as unorthodox as the man,* Lowell mused, *and therefore entertaining.*) "But at a later date, I'm afraid." He glanced at his watch. "I apologize, but I have another appointment to keep."

They shook hands at the door, Dr. Lowell assuring Ellen that she would hear from them within three weeks' time and bustling off down the sidewalk, with Ellen's papers snugged securely under his arm.

When Lowell was out of sight, Ellen looked up to see Garrett watching her. "Oh, what you don't get me into!" she scolded. She felt like kicking his finely booted shins.

"What is it I have done, fair Ellen?" he asked congenially as they walked back toward the car.

"Those papers!" she exclaimed "I had not meant to submit them as research."

"But you wrote them."

"Yes, but only as subject dissertations—theory—I have no documentation to prove them—except *you*." She flashed a look at him over the car as she yanked open the door.

"I do not understand," he said ruefully.

"No. You couldn't," she sighed, settling into the seat and tossing the briefcase into the back floorboard. She smoothed the hair out of her face and regarded him. "You see, Garrett, research has to be based on facts and knowledge that other people can check your work by—so they know you didn't just make it up."

Garrett's brow furrowed as he began to understand.

"When they ask me for resources, I will have none . . . only *you* . . . And that won't hold water . . . not a nice spot to be in."

"What, then, would suffice?" he asked.

"Oh," she shrugged, starting the engine. "Some fantastic find in the Garrison Keep attic, I suppose, handwritten original scripts, five hundred years old, in your own language and hand." She meant it facetiously: he did not take it so.

"This would gain you the position you desire?"

At this serious tone, she looked at him and shrugged. "I can't even know that. Don't worry about it."

But as she gazed down the road ahead and the town fled away behind them, his thoughts were on her words. He could do this easily, if there were time. The ink and quill, he could make. The parchment, he could salvage from the stacks left in the Garrison Keep attic by the scribes. He could do this if it would be of help to her, just as she had aided him. Through his reverie, he realized that she was speaking to him . . .

"So what I found while I was in the library is that those coins of yours are worth even more than I guessed. Each one probably three hundred pounds, if they're worth a nickel."

Garrett did not answer. He saw no need to.

"So. How many do you have?" she asked.

"Several."

Ellen rolled her eyes. "Look, it's not that I care. You'll need them as they are if you return home. But . . . you know . . . if you're stuck here, you could live quite well for some time off such as that."

When he did not reply, she sighed in exasperation. "Look, I'm only trying to help you!" she insisted.

"I know," he replied calmly. "And yes, there are plenty more should I have need of them."

"With you?"

"No. Hidden."

"Good. Hidden treasure is always a good thing," she said. "Wish I had one stashed somewhere," she muttered to herself under her breath, but Garrett heard her and he remembered things spoken of a week ago: the taxes the old seamstress had mentioned, the unpaid bills Ellen had spoken of. He realized that in his own trouble, he had little thought of hers, had not thought she truly had any.

"Tell me," he said quietly, "why does Lady Ellen desire a treasure?"

She thought to pass off this inquiry with a bluff remark, but then thought better of it. It would not hurt for him to know how things were. After all, he would need to be prepared if circumstances didn't work out and she was unable to hold the estate, if she was required to relinquish it before he had found the right "hocus-pocus" to get himself home.

"My uncle willed me this estate," she said tiredly. "I have no great wealth. I have a home and a horse in Texas, together, worth about four thousand. And I owe the queen about thirty thousand in estate and inheritance taxes. You can do the math . . . Six thousand is due by the end of this month, the rest by October. And at present, I have no way to pay." She paused, hating the sound of despair in her voice, liking less the concern she saw in his face.

"But don't worry with me," she said with a forced cheerfulness. "If that job comes through, well, then I'll find a way to borrow the money for taxes. Maybe there's grant money available for the upkeep of historic buildings."

"And if you do not 'get this job'?" he asked.

"Then I'm off to Texas by the first of August, and there'll be a fine old castle for sale to the first person with enough hidden treasure."

Garrett leaned back, watching the countryside flash pass as he thought of all she'd said. "Enough buried treasure . . ." Yes, there was more than enough. If he was forced to remain here—he scowled at the thought—he would have no place to go if the Garrison Keep was sold; and if he were able to go home as he hoped, his stores and coffers would yet be full in his own castle in his own time. He could afford to use them here. Before they had reached the outskirts of Briarwick, he had determined what he would do. He wished his charity were completely selfless, but he knew it was not so.

THE BARON'S TREASURES

In the week that followed, Ellen often found Garrett at the table by the hearth in the Great Hall, poring over the almanac and a calendar from the kitchen wall and scribbling notes on scraps of old parchment with a quill pen and a bottle of ink.

"What is all this?" she asked finally, picking up a torn scrap of parchment he had just blotted and set aside.

"It is your documentation," he said, leaning back in his chair and lacing his fingers behind his head as he stretched. A glimmer of amusement flickered in his eye as he watched her finger the small stack of papers in amazement.

She looked up at him wonderingly. "You . . . do this for me?"

"Of course. It is a small thing, if it may help."

"Help? Yes, thank you. It is a great help." He watched as she wandered from the room, reading as she walked.

That Saturday, Ellen was surprised when Garrett insisted they ride to the Coltstone Keep at four thirty in the afternoon. He would not say why, but was quite adamant that they go, and she wondered whether it had to do with the almanac and the moon phase. Perhaps he had at last found a hidden clue, she thought, or was going in search of one.

To her questions, he gave no reply, only, "Bring a torch and your satchel," which she did.

They arrived at Coltstone Keep by five o'clock as the last tour was in progress and the staff busy counting and closing and finishing up for the day. Garrett had led them onto the grounds by a circuitous path that wended its way around behind the stables and ended at the walled gardens below a green house. Sheltered from view by the garden wall, they tied their horses there and walked up through the gardens toward the back of the castle, where lights were shining from shuttered high windows and through a doorway propped open.

"Where are we going?" asked Ellen, only to be silenced with a look from Garrett. She watched as he walked slowly, parallel to the castle wall, though twenty feet out from it. He studied the ground, the angle of the castle wall, and the gardens roundabout and frowned in consternation.

"What are you looking for?" she hissed, feeling like a trespasser.

"A door," he said.

"Why not use that one?" she pointed to the open door in the castle wall.

"I do not pay to enter my own house." He stepped into the midst of a hawthorn thicket and paused, kicked at the dirt with his boot, then he knelt on the leafy mold, motioning her to join him as he brushed back the dirt and leaves. There, under his hand, was a smooth, flat regular-shaped stone that looked, for all the world, as if it had lain there since the flood. But as Garrett cleared its edges from the sod, Ellen began to surmise otherwise and knelt across from him, digging with her fingers and a stick until the dirt was cleared away. When at last all was clear, Ellen saw that the stone was little more than two foot in diameter and rested on a frame of stone masonry much like the top of a well.

Prying his fingers underneath the stone slab, Garrett pulled upward, lifting and straining until, inch by inch, the dirt and twining roots beneath gave way; and he pushed the stone aside. Below gaped a black hole that smelled of stagnant air, wet earth, and mice. Ellen looked up at Garrett querulously, but he only searched the depths below, holding out his hand to her. "The torch . . . ," he said.

Pulling the satchel around, she quickly pulled out a flashlight and handed it to him, and without a word, he flipped it on and slid feet first down into the narrow opening, beckoning her to follow. Looking down after him, she saw him kneeling on a stone paving perhaps six foot below her, the three-foot tall opening of a tunnel before him.

Taking a deep breath, she gripped the sides of the stone curbing and lowered herself down as Garrett quickly slid into the tunnel ahead, and she followed close on his heels. His form blocked most of the light from the flashlight as they crawled through the cramped space, but Ellen was glad she could not see what manner of things she crawled over and through in the stale darkness. The walls of floor of the tunnel were paved and shored with heavy stonework and felt secure; and Ellen only hoped that, wherever the tunnel led, it still ended somewhere in a door and not at bricked wall.

They had not crawled far when Garrett stopped, and she heard him working at something that sounded like a metal-and-chain latch. He muttered to himself; and then sitting flat on the floor, his back braced against her, he pushed with his booted heels and kicked hard upon what appeared to be a solid stone wall. She was almost certain that they'd be crawling back down the tunnel, when at last she heard a cracking sound and the grating of stone sliding over stone.

Following Garrett as he crawled forward, she came to a square opening where a stone fitted with an iron ring had been pushed out from the wall to reveal a portal. She slipped through the opening and rolled out onto a paved floor, where Garrett lifted her to her feet and they stood in a square alcove where an arching buttress did not meet the wall and neatly hid the tunnel end within its shadowy niche. They waited pensively for any sound in the corridor beyond until moments had passed in silence and finally Garrett took a deep breath, slipped from the alcove, and strode stealthily away down the dim hall.

Longing to ask just what exactly they were doing in this place, Ellen followed after him as closely and quietly as she could. They passed other corridors and several doors before he paused at an arched doorway and descended the steps leading down into a dark cellar.

As the flashlight beam flickered over the stone paving, it revealed the fallen and rotting wooden racks and bins that Ellen assumed had once been the fixtures of a wine cellar and the castle's storage rooms. Garrett stepped carefully through the debris and through the broken-hinged door at the back of the cellar. Standing behind him, Ellen gazed in wonder at the small room with its heavy stonework and barrel-shaped ceiling. "Where are we?" she whispered close in Garrett's ear.

"My store room," he replied quietly. "My treasury."

She looked around again at the littered floor, the broken wood and the old rags that the mice had carried in.

"So much for a baron's wealth," he agreed, reading the look in her eyes. "Wealth is fleeting, and beauty is vain . . . ," he quipped with a wry smile.

"I'm sorry," she said.

"Don't be. I never counted on it being here. Not in this place anyway." He turned to the wall and fingered the mortared stones. "Only that which was better hidden . . ."

Ellen watched aghast as he levered a heavy stone out of the wall and lowered it to the floor. He handed her the flashlight peremptorily, and she shone it over his shoulder as he reached his hand far back into the black niche and pulled out a crumbling leather bag that weighed heavily and rang of coin. He pulled the satchel off her shoulder and plopped the pouch into it unceremoniously and reaching back into the space beyond, he brought out a finely carved and inlaid box with gold hinges and a golden latch fit with an ivory pen. He fingered it a moment and brushed the dust from with it with his hand before placing it inside the satchel also. Then, turning to leave, he paused and looked back. The empty hole, robbed of its wealth, gaped there accusingly like a wordless mouth. Strapping the satchel over his shoulder, he knelt and lifted the stone back to its place, carefully smoothing the joining of the mortarless masonry.

Wordlessly, then, they hurried from the tomblike silence of the place, up through the cellars, over the arched stairs, and into the hall. They were moving quickly along the hall when the strand of white light bulbs wired along the ceiling suddenly flicked on and voices were heard approaching.

Without hesitation, Garrett grasped Ellen and shoved her through a narrow door into the stark blackness of windowless chamber. Ellen could not tell the size of the space around them with only the light seeping under the heavy door to illuminate, but it felt to her as though she stood on the edge of a great precipice for all that she could not know otherwise. Garrett stood with his back to the wall, breathing easily, while she huddled beside him, trying to mimic his calm and imagining all the trouble they would be in if they were discovered.

The voices and footsteps passed; the corridor was quiet for a time, and then the footsteps returned back up the hallway. It seemed forever before, at last, the echoes died away back up the passage and the light flickered off.

Ellen sighed with relief as they waited moments longer before venturing out into the hall and back along it to the tunnel's hidden entrance.

Motioning for Ellen to go first, Garrett waited for her to crawl into the tunnel opening before he slid into the opening backward and pulled the stone in behind them, seating it carefully. Back through the tunnel, they crawled, seeing the sunlight's lowering rays above the Hawthorne branches, when at last they stood at the tunnel's end and Garrett gave Ellen a leg up onto the sod and leaves above, pulling himself up behind her.

"What," she said, breathing deeply, "did we just do?"

Garrett grinned at her conspiratorially as he slid the capstone carefully back into place. "We have just robbed a castle."

"More like a tomb . . . ," she muttered. "We could hang for that, you know."

"You would have, in my day," he assured her. "But not today." He took her by the hand to help her to her feet and left her dusting herself off as he strode off down through the gardens to the horses. She shook her head at his arrogant self-assurance as she hurried after him.

Back at the Garrison Keep, Garrett lit an oil lamp and placed the coin pouch and wooden casket beside it upon the table in the Great Hall. Perching on her knees on a chair across from him at the table, Ellen watched as he pushed the papers and calendar and books to one side and opened the drawstring of the leather pouch. The golden coins glimmered brightly as they rattled out upon the burnished boards in a cheery little heap.

Amazed, Ellen picked one up and fingered it, turning it over in the soft lamplight and Garret eyed her askance as he stacked the coins with ease of practice. It was odd, he thought, how a coin of gold could look so pretty to a woman and yet lend no beauty to her. She placed the coin down again carefully on the table, and he placed it upon a stack.

"Five stacks of ten . . . fifty," he muttered. "Plus four here." He pulled the coins from the pouch at his belt.

Ellen's eyes widened in amazement, "That's forty—perhaps fifty thousand dollars!" she said, awed. "Garrett, you are rich!"

He grimaced. "Yes. In some respects." He sat a moment, contemplating the golden stacks before moving them aside with the back of his hand and placing the wooden chest in their place.

Sliding a small drawer from beneath it, he removed a key which fitted behind the ivory pin and opened the lock with the tiniest little *snick*. When he lifted the lid, it hinged toward Ellen so that she could not see in, and she had to resist the urge to stand on the chair and lean over.

Garrett reached within and held something in his hand a moment before he laid it out upon the table: a necklace of two chains binding large emerald stones between them, each stone ringed in blood-drop rubies. He set a matching ring within its circle.

"My mother's," he said as Ellen gazed admiringly at them. "A gift from my father. She wore them ever while he lived, but only at Christmastide after his death."

Beside these, he placed a circlet of emeralds and diamonds and three rings of intriguing craftsmanship, each unique and each of great value even in his day. Lastly, he set forth a rough stone of russet hue—a ruby, Ellen assumed—and five cut diamonds that dazzled little circles upon the table in flashing splendor as he rolled them from his palm like dice.

Leaning back with his hands behind his head, Garrett considered the wealth before him while Ellen leaned upon the table, chin in hands, and stared dreamily at the treasure.

"It's like a fairy tale," she murmured, touching a green stone with her fingertip.

Garrett scowled at her, not liking her fixation on the things before her. *Money,* he thought. *Most men—and women—were better off with far less of it than they desired.*

"Does this make you happy?" he asked sarcastically, waving his hand grandly over the table.

"Oh yes!" she exclaimed lightly, not noticing the look on his face. "Doesn't it you?"

"Perhaps."

"Perhaps! Why, Lord Garrett, you'll never need to worry about a thing with all this to live on."

"All of this could never buy the things I want," he said gruffly, and meeting his measuring gaze, she sobered in understanding.

"Still . . . ," she faltered.

"What would you say," he asked, squinting at her, "if I were to give all of this to you?"

Ellen sat back from the table, pulling her feet from beneath her.

"To me?" He met and held her gaze above the glimmer of the gold. She swallowed hard, feeling as if too much hung in the balance at her words. What, she wondered, could she possibly say in answer to his question? Was he offering this to her or testing her? She smiled thinly and sighed. "I would have to say no."

"No!" he scoffed. "And why so?"

She shrugged, her gaze falling to the tempting horde. "It is too much. I could not accept it as a gift, and if I owned it I would not know what to do with it."

"I dare say you'd figure it out . . . ," he said dryly.

"Perhaps, but I might find it a burden . . . having so much. I think it might be hard to know the best thing to do with it . . . it might . . . ," her voice faded in thought.

"Might what?"

"I don't know, but I do think it could cause me a world of trouble if I let it. I'd rather not have more than just enough and manage that."

Garrett leaned forward. "And how much is just enough?"

Ellen laughed. Reaching across, she picked one of the stones from the table. "I don't know, but a lot less than one of these." She turned it over and placed it back. "No, this stuff is yours, Lord Garrett, and I am glad you have it. What are you going to do with it?" she asked, without noticing the appreciative look he gave her.

He rose slowly from his chair, crossing his arms upon his chest as he walked around the table and stood looking down at her thoughtfully. "I should like to exchange it for some of your paper money."

"Well," Ellen replied, "You'll have to go to London to do that . . . find a collector—or jeweler. There's not that kind of money around here."

"London," he said flatly, thinking of the years he had spent there, always by another's bequest. "Yes, I will go to London." he said, "And I will take you with me."

Ellen looked up at him, perplexed. Of course she would go with him, she thought. How would he ever negotiate the railway and metro without her along? She wondered why it seemed a point of discussion to him. She did not understand the thoughts behind his words and she could not know that for this one thing, his Lady Leticia had pleaded and begged, threatened and cajoled, and that this one thing he had always denied her, knowing that the power and wealth and intrigue of court could only create a deeper, more insatiable hunger within her for those things she so desired. Ellen could not know that in those six words, he conveyed his highest confidence and esteem.

"When?" she asked simply.

"Before next week's end," he replied and walked away through the tall double doors out into the Close. He left Ellen sitting at the table, the treasure of a baron before her. She gazed at it, wondering if he intended for her to just leave it there, or did he wish her to put it away somewhere safe? She stood slowly and stretched and then shrugged. Where could it be more safe she asked herself and she left it there; but it was late that night ere she could sleep, thinking of the secret tunnel, the treasure room, the hidden niche, and the baron's treasure on the table in the Great Hall.

OF GYPSY SPELLS

Ellen spent some time in the days of the following week, making phone calls to strangers in London: collectors, appraisers, and jewelers, those most likely to pay well for items of such value as Lord Garrett had to offer. And through those days, she watched in concern as Garrett became more restive and thoughtful, riding out often on his own or walking for hours through the country roundabout. In the evenings, he was most likely to sit quietly in the study listening as she played the piano or read, and he often seemed to be in some distant reverie, his mind envisioning things that she could not see.

On Wednesday morning, she suggested he ride into town with her: she needed to buy a number of grocery and feed items, and they would take the car. Garrett agreed readily after she offered to drop him off at the Bowl & Pitcher while she made her purchases in the village, and they set off down the winding road a little before noon.

As they passed the branching lane that led to the Coltstone Keep, Ellen thought again of their foray there through the tunnel and the dark cellars. "Who built the tunnel?" she asked suddenly.

"My great-grandfather."

"Why?"

"As means of escape, of course, should one so need. It is a bad thing to be captive within your own walls."

Yes, indeed, thought Ellen. "Who knew of it?"

"My brother and myself."

"Anyone else?"

"No."

"Not even Leticia or your mother?"

"No. My father told only David and me the year before he died."

"Why did you not use it when they came for you?"

"There was no time, no warning." He sighed. "Most of the most momentous things in my life, Ellen, have happened to me without warning."

Seeing the hard set of his jaw, Ellen wondered to herself if he would have used the escape even had he known. She doubted it.

Leaving him in the dooryard of the Bowl & Pitcher, Ellen told herself that he could stir up little mischief there among the lunch crowd and chess players while she drove away to complete her list of errands. Bags of grain were loaded into the boot of the car and groceries into the backseat. She met Mrs. Sayer at the green grocers and was obliged to stand and chat at great length, answering questions about her Kingston interview, her research, and that 'nice gentleman, Mr. Coalson.'

Breaking away at last, Ellen set her basket, heavy with purchases, into the backseat of the car and drove back to the yard of the Bowl & Pitcher, thinking to have a plate of shepherd's pie before heading home. She looked around the dim interior as her eyes adjusted to the light but could see Garrett nowhere among the few tables of late-lunch customers and pipe smokers and chess players.

"Looking for your gentleman friend?" winked Mr. Gavin, the pudgy middle-aged proprietor.

"Yes, sir," she replied. "Has he left?"

"Aye. Sometime ago. I believe he went over to Ebenezer's shop."

"Ebenezer . . . Mr. Grimmel?"

"Aye. Seemed some curious about the gypsy. Seemed like he might know Grimmel or some of his family or some such like. Right anxious to meet with him he was. Old Grimmel probably has him set down to tea the way he likes to talk, that old rot, about the old times and such."

"Thank you," said Ellen, hurrying out and leaving the company there to their own conversational surmises. When she walked into Grimmel's shop, she did not find the two "set down to tea." Indeed, she halted in the doorway, astonished to see Ebenezer Grimmel backed into a corner behind his trade counter, his face ashen, his form ridged, stricken as if with a vision of horror, his hands uplifting before him.

"That is all I know. It is all I remember!" he was declaiming in a voice that trembled.

"You are certain?" demanded Garrett, who stood over the cringing man threateningly. "On pain of death, man, tell me all you know!" commanded Garrett.

"That is all. If there is more, I do not know it."

"Your own curse be upon you if your memory proves false," muttered Garrett, turning away. He drew up in surprise to see Ellen wide-eyed at the door, but strode wordlessly past her. With a look at the trembling Mr. Grimmel as he scurried away through the curtained back-room door of his shop, Ellen hurriedly followed after Garrett. Catching up to him as they reached the car, she took one look at his face and held her peace until they had driven some distance in silence.

Finally, at the curve before the churchyard, she pulled the car to the roadside. Garrett made no comment, knowing what was coming.

Setting the hand brake, Ellen swiped the hair back from her face and took a deep breath. "OK." she said. "What was that all about?"

"That," he replied, "was all about a curse."

"A curse?"

"Yes. Gypsy magic."

"You believe in that?"

"Yes," he said dryly. "I have to. I should think you might also . . . considering."

Ellen sighed and nodded. "So what did he say?"

"Grimmel," replied Garrett, "was the sir name of the man I slew and of the son I raised for him."

"Your scribe?"

"Yes."

"And . . . ?"

"And according to this man Ebenezer, my scribe was responsible for the etchings upon the tomb. Knowledge of it has been passed down in his family through each generation."

"Imagine that!" exclaimed Ellen incredulously.

"Yes, imagine that," mused Garrett. "Gypsies are odd folk, their loyalty to their family is strong, their traditions sacred, and their knowledge of the past extensive. They are not to be meddled with lightly."

"Obviously . . . But what else did he tell you? Did he know how to send you back?"

Garrett looked down, studying his hands and scowling. "He knew some things and perhaps they are enough. And he claimed that he had forgotten other things, though I think he simply knew something about the curse that he would not tell."

"But can he get you home?"

"He cannot, but what he knew might."

"And what is it that?"

Garrett squinted, looking out the window at the old stone church. "It has to do with moon phase, as I guessed. 'The hart goes home at dawn' is perhaps what is symbolized by the sunrays in the drawing. Perhaps it means between sunset and dawn, he could not say which, at some time within that particular moon phase when the moon and the star are aligned as in the stone etching."

"That is the meaning of the drawing?"

"As well as the old man could explain. He seemed to believe there was more play of word involved.

"How so?"

Garrett shrugged. "The hart . . . and the heart. The hart knows its home . . . the heart (he touched his heart) must also."

Ellen frowned and nodded, thinking it all very vague and sketchy to her. "So when is it?" she asked. "When is this moon phase?"

"The waning quarter moon, as you drew it, will occur next week . . ."

Looking away, Ellen swallowed hard and wondered why she felt such mixed emotions at his answer. "So what will you do?"

Hearing the edge in her voice, he turned to her and stated flatly, "I will take my vigil then, at the side of my tomb, and I will go home. I must."

She nodded and bit her lip as she ground the car back into gear, released the brake, and pulled back onto the road. Once home, Garrett retreated to the Great Hall to study the almanac and figure and refigure the dates and moon phases based on the calendar and the drawing and the almanac.

The gypsy had declared that there was no incantation, no particular words involved to reverse the curse's effect; but then the gypsy had definitely been loath to tell all he knew. Garrett wondered what more there might be that the gypsy had claimed to have forgotten. What more was there that he feared to tell? He could only hope that what he had been told would be sufficient and only trust that his figures were correct. In order to compensate for a chance of error, he was determined to spend the whole of three nights during that particular moon phase at watch in the church sanctuary, and he would begin the vigil at sunset on the coming Monday.

He told Ellen of his plans the next afternoon as they saddled the horses in the paddock, and if she was not at all surprised when he told her of his proposed vigil, she was altogether speechless when he announced his plans to travel to London and back on Friday.

“Friday!” she exclaimed. She had been examining a worn place on her off stirrup leather and thinking that she would need to purchase a replacement soon, but his words distracted her from that consideration.

“Yes, Friday . . . It is a journey of a single day by train?” he asked, although he knew she had already said it was so.

“Yes, but why go?” she asked. “You won’t need the gold exchanged if you are able to leave.”

“Yet I will go to London,” he said as he pulled the grey’s head around and spurred him from the yard. With a shrug, Ellen mounted the filly and galloped after him.

LONDON

The grey dawn of Friday morning found them seated in the plush red cushioned seats of a railway car as the train swayed and its wheels clackity-clacked over the joints of the rails. Garrett watched entranced as the fields, farms, and trees flew past the windows; and he seemed to be enjoying himself immensely. Curled up in the seat across from him, Ellen tried to sleep but couldn't and watched Garrett's face from under her eyelashes, thinking smugly that London was going to be great fun. The taste of chocolate had been so novel to him only three weeks ago; then it was cars, and now trains. She would take him to Gatwick Airport, she decided, and she would show him an airplane.

They changed to a commuter train outside of the London city limits and found themselves holding to the chrome rail overhead as they stood crammed among the rush of morning commuters. Ellen noticed that people made room for Garrett, moved away at the suggestion of his glance; and she stuck close to him. It was nice, she thought, smiling to herself, to have a medieval knight clear the way for you when disembarking from a commuter train at rush hour. They stepped from the train with ease and out through the depot to the taxi stands.

Hailing a taxi, they climbed in, and Ellen gave direction to the address of a dealer of antiquities near downtown. There were several dealers, an auction house, and one private collector, who had expressed interest in Garrett's coins and the gemstones (he had not wished to sell the jewelry); and Ellen hoped Garrett's dealings would go well. She did not want to goose chase through the city meeting with all of these for the whole day.

But the first buyer was skeptical and his offer low. Ellen stood casually at one side, trying to mask her interest as she listened to the bargaining. When Garrett at last shook his head and scooped the coins back into the pouch at his belt, Ellen was pleased. She knew he would strike a better trade elsewhere and was glad to find him adept in his bartering skills; now she need not worry that he would be cheated. Indeed, she thought, she might rather fear for the other party; Garrett was well seasoned in barter and trade from a time when every word counted and every penny bought bread.

Her penny bought a doughnut and carton of milk from a street vendor while Garrett hailed a taxi, and they were off to another part of the city to an appointment with a private collector. His house was opulent; his manner, ingratiating. With the coins, he was at first incredulous and then impressed and at last enamored, until he had bought the half of them with one-hundred-pound notes cash money and looked longingly after the others as they slid back into Garrett's hand and into the pouch.

"Try Winchester Street Auctioneers," he advised at Ellen's inquiry. "They will be most intrigued to see these." And he hoped he might purchase the others there later at a better price. He called a cab for them and shook hands warmly as they left his door. Fingering the coins, he wondered where Garrett had come by them and though he seriously doubted the explanation of an old family cache, it was better than believing they were stolen.

The Winchester Street Auction House was quite equally impressed, although obliged to ask more questions and loath to pay in cash. "A bank draft?" suggested the tall man in the dark suit who sat across from Garrett at a large mahogany desk, eyeing a coin he held on edge between his finger and his thumb. Garrett glanced toward Ellen, whose back was to him as she stood perusing a glass-encased vase upon a pedestal; and catching her oblique nod, he agreed and casually invited her to join them at the table.

"I have an account here in town," she volunteered. "It was my uncle's and is now in my name. I can deposit the funds there for Mr. Coalson, if he wishes, although the draft would need to be made to me," she said with a meaningful look for Garrett, who leaned back in his chair and nodded his approval.

The transaction was complete and the deposit made. Thirty thousand pounds of Garrett's money would be available to him after two banking days.

"Why not today?" Ellen asked impatiently.

"Bank policy," replied the clerk.

"But this money actually belongs to my friend . . . ," she began to protest, but Garrett took her arm and pulled her away.

"I will not require it today," he said as they left the bank lobby. "And I know where you live." he caught his sly wink.

They lunched at the Black Swan.

"So what has changed most in London?" asked Ellen over her plate of corned beef.

"Everything but river and stone," he said. "Everything. I find it odd that people pay to see the inside of the Tower of London!"

"I will show you the shipyards and the airport after you finish with your business," she said.

At the jeweler's on Monk Street, Ellen waited in the showroom as Garrett was led to a back office by a trim young clerk. She was surprised when he returned shortly, his face unreadable as he joined her, taking her by the arm to lead her to the door.

"Come. Let us go," he said. But they were yet shy of the door when the young clerk, hurrying from the door of the back office, stopped them.

"Sir," he said, flustered. "The master of the house wishes to reconsider, if you would please return."

With a knowing look only for Ellen, Garrett followed the clerk back to the master's office and returned soon after without the gemstones and bearing a handful of large denomination bills.

"Satisfied?" she asked

"Um," he grunted. "Anything here that thou dost fancy?"

"No." She shook her head.

"Good. Let us depart." And from thence, he directed the taxi driver to the government offices.

"Whatever for?" asked Ellen.

"My own business. And while I am about it, I hope you will search out the archives," he said archly. "If they have such and so far back as 1460, I should like to see again those letters of my betrayal."

Eyes alight with enthusiasm for the novel quest, Ellen crossed the street to the government library and archive while Garrett mounted the steps to the pillared portico of the government office building. An hour later, he found Ellen leaning over a microfiche viewer in a large open workroom. She reported having no success.

"A needle in a haystack," she muttered after explaining the apparatus and library system to him.

"No matter," he said, unzipping the satchel upon her shoulder and sliding a large bulging envelope within. "It was only an off chance, though I should like to have seen the writing once more."

Ellen wondered what he had put in her satchel, assumed it was the money from the jeweler's; and as she followed him out of the library and into the busy street, she gripped the satchel's strap tightly—it made her nervous to be responsible for so much.

As the afternoon progressed, Ellen enjoyed herself tremendously, feeling like some fabled genie as she showed Garrett all the wonders of the modern age. She watched wonder and amazement play across his features when they stood on the street side above the docks and watched the great freighters unloading upon the quay. Huge cranes levered cargoes up from the ships' holds, and mountains of grain poured from silo pipes into the cars of waiting trains.

"All of this . . . ," murmured Garrett, overwhelmed. "So much," he said, eyeing the mammoth height of the ships' sides and conning towers with awed respect bordered with fear.

"They go everywhere, all over the world," said Ellen. "That one is from South America," she said, pointing.

"To go where they go . . . ," he said at last, wistfully. "To see those far lands."

Ellen felt a moment's apprehension. "Would you go there?" she asked quietly. "Would you trade that for Alice? For your son?"

She thought he hesitated just one moment too long before he shook his head, and she thought again of "duty and sacrifice." It had always been so for him, and perhaps it always would be. She wondered if it were duty that drove him to seek a way home or if it were truly the desire of his heart. She felt, somehow, that this was very important.

From the quay side, Ellen asked the taxi driver to find them a restaurant near the airport and he obligingly drove the busy streets to a large hotel near the terminal entrance where a restaurant on the twelfth floor boasted wide windows overlooking the ramp and runways below. In the thoroughly hip atmosphere where the ballads of Crosby, Steeles, and Nash blared over the hi-fi system, they ate hamburgers and french fries while watching the jets taxi by and roar away into the sky.

Garrett looked tired, rubbed his eyes, and pressed the aching throb in his temples. There was so much to see and so much to know; but somehow, it only made him long all the more for a place where things were all known and understood, a place comfortable . . . like home. Watching him, Ellen understood.

"Here, take these," she said, sliding two aspirin across the table to him. He eyed them doubtfully. "They'll help your head," she explained, and checking the time on her watch, she got up to pay the bill. They would need to hurry if they were to make the eleven o'clock to Briarwick.

The commuter train was not crowded at ten in the evening, and they sat on the hard wooden benches as it clacked along past the industrial suburbs, and they watched the city's lights give way to the dark silhouettes of the countryside where the night was more at peace with itself.

At the transfer depot, they stepped out onto the platform to find that the train to Briarwick was already boarding and would be leaving shortly. Garrett joined the queue of people waiting beside the train while Ellen walked to the depot office to purchase their tickets. There he waited beside the train until most of the travelers had filed aboard and only a few remained on the platform; and still Ellen did not join him. He glanced toward the ticket office, but Ellen was not there; she was nowhere to be seen on the lighted depot platform.

Ellen had walked to the ticket office and stood in the back of a short line as she waited to purchase tickets for herself and Garrett, and she was alone at the window as she made her purchase quickly and turned away, counting her change and slipping it into a pocket of her satchel. She did not see where the young man came from who was suddenly beside her, grasping her arm roughly, his voice hissing in her ear. "Listen up and don't scream."

Something sharp and cold pricked against her ribs. Startled, she tried to jerk her arm away; but his grasp was firm, and the youth's face near hers was unyieldingly cruel and determined. From the dusky alley beside the depot, two men separated from the shadows and walked toward them, one stepping close up behind her while the other pressed close on her other side. Thus ringed about, she was forced to walk with them out of the glow of the lamplight and away from the trafficked area. Thinking frantically, Ellen considered what she could do and what they could want from her. *Money,* she thought. *They would want the money, and they would be willing to kill her for it.*

"Now stand real quiet like," said the man behind her, "and act real friendly."

The man at her shoulder slid her watch from her hand. "No rings," he grumbled as Ellen tightened her grasp on the satchel strap. She looked for Garrett and saw him standing in the queue, oblivious to her circumstance as he watched the other passengers board. The train's whistle blew as he glanced toward the ticket office.

"Here!" she willed toward him, "Turn and look here!" The train brakes hissed as they released: the man beside her grabbed roughly at the satchel, as Garret turned to look along the platform for her. All in a moment, he saw her standing backed to the wall of the depot with three young men close about her. The stricken look upon her face told him all he needed to know, and he quickly stepped from the queue and walked along the siding in her direction. For all the world to see, he appeared as nothing more than a passenger who had suddenly remembered that he needed to be doing something important somewhere else, and he strode along purposefully as if to pass by the four people standing beside the depot wall without noticing them. A quick glance assured her of his intentions.

Ellen held her breath now as anger welled up inside her. The man was trying to yank the satchel strap over her head, and she held to it tightly with her arm through its loop as he glared at her and raised his hand to strike. She ducked just as Garrett stepped up from the shadows behind and, quick as a cat, deflected the blow, shoved the man off balance and lunged for the man with the knife.

Garret struck with the skill and efficiency of a man born in a time when such abilities were used more often than skills for finer things. The knife flew from the man's hand, rebounded from the boards behind, and rattled away over the platform. Ere the knife stopped spinning its owner lay unconscious upon the platform and the third attacker, assessing his odds, released Ellen and bolted away only to be caught in Garrett's viselike grip, lifted from his feet, and flung down upon the bricks with a bone-jarring *crunch*.

Loosed from her captors, Ellen grappled with the man who had seized the satchel and who now dragged her along the boardwalk as he struggled to escape with it. Breaking her grip he sprinted away with Ellen close on his heels and Garrett just behind her. With a desperate effort she sprang onto his back, and tangled his feet so that they both fell headlong upon the boards with Ellen uppermost and the man slamming hard onto the pavement as Ellen rolled uppermost and broke away from him with the satchel in her grasp. He curled up buglike on his side, grasping a bloodied nose in his hands while Ellen struggled to her feet.

Garrett was striding toward her, but the train was beginning to pull away, and Ellen motioned for him to run for the train instead. He reached the stairway of the last car just ahead of her and leaped aboard, grasping the rail and leaning down to catch her by the wrist and swing her up beside him. The train lurched and tugged and swayed away down the tracks, leaving the platform with its one dim lamp and the three still forms lying in the shadows there.

Instinctively, Ellen clasped her arms around Garrett's solid strength, her fists clenched tightly in the folds of his robe. He could feel her heart racing. "Are you hurt?" he asked, looking down at her with concern. "No," she replied breathlessly, "only my pride."

He grinned. "That is easily mended."

"Yes," she said and tried to laugh, but shuddered instead. "At least they didn't get the money," she said, looking down at the leather satchel in her grip.

"That is not what I feared to lose," he said with a sincerity which surprised him as much as it did her.

"Let us go from here," he said and ushered her through the door into the train car where the few people seated paid them little notice. Garrett took an aisle seat and Ellen, the place beside him next to the window. As she tucked her legs up under her skirt and placed the satchel's strap across her shoulder once more, she considered that they had managed fairly well. They were both unharmed; the money was safe, and there would be no sticky police questions.

She caught Garrett watching her and grinned wanly.

"Thank you," she said simply and leaned her head against his shoulder. They sat thus as the coach's lights dimmed and the train wheels rumbled along the tracks through the darkness. Ellen's eyes closed, and her hand loosened on the satchel strap.

Garrett leaned his head back against the cushions and realized that this was not at all as he had intended. This was not his place to live, and she was not his to care for; but he was alive, and he found he did care for her very much. The hours to Briarwick passed quickly, and it was with mixed regret and relief that he saw the station lights approach and felt the train slow.

"Ellen," he said "Awake . . . we are here."

His voice was a deep rumble beneath her ear as she fumbled through her dreams and blinked her eyes awake. She sat up, rubbing her hands over her face. "Where are we?" she mumbled.

"Briarwick," he said softly and kissed her hand as he helped her to her feet. Startled, she pulled her hand back. "That's not fair!" she stammered.

"It was not meant to be," he said and turned away.

Taking a deep breath she followed him from the train and through the pale light of the station. She looked down to check the time and remembered why her watch was not there. The clock above the station door read 1:00 a.m., and the night was heavy and still with thin wreaths of fog around the two hanging lamps.

She pulled her keys from a pocket as they walked to the car and was surprised when Garrett held out his hand for them.

"May I?" he asked.

Dumbfounded, she did not answer.

"I should like to try," he persisted. And with a shrug, she handed him the keys and walked around to the passenger side as he climbed in behind the wheel.

At least there would be no traffic, she told herself, and she'd already faced worse that night . . . maybe.

He slid the key into the ignition, engaged the clutch without prompting, and pulled the gear shift into neutral. "You've been watching," she commented with approval.

"Yes," he said, "I've been watching."

She took a deep breath. "OK, then. Keep us out of the ditch, and get us home, cowboy." She cringed as he ground the first gear, and the car lurched forward; but within the mile, he had the hang of shifting, and they reached the stable shed at last without mishap.

"You are a wonder," she muttered as she climbed wearily out of the seat. She unlocked the dark kitchen door, flicked on the light, and cast the satchel onto the table as she glanced around the room. Garrett did not follow her inside. He stood on the stone stoop just beyond the open door and looked up at the waxing fingernail moon that hung just above the green branches of the trees, and Ellen could guess his thoughts when at last he entered the bright room, closing the door behind him.

"When will you go?" she asked simply, wondering if he could truly know.

"Monday," he replied. "I will begin vigil on Monday eve."

She nodded and looked away. "You know," she whispered. "I'm going to miss you."

"I know," he replied, "But you do not need to. I'll be no further that one history book from you." She laughed as she walked to the doorway, paused to say good night, and was gone. While she walked to her room, kicked off her boots, and fell exhausted into bed, Garrett picked the satchel up from the table and pulled out the bulky envelope he had stashed there. He walked with it to the study where he sat at the desk for some time, writing, studying over the words with painstaking diligence. Carrying the letter and the envelope to his quarters, he placed them atop the dresser, and then reached into the top of his boot to pull out a bundle of paper bills. They had never been in Ellen's satchel, and he weighed them thoughtfully in his hand before he dropped them upon the dresser beside the envelope and the letter. His dreams that night were filled with train cars, autobuses, ships, airplanes, and Ellen.

THE HART FLIES HOME

The weekend flew by for Ellen; an early call from Professor Lowell on Saturday prompted her into energetic efforts to sort and catalogue the scraps of journaling Garrett had begun in her behalf. The Kingston staff liked her writings, and they wished to review her documentation. She could only hope it appeared as authentic as it was and could only pray it was sufficient as she prepared notations, explanations, and a brief bibliography of the journal pieces to be sent by post to Kingston on Monday.

For Garrett, who lingered only to leave, the days passed slowly; and he was glad when, at last, Monday's eve drew nigh. They ate a light supper in silence before Garrett went to his room to set all in order there. The letter, the envelope, and the notes lay upon the dresser; his sword and dagger, he belted on. He placed the necklace and rings within a bundle in the pocket of his cloak. The bronze horse, he held a moment, before placing it there also; and with a last glance around the room, he pulled the cloak over his shoulders and turned to go.

Ellen waited for him in the Great Hall at the doorway to the Close, and she smiled bravely at his approach.

"Ready?" she asked when he stood before her, and he nodded as he opened the door and ushered her out. Through the slanting rays of the late afternoon sunlight, they crossed the Keep grounds and traversed the shadowy belt of woods beyond to the field above the church. Pausing there, he turned to her.

"You are certain you wish to be there?" he asked, studying her face earnestly.

"Yes," she said. "I must know."

He nodded and led the way across the field to the church, mounting the steps, and entering without hesitation. Ellen glanced around the still sanctuary as Garrett strode to the alcove of the crypt. She heard the clear ring of his sword as it cleared the scabbard, and he braced it before him upon the flags, his hands resting on its pommel. There, he stood in ready stance, head bowed, as he began his patient night-long vigil even as the sun's last rays dimly lingered in the multicolored prisms of the windows high above.

Everything once again seemed terribly unreal to Ellen as she settled herself into a pew just behind him. Like a knight before some chivalric quest, he stood there, a figure from a fairy tale; and Ellen wondered if he could really just vanish away or if he would melt back into the stone as mysteriously as he had appeared. She pulled her feet up onto the wooden bench and leaned back into its corner, fixing her eyes upon the center of his back where the braid of hair bound in leather hung between the broad shoulders of the cloak. If he were going to vanish, then she must see it, else she might never believe it had happened at all.

All through the long watches of the night, she struggled to stay awake; and sometimes, she failed. But ever when she looked again, there he stood as unmoving as his own statue. Once she heard him humming a low, mournful Gothic chant; and sometimes, he murmured a liturgy. But most often, he was silent—silent and still—until at last the cool of morning was warmed with the first rays of sunlight. The night was done.

Then he stirred, lifting the sword stiffly, and sliding it into its scabbard with a resolute *snack!* Turning away from the crypt, he slumped wearily onto the pew beside her, rubbing his face with his palms.

"What now?" she asked softly.

"We go back to the Keep . . . for today," he said with a wan smile. "And try again tonight."

She nodded and rubbed her aching backside as she stood and yawned and stretched. "I'll cook breakfast," she offered as they made their way back through field and wood wet with mist and morning dew.

Garrett slept most of the day after reviewing the calendar and the almanac charts, and evening found them once more entering the church's sanctuary. But this night of vigil ended as had the night before, and Garrett again sat dejectedly at the kitchen table on the following morning.

Setting a plate of honeyed toast before him upon the table, Ellen placed her hand upon his shoulder and wished she could say something encouraging, but all the words she could think of sounded shallow and silly to her. Instead, she sat down across from him and drank her tea in silence.

The third night seemed the longest and the most wearying as the quarter moon climbed over the sky and a chill wind fingered through the windows and doors, heralding a change of weather. Ellen fell asleep and dreamed that Garrett had vanished, that she was searching for him desperately among the tombs as a heavy fog encircled her. In the dream, she tried to call to him, to call him back, to tell him something she desperately needed him to know. She awoke with a start to find him still there, bowed and weary, leaning on the stone of the crypt, a queer rosy light hinting of dawn falling like an aura around him.

"Garrett?" she asked in a whisper.

He stirred. He turned. He shook his head, weighing the sword tiredly in his hand before he slid it resignedly to its scabbard and pulled the cloak close about him. "Perhaps, he murmured. "Perhaps it is no use. For all that I have tried. Perhaps it is the wrong time."

He helped her to her feet, and they walked together from the silent sanctuary and out into the morning. At the verge of the wood, he took her hand and faced her to him, looking down at her in trouble of thought. "Perhaps, Ellen, this is how it is meant to be," he said at last, looking past her to the low-hanging moon riding just upon the horizon, the bright morning star nestled close within its curve. She saw only a tired longing in his face as he spoke.

"I would not have you feel that I choose your hospitality as my last resource, when you are not so to my heart, and so I believe I must leave you now to find my way in this present age as best I can."

Ellen swallowed hard to control her voice. "Why?" she asked, though she thought she knew the answer.

"Lady Ellen," he said, his voice soft and full of compassion. "I have tried in this quest to win my way home, to save my family, my son, and Alice. I have tried, and I have failed. But I will never cease to search for another way, and as long as I remain in this age, I will grieve for those in my own."

"I understand," she said, knowing that what he said was true, but still having to steel herself against feelings of disappointment. "Really, I do understand, but there is no reason for you to have to leave."

He started to protest, but she stopped him.

"No, Garrett. You really should stay here. This was, and is, *your* home—not mine. I have a home in Texas. I have a life there that I really need to get back to." This was sounding convincing, even to her. "I will leave as soon as I make the arrangements. You should be able to manage the estate," she said with a forced grin. "I'll get some ID for you and a power of attorney. You could probably even get a great job . . . the CIA would love to have you." She stopped short, realizing that she was beginning to babble.

"CIA?" he asked quizzically, but she shook her head.

"Never mind that, just a stupid thought."

He stood a moment, regarding her as she wiped impatiently at her eyes with the back of her hand and gazed determinedly away through the trees.

"Lady Ellen," he said finally, "why would you do this for me?"

With a heavy sigh, she shrugged and faced him. "Because I love you. And because if you had chosen to do any differently than you have, it would have made me *very* happy . . . and *very* disappointed. Does that make sense?"

At his noncommittal shrug, she continued. "If you *could* do any differently, I could not love you as much as I do. So I will do what I can for you, and then what I must for myself. We both need to go home."

He smiled then and, to her surprise, took her hand in his. She watched in amazement as he slid a ring upon her finger, the emerald ring with the rubies flashing all around it. He folded her into a kind embrace, and she leaned her head against his shoulder.

"Dear Ellen," he whispered. "I do love you. I always will. But dear as you are to me, my heart will always be with them. It will always hope to fly home. It always will."

It was then that the first golden sunlight fell, dazzling through the trees in a single ray of brilliance. It spangled in shimmering gold around them. And it was then that Ellen felt his form grow cold as ice beneath her hands. She shrank away in horror as his image began to waver and fade, like water into steam, and the last look upon his face was one of terrible pain and anguish. She heard a rending cry like as one betrayed to death, and she heard the sound of the ax falling with a resounding ring that echoed through the woods. She could not know if the sound came from within her or from the woods roundabout, but it struck her with such horror that she fell, cringing on the damp leaves beneath her.

She huddled shivering there for some time, her eyes closed to shut out the morning light, her ears still hearing the horrible anguished cry and the chilling ring of the blade. She numbly searched for an acceptance of what had just happened, until finally, the sunlight's warmth and the songs of the woodland birds stirred her back to reality.

Staggering to her feet, she brushed her damp hair away from her face; and as she did so, the ring upon her finger caught her eye with its flash and twinkle. She stared at it. She rubbed it with her finger. She touched it to her lips. It was real. It was all real. And he was gone. *The hart,* she thought, remembering the word play. *The heart flies home.* She stooped to pick up the green cloak where it had fallen from Garrett's arm, and clutching it to her, she stumbled away through the woods to the Garrison Keep, where she curled on her bed without removing her boots and lay staring in wakeful exhaustion, trying to fathom all that had just happened. At last she fell asleep.

WHAT THE GYPSY KNEW

The clock upon the mantelpiece was chiming nine o'clock when she awoke, and she thought it yet morning until she looked groggily out of the draped window and saw that all was dark outside. She had slept the day through. She was hungry and fixed herself a peanut-butter-and-jelly sandwich in the kitchen before she stepped out into the night and walked to the stable where the horses whinnied a greeting, waiting to be fed. The air was damp, the night wind cool, and the moon strafed over by ragged clouds. It all looked much as she felt, thought Ellen, leaning on the paling to watch the horses eat and taking small comfort from their warm presence. Rubbing the grey's neck thoughtfully when he turned to nuzzle her, Ellen decided that she would return him to the Coltstone riding stable on the morrow. There was no reason to keep him, she mused, when he was now only an added expense; and he was "old and slow." She smiled wanly to remember Garrett's deprecating words.

Back at the Keep, she stood in the center of the kitchen, feeling ambivalent about what she should do now. She'd been alone before, she admonished herself, and never minded it much. She decided she'd have a cup of tea and a hot bath and find a book to read; but when she walked into the library, she felt drawn to the study and from there, to the door of the rooms that had once been her uncle's and that Garrett had occupied.

She turned on a lamp near the door and stood there a moment, gazing into the room where all was neat and clean and orderly, except for a towel that hung on the bathroom doorknob and an envelope and some papers that lay upon the top of the dresser. She walked across the room and looked at them for a thoughtful moment before she touched them. There was an envelope that was sealed and addressed to her, the bulky manila packet he had put in her satchel in London and a tall stack of five-hundred-pound notes.

Gingerly, she lifted the envelope and weighed it in her hand, holding it there for a long moment before she turned it over and broke the seal with her thumbnail. Sitting down in the chair beside the lamp, she tilted the letter toward the light to read.

Dear Lady Ellen,

If you are reading this, then I can only hope that I am returned to the place from whence I came, and that our endeavors to right the wrongs of the past have been accomplished. While our parting brings me sorrow, you must know that to this end I am bound. I am forever indebted to you.

Please accept these few things as token of my fealty. I give them in the hope that they will further your happiness in this place, although they pale in comparison with all that I should wish to have given.

May you find your heart's desire.

God prosper you,
Lord Garrett, Baron of Coltstone Keep.

Ellen smiled through tears as she read the script of his signature and the imprint of his signet ring below it. She read the letter again, and then once more, before she shook herself from her reverie and folded it away. She picked the manila envelope up from the dresser and slid a bulky folded stack of legal documents from it: they were the receipts of taxes paid, all stamped and notarized. Her inheritance taxes, her uncle's taxes past due, her own for the next year were all paid in full; and the stack of money on the dresser top was enough to rebuild and maintain the estate for years to come. This, she then realized, had been his whole purpose in traveling to London to exchange the coins and stones: this was what he had intended all along. Overwhelmed, she walked from the room, the letter and papers in her hand, the bills left in their stack where he had placed them. She placed the papers upon her bedside table, poured up a hot bath, and took two aspirin. She felt like she was getting a cold.

The next morning, early, she arose to a day gray and misty and cool. She ate a piece of toast as she pulled on her boots in the scullery and looked at the cloak that she had hung on a peg beside the door the night before. She fingered its deep green woolen folds, took it down, and pulled it on. It would be warm against the day's dampness, but she knew the warmth was more for her soul; it still held the lingering feel of friendship. It was too long; it made her feel good.

Saddling the filly, she led the grey along the path through the field where the Coltstone stable horses grazed, their coats frizzled with mist. The stable hostler greeted her cheerily, talked of the weather, and tallied her bill while she wiped down the grey and led him to a stall. It was not until she was halfway home by way of the county road that a vague feeling began to steal over her that something was wrong or, rather, that everything simply seemed *too right*. The Coltstone stable, the grounds, the "Parks and Tourism" sign by the roadside . . . Shouldn't it all somehow be different? If Garrett had returned to his time armed with his knowledge from the future, wouldn't things now be different?

Her feeling of unease grew as she returned to the Keep and wandered through its rooms, studying and thinking. Garrett's papers of scrawling notes and figures were still upon the table in the Great Hall, her drawing of the tomb's etching alongside them. As she looked at her pencil sketch, she wondered if perhaps something had gone wrong. The sunlight, the trees, the moon and star; they had all been there in their right places that morning, but she still remembered the haunting cry and the sound of the executioner's ax with a clarity that made her shudder. She could still see the stricken look on Garret's face as his form shimmered and faded. These things *couldn't* be right.

Dropping the sketch back to the table, she returned to the scullery to pick up the satchel from the chair and the cloak from the table where she had dropped it. She would ride into the village, she decided; she needed some things from the shops, and she wanted to talk with the old gypsy. He, of all the people she knew here, might know the answers to her questions; and he was the only one who might not think her crazy.

The company of the Bowl & Pitcher was congenial, and the fire in its hearth warm as Ellen ate lunch there before pulling her list from her pocket and setting off down the drizzled street. A bottle of aspirin, bar of soap, small jar of cinnamon, matches for the stove, batteries for her flashlight—all trivial items compared to the weight of her thoughts. She purchased them, stuffed them into the satchel, and walked down to the gypsy's small shop at the end of the street.

He was working in the backroom when she entered and stooped through the curtained doorway behind the counter at sound of the front door's jingly bell. At sight of her, he offered a guarded smile and a short "Good afternoon, may I help you?"

"I hope so," said Ellen, walking to the counter. She gazed down absently at some items there, wondering how to broach her subject. She decided to be direct.

"Mr. Grimmel, do you remember the man you spoke with here last Wednesday, a week ago?"

The gypsy nodded, his dark face creasing in a worried frown.

"Did you know him?" she queried.

The gypsy studied her a long moment in pensive silence before he answered. "That one," he said guardedly, "should never have been here." He shook his head. "You cannot know of these things." He meant to turn away, but Ellen stopped him.

"But I do!" she exclaimed urgently. "I do know, probably more than you, and I *must* know more! I need answers."

He turned back to her wearily. "Why, miss? They are old stories, old troubles. The curse is of my family—do not make it yours."

"It already is," she said morosely. "Now will you please tell me what he asked of you and what you told him?"

The old man pulled a stool from under the counter and settled upon it. "That one," he said at last. "I know not if he were truly spirit or flesh."

"Flesh," she said succinctly, "absolutely flesh. But spirited here out of his time," she added to his guarded look.

"Ah," he said. "Then it is true."

"What is true?" asked Ellen. "What did he ask you?"

"He asked me of the etchings upon a tomb, their meanings, the magic he suspected there in."

"And?"

"And so I told him," he sighed and rubbed his temples distractedly. "I told him what I could."

At her expectant silence, he continued.

"My family is very old here: we have much history. Some many generations ago, a man of my lineage was slain by Lord Garret of the Coltstone family in sentence for the death of his brother, Lord David."

Ellen nodded her understanding, and he continued.

"Lord Coltstone soon learned of the man's innocence and repented his deed, taking the slain man's young son in his charge to raise, train, and provide for in recompense. He made him a scribe and accountant in his house. But the youth had sworn bitter vengeance upon the Coltstone family for the death of his father and later sold his service to another to betray Lord Garret Coltstone to his death. He wrote letters of treason in craftily forged hand and saw his lord beheaded."

Ellen shuddered. This then was the answer, just as she had suspected—the scribe was Leticia's accomplice! "Did you tell him this, Garrett, the man you spoke to last week? Did you tell him?" she asked urgently.

"No," said the gypsy. "I did not. He did not ask of this . . ."

"But you must have known, must have thought that he should know, if he asked about the crypt and the drawings there?"

"This legend has long been in my family. Some things have been lost, but not the fear of its curse."

"Curse?" Ellen prompted.

"Aye," he muttered. "Too late the young scribe would learn of his own father's betrayal by the very hand of the one who had paid him."

He watched Ellen struggle to understand. "The men who witnessed against the gypsy's father, the ones who condemned him before the Lord of Coltstone, were in the hire of her who purchased the letters writ. Too late the young scribe knew this, too late he grieved the actions of his hand and the fell deeds that had followed. The irony of fate heavy upon him, he took his own means to ease the burden of his soul."

"How?" queried Ellen, intrigued by the gypsy's words.

"Magic," replied the gypsy with a wry twisted grin and an appraising glint in his eye.

"Magic?"

"Aye, a gypsy art we've often been burned for and never understood completely . . . so much is lost."

"What was this magic?" asked Ellen.

"An etching upon the tomb, nothing more I suppose. If there is more, it's lost now, over the years. But the boy carved it there and wove its spell so that at some distant point in time, the doors of eternity would open and Lord Garret Coltstone would walk again. It gave a chance only, that in this loop of time, fate could be reversed and evil undone." The gypsy paused as if he might say more, but fell silent.

"And you told him this?"

"He asked of the etching, of its spell, its power for his return. I gave answer to what he asked."

"And?"

"And I told him what I knew, all I remembered from the legends of my family." At Ellen's querulous look, he shrugged. "It is all of time, of moon phase, having the things of the drawing all in place. It could only happen once. Once in many centuries . . ."

Ellen nodded. "It has, then," she murmured.

The gypsy gave her a calculating look. "He is gone, then?" he asked as if all hung on her answer.

"Yes" she said. "He is gone. Yesterday morning."

The gypsy wiped a hand over his face and blinked. "And the curse has not yet fallen," he said quietly.

Ellen squinted. "Curse?" she asked. "What is this curse you keep talking about?"

"The fear we have owned through the centuries that should the magic work its spell, our own family would find its doom in Lord Garret's reprisal for his scribe's treason. If he should know, should find out, and then should return to his time with that knowledge, our family would forever be lost."

"And you believe that this has not, and will not, now happen?"

The gypsy shrugged. "I am still here."

Ellen gazed at him, appalled, "And that is why you did not tell him about the scribe?"

The gypsy's silence was in itself an eloquent reply.

"Then it's done," she said finally. "Whatever happened is done, and he is back in his own time to work through his own fate and find the answers for himself."

Still, the gypsy did not answer; and she struggled within, feeling as if something was missing. "But it doesn't feel right," she finally exclaimed.

"Why?" he asked, rubbing his cheek with a long bony finger.

"Because he is gone. It's all done, and yet nothing has changed. You're here. Your family is still here, but his is not. Shouldn't something have changed here in this time, if he were able to change the events that were happening then?" She wondered if she knew anything of time, of eternity. Everything seemed in question, and everything was too confusing. Maybe realities ran parallel. She shook her head. She could not rid herself of the horrid anguish of his last look and the horrible cry.

She looked up to find the gypsy watching her intently. "Perhaps," he said softly, "the magic is not yet finished. Such magics are old and much is forgotten, and there may yet be something to be done. His history is written, but yours is still an open book. You too must follow your heart."

Ellen smiled wanly. What she felt in her heart now was far from comforting. Garrett had returned without knowing the origin of the letter, but that was not what troubled her: somehow, she felt something else was much more deeply wrong. "Thank you," she said to the old gypsy man. "Thank you for not saying I'm crazy."

He shook his head and grinned toothily. "Speak of it no more," he said, "and to no others, or I will proclaim you so." She nodded agreement to the silent pact between them. He did not rise to open the door for her as she left, though his eyes followed her out of sight, and he sat long and quietly in thought after she had left.

At the courtyard of the Bowl & Pitcher, Ellen untied the black filly and mounted quickly, setting her course across the downs to the old church, knowing what she went to seek and dreading what she might find. All in the cemetery remained as it had been: Alice and her son still buried in their common grave beneath the eves of the church wall. Inside the sanctuary, the statue still stood beside the crypt in its gloomy alcove, and Ellen read the dates inscribed there with a sinking heart. Nothing had changed.

She cast about in her mind for answers, wondering what could have gone wrong. Why would Garret have been sent into the future by this enigmatic gypsy magic if he were meant only to return to the time of his own execution? Was there some fault of the magic, or some fault of their interpretation of it, and if there was, could she do anything about it now? She thought of the etching on the tomb and of her drawing of it. On impulse, she pulled her flashlight from the satchel and scrambled back into the dirty cobwebbed corner of the alcove, shining the light into the cramped space beyond.

The etching was all there; she had half expected it to have disappeared. She studied the sunlight rays, the trees, the leaping antlered deer, the moon and star. She had drawn it all just so: except, perhaps, could it be that she had transposed the moon in its phase from waxing to waning? She thought hard, hoping her memory would tell her it was not so: but there it was, and she was not certain she had portrayed it accurately. She sat back on her heels, wondering if, by her own oversight, she had helped Garrett back through time only to lead him back to the bailiff's block. The thought was too horrifying, and she hurried from the sanctuary, away from the silently accusing gaze of the man in statue.

She would go back to the Great Hall and find the etching on the table. She must know whether her foolish ineptitude had doomed him to the very fate they had hoped he could escape. Then she would search the history books, she thought desperately, the history books would tell her if anything had been changed by his sojourn here. They would be her final answer. With energy born of anguish of heart, she leaped astride the filly, pulled the cloak close around her, tightened the satchel's strap across her back, and set her heels to the horse's flanks. Away they flew across the green field and into the wood at a headlong gallop. Forsaking the thin trail, Ellen sought the openings between the trees, bending under the low branches, and pushing through the scratching scrub. The bole of a tree lay across the way before them, its smooth straight trunk spanning across their path at no great height; and Ellen set the filly to it, leaning over her crested neck for the jump.

But this was not her brave sorrel trained to her confidence and firm to her hand and was not a Texas-field trial jump. The black filly balked and swerved to one side; and Ellen's weight, thrown so suddenly upon the off stirrup, tore through the worn leather that she had neglected to replace, and she was flung off over the horse's shoulder and struck the downed tree with a force that sent a blinding flash of sparks and pain through her head. She groaned, curled up on the wet leaves, and lay unconscious there as the filly stood by uncertainly, fidgeting at her bit. The grey mists wreathed over them and drifted away through the trees.

The Earl of Marche's Daughter
A ballad

William Blain is from hunting's hame and gallant are his deeds
But he's tane the heart of Lady March—the finest maid ere seen.
Her father, he has banished him, for he's below her station
William Blain's awa to France to fight for king and nation.

When the Lady's come to know that her own true love has fled
Now she's looking pale and wan and taken to her bed.
A physician's come to see her. For a season she's been crying.
He says she's got a broken heart and I fear your lady's dying.

Then her father, he's conceded. He's want to take the blame
And a messenger is sent away to fetch young William hame.
And the Lady's feeling better. She's risen tae her feet
And she's tane a horse to Paebles town her true love there to meet.

But the Lady's looking pale and wan; her cheeks have lost their glow
And she's no the handsome beauty that she was a year ago.
And when her love rode through the town his horse he did no tether
He swiftly passed the Lady by, he's mistaken her for another.

And he galloped to her father's house to see his love again.
He spurs his horse in anguish, but he spurs his horse in vain.
For the Lady lies in Paebles town. It's there she's passed away
And her wounded heart no longer beats for handsome Willy Blain

She's the Earl of Marches daughter and the fairest of them all
But the humble squire, William Blain has tane her heart away.
(Child's ballad, 1423)

A TURNING OF FATE

Ellen slowly became aware of a great roaring in her ears and a dull throbbing in her head. She felt, more than heard, the thudding of horses' hooves from the ground beneath her and pushed herself up from the damp leaves to sit dizzily, trying to remember why she was here. Her stomach felt queasy. Something on the side of her face felt stiff and warm, and when she drew her fingers away, they were red.

She groaned and shivered, staggering to her feet as she began to remember what had happened and looked around for the filly who she figured should be nearby. But the filly was nowhere in sight and what she heard perplexed her: hounds were baying and horses were galloping at the hunt. The sound was near her, nearer all the time, and she looked through the trees in dismay as a pack in full sound bounded into view and rushed toward her with teeth bared and tongues lolled out.

With quick thought and quicker feet, Ellen leaped to put her back against a tree and flayed about her savagely with her riding crop as the pack circled her, barking and snapping.

"Haw now! Get down!" she cried, and she cut the leader across the nose with her crop until he cowered and the pack backed away in a whimpering mob. The band of horsemen that galloped upon the scene pulled up sharply and stared at the strange scene before them as the horses stamped their hooves and champed their bits.

"Ho there! Back down!" commanded a rider, and Ellen startled in wonder and relief to hear a voice that she knew well.

"Aha! My lord," cried another voice amid laughter, "me thinks thou hast treed thee a rare pretty bird!"

"So it would seem," said Lord Garrett as Ellen rushed toward him.

"Garrett!" she cried. "You're here! You've come back!" She ran to his horse's side only to step back in bewilderment when she met his gaze and found it bereft of recognition and lit only with amused curiosity. "Garrett?" she stammered, glancing at the strange horsemen that surrounded them. "It's Ellen! I found out who wrote the letters," she continued in a rush of panic and confusion. "Don't you know me?"

"Know you?" he laughed as the horsemen around him joined in the jest. "Maid, I have never before set eyes on you." He gazed at her strange raiment: the overlong cloak, her breeches and shirt. He'd never seen a woman in such garb, and her long hair flying loose and unkempt struck him as outlandish and vulgar. "Who art thou?" he asked, leaning down from his saddle. "Whence comest thou, and what business have you in my lands?"

These were all questions a man would ask a trespasser, thought Ellen, as she stepped back and stared at this Lord Garrett astride a magnificent, tall bay charger. Something was definitely not right in never-never land she told herself, and she decided she'd best get a grip on the situation fast before things got out of hand.

With one last vain effort at denial and a sinking feeling in her heart, she looked up into Garrett's face and knew that this was indeed Lord Garrett, but certainly not the one she'd known. There was no grey in the long brown hair; there were no lines of care around the eyes that returned her gaze without recognition. This was a man of fewer years, the arrogance and confidence in his demeanor untempered by the sorrow and sacrifice he might one day know.

She looked from him to the horsemen who sat their mounts roundabout and watched the scene with passive interest as their horses stamping impatiently, and she knew that Garrett had not come back to her. The black filly was not here. The fallen tree was not where it should have lain, and Garrett had not come back to her world at all: somehow she reasoned (and the thought made her close her eyes and swallow hard), they were caught again in the strange magic timescape, only this time he had not come into *her* world; she had gone back into *his*!

That must *be what's happening,* she thought apprehensively, and the very impossibility of it made her head pound. Experience told her it was too much to hope that this was all a dream.

"Speak, maid," ordered Garrett. "Do not try my patience." And by the tone of his voice, Ellen knew that this was going to be much more dangerous than fun.

"My Lord," she said, fumbling at what she thought might be a respectful curtsy. "My name is Ellen," she hesitated. "Tell me, please, what date . . . what year is this?"

The horsemen found her amusing, and Garrett grinned. “It is the quarter moon of June, in the year of our Lord 1449. Art thou moonstruck, wench, that thou dost not know this?”

Ellen squinted hard at him. So that’s how quickly it went from maid to wench, she thought, and she supposed “witch” would not be far behind. “Then David?” she asked urgently. “Is he still alive?”

He looked at her sharply. “But of course! What meanest thou?”

“And Leticia? Are they married?”

“Enough of your questions!” he barked. “Who art thou that thou wouldst know?” “You must believe me,” she said, telling herself even as she spoke that she was rushing into this much too fast. “You must believe me. I am not from this time. I must have come to warn you,” she stammered, knowing she was saying all the wrong things as an indulgent frown played across his face. Of course he did not believe her. He thought her crazy, a simpleton. He would leave her here in the woods, lost in the fifteenth century. She shuddered. It did not sound like a nice prospect.

“Please,” she said, reaching up to grasp his arm impulsively. “Please, hear what I have to say . . .”

But she got no further and gasped in surprise and pain at the viselike grip of his hand around her wrist. He yanked her hand from his arm and almost lifted her from the ground as he pulled her against the horse’s shoulder.

“This!” he hissed, his face hard with anger as he grasped the ring upon her hand and twisted it cruelly from her finger. “Where did you get this?”

“Ouch!” she cried reactively. “You gave it to me!”

“Gave it to you!” he spat vehemently as stern silence spread among the watching horsemen. “Thou art a thief and a liar!” he cried, flinging her back so violently that she landed on her rump in the dirt.

“Not much different than the first time,” she thought unhappily as he ordered two men forward and had her pulled to her feet and bound.

“Take her to the Keep.” he commanded. “Lock her there. I will see to this later.” He rolled the ring in his gloved hand and slid it into the pouch at his belt, his face dark with anger. They lifted her across the pommel of a saddle in front of a young soldier who held her there as they rode away toward the castle.

And as Lord Garrett continued his hunt, his mind yet lingered in querulous thought of the half-wit maid and the stolen ring. He did not believe that she had the ability to plot such a theft or the wit to carry it through, but she would know who had. That someone, he believed, must have had access to his mother's private chambers; and that thought greatly disturbed him.

More than thoughts disturbed Ellen as the horse jolted heavily along; the blood pounded in her head as she hung face down over the saddle with its hard pommel in her stomach. Past the horse's shoulder, she could see the road ahead and the gates of the great castle above them: the Coltstone Keep, in the year of our Lord 1449.

There were no terraced gardens, no paving, and no fancy electric lamp posts, only a wide, rutted, muddy track through the green sward where sheep grazed. A smoky fire was burning near the castle gate, and a woman lifting dyed wool from the pot suspended there paused to stare as they rode into the Close.

"What ho?" cried a voice nearby, and Ellen craned her neck around to see a stout, good-looking young man standing beside a horse. She thought he was smiling, though it was hard to tell, since he was upside down. "Is this what my brother brings home from the hunt?" he quipped, walking over to them.

"Aye, my lord," rejoined the young man who held her on the horse. "A thief found in the wood."

"Ah. Roast thief," laughed the man that Ellen thought must the Lord David she had read about in the history book. He slapped her roughly on the back. "I prefer roast *beast*." And he walked away laughing as they lifted Ellen from the horse and stood her on her feet.

"And I prefer better jokes," she muttered tiredly as they led her away. They passed through the entry where liveried soldiers stood at arms, traversed the Great Hall, and entered a corridor beyond. They passed halls and doors, the pantries, kitchen, and scullery—all places Ellen knew and had seen before but that were now all quite different, filled with the sights and sounds of a place peopled and lived in. The castle was alive; it breathed with activity: it smelled of food, of fires, of candle smoke, and the rush matting on the floors. Ellen saw everything around her with amazed bewilderment and could almost have forgotten her sorry plight for the thrill of it all had it not been for the guard who hurried her along the passages with a hard grip on her elbow.

"In here!" he said gruffly and pushed her along down a flight of steps, which she knew were only one doorway shy of the storerooms, and into a narrow dark space off which two doors opened. He guided her through one of them, banging it shut behind her, and she heard a drawbar drop into place. “Wait,” she cried, banging against the door in sudden panic. “Come back! I must speak to Lord Garrett!” she called but knew it was futile. The soldier made no answer, and she heard his footsteps retreating up the stairs as the silence settled heavily around her. “Is anyone there?” she called to the silence of the cell but got no answer.

She looked around then at the tiny space of the dirty cell. A narrow cut in the wall high above her admitted a little light and as little fresh air, its dim light showing four stone walls and a flagged floor, but not so much as a wooden stool to sit upon. A bucket in the corner reeked so pungently she easily guessed its use and the floor was dirty and damp.

“Well, Toto,” said Ellen to the four walls as she slumped dejectedly against the wall facing the door, “we definitely aren’t in Kansas anymore.” Her head hurt and she ached all over, and she would like to have just curled up and slept to ward away the weariness and despair that threatened to overwhelm her; but she knew she had no time to indulge in such self-pitying. So instead she pulled the satchel into her lap and unzipped it, realizing that what had been trivial purchases only hours ago now represented a treasure trove of all the assets she had for survival in this strange new world. She shook two aspirin out of a bottle and chewed them down, closed her eyes for a moment, and took another for good measure; labels were not meant for times such as these, she reasoned as she snapped the lid back on the bottle and stashed it away again.

Sorting through the satchel, she pulled out her pocketknife and put it in her pocket. Pen, flashlight, matches, soaps, aspirin . . . She inventoried everything she had carried with her, evaluating it all in the light of her new circumstance and then she closed her eyes and leaned her head back, trying to think. She must think, she told herself, she must plan, before things simply happened to her. She tried to remember all she could from her studies. What did they do to thieves in the fourteenth century? Did they cut off your hands or just your thumbs? Did they brand you or hang you from the castle gate? Nothing she could remember seemed very pleasant.

“I must find a way to speak to Garrett,” she muttered to herself. “Got to convince him there is more to me than he thinks and more going on here than the ordinary. But now, how am I going to do that?” she mused, and soon began to form her thoughts into a plan. Thinking over the events of the past month, she mentally cataloged all of the things she knew about Garrett and about his family. There were things she knew about Lord Garret that perhaps no one else did, and that knowledge might just be the key to her survival she surmised. And now, of course, there was also Lord David to contend with since it *was* 1449 and he was still alive; although, if her memory served correctly, he had died in early July of that year.

From these vague thoughts Ellen began to form a strategy; and in the dismal dark of the cell, she plotted its course and planned her next move. She resolved to tweak Garrett's interest and keep it with the small curious details of personal information that she knew no one else could know, and once she had him listening, she would play the prophet and foretell David's death. Maybe then he would believe her, and they could prevent the very tragedy that had set events in motion for his eventual demise.

It seemed a monumental challenge as she huddled against the hard stone wall, her head aching and her thoughts in unruly turmoil, but she knew she had no choice. Perhaps this was what old Grimmel had meant by the magic not being finished, she mused. Perhaps Garret had been sent forward in time only so that she would know what to fix in a time prior and could set all to rights before the fell deeds were done.

She sighed. The gypsy had said that her book was still open. Well, she figured, it might take some creative thinking to keep it that way now.

Thrown in a dungeon, she thought wryly to herself, *just like Uncle said.* Now if only she could pull through without being burned for a witch . . .

Pulling her checkbook from the purse within the satchel, she penned a short note on the back of a debit slip, reread it, scratched it out, and wrote it again in as close to Old English as she could muster. She would send it to Garrett by the guard, if and when he brought her some dinner.

SHIPS THAT SAIL

Garrett and his men rode in late that afternoon from a successful hunt. A red deer was tied across the rump of a horse and, although the riders were all damp and weary, they were all in high spirits as Alice met them in the Close.

"A good evening, my lord," she greeted Garret warmly, holding a mug of warmed mead in one hand and Edward's small fist in her other.

Swinging down from the saddle, Garrett tossed the reins to a hostler and lifted the small boy onto his hip before he took the cup from Alice and tasted it.

"Your hunt was successful," Alice observed.

"Aye. It was a good day. And how is my mother?" Garrett asked as they walked from the Close through the wide entry doors.

"She remains ill. I left her asleep," replied Alice, taking the empty cup from his hand.

"You are good to her, and I thank you," said Garrett. Alice only smiled as he hugged the little boy and set him down beside her. Touching her cheek in a momentary caress, he left them there: she to return to her duties at his mother's side, he to the castle's administrative matters. There was nothing more to say between them just now; there was nothing more they *could* say, just now.

Later, when Garrett sat down at the table in the long dining hall where all the household sat down to meal, he was joined by his brother and his brother's wife, Leticia; his mother's place was vacant across from him.

"I hear my brother has brought in the game this day!" quipped David with a wink to all those around.

"Aye," replied Garrett, "A strong four point—he ran well."

"Nay," laughed David. "I speak not of such, but of a green cloaked creature that goes on two feet."

Leticia looked up intrigued. "A what?"

"A fairy wench he claims is a thief . . . ," ribbed David.

Garrett continued cutting his meat, unperturbed. "The hounds bayed her in the wood above the kirkyard," he explained. "I found this in her possession," he said, pulling the emerald ring from his belt and holding it between his finger and thumb.

"Your mother's ring!" exclaimed Leticia.

"Yes," said Garrett evenly. "The great wonder is how she did come to gain it?" He looked questioningly at Leticia, who made no answer. "Alice tells me our mother has been in her chambers all this day."

"Yes," replied Leticia. "With only Alice, Emaline, and myself to attend her."

"None other?"

"No."

"And have you seen anyone else, any stranger, within the Keep?"

"No." Leticia replied, eyeing the ring as he slid it back into his belt.

"Say no word to Mother," Garrett said to Leticia, and his brother nodded agreement. "I would not have her worried."

"I'm up to the north holdings tomorrow," said David "I leave this matter to your hand." And no more was said of it over dinner.

It was later that evening when Garrett sat alone, thoughtfully perusing the accountant's books laid out upon the worktable where his scribe usually labored, that the matter was again brought before him, again annoyingly unbidden when a guard entered the room and stood hesitantly at the door before addressing him with a bow.

"My lord," he said.

"Yes, what is it?" Garrett asked, leaning back in his chair and rubbing his eyes. It was too late and the candle light too dim for such work.

"My lord, the wench in the dungeon bid me give you this," the guard said querulously, holding out a white slip of paper

"Since when, Derrick, have you taken orders from prisoners?" Garret asked the guard, a note of patient indulgence in his voice.

"I would not, sir, but . . . she . . ."

"She what?" demanded Garrett, taking the paper in his hand.

"She threatened to do me harm, sir, if I did not do her bidding."

"Really?" asked Garrett, raising one eyebrow.

“She has powers, sir. She holds fire in her hand with a terrible flash and smoke . . . and she bid me give this to you without fail.”

Powers! Fire and smoke! Garrett thought with sarcasm. Still he’d never seen Derrick so spooked; the guard was truly shaken. He held the paper carefully in his hand, fingering its curiously smooth texture. It was edged in gold with a bold clear print such as he had never seen. Only the very wealthy could obtain such parchment as this, he deemed, and only the very influential could employ such a scribe or cleric to print so. He wondered how the wench had come to have such an item in her belongings and surmised that she had probably stolen it even as she had stolen the ring. She must be much cleverer that he had first thought, he decided as he held the paper to the candlelight to inspect it more closely and noticed that there was writing on both sides. Flipping it over he found what appeared to be a message written there in a curious scrawling script that twined like some unreadable incantation written and then crossed through, and below this, legible words written in block print:

“I know of Turret of the Garrison Keep Tower from whence the mighty ships once sailed,” it read.

“The ships . . . from the Garrison Keep Tower,” Garrett mumbled the words over, mystified, and then he read it again and dropped the paper quickly upon the table as if stung. The ships in the Tower Turret, the parchment drawings that he and David had secreted there as children—how could she have known of these. Who was she that she could know so much? It aggravated him—no—it made him nervous. (He would not use the word *fear*.)

“Where did this come from?” he asked the guard. “This parchment . . .”

The guard shrugged. “She carries a leather pouch under her cloak. That is all I know.”

“And you left it with her?”

“Aye, my lord, I saw no need to take it.”

“No need,” muttered Garrett, “and yet you speak of fire and powers . . . Bring me the pouch,” he said at last. “And aught else she has about her.”

As the man left the room, Garrett leaned back in his chair. The maid *might* be a witch, he mused, though he did not think she had the fell look of an enchantress. Then he considered half amusedly that he was not sure what an enchantress was *supposed* to look like. But how else did she come into possession of a ring that had never left his mother's room, and how did she hold fire in her hands and not be burnt, and how did she know of the long-ago secret hideaway of two boys and become privy to their childhood councils? He rubbed his hands over his face and shrugged away the troublesome thoughts as he rose from the table, deciding that he would deal with the witch on the morrow when the sun's light could brighten his councils, and picking up the candle, he ascended the tower stairs to his private quarters.

In the dingier depths of the castle Ellen's heart leaped when she heard footsteps returning upon the stairs outside her cell. It had be an interminably long time since she had coerced the guard into carrying her message, motivating him with fear of magic by the simple act of lighting a match in her hand. Ingenious, she congratulated herself, glad of the man's ready superstition as he hurried away on her errand. Now as she rose to her feet, she hoped that this would be Garrett come to speak with her or at least the guard to take her to him. She was nonplussed when the door creaked open and the guard entered, his face ashen and tense, a torch in his hand.

"The scrip!" he demanded, holding out his hand. "Give it to me!" He brandished the torch at her even as he advanced, pushing her back.

"Stop it!" she cried. "What . . . ?" she had her back against the wall, her hands raised to ward the torch's heat from her face.

"The scrip that thou dost carry! My lord's orders," he demanded, and Ellen quickly pulled the strap over her head and cast the satchel to the floor at his feet.

The guard stooped, snatched up the bag, and backed away out the door, slamming it closed behind him and banging the bar into place as if seven demons were pent within. His footsteps echoed down the corridor as he hurried away.

Ellen slumped back against the wall in the darkness. "Great, just great!" she muttered. Things were definitely not getting better. "Could at least have left me a tissue," she said to herself as she slid down to huddle against the wall, pulling her knees up under the cloak and resting her head on her crossed arms. It was going to be a long, cold, comfortless night.

The guard, hurrying away up the corridor, through the Great Hall and up the tower stairs came to Lord Garrett's chambers just as Garrett had once again dismissed the matter, cast off his sword belt and robe and sat down to pull off his boots. The knock on his door was perturbing, as was the guard who stood there, holding a leather pouch by its strap at arm's length as if it were a dead rat.

"As you requested, my lord," he said, proffering the bag, and Garrett took it from him with a nod.

"Thank you, Derrick," he said in dismissal, and the guard bowed.

"Good night, my lord," he said and was gone.

Garrett eyed the leather satchel with a reserved curiosity, holding it from its strap at arm's length much as the guard had done.

"Humph!" he grunted, tossing it onto a small table beside the door. It rattled mysteriously and he poked it cautiously with his finger, studying the smith work of its buckles and strap rings, rolling it over, and then quickly pulling his hand away. The thing had a row of grinning bright metal teeth all across its top with a tab like a tongue at one end, and he eyed it with grave distrust before he turned away resolving that such mysterious things were better studied in broad daylight. He slept uneasily through the night.

Ellen spent a wretched night of frightful dreams and no comfort, to awaken curled upon the flagstones sore and weary when the guard opened the door that next morning to set a half loaf of bread and a cup of water inside the cell. She felt like she'd slept upon a brick, and she rubbed her aching ribs and felt among the wadded folds of the cloak where she had lain upon it. Something solid met her prodding fingers, and quickly, she pulled the cloak open to the pocket Garrett had asked old Mrs. Sayer to sew into the lining. Finding a folded packet there, Ellen pulled the soft felt cloth envelope from the pocket and unwrapped it upon her lap.

She gazed in dismay at the tumbled pile of glittering gold and jewels. She would rather it had been a peanut butter and jelly sandwich, she thought to herself, as she picked the small bronze horse out of the tangle of jewelry and rubbed its smooth metal back. She knew that these things could only bring her more trouble if they were discovered missing and then found with her; and she carefully folded the cloth back over the jewel's glimmer and slid it back into the pocket of the cloak.

"So what do I do?" she asked of the little bronze horse, who only stood on her palm, prancing valiantly. She shook her head and tucked him away in a pocket as she picked up the bread and cup of water from the floor. Things really couldn't get much worse, she thought, and they sure could stand to get a lot better.

After breakfast that morning, Garrett walked with David to the Close, where the horsemen were assembled to ride forth with his brother to their northern land holdings. Garrett saw with approval that Shawn, the captain of the guard, and Remmel, his lieutenant, were among them.

"God speed thee, brother," he said as they embraced and David mounted his horse.

David laughed brightly. "And thou, watch after our mother. And keep my lovely Leticia out of mischief," he said derisively.

"Aye," agreed Garrett.

"I'll look forward to hearing what you learn from your lovely jewel thief, when I return on the morrow."

Garrett looked up with a studied frown, placing a hand on David's rein. "Brother," he said, "have you ever spoken aught of the Garrison Tower turret to anyone?"

"No," replied David, perplexed. "I had not thought of it myself for some time now."

"And the things we did and spoke of there?"

"No. Why?"

Garrett squinted. "She knows of them."

"Not by me," said David, wondering at his brother's concern. "I'm certain thou wilt find the meat of the matter," he said offhandedly. "Thou always dost." And he smiled gallantly as he spurred his horse away through the gates with his band of horsemen riding behind.

Going thence to his mother's rooms, Garrett sat with her for some time as she asked news of the household and matters of estate business. She felt better, she said, though her head still hurt; and the shutters were kept closed to dim the light of the room. She often suffered from such pains in her head these days and spent much time here in her rooms, with Alice's quiet cheer and Emaline's dreamy musings and incessant tuneless humming, but she would much rather have been out among the goings and doings of her family, enjoying the fresh air and sunlight of summer as she was once wont to do. Pressing a cool cloth to her forehead, she took Garrett's hand as he rose to go.

"Thou art a good son," she said with a patient smile, and he kissed her cheek ere he gave a wink to Alice and tousled Edward's hair in parting.

"I'll take thee with me when I ride forth this noontide," he whispered to the boy, whose eyes brightened at his words.

As Garrett walked past the drawing table on his way to the door, he eyed the small wooden jewel casket that rested there. Casually, he placed his hand upon it and tried the lid. It was locked.

Back in his room, he picked up the leather satchel and carried it carefully into the large open library that joined his chamber and laid it upon a table there. Studying it closely, he touched the toothy closure cautiously, tugged at it, and—at last discovering its mechanism—unzipped it with a satisfied grin. No magic, he thought to himself, only clever design, and yet he did not venture to reach between the teeth to explore the depths inside. Instead, he gazed there a moment, perplexed, before tipping the whole thing upside down and dumping its contents out upon the table.

A curious collection of oddities tumbled out and rolled and rattled upon the table until they found their places to lie quiet. He looked at them; he poked them into a line upon the table with his finger, and eyed them mistrustfully; but he could not begin to discover what they were and at last he backed away and called a guard to bring his prisoner to him for questioning.

Ellen was delighted when the door of her cell opened and the guard beckoned her out, granting plenty of room for her to pass before him, and guiding her up and out of the cellars, through a back passage and up the tower stair.

This was it then, she told herself, smoothing her frizzled hair back and brushing the dirt and straw from her cloak. With any luck, the guard would take her to Garrett, and she knew that this might be her one and only chance to speak to him. She cleared her throat nervously when they reached the library door and wiped her sweating palms on her breeches.

Garrett stood at a sunlit window at the far end of the room, the fresh breeze over the open lintel tugging at his cloak as he gazed beyond the Keep wall to the sheep grazing out upon the green. The warm air smelled freshly of apple blossoms, and Ellen took a deep breath in relief. It was much better than dungeon smell.

"My lord, I have brought her," said the guard with a bow, and Garrett turned to face them.

"Thank you. You may leave us," replied Garrett to the guard, who bowed again and retreated, closing the door behind him. Garrett crossed his arms upon his chest and frowned as he studied her.

She was thin and tall—taller than most women he'd met—though the cloak she wore was too long for her. Her hair was long and dark and pulled back tightly except for damp curls at her neck and forehead. He remembered the blood on her face when they'd found her in the wood. It had dried and flaked away, except for a bluish gash at her temple.

Her clothes were extremely peculiar, and he studied her up and down disdainfully, and would have turned away, but the startling familiarity of her eyes arrested his gaze.

He stared at her a moment, and yet her air of confidence did not falter and he wondered at her audacity. She looked at him as though she knew him well. No, more than that; she looked at him as if she had known him for a very long time and shared the secret thoughts of his heart, perhaps his very soul. The feeling was unsettling, and he scowled.

"Who art thou?" he asked gruffly.

Ellen swallowed and took a deep breath. It was odd to stand before this man and want to say so much: to have so many memories in common and yet none she could share. She looked boldly into his proud, handsome face, and smiled as she would at a very old friend.

"I am Ellen, Ellen Lancaster," she said matter-of-factly.

Garrett blinked, disbelievingly. "You claim to be of that great house?!"

"No," she said. "And if you ask *them*, they will not know me from Adam's house cat."

"You admit this freely?"

"Of course. What good could it do me to lie?"

"Some would think much," he muttered. "You have threatened my guard until he fears you. He claims you have 'unnatural powers.'" Garrett eyed the items on the table. "What say you to this?"

"That he is a superstitious man, and I did what I thought necessary to get him to carry my message to you. I really am *not* a witch!" she said forcefully, crossing her arms in imitation of his own stance.

"Can you hold fire in your hand?" he challenged.

"Yes," she said. "Like this." And she grasped a match up from the table and struck it before he could move to prevent her. "It's a match," she explained to his wondering gaze. "Not magic."

Cautiously, he took the box of matches from her hand, inspected it carefully, and placed it back upon the table beside the burnt match.

"And these other things?" he asked.

Stepping to the table, she fingered the items one by one, explaining as he watched her warily.

"Flashlight," she said, flicking it on and off. "Works on batteries—electricity—you know." He only shook his head.

"Matches . . . pen." She scribbled a line on a piece of paper. "Soap—something you all definitely need more of—matches, and—aha! Aspirin!" She shook the bottle and opened it.

"What is it?" he asked, eyeing the pills suspiciously.

"Medicine," she said, popping two into her mouth before he grabbed the bottle from her hand. "It makes pain feel better," she said, lightly touching her temple by way of explanation as she handed him the lid. He snapped it on and dropped the bottle back on the table as she continued.

"And this is money from my time," she held a note out to him. "Look at the date," she prompted, but he did not and carefully placed the paper note back down on the table.

"How," he asked measuredly, "how do you know of the turret of the Garrison Keep Tower? How do you know of the drawings of the ships?"

Leaning upon the table, Ellen shook her head. "That I will not tell you, not until I know that you will listen, not until I know you will believe what I say."

"Do not toy with me!" he said, eyes flashing.

"I would not dare to," she replied.

"I could have thee hung as a thief . . ."

"I'm sure you could. I think you might, though I would rather you didn't," she said, and he found the lack of fear in her eyes disconcerting. "But I would have you know," she continued, "before you do so, that your brother will be dead within two weeks' time, you will never marry Alice, and you will be executed for treason at the age of forty-two if you do not hear me and heed what I say."

"You threaten me?" he said incredulously, glowering over her.

"No. That would be preposterous. I only tell you what I know." She took a deep breath and looked up into his hard, unyielding face. *Well, here goes nothing*, she thought to herself and said aloud, "You see, Lord Garrett, I am not from your time—this time. I lived—or actually *will* live—in the Garrison Keep in the year 1963." She steeled herself against his disbelieving glare and continued on hurriedly. "I am a student and a professor of history, and I have read the histories of your family extensively. I know all about you, probably more than *you* know at the moment and I know what happens to you and your family. Somehow—no, I cannot explain how—I have been sent here to warn you. At least, that is what I suppose I am here to do." Her voice trailed away as her words began to sound too strange even to her own ears.

"You are mad!" said Lord Garrett, turning away in disgust.

"Yes. I probably am," she sighed. "Or will be soon for trying to convince you of these things before they happen. Still"—she touched his arm lightly, and he flinched—"How else could I know the things I do about you? How else can you explain these things?" She motioned to the items on the table. "The dates on the money—could I have made that up?"

He shrugged. He was obviously not yet convinced, and Ellen decided to play another trump card in trying to win him over. Stepping close with a conspiratorial look, she whispered, "Where do you keep the dagger you stole from your father's corpse?"

Ellen knew she had said too much when Garret stiffened as if struck and backed away.

"Guard!" he roared, and the door flew open as the soldier rushed to his summons. "Take her away! Lock her away!" he said with a dismissive gesture.

Ellen made no resistance and said no word as she turned away, but at the door she glanced back to see that Garrett had sunk onto a wooden chair beside the table, with his elbows upon his knees and his steepled fingers pressed against his lips. At least he was thinking, she said to herself, and hoped that was a good thing as the dungeon door slammed closed behind her once again and she sat down on the floor in the small spot of sunlight that braved its way through the crack high in the wall.

And indeed, Garrett was deep in thought. The wench knew too much; he felt she was a nuisance, possibly even dangerous, and he wished he could simply be rid of her, but he felt he dare not ignore the things she had prophesied.

She had said that his brother would die in two weeks' time and that he and Alice would never wed, (he grimaced at the thought), and if her words were true, death for treason would be his future. Still, he wondered how she could know any of this to be true. Her claim to be from a different time was too preposterous to entertain, and yet it was the only plausible answer for her extensive knowledge. He picked a paper bill up from the table and rubbed its smoothness between his fingers as he studied the strange pictures on its face and read the date: 1959. He laid it back upon the table.

A different time, he mused. Picking up the box of matches, he held it in his hand as she had done, struck a match, and held it aloft as it flared and settled, burning bright. It scorched his thumbnail before he blew it out and cast it upon the table. She knew of the dagger. She knew too much.

LETICIA

When Garrett rode out that afternoon across the green sward before the castle gates with his young son, Edward, upon a pony beside him, two persons watched from the windows of the Coltstone Keep: one with eyes full of a mother's love and a heart's soft yearning, the other with a cold, calculating gaze full of stony purpose.

Alice sat at a window of Lady Eleanor's chamber, her needlework fallen upon her lap as she gazed across the spring-green fields to watch the man she loved and the child she adored ride away toward the river woods.

"What is it, child?" asked Lady Eleanor.

"Garrett, Mother," Alice replied. "He and Edward are riding to the river."

Lady Eleanor smiled. She loved Alice well, and knew no other of such sweet and gentle charm; and Edward, a boy yet only four, was a thoughtful and obedient child. She hoped yet for their happiness and thought it justly due their patience in waiting for Leticia to provide a noble heir, an event which seemed more and more an unlikely event even to Lady Eleanor. Watching Alice at the window and seeing the wistful light in her face, Lady Eleanor resolved to no longer hinder the wishes of her youngest son who was always so serious and always so responsible. Perhaps it was age, she considered, or the dull ache in her head that made her less concerned with the proud lineage and prosperity of her family and more concerned with their happiness.

Leticia had no such charitable thoughts as she watched the pair ride away from the Keep. Garret's older brother, her lord and husband, she despised. He cared more for his tenants and their sheep than he did for the things she desired, and he insulted her openly with his light regard for her and her wishes. Lord Garrett, she considered, was a more thoughtful and considering man and perhaps more malleable to a woman's artful, persistent, and creative persuading. He certainly held a nobler sense of duty, she reasoned, as she thought scornfully of his long fealty to Lady Alice and her son. *Their* son, she reminded herself.

Edward, in all his sweet childish innocence, was irksome to her, more so because he was so loved by the entire household than for any other reason. Leticia would have preferred him a tiresome brat and all the more easily got rid of, but she felt confident that rid of him she would yet be, given enough time and patience.

Lord Garrett had been troubled of mind that morning, thought Leticia, turning from the window of her high chamber as the pair rode from her view among the trees. Some matter concerning the pretty young jewel thief, she presumed, and wondered what it could mean.

She had not seen Ellen when she was brought in by the soldiers, but she had heard plenty of talk among the kitchen maids. Even knowing that such talk was rarely more than half true, it yet pricked her curiosity, and Leticia wondered who this strange creature might be and how such a one had come in possession of her ladyship's favorite ring.

Most intriguing! thought Leticia. One who could plan and bring to fruition such a theft must be canny indeed; and even Lord Garrett, by the look of things, had yet to discover the woman's means or accomplices. *Such a one,* she thought, *could bear no great love for the Coltstone sons. And if she could be obligated to an allegiance of gratitude for, say, deliverance from her present plight, then she might be a worthy ally to include in other clandestine plans,* surmised Leticia. With such thoughts in mind, she made her way to the dungeon cellars.

If Ellen was not surprised at the dungeon door's opening, she was quite perplexed by the figure that stepped through its narrow sills. She had expected the guard, perhaps, or maybe even Garrett, at an off chance, but never the elegant woman of rich dress and haughty demeanor that stood there. That this was the Lady Leticia, she knew without need of introduction, but she was greatly intrigued to know to what she owed the honor of this visit, doubting that it was for her own good.

"Arise, thou wench," said Leticia crossly. "Hast thou no respect, or know you not who I am?"

"I know who you are," said Ellen, rising slowly and looking past Leticia's beaded and brocaded finery to the open door beyond. Thoughts of escape filled her mind momentarily, but she dismissed them, knowing a guard could not be far from the cellar steps along the corridor.

"You are the thief Lord Garrett brought from the wood above the kirk . . . ," Leticia was saying.

"My name is Ellen. I am no thief," said Ellen shortly.

Favoring her with a disdainful look, Leticia smirked. "You had a ring in your possession, a very valuable ring, the property of one of this house."

"Um," shrugged Ellen.

"How did you get it?" asked Leticia, her keen eyes flashing.

Ellen studied her then a moment before answering. What could Leticia want from her? Certainly not just information.

"It was given me by a great and noble lord," she said evenly, meeting Leticia's hard gaze.

With a scoffing laugh, the Lady looked her up and down with measuring scorn. "You!" she said. "The likes of you would receive no such gift from the great and noble!"

The likes of me, thought Ellen, *could buy and sell the likes of you.* But she reminded herself that it was best not to brag of the hatband before the snake was skinned.

"Tell me!" cried Leticia, impatient with Ellen's silence. "How came you by the ring?"

"And what shall I earn from such a noble lady for my information?" asked Ellen.

Leticia smoothed her features and her dress. Now this sort of bargaining was to her liking. "I can promise no harm will come to you. I have great influence," she said smugly.

"Really?" replied Ellen, faking interest. "And if I told you I had taken it from the very chest where its brethren lay . . . ?"

Leticia's eyes brightened. "How?"

"*That* I will not tell but only that it was secretly and easily done."

With guarded enthusiasm, Leticia simpered sweetly. "And what of those others?"

Ellen only raised one eyebrow querulously. "Others?"

"My Lady's jewels, you fool! Where are they? If you could take the ring, you could have them all."

So that was it, thought Ellen. *Leticia wanted in on the deal. She wanted Lady Eleanor's jewels, but why? Perhaps she needed rewards for those in her pay? That,* thought Ellen, *would explain the soldiers among the Coltstone garrison that were yet loyal to her orders.* "Those," replied Ellen, evasively, "are yet well within Lord Garrett's keeping, I should presume."

"And could you possibly acquire them?" asked Leticia.

"For what reward?"

"Your life," said Leticia.

"You think I value my life highly."

"Most do," said Leticia acidly.

"Yes, though some more than others," replied Ellen. "And I will not do what you ask, though it be well within my power."

"Fool!" hissed Leticia. "I will see you're hung for your insolence."

"More to keep my silence," said Ellen softly. "But you will never be able to see it done."

"You think not."

"I think not."

"Why?"

"Because by the same power that I spirit jewels from coffers locked and hidden, I can find your pretty throat on any dark night," Ellen bluffed. "And you will never have enough power or influence to see me slain." She was spinning a web with the thin thread of superstition and could only hope Leticia's fears would outweigh her venomous animosity at the moment.

Leticia seethed; she glared, and then she wavered. The woman before her showed no qualm; her eyes held no fear. Indeed, her self-assurance was quite unsettling, and Leticia backed away mentally and physically. "What value was this woman anyway?" she said to herself. Lord Garrett had caught her in theft. His judgment in that matter would be swift and certain, and no plea or threat from the wench would change that. Surely, the claims this woman could make to incriminate her would be taken for nothing more than slander.

Smiling smugly, Leticia backed to the door. "Lord Garrett will see to you," she said quickly. "And then you will plea to me in vain."

The door closed heavily, muffling the sound of rustling shirts and Leticia's light step in the corridor.

"*Any* plea to you," muttered Ellen, "would likely be in vain."

Leticia took her meal in her private chamber that night, and Lord Garrett dined alone at the table in the Great Hall. Ellen ate her lump of bread sitting cross-legged upon the cellar floor and wondered wearily what the morrow would bring.

"Two days in Camelot," she muttered, "and I'm ready to go home." She wondered if she ever would.

GUEST OF THE HOUSE

Garrett arose the next morning determined to resolve the matter of his unwanted guest, thief, clairvoyant, or whatever she was, and to clear her from his plate of business before his brother returned at nightfall. To that end, he made his way to the cellars at the first light of dawn.

The mouse Ellen had been tossing crumbs to startled and scampered away at the sound of approaching footsteps. Ellen sighed, munched a crumb herself, and wondered how long it took to tame a mouse and whether she'd be finding that out. The mouse scampered to a corner and hid under a stone slab as the door opened.

"Like Grand Central Station here," Ellen muttered, looking up in surprise to see Garrett standing over her.

"Good morning," she greeted smiling tiredly. "I hope you slept well . . ."

"I wonder that thou jest so," he observed as she nibbled another crumb of bread and remained seated cross-legged on the floor.

"A merry heart doeth good like medicine . . . ," she quoted blandly.

"And sadness drieth up the bones . . . ," he finished.

"Exactly! Never have liked that part," she said, rising to her feet stiffly. Garrett resisted the impulse to smile and crossed his arms instead.

"The dagger you spoke of," he said seriously, "describe it to me." His face creased in thought as she did so.

"And how do you know of it?" he asked, "When none in my own household does, save myself alone."

Taking a deep breath, Ellen leaned her back against the wall and thought for a moment before she spoke. "I know of it because you showed it to me—once upon a time . . ."

"How can this be," he asked, "when I have never seen you before in my life?"

"Because," she said "when you are executed at the age of forty-three, you have a scribe, a gypsy boy by the name of Grimmel. He places a spell on your tomb that sends you five centuries into the future . . ."

"Where I meet you . . . ?"

"Yes."

"That's preposterous."

"I know. It's as preposterous as my being here now," she went on quickly. "But while you are there, you show me turret of the Garrison Keep Tower and a lot of other things."

She watched as he leaned back against the wooden door. He did not seem as imperatively unbelieving as he had the day before.

"You showed me a secret passage to these cellars," she said quietly. "And a hidden niche in the store cellars of your treasury."

"You know of the passage?" he said, more to himself than to her. Her knowledge of such began not to surprise him, "But of what hiding place?" He raised one eyebrow. "I know of none."

Hmmm, thought Ellen. "Perhaps you don't yet." She had not thought of that, she mused.

"Show me," he said curtly, grabbing her by the wrist and pulling her behind him through the doorway and up the cellar steps. In the corridor, he grasped a torch from its sconce upon the wall, and she took the lead down the steps into the amply stocked storerooms that smelled sweetly of wine and grain and apples.

When she indicated the treasury room door, he unlocked it, shoved her in ahead of him, and closed the door behind. The flickering torchlight revealed a barren room in which only three large wooden caskets rested on the floor along the far wall. Garrett held the torch up high and looked to her questioningly.

"It's here," pointed Ellen, counting three stones over from the support pillar at shoulder height.

"That is a solid stone wall," Garrett said dryly.

"So you think," she said tartly. "Hand me your knife."

At his hesitation, she shrugged. "OK, *don't* hand me your knife. You try."

With a look of extreme tolerance, Garrett pulled a thick blade from his belt and pried halfheartedly at the stone's seam work. For one anxious moment, the stone did not budge; and then to Garrett's chagrin and Ellen's triumph, it gave and began to slide from its place. Ellen stepped back as Garrett grasped the stone's smooth edges and pulled it forth to reveal the hidden niche behind.

"That," said Ellen "is where you had hidden the dagger, a bag of gold coins, and these." She pulled the cloth packed from her cloak pocket and handed it to him, backing away to sit on one of the chests against the wall as he weighed the packet in his hand, glanced at her, and pulled the cloth folds back curiously. His face darkened momentarily when he saw the torchlight glimmer on the jewels within.

"Your mother's jewelry," acknowledged Ellen. "You kept them here, although they were in a wooden casket then, a small casket, inlaid in gold, closed with an ivory pen, with a little drawer for the key hidden underneath."

Garrett's face was grim. "And thou wilt say I gave you these also?"

"No. You left them by accident when the gypsy magic took you home."

With a heavy sigh, Garrett laid the precious stones within the dark niche and pushed the stone back into place, brushing his fingers over its face thoughtfully. This woman, he decided, definitely had more about her than could be explained away or ignored. And he began to feel he should entertain her peculiar madness for a time longer, at least until he could be certain of her intent and the validity of the other things she had spoken of.

Those other things . . . He turned to her, considering. "You spoke of my brother," he said. "Of his death. Tell me what you meant by this."

Pulling her knees up and hugging them to her chest as she leaned against the hard stone wall, Ellen nodded. Now, she felt she was getting somewhere. "I will tell you, and I will help you prevent a lot of your misfortune," she said quietly. "But first, you will do some things for me."

"Like what?" he prompted.

She rubbed her nose on her sleeve. "I have been dropped into a time five hundred years before my own," she said tiredly. "I have no friends here, no kin, and no way of surviving—very well. I want your hospitality and your protection." She saw patient tolerance in his face. "I wish to be your guest here. I want a soft bed—in my own room. I want a hot bath and a hot meal and clean clothes."

"Tell me of David," he said.

"Promise me these things first."

"I will not, but I will treat you fairly."

"You will treat me as I ask."

"Your demands are great for one of your station."

"I have a right to them," she returned and, at his doubtful look, continued. "When you came into my time, you had nothing but a lot of trouble and a need to return and save Alice and your son from a terrible fate. I helped you, gave you sanctuary, food, clothing. In comparison, I find your hospitality deplorable," she said with alacrity.

Garrett stifled his retort at her deploring look. He found that with her indomitable lack of fear and unique lack of humility, she managed to amuse him and aggravate him at the same time. He smiled. "Fine, then," he conceded. "You tell me of David . . . and I will reward you with what aid I feel commiserate.

Deciding she would press her advantage no farther, Ellen nodded and cleared her throat as Garrett leaned back against the wall, watching her.

"Do you trust Leticia?" she asked.

"Trust her?" he pondered. "I know not. She is not mine to manage . . ."

"But she will be, if David dies. Do you trust her?"

He shrugged, eyeing her closely.

"Are you aware that she visited me yesterday and asked after those same jewels that I have handed you?"

"I would be careful, miss," he said quietly, "how you slander those of this house."

"Believe me, I *am* careful. And I do *not* slander, if I only speak the truth." At his silence, she continued. "I say this because you must know that Leticia has those loyal to her among your armed garrison, and I now have an idea how she keeps them loyal." He gave her a hard look, and she spoke quickly. "Sometime within the first week of July (she crossed her fingers and prayed her memory served her well), you will be wounded *accidentally* by one of these men while training in the practice yards. David will ride out to the hunt that day without you, in the company of his squire and three others of his guard. He will be shot, struck upon the head, and then drown in the Gulforth. His men will vow that a young gypsy man is guilty of his murder, and you must *not* believe them."

A heavy silence hung over the room when Ellen finished her tale. Garrett stared at the floor, his thoughts unreadable until at last, as one shaking off a bad dream, he wiped his face with his hand and looked up. "In two weeks?" he queried.

"If my memories—and the history books—serve me right."

"Then thou wilt be our guest here, as you request, for two weeks. By the end of that time, we will know if thou art a prophet or an imposter." He gave her a scathing look. "Press not my patience, and know that, shouldst thou prove to be the latter, you will suffer greatly."

Ellen sighed, nodded, and unfolded herself from the trunk. "Fair enough. I will try not to annoy you," she said amicably.

"Too late for that," she heard Garrett mumble under his breath as he led her from the treasury, locking the door behind them.

Leading her to the scullery where the household staff was busy at the day's tasks, Garrett gave quick orders in Ellen's behalf; and as two maidservants hurried to heat water and pull out a round wooden tub in which laundry was washed weekly and the persons of the family less frequently, he brandished an admonishing finger in her face.

"Do not thou make trouble for me," he said and turned to leave.

"Lord Garrett," she said, stopping him. "Thank you." He nodded and turned to leave again. "And Lord Garrett . . ."

"What!" he snapped.

"Please, may I have the bar of soap from my pack?"

With a grunt and a roll of his eyes, he stomped out the door; and she was unsure of his answer until, as she sank under the lukewarm water in the tub (reconciled to the fact that she would have no privacy from the castle's working staff), a housemaid entered carrying the soap in one hand and a set of clothes over her arm.

"Thank you," exclaimed Ellen happily, taking the soap as the girl draped the dress and apron over a chair back. "What is your name?" she asked, studying the young woman's youthful beauty, quiet demeanor, and genteel dress. This was not a scullery maid, but nor was she a lady of the house.

"I am Alice," said the young woman, folding her hands uncertainly. Alice Sheffield. My lord Garrett asked me to help with you."

So this was Alice, thought Ellen with new appreciation as she gingerly scrubbed at the dried blood in her hair. The Alice! And as pretty and sweet as Garrett had once described her. Ellen squelched a tremor of jealousy peremptorily. She was not here to make trouble, she scolded herself and squared her resolve to maintain the perspective of uninterested observer.

She smiled at Alice. "I hear you have a son," she said, determined to make Alice her friend.

And by the time Alice was helping her into the dress of finely woven rose-tinted linen cloth and belting the apron of chocolate brown linsey-woolsey over it, the two were chatting easily. Alice combed out Ellen's long hair, braided it artfully, and thought to herself as she worked how pleasant it was to have such an odd and refreshing person brought into her secluded existence. She decided that she would introduce Ellen to her ladyship that afternoon after she had shown Ellen to her room as Garrett had requested.

Ellen's room was actually an alcove off a larger bed chamber which Alice and Emaline and Edward shared. Its narrow space was just sufficient for a cot, straight wooden chair, and small table; but Ellen smiled gratefully at her accommodation. It beat the 'comforts' of the dark smelly dungeon hands down and even had a tall narrow window opposite the door where the apple-blossom breeze drifted over a wide sun-drenched stone sill.

Dropping her freshly washed clothing in a damp pile upon the chair, Ellen walked to the window and leaned out past its shutters to see the view it commanded of the side yards below where the stable gates opened to paths over the greensward and away to the river beyond. She took a deep breath and smiled. A two-week vacation in Camelot, she told herself, all expenses paid, was going to be lovely while it lasted.

At Alice's suggestion, they hung her wet cloths to dry upon pegs in the wall; and then, intrigued by Alice's enigmatic beckoning, Ellen followed her down the corridor to the heavy doors of a well-appointed but darkly shuttered chamber.

Ellen squinted as they entered, trying to adjust her eyes to the poor light as Alice led her forward by the hand.

"Lady Eleanor," she heard Alice say, "this is Lady Ellen Lancaster: Lord Garrett has made her our guest!"

Lady Eleanor! Ellen's mind raced ahead of her. She was being introduced to Lady Eleanor Coltstone, matriarch of the family! She curtsied low, bowing her head to hide her momentarily discomfit as she wondered what exactly she was supposed to do and say, but when she saw the look of surprise and appraisal upon Lady Eleanor's face, she decided she would just be herself and hope that would suffice. Garrett had once said that his mother would like her wit and resourcefulness, and therefore, witty and resourceful she determined to be.

"Ellen . . . of the house of Lancaster," said Lady Eleanor with some amazement. "How are we so honored?"

"Oh, just dropped in you might say. Found myself in your woods, thought I'd say hello."

Eleanor's eyes widened at the strange speech and demeanor of her guest, but motioned for her to sit in a plush chair at her side and for Alice to take the chair beside her. "Sit, Lady Ellen," she said. "Tell us what news of your family."

What news of my family? Ellen thought to herself with a moment's trepidation and almost laughed out loud to think of news from the ranch in West Texas. "My family prospers well as usual," she said brightly. "Not much news there . . . But we are greatly entertained by stories of late about . . ." And she forged ahead with all the colorful anecdotes she could muster from the volumes of history she had committed to memory. Years of lecturing at the university stood her in good stead. If her students had always found her tangents and impromptu enactments entertaining, Lady Eleanor and her maids were enthralled.

Lord Garrett was much disturbed to find her there hours later, ensconced on a chair beside his mother, telling artful tales and stories which both thrilled and enchanted the ladies present.

"What is this?" he asked quietly of Alice when his mother had raised her hand for him to keep quiet until Ellen had finished her latest story.

"Oh, she's wonderful!" exclaimed Alice. "She tells the best stories of the oddest things . . ."

"No doubt," muttered Garrett as Edward climbed up onto his lap.

"And she sings. She knows some very pretty new melodies. I believe she is greatly educated."

"Mmm," grumbled Garrett.

His thoughts were interrupted by Lady Eleanor's preemptory command. "Son, Lady Ellen claims you have a satchel that she carried here with her."

Garrett looked at Ellen sharply, but she only smiled demurely at Edward upon his knee.

"Would you please bring it to her," continued his mother. "I should like to see some things she has told us of."

Garrett did not think it wise to give the satchel back into Ellen's hands and thought to make excuse, but his mother's impatient gesture dismissed his words and sent him forth to do her bidding. He returned soon to place the leather bag and its odd contents at Ellen's feet, casting a warning look for her benefit alone as he did so.

From the corner of the room, he watched as Ellen showed Lady Eleanor the odd coins and paper money, the match box, and a small jar of sweet spice that she called cinnamon and which gave as a lavish gift to Lady Eleanor.

"This, Lady Eleanor," Ellen said, showing her the bottle of aspirin and putting two white tablets into the Lady's hand. "This is medicine. It will help your head feel better . . ."

Garrett almost spoke out in apprehension as his mother swallowed the white pills, but then held his piece. Ellen had, after all, taken two herself the day before and suffered no ill effect.

"I think," said Ellen to Lady Eleanor, "that you have allergies, an illness caused by the mold and mildew in this damp room." She sniffed, rubbing her own nose. The rush matting smelled stale and old; the air was musty and stagnant. "It gives you headaches and itchy eyes?"

"Oh constantly!" exclaimed Lady Eleanor, readily agreeable to commiseration and sympathy and as eager for a solution.

"Well, then," said Ellen. "Tomorrow, if you like, we will clean house. And I think you will feel much better."

So much for keeping out of trouble, she thought to herself as Garrett glowered darkly and left the room. But at least she could help the old lady feel better, and that certainly would not injure her own chances of survival in this place.

"My, but thou dost look like a storm cloud, brother," laughed Lord David when he rode in that evening and met Garrett in the Close. The men dismounted, and the horses were led away. "What troubles you?" he asked.

"You'll know soon enough," muttered Garrett, and then brightened. "How are things to the north? Be there a good crop of lambs?"

"Aye, brother, and the barley growing well. We shall prosper well this season I think, though, there is rumor among the crofters of a band of brigands in the hills, thieving along our borders."

"We can easily see to that," said Garrett, looking almost eager, and his brother nodded agreement. They walked through the darkening halls toward the sound of people and the smell of food.

"And how is aught here?" asked David. "Mother?"

"Improved."

"The household?"

"As usual."

"And the matter of your ring thief?"

"See for yourself," said Garrett with a cutting glance as they entered the dining hall, "though I shall tell you all later."

And there, much to David's surprise and Garrett's disgruntlement, sat Lady Ellen Lancaster at the right hand of Lady Eleanor, a very pale and subdued Leticia across the boards.

"What ho?" laughed David as he advanced, and Ellen rose to curtsy as she thought appropriate. "My brother has indeed retrieved a fair gem from the kirk wood!" he ribbed, but bowed discreetly at his brother's warning glance. "I look forward to hearing of your plight," he said with a wink.

"You are as charming as I always thought you'd be," replied Ellen, carefully withdrawing her hand from his as she watched Garrett's face amusedly. Truly, this family was a fun deck of cards.

As they all sat down to eat, Ellen wondered what Garrett had told his brother of her, and how much more he would tell, and whether he would warn David of the coming attack. His guarded expression told her nothing.

FAIRY TOWERS ON A HILL

The week that followed passed quickly for Ellen as she spent her mornings exploring the Coltstone Keep and learning all she could of its odd and intriguing daily duties and routines. Her afternoons were spent entertaining Lady Eleanor as Alice and Emaline helped her cleanse the Lady's chambers of mildew and mold. Lady Eleanor's health and temper improved remarkably, and she was now more often out about the castle gardens and grounds, managing her household with much of her once-exuberant interest.

The change was noted and remarked upon by both of her sons, and Ellen grew in the favor of all the household, until there was not a scullery maid or a horse boy who had not made her acquaintance and been amused by her multitude of questions. Only Leticia avoided her like the plague, framing her in as ill a light as she could to the few who would hear her; and only Lord Garrett met her with guarded favor, always wary of her and still waiting for events to prove her genuine.

"My brother is some troubled by you," Lord David said to Ellen one fine sunny morning when he met her in the garden. He had seen her walking with Alice and little Edward and chose to meet with her as she sat alone under an arbor near the stable path after the others had returned to the Keep.

Looking up at him, Ellen wondered once more how much Garrett had told him.

"Lord Garrett thinks I am not yet to be trusted," she said finally.

"And are you?" David asked

"I think so."

"With whom and how much?" he asked in jest.

"I have always trusted myself with much," she replied. "Of others, I do not know."

David smiled, "You have a quick wit," he observed.

Ellen did not answer.

"Garrett tells me that you have no family here, that you have requested sanctuary with us . . ."

Ellen nodded.

"I find this odd, knowing your family name well. I would know more of your plight, of what you fear, or what thou hast fled, if you would so tell."

Seeing the sincerity of his interest, Ellen considered the man before her and knew that he was not the irresponsible older brother she had once read of in history books and that his words were neither flirtatious nor lightly spoken. He wished to know her situation lest it affect the safety of his household, and he would offer her protection if she claimed need of such. She favored him with a friendly smile as she arose. Garrett had obviously not told him much about her.

"I thank you, Lord David," she said earnestly, "for your kindness and your hospitality. I am in some trouble, but it is much of my own making, and I hope that I will not long burden your household before I am able to return to my home or some other place."

"For my part," he rejoined, "you are welcome here as long as you choose to stay. You have brought health and happiness back to my mother, and for that, we are all grateful. Do not mind the doubt of my brother—he is always one to think overmuch."

"It is a virtue of his," observed Ellen.

"Yes—and oft serves him to good end," said David. "And I actually think he likes you well."

Ellen only shrugged and quickly changed the subject.

"Lord David, I confess I weary of sitting around all day. Might I borrow a horse from your stables? I should like to see somewhat of the countryside here about."

"Certainly," he said, amused at the thought of a lady making such a request. "The hostler, James, will set you upon a suitable mount if you so desire. Tell him I give you my leave, but do not ride far without escort until you are familiar with these lands. They are not as safe as your lowland home."

Ellen was not certain of exactly where her "lowland home" was supposed to be, but thanked Lord David all the same for his concern, assuring him that she would watch her paths carefully.

Watching from a high window of the library, Garrett saw them clasp hands in parting, as Ellen strode away toward the stables and David stood watching her go.

Later David teased him saying, "Brother, I find your Lady Ellen quite a winning creature," and enjoyed his brother's discomfit, punching him roughly on the shoulder as Garrett gave him a morose glare.

"You too trusting," grumbled Garrett.

"You are too suspicious, brother," he ribbed.

And Ellen, unaware of it all as she walked to the stables, intent on making good David's offer of a horse, thought only that surely there was some unclaimed animal in the Coltstone stables that she could borrow for a week or two. But the pony the responsible James pointed her to was not to her liking. "Old and ugly," she muttered, looking at his scruffy coat. "Nice for Edward—not for me." And she strode away with James following as she looked at the stalls of stabled horses.

"What about this one?" she asked of a bright-eyed roan mare that nodded her head over the stall partition when Ellen approached.

"Oh, my Lady," said James depreciatively, "That one is not often ridden—a bit mettlesome for a lady, I think."

"Ah," replied Ellen, "then probably about right for me." And she had the groom bring her a halter and bridle as she looked the mare over and smoothed her coat with her hand. The mare was well built and sound, stocky and well-rounded; four white stockings and a broad-blaze face marked her blue roan coat handsomely.

"What about a saddle?" she asked the hesitant James when she led the mare from the stall. What he brought her was an oddly shaped and cumbersome lady's sidesaddle, which she eyed with misgiving, and decided for the time that she would ride bareback.

Working the mare on a long line, and studying her temper and gait Ellen decided that this horse would be fun to work with and easy to train, and James was not the only one watching when at last Ellen loped the mare around the paddock several turns and took the track to the river woods. She spent all of the day riding through the countryside near the Keep, marveling at the changed but still familiar landscape, and returning in the late glow of afternoon, windblown and sunburned and radiant with the joy of freedom. She met Garrett in the Close as he was riding out.

"That was wonderful!" she exclaimed at his greeting. "The countryside looks just like a picture in a story book, and the village is a perfect study in medieval social structure." He looked at her frazzled hair, rumpled dress, and exuberant stance and thought she could not have looked less ladylike.

"You smell like a horse," he said gruffly, but could not resist smiling to himself when she only curtsied gracefully and replied, "Thank you."

That Sunday, when she rode beside Lady Alice on the road to the kirk for mass, Ellen rode the sidesaddle as was proper, and decided it was not as precarious a rig as she'd feared, and that she would perfect her use of it in the week to come. And in the sanctuary of the Kirk she found herself seated between Lady Eleanor and Lord Garrett in a *very* familiar wooden pew with Lady Alice and Edward seated at Garrett's right hand. The service was enchantingly simple with its archaic liturgies and stilted hymns, and Ellen was intrigued by the patient observances of the old priest who moved through the ceremonies with rhythmic ritual as mystic as his Latin texts. It appeared as though he had performed those same actions and said these same words by rote for all his many years.

When at last all the assembly had filed out of the stone-paved aisle (that was not yet so smoothly worn), Ellen stood alone near an empty alcove, contemplating its shadowy space.

"What do you see?" asked Garrett at her elbow, startling her.

"I am looking at the place where they will bury you," she replied quietly.

"I am not dead yet," he whispered.

"No, and I hope you will never die *that way*," she murmured.

"It grieved you, then?" he asked, taking her elbow to lead her away.

"Yes," she said simply, "it did," and she stepped away from him and out the door.

Looking back at the dim alcove, Garrett shrugged. Either she was crazy or . . . He shivered. He would know soon, he told himself. He would know.

In the Kirkyard, as Garrett lifted Alice onto her grey palfrey, and David assisted his mother and Leticia, Ellen mounted the grey roan unaided and Garrett watching her, decided that whatever else she was, she was simply much too independent and aggravatingly self-sufficient for a female.

As the spring bloom of June drew to a close Ellen was confronted late one evening by an angry Leticia as they chanced to pass in the corridor from the Great Hall.

"You!" hissed Leticia, when Ellen would have passed her by with a polite nod. "I know not what game it is you play." Ellen stood firm as

Leticia leaned menacingly close "but I will expose you for the imposter you are—a scullery wench in fine clothes."

"Whatever I am," replied Ellen evenly, "I am not your game, nor will I fear you."

Leticia sneered. "You will fear me yet, and you will serve me soon."

"Not on your life," muttered Ellen to herself as she watched Leticia stalk away with a swirl of silk skirting. "How did David ever get tangled up with you?" She was still fuming when she entered the study where Lord Garrett and Lord David usually worked with their scribes when accounts were to be reconciled; and she meant to pass through to the tower stair, but paused in surprise at finding Garrett there. All the family had left the dining hall after dinner, except for Ellen, who had lingered to observe the serving staff and men of the garrison who dined after the family. She had assumed that Garrett had retired to his quarters or to a pint of ale with David in the library.

"Good evening," she greeted when he looked up from a parchment piece spread over the table under the candle stand, and he nodded a quick greeting as if he did not wish to be distracted and half shielded the paper with his arm, laying his quill beside the blotter.

Curious, Ellen glanced at the table as she passed, and then paused. "Your plans," she murmured, "I did not know you had already started them."

Exasperated, Garrett leaned back in his chair and regarded her for a moment. "What do you know of them?" he asked finally.

"I know that you dreamed of great things that you wished to build. I have seen the ruins of a great manor house you once began but never finished, up on the tall hill to the north." She looked at the rough-draft beginning of a plan plotted on the parchment. "I've ridden there often."

"You ride too far by yourself," admonished Garrett.

"Perhaps so," she said, unconvinced, then chanced a bold thought. "Why not ride with me?"

He made no reply.

"I could show you where you will one day build . . . perhaps," she said.

Garrett considered her proposal a moment and then leaned forward, "All right," he said. "I have other matters to see to, but they can wait until another day."

"Good," replied Ellen. "After breakfast? From the stable?"

He nodded as he picked up his quill. He assumed she would now leave him to his work, but she lingered a moment longer, studying his draft.

"I have always wondered what you intended with the roofline here," she pointed. "You said you wished you had made the bank of windows rounded and larger." Seeing his look of mild annoyance, she backed away, smiled an apology as she curtsied, and turned to leave.

"Good night, Lord Garrett," she said

"You are going to retire, then?" he asked, wondering why he prolonged the interview.

"Oh, I thought I'd sit and chew the fat with the womenfolk for a while," she replied with a wry smile, "if Leticia is happily not present."

"Does she trouble you?" he asked

"She dislikes me intently," Ellen replied.

Garrett gazed absently at the flicker of the candles. "Her dislikes are always more intense than her likes," he observed.

"Yes, but you do not seem to credit her with as great an evil as I do."

"Perhaps not," he agreed, "or perhaps I credit myself with the ability to contain it."

"I hope so," Ellen replied, not without misgiving. "I do hope so."

The next morning, when they rode out from the stable paddocks, the dew was yet thick and fragrant on the meadow grass and the sheep were still in their fold. The roan mare was full of mettle and heavy on the bit, forcing Ellen to work her in tight circles to keep her alongside of Garrett's rangy bay, and as Garrett watched her manage the roan's unruly energy, he thought to himself that Ellen and the horse made a suitable match—both were troublesome.

They entered the wood along the riverbank not far from the castle, and Ellen was reminded of a day not so long past but world's away from here when the sun had shone just as fairly and the birds had sung just so sweetly and she and Garrett had ridden much the same track under the high canopy of the forest green. The Garrett she had known then had been older and his arrogant confidence had been tempered by the wisdom of experience. Now she wondered how much her memory of that person colored her trust in his younger self, and she found the irony of it all amused her.

When they reached the pool below the shoals, Ellen reined in and allowed the mare to drop her head and graze. Garrett halted alongside and looked at her questioningly.

"This is the place—Brigham," she explained, confounding him all the more. "Brigham . . . ," she repeated. "Brigham Young . . . Mormon . . . Salt Lake City . . . It's an old saying . . . Oh, never mind!" She found it exasperating how time changes continually stole the punch line. "This is the place where once your brother drowned," she explained matter-of-factly.

Garrett frowned at her and then looked at the shoal crossing with the pool below. He knew it well; they used it often. He could find no threat in its placid setting.

"Have you told him?" asked Ellen.

"Told him . . . ?" Garrett shook his head. "What have I to tell him—certainly?"

"That his life is in danger," replied Ellen impatiently.

"When I have only your word in that?"

"And you do not trust me—yet?"

"I find you very strange. I confess I know not what to think of you," Garrett replied.

"Well, you're as honest as you ever were," Ellen said with resignation. "Still, if my life were threatened, I should think I would like to know of it."

"And what if your prediction proves false?" Garrett responded.

"You," she said, appalled, "are more worried about being made to look foolish than of losing your own brother?!"

"No, but I believe I am quite able to prevent this thing you prophesy of, should I need to."

"You credit yourself with great providence and leave your brother vulnerable." She gave him a scathing look and crossed her arms with an impatient gesture.

Garrett only smiled patiently at her reprove. "If it makes you feel better," he said, "I have told him that I have some reason to question the loyalty of several of our men-at-arms."

"Did you now! And what did he say?" asked Ellen, glad at least of this concession.

"He laughed," replied Garrett. "He has never seen reason to question our garrison's integrity . . . nor have I."

And that, thought Ellen, gazing into the placid depths of the clear pool, is exactly why this calamity might still happen.

At the far sweeping bend of the Gulforth where its placid tide curved first west and then sharply to the north, they quit the banks and rode up the sloping ridge that joined to the tall north hills. Upon that first highest crest, they halted, and Garrett lifted Ellen down from the sidesaddle into the shade of the tall spreading oaks. Tethering the mare to a sapling to graze, Ellen untied the satchel from the saddle rings and brought out a lumpy bundle wrapped in a napkin, from which she handed Garrett a small loaf of barley bread, a lump of cheese, and a very shriveled dried apple. He nodded his thanks as they sat upon the grass to eat.

The sun was high and warm and the hillside fragrant with heather and gorse bush. A pleasant breeze bent the nodding heads of grain around them as they ate in silence. While Garrett retrieved a water flask from the bay's saddle, Ellen stood to survey the wooded hilltop around her, searching for a landmark: a tree, stone, a slope of the land, anything that might remain over the five centuries that would pass.

"There," she said as she took the flask Garrett offered her and drank the tepid water. "Right over there." She pointed to a large angular boulder that jutted from the mossy bank some distance up the ridge. "Just up from that boulder about a hundred yards is where you will begin construction. The front of the structure faces south." And she then described to him each angle, each artful curve of the architecture, the rooms and halls, tall arched windows, towers and turrets. His eyes followed the sweep of her hand as she painted a vision of the structure he knew only he had dreamed of and of which he had spoken to no other.

And seeing all that she described and knowing it of his own design, Garrett felt first amazement and then a terrible unease. He watching her as she spoke with the voice of a seer, and he wondered by what enchantment she could know the very thoughts within him: to know of a dagger or a ring was cunning and crafty, but to know the paths of the mind was near to owning the very soul. He shuddered, and Ellen, suddenly aware of his distress, stopped in midsentence.

"I'm sorry," she said hesitantly, unsure of what she had said to disturb him so. "What is it?"

He gazed out over the wooded ridge at the fairy vision she had painted there for him.

"How can you know these things," he asked gruffly, "when I have spoken of them to no one?"

"Because, I have seen them," she said with a sigh. "You obviously still don't believe me, but I have been here with you before, and you told me all the plans you once dreamed of—all that you desired to do but never could."

"I esteemed you highly, then, to have shared so much," he said, thinking that even now, he had none with which he would share these dreams.

"Yes, I suppose you did," she said wistfully. "In that months' time, we shared many things and I . . . well, we were good friends." She thought to say more but checked herself, seeing in her mind's eye Lord Garrett at her kitchen table, at the pub in Kingston, at a railway station in London. Those were *her* memories now; there was nothing of them that she could share with *this* Lord Garrett. With a self-conscious shrug, she smiled half apologetically and turned away.

The things that she'd obviously left unsaid gave him all the more to think about as they rode together back to the Keep. What he found most peculiar about Ellen was that she knew so many things about his life and yet made no claim over him; and, although he had set his mind not to, he was beginning to think more kindly toward Lady Ellen Lancaster. When they left the horses with the stable grooms and walked the path to the wall of the Keep, Garrett offered her his arm and she placed her hand lightly upon his sleeve.

"The house that I would build," he said as they walked thus along the path, "why do you call it the ruins? Why is it never finished?"

"Because," she said, facing him at the gate, "when David dies, all the things you wish to do are left undone. The estate and Leticia keep you occupied. You will work three years to build and die before it is half finished."

"Your prophesies are grim," he observed.

"And that is why they must not happen," she replied earnestly, pressing his hand in hers ere she left him there.

It was Alice, walking beside the garden hedge with young Edward, that watched their parting with the greatest tremble of heart. She had learned to like Ellen well, had admired her strength and self-confidence, had envied the wit and charm that won the friendship of all the household; but now she knew a dull fear that this same person might take from her the hope, the joy, the one happiness she had longed for. Over four long years, she had waited, never doubling her beloved's faithfulness. Now in this one instant, she knew fear, and she knew the bitter taste of doubt.

Edward, tugging at her hand to show her a pretty flower he had pulled, could not guess why her thoughts were so far from him.

AT THE SHOALS OF THE GULFORTH

The waning days of June rolled into July without event as the weather settled in dull and grey, and barred all inside that would not brave the windy damp. Ellen spent her mornings in the kitchen and scullery and stables (much to the amusement of their staffs) and wiled away the afternoons and evenings with the ladies in the drawing room of Lady Eleanor, writing notes she suspected she might never use and drawing sketches of the rooms, and people and activities around her.

And as the week dragged slowly on without event, Ellen began to feel edgy and cross and avoided Garrett whenever she could for all his looks of amused query at her expense. She considered that she might have remembered the dates wrong, or perhaps the books had recorded it wrong, and though she felt plagued by her doubts she had no remedy for them.

The dull weather finally broke and on the morning of the fifth of July Ellen awoke to patches of sunlight warming the stone floor of her room as the clouds ran racing in heavy, ragged rovings across patches of blue sky. Garrett and David were not in the dining hall, and she found Alice and Emaline at breakfast with Edward in Lady Eleanor's chamber. At her query, Lady Eleanor laughed. "Oh, I suppose those boys are out in the fields by now or training with the men in the yard. They've been caged in so long." And Ellen's heart leaped suddenly with renewed foreboding.

"Perhaps this was the day," she thought, and the ladies wondered at her worried expression and distracted excuses as she quickly left the room. Not thinking how her presence there might change events, Ellen quickly ran from the Keep and down the stable path to the tall stone wall above the field where she perched to watch the game on the practice yard below.

Garrett saw her sitting there and knew why she had come to watch. His thoughts were distracted momentarily from the melee of the horsemen and the blow that was meant to injure him was dealt without effect as he pulled his horse's head around at just that moment, and in glancing up toward the place where Ellen sat, saw the blow coming and ducked under the blade. Momentum of the charge and change of course overbalanced the poor horse for one fateful moment; and the bay slid on the muddy turf, careened into another's mount, and fell heavily upon his side, penning Garrett's leg beneath the metal cinch buckles. Horses and riders leaped over and clear as the bay struggled on the rain sodden ground and Garrett worked to free himself from the frantic beast. His boot was caught in the stirrup when the bay at last scrambled to his feet and bolted a short distance, dragging Garrett over the muddy sod until training overcame panic, and the horse halted and stood stamping nervously while Garret pulled himself up by the stirrup leather and wrenched his boot free.

Ellen jumped down from the wall as a group of men gathered around him, lifting him carefully when his leg would not bear his weight and supporting him as he limped painfully from the field to sit upon a wooden bench against the stable wall.

"I am well enough," he was saying as she approached, and he waved their attentions away impatiently. "Leave me be. I shall be fine."

David, seeing his brother more annoyed at their attention than in distress of pain, called the men back into the field after a tactless jest about "leaving him in good company" and a wink for Ellen, who stood nearby. All remounted and rode back into the field while Ellen stood uncertainly and studied Garrett's face. His teeth were clenched and his lips were white with pain.

"How can I help you?" she asked.

"Ach, I think you cannot," he said, grimacing as he pulled the breeches leg out of his boot to reveal an angry blue swelling just below the knee. Though his leg was not broken it was badly sprained and painful and would take some time to heal.

"I should have brought several bottles of aspirin with me," mumbled Ellen as she knelt beside him upon the grass examining the injury. "James," she called to the groom who was leading Garrett's bay past them into the stable. "Bring me the liniment jar, will you, and some wraps?"

"Yes, my Lady," he answered, hurrying away.

Garrett brushed her hand away from his leg and complained that he "was no horse and need not be treated so."

"No," she agreed, "You are less patient than a horse perhaps, though I do hope you will heal as well, and James will know best how to wrap this to keep the swelling down." She stood and wiped her hands on her skirt.

Garrett smiled grimly, leaned his head back against the stable wall, and looked at her from half-closed eyes. "It is not the wound you expected," he said.

"No," she looked at him with a troubled expression. "Though it may yet suffice."

Garrett did not reply as the groom's hurried footsteps approached. He bore a crock of liniment in one hand and horse's leg wraps in the other, and Garrett leaned forward at his bow and questioning look.

"Wrap it up, man," ordered Garrett. "Do as you know best." His voice was gruff, but his confidence in the man was a great compliment.

"Yes, my lord," replied James, kneeling to his work as Garrett gritted his teeth, Ellen's hand steady upon his shoulder.

"What is that stuff?" Ellen asked as the groom smeared the pungent lineament.

"Comfrey and rosemary in lanolin," answered the groom, wrapping the cloth firmly to suppress the swelling and pulling Garrett's breeches leg back over the bandage when he was done. He bowed to Garrett's word of thanks and returned to his work in the stables as Garrett watched the horsemen in the field with studied contemplation. His brother was a skilled horseman, a better swordsman; he parried blows with the ease of practice and training.

"The sword will not wait while you consider . . . ," muttered Ellen, following his gaze.

"What was that?" he asked, glancing at her.

"Something you once told me," she said, "when you tried to teach me this."

They remained watching the mock battle in the field before Ellen silently turned to leave.

"Ellen," said Garrett suddenly, and she paused, glancing back to him. "I will be watchful."

She nodded—"I also"—and walked away up the stable path to the Keep.

There was quite a stir in the household later that morning when Garrett limped in through the Close, leaning heavily on David's shoulder as the two of them laughed and staggered as if drunk.

"Papa!" cried Edward, running forward. "You are hurt?" And Ellen saw Alice's look of concern and Leticia's sardonic smile as she watched them from the fringe of the small group.

"Not badly and not for long," replied Garrett reassuringly, tousling the boy's hair and smiling at their fearful fretting. "Though I may get worse for all the attention it gets me . . ."

By afternoon, the weather had settled in, dull and grey once more; and there was no word of a hunt party as Garrett kept David occupied over ledgers and accounts, the two of them closeted with a scribe in the study downstairs all that day and into the evening. When Ellen retired to her room that evening, it was with a feeling of great relief that nothing she had feared had come to pass that day.

It was young Edward who woke his uncle at sunrise the next morning by pouncing on his bed and begging to be made some breakfast while his mother slept and all the house was quiet. David, who always enjoyed the company of his nephew, obligingly arose, dressed, and pulled on his boots while the lad chatted of his plans for the day and pretended the end of the tester bed was his noble steed to ride. In the kitchen hall David met with his squire, who sat at the table with Remmel and two other members of the watch.

"It is a fine morning, my lord," observed the squire.

"Aye," agreed Remmel, glancing at the two others, "a good day for a hunt."

David's eyes brightened enthusiastically. He'd been too much inside these last days and to be so sedentary irked him. "A fine idea," he agreed, and plans were quickly made and set in motion to quit the Keep that very hour before the household was well awake and matters of the day could prevent them.

"May I go with thee, Uncle?" asked Edward, pouting his disappointment privately when he was firmly told "no." He stood in the dooryard to watch his uncle and the four men as they rode across the field at an easy jog trot with their bows and arrow quivers slung across their backs, bridle bells ringing and the hounds running out before them.

When Ellen entered the hall later that morning, she found Alice and Emaline at breakfast while Edward played among the chair legs under the table and Leticia occupied a place apart at the far end of the table. Lady Eleanor was taking breakfast in her chamber, and Emaline e offered Ellen the chair nearest her and a place in the morning's conversation.

Garrett, walking in shortly thereafter, limped stiff legged to the chair opposite and motioned a kitchen maid to fill his empty cup.

"Where is Lord David?" asked Ellen with a small feeling of apprehension as she noted his absence.

Garrett looked around the room and shrugged. "Perhaps still abed," he mumbled, though he knew his brother was not a late sleeper.

"He's gone," piped up Edward, peaking over the table's edge near Leticia's elbow. Leticia looked down at the boy with a smug expression that Ellen disliked immensely.

"Gone where?" asked Ellen quietly.

"Hunting!" cried Edward, jumping up and down. "He and Harold and Remmel and Hotchkiss and the other guys."

His words brought Ellen suddenly bolt upright in her seat, and her eyes met Garrett's sharply. "When, Edward?" she asked breathlessly "How long ago?"

"Oh, early, Ms. Ellen. He wouldn't take me with him . . . ," the boy prattled on, but Ellen wasn't listening. Instinctively, she glanced at her wrist; but her watch—of course—was not there and she wondered why knowing the time would matter: the sun was already well up. "Garrett!" she cried with a feeling of panic as she stood abruptly, knocking her chair backward in her haste. And as all the company watched in amazement Ellen bounded from the hall, her boot heels ringing on the flagstones of the corridor as Garrett rose quickly to follow.

Out of the Close she flew and away down the stable path. Outdistancing Garrett as he struggled along behind, she reached the stable well ahead of him, charged headlong through its doors, and ran pell-mell into James as he carried the rations of morning feed.

"Aye there, miss!" he cried steadying her. "What . . . ?"

"Get Lord Garrett's horse!" she yelled, pushing past him and leaving him to stand in bewilderment as she ran to the roan's stall and flung its gate wide. "Now!" she screamed at him, grabbing a halter and flinging it over the mare's head.

Moved by the urgency of her voice, James dropped the buckets on the floor and grabbed the bay's bridle as Ellen leaped astride the roan who reared and leaped forward at Ellen's booted heals in her flanks. They reached full stride ere they'd left the stable run.

Garrett had just reached the paddock gate as the roan mare sailed over it, eyes white ringed and Ellen clinging like a burr to her neck with her fingers laced tightly in the long thick mane.

"My horse!" he yelled to the groom as he flung wide the gate, and James was ready to hand him the bay's reins as the sound of the roan's hoof beats retreated toward the river across the field.

The groom ran back toward the stable. "Your saddle, sir," he called.

"No time, man!" Garrett shouted after him, and leaped up astride the bay, spurring him away through the gate as the groom stood aghast, watching the two race away.

The roan had reached the river woods as Garrett galloped the bay headlong across the field, but he knew the path Ellen would take, and he knew a shorter way to the pool below the shoals. Through the greenwood trees they flew, the bay's long strides eating up the ground until in an open glade ahead, he saw that they were gaining on the roan. Near the tree line just beyond Ellen, Garret saw David's squire and a soldier of the guard who were bending over the lamed hoof of the squire's horse straighten and shout out to Ellen as she swept by them never slacking pace. As they gazed after her in startled amazement, the thundering hooves of Garrett's bay bore down on them and he yelled for them to follow as he too galloped wildly past. The two made haste to mount double on the soldier's horse and pursue the bay at what pace they could.

Pushing her mare relentlessly through the trackless wood, leaping over downed trees and through whipping brush, Ellen at last saw the clearing ahead where the great trees thinned along the road to the ford. Two men sat their horses beside the water's edge, and Ellen's heart faltered as she inwardly cursed their damning inactivity. They sat their horses and gazed attentively out over the water of the pool below, but at the sound of the galloping hooves approaching, they drew up in sudden activity: one dismounting, the other riding toward her as if to bar her way.

"No! You won't!" she shrieked at Remmel, striking him full in the face with the knotted end of the mare's lead rope as he grabbed at the roan's halter. She ducked under his arm as he tried to grab her, and then spurred the mare to the river's brink, plunging her down the embankment and into the stream.

She looked for David frantically as the mare lunged deep into the water, reared and balked; a fearful dismay gripped her heart. David's horse stood riderless with reins trailing in the water near the far bank, and the feathered shaft of an arrow rode like a beacon floating above the rippling water near the center of the deep pool. The mare could be forced to go no further, and in exasperation Ellen leaped from her back into the cold water, unaware of the soldiers behind her who spurred their horses across the ford in pursuit of a man they had sighted scrambling to her aid from the thick undergrowth of the of the opposite bank.

Beneath the shaft of the arrow, facedown, with the long strands of water weed twining around his boots, David floated motionless beneath the water as Ellen struggled toward him, her cumbersome skirt and riding boots pulling her down as she tried to swim. Reaching him at last, she dove down to grasp him under the arms and planted her boots in the gravel of the riverbed to push upward toward the surface with all her strength. When they broke the surface, Ellen gasped for breath and knew that her struggle was desperate. "Garrett!" she screamed with what breath she had, and choked as the water closed over her again. She could not swim, hampered as she was by her heavy skirts, and pull the body of the drowned man, inert and weighted with gear. Indeed, she began to fear that she would not save even herself as the water closed over her head a second time. *Third time is all*, she was thinking as she felt her strength begin to wane.

And then she knew Garrett was beside her; his strong arm caught her around the shoulders, lifting her as they swam and together pulled David to the river's edge. Garrett dragged David's body from the water and out upon the grassy bank and knelt beside his brother's pale, still form with dull anguish of heart. David was not breathing: his brother was not alive, and Garrett knew that he had failed. Ellen had warned him: he had known the prophecy, and still he had let it had come to pass. He bowed his head in grief.

Ellen struggled up from the water, coughing, and tripping over her sodden skirts and knew from Garrett's broken demeanor that the situation was dire, but her heart refused to accept the defeat or give over all hope. Not yet. Not without trying . . . something.

She reached David's side and quickly assessed the situation as she knelt there: he was not breathing: there was no pulse. "So what do I do for a drowned man?" she asked herself and wished she felt more certain of the answer. All she knew was that she needed to act fast if she were to make any difference, and she rolled him over on the grass to press the water out of his lungs before she placed her palms over his chest and pressed down hard three times as she counted. "Garrett," she said breathlessly. "Watch! I will need you to do this." But he looked at her blankly, grief and despair in his face as he knelt head bowed across from her beside the prone form. "Ellen," he said hoarsely, "he is dead."

"Yes, mostly," she said as she worked, "But we may yet save him." And to the astonishment of all, she placed her hand upon David's brow, closed his nose with her fingers, and tilted his head back as she took a deep breath and pressed her mouth to his.

"She kisses the dead!" gasped the squire, appalled, as Ellen forced her breath into David's lungs, once, twice, three times. Struggling to remember a CPR class from long years past, Ellen prayed, and wondered if she were doing the right things, and dared not pause to entertain the doubt. "If ever I get back from here," she vowed to herself, "I will broaden my knowledge of a good many things."

As Ellen gave three more chest compressions, Garrett watched with a slow-growing understanding of what she attempted and at Ellen's silent pleading look, he folded his hands upon his brother's chest and pressed down hard as she had done—one, two, three times—while Ellen checked for pulse, for breath, and continued the sequence. Together they worked over the still form upon the grass, oblivious to the sounds of the two soldiers returning with the gypsy man bound and gagged between them, oblivious to the anxious questions of squire Harold. Eternity was held in the long minutes that passed until Ellen began to doubt their success and wondered how much longer they could hold to such a thin thread of hope. At the very moment when she sat back upon her heels, wiping the matted wet hair from her face and dared not meet Garrett's gaze lest he read her thoughts and lose all hope . . . David coughed and gagged and coughed again.

With a glad cry, Ellen quickly rolled him to his side and Garrett knelt over him, holding his brother's head, as David coughed and wretched out the water he had swallowed. Watching them and seeing Garrett's eyes so bright with tears of joy, Ellen knew then the love of these brothers so close and strong and the depth of the grief so narrowly avoided.

When at last David lay quietly, his breathing rough but deep and even, they carefully lay him again upon his back to inspect his wounds. The arrow shaft firm in the flesh of his shoulder had snapped off short when they had laid him upon the green, and a cruel blow to the head had left an angry gash over his ear and kept him in the painless world of unconsciousness. As they worked over him, their faces close together, Ellen glanced at the men standing beside the gypsy and whispered quickly for Garrett's ear alone.

"The gypsy . . . do not let them harm him! He is innocent and can tell you everything . . . He *must not* come to harm." Memories of old

Grimmel behind the counter in his store came to Ellen's mind as she spoke. So much hinged on this one moment and the decisions made in it; Garrett, seeing the earnest plea of her eyes, nodded as he rose stiffly to command the situation.

He ordered David's squire to cut poles and make a sled to carry David behind the bay, then motioned Remmel and Hotchkiss to lead the gypsy forward. He looked from Remmel to the gypsy man, whose eyes were staring wide with fear and took a deep breath.

"Tell me all you know," he said to Remmel.

"This man was at the ford before us," Remmel replied evenly. "Lord David outdistanced us, and the arrow found its mark ere we could warn him."

"This man would have slain my brother?" said Garrett, his voice tight with anger, but not for the reason Remmel supposed.

"Aye, my lord," he lied glibly, wrenching the man's arm as the gypsy shook his head violently in denial.

"How then came the arrow to strike him in the back?" muttered Garrett with a glance at the gypsy that served to allay some of his fears.

"My lord!" exclaimed Hotchkiss, but Garrett silenced his declamation with a raised hand.

"Bring him with us to the Keep. I will deal with the matter there," he said and turned to assist the squire and Ellen as they prepared to lift his brother to the improvised travois. He did not see the look that passed between the lieutenant and Hotchkiss, but he knew already that things were not going as they had planned.

The trip back to the Coltstone Keep was long and torturously slow. Garrett rode upon the bay, pulling the travois behind, while Ellen walked beside it to steady the sled poles over rough ground. Garrett had sent David's squire on ahead to fetch a physician from Briarwick, and the Keep was all astir with preparations. Anxious eyes were watching from the casements when at last the small cavalcade rode into view. From the Close, David was carefully lifted from the stretcher and borne away through the pensively quiet halls to the sanctuary of his own rooms. As he was borne away, Garrett ordered the prisoner to the dungeon cell under guard of the trusted soldier Derrick and directed Remmel and Hotchkiss to remain in the Keep for further questioning. Then following the beckoning Alice, whom his mother had sent to hurry him, he strode through the lower halls and up the tower steps to his brother's rooms.

All there was a flurry of activity as he took his place at his brother's bedside. His mother stood close, weeping and wringing her hands as Alice and Emaline worked quietly, bringing towels and bowls of water and bandages as the physician required; and Ellen knelt at the bedside, closely watching the physician's every move and (much to that good man's annoyance) washing every scalpel and knife and tool that he requested as he worked the barbed arrow free of tissue and bone.

At last the wounds were cleansed and bandaged; and still, David lay pale and deathlike as his wet garments were stripped away and the soft wool blankets were pulled to his chin and tucked carefully to ward off the chill of shock.

"His wounds are not mortal," the physician said at Garrett's anxious look, "but he must be carefully watched until he regains consciousness. Fever, infection . . . these things may yet claim him." His scarecrow features and owlish eyes added emphasis to his words. "Send for me should either arise."

Garrett nodded and extended his gratitude as the man gathered his knives and sutures, stowed them carefully in his case, and left quietly.

The silence that hung over the room was broken only by David's rough breathing, until Leticia stepped forward from the corner where she had sat quietly watching throughout.

"I will watch over him," she volunteered sweetly. "As his wife, it is my rightful duty. There is no need for others to trouble." She glared at Ellen, who seemed to have suddenly been seized by a fit of coughing.

"No," replied Garrett, fixing her with a measuring gaze. "An attempt has been made upon his life. There must be two to watch over him now—always." He turned to Lady Eleanor. "Mother, you will stay with Leticia this first vigil. Do *not* leave this room for any reason. I will post a guard at the door by which you may send for me if you have need."

Then quickly, he directed all to leave that his brother might rest: Alice and Emaline to bring Ellen dry clothing, Edward to fetch and carry between kitchen and sick room as needed, and himself to dry clothes and other matters more pressing and the questions to be asked and answered.

THE WHOLE TRUTH

Ellen did not see Garrett again that day. As Alice and Emaline led her away to fuss and fret over her, drying and combing and braiding and dressing, Ellen answered their many questions as best she could without revealing too many of the very odd things she knew and the implications of all involved. She would let Garrett explain all these things if he wished. When they were done, she found herself in a very pretty silk brocade gown of midnight blue, all trimmed in gold, and her braided hair intertwined with beads of pearl.

"This is too much!" she exclaimed, smoothing the thick pleated folds of the skirt. "I shall never keep it clean."

"It is one of Lady Eleanor's old gowns," replied Alice, "and it is as Lord Garrett commanded." Her eyes grew sad for just that one moment as she spoke, and Ellen knew the fear in her heart.

"Then I thank you, Lady Alice," she said, giving the girl a hug, "for your sweet kindness . . . though such as this is too grand for the likes of me. I shall want the others back, when they are dry." She was glad to see Alice smile and wondered how she could assure her that these fears were unfounded. At least, she hoped they were.

As David yet lay fitful and unconscious, beset by the low fever from his wounds, a schedule developed among the gentlewomen attending him: Lady Eleanor and Leticia watched through the morning, Emaline and Alice through the afternoon—with Edward wandering in and out at whim—and Ellen with a young waiting maid named Elspeth, through the long watch of the night. Ellen had chosen it that way, believing that if any mischief was about, it would likely be afoot when all else slept; and they could not chance that slumber now with David defenseless upon his bed. It was not easy to stay awake with Elspeth nodding in the chair beside the windows and Ellen resorted to singing softly and talking to herself and telling odd stories of her life to David, who lay unresponsive upon the white pillow as she smoothed his fevered face and hands with a cool, wet towel.

"You are not the man I expected," she said softly, leaning over him to wipe the greasy ointment of the dressing from the hair above his ear. "You were supposed to be a weak, flirtatious fool, and not such a good and strong and kind and handsome gentleman . . . I shall have to rewrite the books . . . one day . . . one day when I go home."

She had not heard the door open; and she startled to hear it close softly, and turned quickly to see Lord Garrett standing there. He wore boots and breeches and gear, and his sword belted under a dark brown cloak that showed the dirt and wear of long and weary ride.

"Elspeth," he called, waking the half-dozing girl, "you may go to your room. I will take your watch." And he opened the door and closed it again as the girl curtsied and scurried out without question.

Ellen, wondering at the look upon his face, wrung out the towel more carefully than necessary and placed it beside the bowl as he walked across the room, cast his cloak over the foot of the bed, and came to stand beside her.

"How is my brother?" he asked, looking down at David's still, pale form.

"As well as may be expected," Ellen replied, touching David's shoulder with her fingertips. "I think he will pull through this all right."

Garrett nodded. "He is a strong man—he will heal quickly." He turned to her. "And how is Lady Ellen?" he asked softly.

"Right as rain," she replied shortly and he smiled.

"I am glad to know that," he said earnestly, "And I know that you deserve my humble apology for not believing you as I should, and not heeding your admonitions."

Ellen shrugged. "Well, I thought you were being a bit thick," she said smugly, trying to keep the conversation light.

He only grinned. "Still I am grateful to you," he said earnestly. "You have saved my brother's life, you have saved me from a grief I shudder to contemplate, and you have saved my house from a great misfortune. I know I will remain indebted to you for all of my life, and I wonder in what way I may ever repay you."

"Well, I can think of a thing or two," she muttered under her breath, but to him said only, "Oh, I think it will suffice if you promise not to throw me in the dungeon again."

He grinned. "It might be a nice place to keep you," he replied, "if we fixed it up a bit. Having our own private prophetess is bound to be as prestigious as having our own private priest."

"Then why imprison me?"

"To keep you from getting stolen, of course. Valuable things usually are."

"Yes, you might even make a decent income marketing fortunes told." She laughed. "In fact, I may have to consider that as an occupation if I am stuck here for a while."

"You are not happy here?" he asked.

"Oh no, it's not that. It's just that this is not my place and I think I have done what I was supposed to do here." She motioned toward David. "I think you and David can handle anything more that comes along, and I really need to find a way to get home before I cause any mischief, unintentionally."

"What mischief do you imagine you could cause?" he asked.

She shrugged. "Perhaps not much, but I think your kindness toward me is troubling to Alice."

"Alice?" said Garrett. "Why should she be troubled?"

"Oh," sighed Ellen. "Don't be so obtuse. She thinks perhaps you are becoming too interested in me."

He laughed. "Well, mayhap that is true, but she would never doubt my faithfulness to her."

"Maybe in her heart she would not. But doubts and surmises are ever troubling, and they make her very unhappy. This," she said poking him in the chest with her finger, "cannot belong to me. If you would grant me one request in reward for my service to your house, marry Alice now, soon, with or without Lady Eleanor's blessing. It will preclude the possibility of future complications and make a more secure happiness for everyone involved, I think."

"You go quickly from prophetess to matchmaker," he laughed.

"If I do so, you should remember that I have the benefit of a history book in my hip pocket and would keep from you one of your greatest regrets."

Garret glanced involuntarily behind her, and she laughed, "No, 'in my hip pocket' is a term from wearing blue jeans—they have pockets in back . . . It's a 60's thing. But really, you get my point."

"Yes, I 'get your point,'" he said, "And I will earnestly consider your advice. It has stood me in good stead thus far."

Ellen pulled a chair up beside hers at the bedside and waved her hand to it.

"Sit with me, please," she said. "And tell me what has happened. What did Grimmel tell you?"

"Grimmel," he said with a wry smile. "You know his name already . . ." He settled into the chair beside her, crossed his arms upon his chest, and began the story as she kept her eyes upon her patient.

He told how the gypsy had sworn it true that David was set upon by his own men as they were crossing the river shoals: the arrow from the hand of Hotchkiss, the blow from the broadsword of Remmel, and how they had then cast David from his horse and into the deep pool below. The gypsy told how he had watched from the concealing thicket beyond as both men sat their horses near the riverside to make certain the deed was done, and seeing Ellen in her distress, he had thought to give aid but was taken and bound instead by those very soldiers who would wish to silence his tongue forever.

Ellen nodded slowly at his words.

"What have you done with him?" she asked.

Garrett leaned forward, his elbows upon his knees as he watched Ellen bathe his brother's face with the damp towel.

"I have set him free."

Ellen glanced at him questioningly. "Remmel and Hotchkiss?"

"Have fled," he said tiredly. "None can know where. They left from the Close soon after we returned here. I should have placed them under guard. There are others disloyal among our men, I am certain, thought I do not yet know who they are."

"You know who owns their allegiance?"

"Yes. I believe it is as you have said, but I have no proof as of yet, and therefore am loath to bring accusation. I would wait until I have David's council. After all, she is his wife. He must know of these things."

Ellen looked at him sharply, a disturbing thought suddenly come to her. "Is Grimmel safe?" she asked. "If Hotchkiss and Remmel find him?"

"He is safe," Garrett answered her. "I personally escorted him to his camp, and from there to a gypsy clan encamped in the hills a day's ride to the west. That is where I have been these last two days and am just returned. They will protect him. He and his family will be safe there."

"Good," said Ellen relieved. "Then all is going well. And although we are not out of the woods yet, at least there will be no Ebenezer Grimmel to curse you."

Garrett leaned back in his chair, contemplating her in the soft glow of the candle stand upon the bedside table. He was suddenly very curious to know more of this time that she had come from and the history that she claimed he had there.

"Tell me of that time," he said softly.

Ellen sighed. "What would you like to know?"

"Everything. Tell me what you know."

"You are ready to believe me?" she asked, eyeing him doubtfully, but his eyes held no mockery.

"I should not have doubted you before," he said. "I apologize for having done so. Now . . . please . . ."

"It will sound very strange . . ."

"I expect it will," he replied, and she laughed shortly.

"Ok, I suppose I should start by telling you that I am not from England . . . Long, long ago and far, far away, there is this place called Texas . . ."

And calling back from her memory all those things that had happened, all the things that were done and said and shared and learned between them in a time that seemed now, to her, a lifetime fabled and far away from her present existence, she told him of the month he had spent in the Garrison Keep in the year 1963. She kept back only those things nearest her heart, knowing they would cheapen in the telling.

"And then you simply vanished," she said at last when hours had passed and the candles had burned low. "But I felt something was wrong—nothing had changed as it should have. I spoke with Grimmel, and he told me of the curse, of the scribe who betrayed you, of the magic the scribe etched upon your tomb. I am not certain still, but I think maybe I drew it wrong," she said, shaking her head at the memory of that wretched moment of doubt. "I think maybe I drew it wrong, and it sent you back to the very moment of your death—again." She swallowed hard, and he saw the anguish in her face even now as she glanced his way. "I was riding back to the Keep—then—to find the drawing on the table and to find out if I had made such a horrible mistake, when my horse balked at a jump over a fallen tree, and I fell . . . and woke up here."

"With my mother's ring," he said thoughtfully after a moment's silence.

"Yes," she said without meeting his gaze.

"You said I gave it to you."

"Yes, you did, just before you left."

He thought to ask why; but when he did not, Ellen continued, guessing the questions in his mind. "We had become close friends, Garrett. For my part, I know that I loved you well. But we both knew that you should continue to search for a way to return home, and you would always be faithful to those first in your heart." She looked away and wiped her nose.

"I am glad to know these things," he said softly. "Your story is as strange as you said it would be, but I am happy to believe it true . . . It is good to know my history is yet honorable in two centuries."

He smiled, and he might have said more; but at that moment David's eyes flickered open, and he groaned, grimacing at the pain in his head. At the touch of Ellen's hand upon his brow, he looked at her, and his eyes focused first on her and then upon the face of his brother. He had heard their voices for some time in his sleep, and Ellen's voice had brought the oddest visions to his dreams.

"Garrett," he said hoarsely. "I have had the strangest dream, all light and dark, and an angel in a watery grave."

With a smile of relief, Ellen bent to kiss his forehead. "Don't talk too much," she whispered, and placing her hand on Garrett's shoulder, she stood to leave. "I'll let you two talk. The morning is almost here." And as she closed the door behind her, Garrett took his brother's hand, thinking of all the things his brother needed to hear and wondering how and where to begin.

ANNOUNCING THE BANNS

The days of that week passed quickly as David began to mend, and he rose from his bed upon the fourth day, to the great joy of the entire household. The servant staff was solicitous of his every need to the very brink of annoyance, and Ellen noted that even Leticia seemed demurely affectionate and gratified by his attention. Ellen wondered whether Leticia might, after all, be capable of such a change of heart; but she felt this new behavior originated more from trepidation at near discovery than from penitence. A mild-mannered Leticia was a Leticia worth watching, Ellen figured, and she could tell by their exchange of glances that David and Garrett felt the same. The whole intrigue was an amusing diversion for her at the moment, and Ellen was in need of diversion.

Now with the crisis she had dreaded past and the great misfortune of the Coltstone family avoided, Ellen was left wondering what exactly to do with herself. As a guest of the household, there was not enough work to occupy her time; and finding idleness wearying, she pushed herself to a more rigorous routine, spending much time with the servants at their work, visiting the near farm holdings until she was a familiar sight amid their daily activities, and talking with the tradesfolk of Briarwick on any and every topic—from brewing ale to the politics of the day. Always asking, always listening, always watching, she absorbed every detail of the social landscape she explored, only to carry it back to the Coltstone Keep and there sit for hours at the scribe's table in the study, journaling, and scratching out extensive notes with the awkward quill pen.

Garrett was kept busy these days, overseeing the estate matters while his brother recuperated, and he was rarely seen within the Keep between dawn and dusk. So if any noticed Ellen's distractions, it was Lady Eleanor and her maids, who passed such things off as fretting typical of the female heart (a thought which caused Alice much more worry than she would admit to any other), and perhaps Lord David, who had knowledge nearer to the heart of her distress.

She was sitting alone, scratching away at her notes at one end of the scribe's table one warm and wind-still afternoon when David entered the room. He was swinging his broadsword lazily in one hand as if relearning its balance and grip. Holding it high, he gave it an arching downward sweep that sang slightly in the quiet of the room, and then winced, rubbing his injured shoulder.

Glancing up at him from her writing, Ellen almost laughed. "Why do you do that if it hurts?" she ribbed him.

"I do it," he said, bowing with much humility, "to condition and remind the body of what it must do . . ."

Ellen only smiled and dipped her pen in the ink to resume her writing, but David precluded her. Tapping the stack of notes at her elbow with the tip of his sword, and then, most annoyingly, resting it in the middle of the sheet of parchment before her, he asked, "Why is it that you do this?" he asked, mocking her own tone of voice.

"I do this," she said slowly, searching for that answer herself, "To condition . . . to remind my thoughts of where they should be." Then she impatiently tossed the quill to the ink-stained wood of the table and rubbed her hands over her face disconsolately. "Although I am not sure why I bother," she said with disgust.

David considered her for a moment, and then sat upon the edge of the table, the broadsword balanced upon its edge as he sighted down its length with one eye. "Garrett has told me about you," he said quietly, his eye still upon the blade.

"What has he told you?" asked Ellen, her heart skipping just one small beat.

"Everything he knows, I suspect."

"And you believe him?"

He turned his gaze full upon her then, measuring and intent. "My brother would never lie. Not willingly."

Ellen met his gaze without falter, and he smiled. "The tale is outlandish, I admit. But its proofs—your proofs—are substantial."

"Lord David," said Ellen with a shake of her head, "you are definitely a different sort of person than I had thought you to be."

He lifted one eyebrow roguishly. "So Garrett tells me." And Ellen wondered then just how much Garrett had said as embarrassment colored her cheeks. David, however, did not pursue the matter. "What I am wondering," he said, "is what you intend to do now?"

Ellen sighed. "I don't know. I truly don't know." She paused a moment but, seeing his sincere interest, continued, "You see, I suppose I thought—after I got here—that once you were saved and the gypsy free, once history was made different and those things set to right, then I would go back; I would go home—somehow—the task, complete." She looked down at the notes before her. "But I haven't, I don't know how, and I'm afraid I never will. There doesn't seem to be any gypsy magic left over for me," she said, feeling a grip of panic as she looked up at him.

"It's so awful then, being here?" he asked, not without a note of understanding in his voice.

"No, it's not awful, but it is like being on vacation too long. One still wants to go home, to know that you can. I'd just like to eat a hamburger and french fries with some ketchup on them . . ."

"Hamburger?" he said, puzzled.

"It's food," she snapped.

"Then cook it."

She looked at him sharply, but he was not mocking her. "Right," she said. "I'll open the first McDonald's . . ."

"Mc Donald's . . ." He scowled. "Scotland is a wild place . . ."

And Ellen laughed, not knowing whether he was jesting truly or if their conversation had derailed over five centuries. He only smiled.

"I envy you," he said at last.

"Envy me? Why?" She could not imagine such a thing: a baron's eldest son envying a homeless waif . . .

"Because you have no set destiny before you. You have no history here, no one you are beholden to or responsible for. You have no one but yourself and a higher God to honor, and therefore, you may be anything you wish to be and do anything you wish to do."

Ellen saw the wistful look of his eye and listened with amazement. Somehow, in the activities and plans and worries of the past two weeks, those thoughts had never occurred to her.

"Think," he was saying, "with all you know, you could be the most powerful person in the kingdom. You could be advisor to the royal court and be as rich as you desire and command all you wish." He paused, reflecting that those were attributes his own wife had constantly striven for and pushed him toward. The thought irked him. Leticia would use such a one as this if she could; if she knew how, and perhaps this one would become like her. Such a thing could be monstrous, he realized, and he looked at Ellen with a sudden qualm of distrust.

But he saw no dawning light of avarice in Ellen's face as she twiddled the quill in her fingers and staring across the room as if at something a great distance away. "No," she said quietly. "I should do nothing like that. I should be afraid of the damage I might do. History goes along pretty well without tampering with kings and queens, but"—and she smiled—"there are things I *can* do that could do no harm. And you are right. I have resources beyond imagining whether I decide to be a gypsy or a farmer's wife."

Relieved, David stood and walked to the window. He put the tip of the sword upon the stone parapet and leaned on it there.

"I owe you my life," he said as he looked across the greensward to the river beyond. "If I have not thanked you before, I do so now." He glanced over his shoulder at her. "You may stay here as a member of our family however long you like, or I will assist you on your way as you desire. Whatever you wish of me, you have only to ask."

Feeling a warm appreciation for this man that she had once thought little of, Ellen shook her head. "What I have done was not for reward."

"No," he replied. "But the gratitude is mine, and the reward mine to give."

Ellen smiled her acceptance of his offer, but when he strode away from the window and would have left the room, she stopped him.

"Lord David," she said, rising from her chair. "Do you fear Leticia's father?"

"No," he scoffed, swinging the sword in a sweeping arch and sheathing it.

"Do you trust Leticia?"

"Trust her?" he repeated as if he'd never considered such a thing important. "No."

"Then if I have one request to ask of you, it is that for the sake of your family and for your own sake, you take Leticia in hand, rule her, and keep her until she is the wife she should be."

David rested his hands upon his sword hilt and stood at ease. His gaze seemed to pierce right through to her heart. "This, I fully intend to do," he said evenly. "But I know you do not request it for me, nor for my family, but for one of our number that you hold most dear."

Ellen blushed. "Am I so transparent?"

"Not to all," he said, coming to stand across the table from her. "And definitely not to him. But I do not flatter myself that you would have come here and done all you have for my sake only or my family's." He placed his hands on the table edge and leaned toward her. "If you wish to marry him," he said, "I will not prevent you."

"Marry him!" Ellen said, aghast, the stark reality of the words awakening her to her own contemplations. "Marry him," she whispered. Then shaking her head violently as if to cast the thought aside, she said forcefully, "No, you must become the great baron of Coltstone that you are meant to be. You must rule these lands and your family so that he can become the builder and architect he dreams of being. Together, the two of you could do great things—build that fleet of ships you planned when you were kids." She looked at him earnestly, and he watched her with mild surprise.

"And he must marry Alice. You must see to that—soon. It's how it has to be," she said adamantly. "I could never hurt her and Edward so."

"And yet you do love him," he said.

"Yes . . . But I could only do great harm—to myself—and to them by coming between them. Don't you see that?"

"Yes, I do," he said, and he thought he also saw what he had missed by his own lack of prudence in the choices of his past. He turned away slowly and, at the door, looked back. Ellen was staring absently at the page of notes, her chin cupped in her hands.

"Lady Ellen," he said, "wherever you go from here, whatever you do, I shall always remember you as a great lady. I hope you find happiness."

I hope so too, she thought to herself as his footsteps faded through the Great Hall beyond; but at the moment, it really didn't seem that way.

The following morning, Ellen rode into Briarwick to spend an hour with the old Chandler, a woman of venerable years and good wit who liked very much to talk. Then to the amused curiosity of the townsfolk, she sat upon the well curbing in the village square with a piece of parchment on a board and sketched the scenes around her with a piece of flat charcoal. She ate her lunch of bread and cheese there before riding back toward the Keep, stopping by the church to walk through its cemetery on the way. She stood in about the place where her uncle's headstone would one day be and looked at the smooth green grass around her and thought how the newness of the stones along the single row under the kirk wall, their dates chiseled sharp and clear, seemed so very odd.

When she remounted, she turned the roan back to the road and then, on a whim, passed the track to the Coltstone Keep and took instead the wide path to the Garrison Keep. She had avoided it before for a vague reason she really could not say. Perhaps for fear the very sight of it might somehow trigger her return home by some magnetic force. But now the thought of that was not absolutely unpleasant, and she was curious to see what the grand old place really looked like in the height of the Coltstone family's power.

There, where the track left the woods and the open green sward sloped up to the massive stone walls, Ellen reined in and dismounted, gazing in wonder at the place she'd last seen so ruinous and quiet. The Garrison Keep of 1449 was anything but ruinous and certainly not quiet. Manned by a large garrison of the Coltstone's men-at-arms, the castle and the grounds surrounding it were clearly kept in orderly repair by military standards. Even the sheepfolds and stable paddock's beyond had not a stone mislaid. The slates of the roof, massive wooden shutters and doors, foundations and towers and terrace walls reflected the care of a lord who knew their worth and had the means to keep all in ready repair. It was impressive; it was beautiful, and it made Ellen sad to think of its decay.

Garrett, who had spent much of his morning there at the Keep, was just riding from the Close when he saw Ellen standing beside her horse beneath the trees below. With a signal for his men to ride on ahead, he reined his horse away down the path toward her, dismounting at her side. He had not spoken with her in several days and not privately since that night in David's chamber, and he greeted her warmly.

Curtsying with a smile for his genteel bow, Ellen answered with ease his questions of her morning, her activities, matters comfortably spoken of, until all such were said and there came that moment of awkward silence that she had never before felt in his presence. It made her nervous; and she looked beyond him, studying again the symmetry of the Garrison Keep, and he saw the incongruence of memory in her face.

"What are you thinking?" he asked.

"I am thinking how different this looked when last I saw it."

At his querulous look, she continued. "The roof was falling in, especially on the far side by the tower. Most of the wooden shutters were fallen off or rotting. The terrace walls had fallen in. Only one stall in the stable could decently hold a horse . . ."

She looked up at him. "I hope it will not happen so now. I would like to think it will always look just this way."

She took a deep breath and turned to rub the roan's neck. "And I was thinking," she said, "that it is time for me to leave."

"Leave," he said with surprise. "And go where?"

"Oh," she said as lightly as she could. "I thought I would go to Edinburgh. I'd like to translate the Bible into English. I find these Latin liturgies difficult. I want to invent penicillin—that would be helpful. Maybe open a pub and sell hamburgers and ice cream . . . or sail to the new world."

"Why?" he interrupted her. "Why leave now?

"Because I need to . . ."

"Need to? You can do all of these things here," he said. "My brother will never grudge your keep, and I . . ." He paused, considering.

"You," said Ellen, finishing the thought for him, "are too handsome."

Garrett laughed, "That has never been a bane to me before."

"No," said Ellen, "but it is to me . . . I know you too well, and I love you too much, and I will not stay here to become the next villain in our history."

He would have laughed at her tempestuous outburst, but he saw that she was in earnest. "I cannot think that you would be so," he said quietly.

"But I," she replied, "know that I am terribly human. And I do not wish to be around to make that mistake." She looked into his face. "You," she said softly, "must marry Alice."

Garrett looked at her earnest expression for a moment before he nodded his head in regretful understanding and turned away.

Ellen attempted a bright smile as she continued quickly. "You have a beautiful son, Garrett. I hope you will have many more and that one day they will be heirs of these lands. I want to see you build your castles and ships and do all the things you dream of, but I must watch from a distance, else you would hate me in the end."

They rode together in silence back to the Coltstone Keep. In the Close, Derrick held the roan's rein as Garrett lifted her lightly down. "How long will you remain?" he asked.

"I will stay for your wedding," she replied brightly. "I would not miss that for all the world."

"Good!" he said earnestly and kissed her hand in parting.

She busied herself with the saddle bag until he had walked into the Keep, and then with a sigh, she turned to the soldier standing nearby.

"Derrick," she said.

"Yes, my Lady," he replied, bowing slightly.

"Promise me that you will guard your masters well. They are good people."

"Aye, my Lady," he said, and Ellen knew by his open and honest face that this was one soldier whose loyalties could be trusted. She liked Derrick, and they had become better friends of late since she had assured him she could never turn him into a toad and had shared the secret of the matches.

Taking her sketches and papers from the saddle pouch, she left the Close for the clerk's rooms and her writings. She had things to plan now, and she found the thought exhilarating: Edinburgh, Glasgow, and the wilds of Scotland, history firsthand, to see it and live it and watch it in the making. This, she thought, was going to be great fun, if she didn't get unwittingly caught in some revolution or die of the Black Plague, she reminded herself soberly. There were plans to make, lists of things to remember—lots of things to remember.

Garrett, upon entering the hall, sent a page boy to find his brother; and they met together in family council with Lady Eleanor that very hour in her chamber. Lady Alice and little Edward were sent for; and while none knew all the words passed between them or all the matters discussed, it was soon known that a feast was planned for the day after the morrow, and all the household and garrison were in a flurry of activity in preparation. All of the town's folk were invited, as were all the tenants, farmers, and herdsmen of the estate and any of near acquaintance who wished to share the celebration. It promised to be a grand event indeed in the cool of a fair evening in mid-July.

Excitement grew throughout the day of the feast as sides of beef and venison were slow roasted over open coals and ovens of bread were baked, and casks of ale and wine were carried up from the cellars. Edward ran from room to room and all around the grounds in an exuberant effort to be into and a part of everything; and Ellen, observing all with keen interest, felt every bit the same.

In the afternoon, the ladies retired to their chambers to rest and prepare for the evening's entertainment, and Ellen felt highly complimented when Lady Alice asked if she would accompany them. Once in her chamber, she offered Ellen the loan of a beautiful gown of forest green velvet trimmed in gold. "It suits you well," she said when Ellen had pulled it on. Alice, in a rose brocade and ivory lace, looked much like a rare china doll, happiness blooming upon her cheek; and Ellen took her hand in the warmth of friendship and admiration. "You," she said, "are the belle among them all this day."

Alice's eyes dropped from her gaze momentarily. "Lady Ellen," she said, "forgive me for once misdoubting your intentions. I . . . was afraid . . ." She paused uncertainly.

"That I coveted the affection of your Lord Garrett?" suggested Ellen.

"Yes," replied Alice, frowning slightly.

"Then you guess right," she said sincerely. "But you need not fear me . . . I am no such fool to cause my own misery. His heart, Alice, will always belong to you."

Alice hugged her and asked her to sit nearby while Emaline braided her hair.

The feasting began early, with all who could not find place in the Great Hall of the Keep spilling into the regular dining hall and some even at tables upon the green. From her seat between Emaline and Lady Eleanor, Ellen could feel no regret or ill will toward any as she watched the company roundabout her. The joy in Alice's face as she sat beside Lord Garrett was recompense enough for any regret Ellen could have harbored. Edward, mostly standing in his chair, was almost as loud as his uncle, who was enjoying a good share of the ale long before the toasts began.

Torches were lit as the sun sank low, and the great chandeliers were lowered and lit and hoisted back to the rafters, before Lord David rose from his chair and, to the amusement and cheers of all assembled, climbed up onto the table, holding up his hands for silence. Ellen noted Leticia's glower of disgust as she looked up at him, but no one else seemed mindful of her.

David, pausing to lift his tankard from its place on the table beside his boot, gave a short speech of welcome and praise to his worthy guests, took a long swallow as all cheered and then, quieting them again, motioned for Lady Alice and Lord Garrett to stand. Edward obliged by climbing up on the table, where Garrett grasped him firmly around the waist lest he tread on the trenchers.

"My noble guests, good friends, and neighbors," bellowed David, "It is with great pleasure that I announce to you this night the betrothal of my dear brother, Lord Garrett of Coltstone Keep, to the fairest flower of womankind, Lady Alice of Sheffield. May they live long and happily together," he said, raising his tankard in a toast, "and may many little Coltstones sit around their table."

Alice blushed at the rousing "Hear! Hear!" from all the company.

"The wedding will be on the new moon eve of August. May you all have the good fortune of attending!" shouted Lord David over the cheers and toasts, and then quickly, the tables were pulled back to the walls and the benches cleared. While the musicians struck up a lively tune, all the assembly formed into circles for country dance sets. To Ellen, it all appeared much like the country square dances and Western reels she had grown up with; and although she did not know the sets or sequences, she soon found herself out upon the floor, being passed gaily from one partner to the next as the dancers twirled and glided and turned and bowed in intricate progression around each ring.

It was lovely. It was intoxicating. She thought she had never been so happy, felt so light, so carefree, so like Cinderella in the fairy tale. And when she found herself on David's arm for a turn of the dance and he held her a bit tighter than the others and kissed her playfully ere he passed her along, she only laughed and winked at his audacity.

When at last, blushing hot and out of breath, she curtsied out of the next dance set; Ellen took a cup of water from the table near the door and stepped out into the cool night air. She walked, as if still in a dream, to that twilight where the sounds of music and laughter blend with the quiet sounds of night breeze and crickets and where the light from the doorway gave way to the dark. She had lingered there for some time, when she was suddenly aware of two figures walking toward her from the shadow of the hedge just beyond, and she recognized the woman's voice as Leticia's. They stopped near her, and Ellen knew from Leticia's low tones that what was said was not for her ears.

"Remmel is with them now," she was saying, "and Hotchkiss . . . They will know your signal. Make it in the fourth watch of the night, if fortune so avails. I will richly reward those who do not fail me."

Remmel and Hotchkiss? thought Ellen, startled by the names. *Who were they with? And for what did they await a signal? And who was this soldier Leticia spoke to so clandestinely?* She feared Leticia would notice her soon and did not want her to know that she had heard what obviously was spoken in secret.

Thinking quickly, she stepped back deeper into the shadow of the Keep wall and then, humming lightly, stepped casually toward them from the light of the doorway. At Ellen's appearance, Leticia startled and looked annoyed as the soldier bowed low and ducked away before Ellen could address him or see his face in the light. As he walked away, Leticia turned on her with an acid smile.

"You seem extremely happy for one who has lost so miserably," she said.

"Lost?" asked Ellen. "Lost what?"

"That which you come here for: an heir of the Coltstones, for which you are better suited than her who has got him . . ."

Ellen laughed. She could not see how, amid all this happiness, anything could now go wrong. "Leticia," she said, "you have an overgrown love of vindictiveness."

"And you of simpletons and squalor."

"You know, Leticia," said Ellen sadly. "Honey draws more flies than vinegar . . . If you really want wealth and power, you should try a different tactic."

Leticia favored her with a look of disgust. "I will be all I wish to be," she said quietly. "And you . . . you will be drawing flies much sooner than I."

Ellen knew it for a threat but could not feel fear at such petty striving. "I pity you," she said quietly as she turned away. "You could not be happy were the whole kingdom in your hands."

"Try me," muttered Leticia, glaring at Ellen's retreating back. And Ellen thought to herself, as she entered the candlelit hall full of sound and music and motion, that Leticia was more mean of spirit than ever she could have imagined, and she wondered just what had made her so. People, she told herself, certainly weren't just born that way.

BRIGANDS ON THE BORDER

The house awoke late and slowly the following morning. The days that followed were peaceful and happy with the busy stirrings of a family preparing for a wedding. Ellen watched those around her happily and, busy with her own thoughts and preparations, forgot much of her encounter with Leticia. When thoughts of it did come to mind, she managed to dismiss them with the positive belief that whatever Leticia's schemes, they could not now do any great harm, with David alive and well and watchful and Garrett and Alice well set on a path to their own happiness.

So the days of a week passed, and thoughts of Leticia's words were further than they should have been on that morning when a lad of perhaps twelve years was seen riding across the green toward the castle gate, crying out for admittance and aid even as he spurred the very jaded and lamed mule to the end of its strength.

In the Close, he was pulled from the beast's back and supported as, fatigued and distraught, he stammered and cried in frantic distress, "They are burning everything—and killing—please help us!" he cried and could not be quieted until he was brought inside the castle and Lord David and Lord Garrett sent for.

"He is a lad from the north holdings," Derrick replied to Ellen's query when the boy was led to the study and closeted there with the Coltstone lords. Within moments, the doors were again flung wide as David strode forth, bellowing orders.

Derrick was dispatched to the Garrison Keep to call forth the full contingent of men-at-arms. "Have them formed ready upon the green within the hour," David barked. "I will inform my captains of matters as we ride." He pushed past Leticia, who stood in the doorway, and called for his squire to bring his armor and sword.

Ellen saw the knowing smile upon Leticia's face, and some urgent alarm seemed to clamor from the back of her mind, but she was quickly distracted as Garrett caught her by the elbow and pulled him along with him. He placed Edward in the care of Alice and Lady Eleanor and sent Emaline to order the staff to prepare provisions for the march.

"Ellen, come with me," he said tersely, and she found herself hurrying after him through the Great Hall and forced to a half run in order to match his stride. In his quarters, he called for his servant to bring his armor, helmet, and shield.

Ellen had never been in these rooms and looked about at their sparse furnishings as Garrett pulled on the long thick tunic the boy proffered him and shrugged into a heavy coat of chain mail. He turned to Ellen as the boy buckled the armor fastenings and strapped the metal greaves.

"There is more afoot here than we know, Ellen," he was saying, "and I fear great evil may come of it."

"Why, my lord?" she asked. "What has happened?"

"Brigands, upon our north border," he said tersely, bending to help tighten the straps of the armor. "They are burning crops, killing the livestock. They have attacked our people, killed whole families." His face was tight with anger as Ellen gasped, appalled.

"Killing . . . ," she murmured.

He stood and took her firmly by the shoulders. "Robbers do not do such things." And she understood the meaning in his gaze. "Stay close to Alice. Keep her and Edward safe. Promise me."

"I will."

"If I do not return . . ."

Ellen shook her head in protest, but he stopped her. "*If I do not return*, take them from here. Take them to her father's house."

"No," said Ellen. "That is where they were last time. It's not safe enough. I will take them out of the country—to France."

"Good!" he said, releasing her. "I trust you, but do you trust no other! I know not which of our men may have been bought." He stroked her cheek once with the back of his fingers before he pulled on the heavy leather gauntlet, grasped up his helm, and was gone.

In the Close, Ellen watched from the shade under the thick wall as David and his men mounted. To her surprise, Leticia stood near her husband's tall charger and spoke a fair and amicable farewell. Lady Eleanor kissed her eldest son in parting, and Garrett held Alice close in his arms and kissed her ere he mounted the rangy bay. Then, lifting

Edward up before him in the saddle, he hugged and teased the small boy until a smile lit the tiny features and the tears were wiped away. Lowering him down to his mother, Garrett took up his reins and cast one meaningful glance to Ellen, who nodded her understanding as the gates were flung wide. Edward's eyes were aglow with pride and admiration as he watched his father and his uncle ride forth at the head of the column of men, their banners snapping and rippling in the breeze and armor flashing bright under the clear summer sky.

All stood in the gates to watch as David and Garrett joined the company of mounted soldiers formed and ready upon the greensward, and the thudding of many hooves and the shouts of the captain's ordering the march rang clear in the morning air. Alice and Edward, Ellen, and Lady Eleanor remained there until the last horseman had disappeared from view and it was not until they walked back through the Close and into the castle hall that Ellen noticed Leticia's absence, and she found that absence strangely troubling.

Walking into the clerk's room, she sat down heavily at the table. Something was not right, and she knew it, and she knew that Garrett had felt it too. He had made her promise to keep Alice and Edward safe and she wondered how she could do that if she had nothing more than a nagging feeling to go on. She felt miserably that she was forgetting something very important.

Glancing down at her stack of journaling notes, she fingered them absently, smiling to herself that she had been so prolific with her writings. She had writing about such a wide variety of topics and had written about the feast in great detail, even setting down the notes of the music and the steps to several dance sets. The revelry had lasted late into the night and as Ellen remembered the cool of the morning mists creeping up from the river as the last guests meandered away down the road from the Keep, the term "fourth watch" sprung into her mind. "*Fourth watch*." She wondered when that was. It must be very late or early morning, she surmised, recalling that Leticia had used the term when she had spoken with the soldier in the dark.

Ellen frowned at the remembrance. "Remmel and Hotchkiss are with them," Leticia had said, and something about a signal—in the fourth watch . . . Ellen sprang to her feet with sudden horror of understanding. "Robbers did not do such things," Garrett had said. They did not burn and kill—but soldiers did. Leticia's soldiers would.

And what of the fourth watch? she thought as she hurried up the steps to her room. *And what of the "signal?"* It rang with the ugly sound of betrayal. How easy to slay a man in his sleep, (she grimaced at the thought,) or call his foes down upon him when he was least prepared.

David and Garrett must be warned, she decided with stalwart resolve, as she cast off the pretty but cumbersome folds of the linen dress and pulled her breeches and shirt from the pegs where they had hung upon the wall for the past weeks. Tucking in her shirt, she buckled her belt, tucked her pant legs into her boots, and swung the satchel across her shoulders while she thought of all that she must do.

"Do thou trust no other," Garrett had warned her. If she couldn't trust a guard to carry her message, then she must go herself. But what of Alice? She had promised to keep her and Edward safe, and she could not leave them here, not with Leticia. With a wry smile, she thought how nice it would be to just lock that pretty viper in the cellar and do the whole world a lot of good, but the thought was impracticable: Leticia would doubtless have her own protection around her, especially now.

She must warn Alice, she decided. They would leave the Keep now, quietly, while no one suspected that she knew anything; and Alice and Edward would ride with her to warn the soldiers if need be. With any good fortune they might catch up with David and Garrett and their troops before nightfall.

With that in mind, she pulled the green cloak off its peg and flung it around her shoulders as she stepped out into the hall, walking quickly toward the open door of the lady's drawing room where she thought Alice most likely to be.

Two men-at-arms were walking toward her down the corridor's length as she neared the doorway, but such was not uncommon in the castle and her mind was not on them as she stepped aside to let them pass. Too late she saw the intent of their steady gaze and felt their hands close roughly upon her arms. She saw Edward in the doorway ere they spun her about.

"Edward," she yelled. "Tell Alice . . . !"

A guard struck her roughly across the face, and they pulled her along the corridor, held fast between them and helpless to struggle. "What is the meaning of this?" she said fiercely but got no answer until, at the door to Leticia's rooms, the guard spoke smoothly, "My Lady's orders," and pushed her before him through the door.

Standing before a tall vanity, Leticia languidly dabbed a sponge of perfumed rosewater at her neck before she turned to smile cajolingly at the seething Ellen, still held between her guards.

"My, my, Lady Ellen," she chortled triumphantly. "You do wear the oddest things . . . Were you going somewhere?"

Ellen glared but answered nothing.

"You see," continued Leticia, "I was afraid you might have heard too much for your own good. You are always asking so many questions." Leticia smiled wickedly.

"You won't get away with this," hissed Ellen.

"Won't I? I cannot see why not."

"Garrett knows," Ellen said, bluffing, "I've told him."

Leticia laughed, only slightly perturbed. "Even if he knew all, which he cannot, I will yet be a very sorrowful widow and you a very penitent witch before anything can be done to mend the matter. And Alice . . . poor Alice. So very sad." She sighed eloquently. "You see, I have very capable men riding among them, well-trusted men. My husband's camp will be guarded *very* well . . ."

"Garrett knows this," said Ellen defiantly.

But Leticia only winked slyly. "Then he will die knowing it, for he knows not enough. And you, my pretty witchling, will never live to tell."

With a feeling of anger and despair, Ellen knew that Leticia's words might easily prove true as she was ordered away and led by the guards down the dark cellar corridor and once more heard the door of the dungeon close solidly behind her and its drawbar fall into place.

She hissed in frustration, kicking at the filthy rags on the floor and scowling as she leaned heavily upon the dank mossy wall. "Here we are again. Just where we started and no better off—worse—if that were possible." She fumed to herself.

Once past her initial tirade and bout of berating herself for blind idiocy, Ellen set herself to thinking—and thinking hard. There was no doubting her fate now if she did not act fast and effectively: Leticia was more than capable of fulfilling her threats, and the history books were witness to just how little her conscience ruled her. In this, Ellen felt the history books were for once infallible.

She had to escape . . . But how? Ellen eyed again the thick stone walls, the tiny crack high in the wall that admitted a thin shaft of light, the heavy wooden door—a very heavy wooden door. Digging through her satchel, she found the box of matches; only a few remained. She eyed the dirty rags on the floor and the wooden bucket and, taking her knife from her breeches pocket, she flipped it open and patiently began whittling away at the dry wood of the bucket, making a neat pile of the shavings against the door. Perhaps, she considered, if she did not succeed in setting the door ablaze, she might at least cause enough smoke and alarm in the cellar to draw the guard. And perhaps, then, she might somehow force her way out. It was a pretty sketchy plan, she admitted to herself as she worked, but sitting on her heels waiting to be taken out and burned would not serve any better.

The sunlight from the niche in the wall above her was slanting its way up the far side of the chamber when Ellen was startled by the sound of a small voice. She paused in her work, listening, only to decide that her ears had deceived her and she had resumed her whittling when she heard it again.

"Ms. Ellen!" it called, and this time, she was certain of it. Rising slowly and turning around to pinpoint from whence it came, she heard the voice once more. "Ms. Ellen, are you down there?"

It was Edward! And he was at the small window, his form blocking the light as he moved.

"Yes! Yes!" she called excitedly "I'm here!" And grasping the bucket, she overturned it and stood on its bottom, trying to reach the opening above—to see him—but the space was too high.

"Edward," she called. "Is anyone with you?"

"No, ma'am," he answered softly.

"Can anyone see you?"

"No, ma'am. I'm under a bush. I heard they had put you here. Are you all right?"

"Yes, Edward," Ellen said, speaking calmly for his sake. "I'm fine. But I need your help."

There was a long silence, and Ellen feared that he had left when at last he answered. "What may I do?"

"Edward, listen carefully," she said. "Come down into the cellar. If there is a guard at the door, leave quickly and come back here to tell me. If there isn't, then come to the door and open it for me. OK?"

"OK," he whispered

"And Edward . . ."

"Yes?"

"Don't let anyone see you . . . like hide-and-seek. OK?"

"OK," he said, and she heard the rustle of the leaves upon the ground as he crawled away.

Time seemed interminable before she heard his light footsteps on the stones outside her cell and, with a sigh of relief, heard his voice.

"Ms. Ellen, there's no one here."

"Good," she said, saying a thankful prayer at their good fortune. "Can you reach the bar?"

"Just barely," he said; and she heard him scrambling about as if stacking boxes or something against the door, until at last the bar scraped upward and fell onto the flagged floor with an ominous clatter.

"Sorry," Edward was saying, his eyes wide and scared as she pulled the door open.

She hugged him close and smiled reassuringly. "That's OK," she whispered. "You did great!" Shutting the door and replacing the bar, she grabbed his hand in hers and led him quickly up the steps and away up the corridor to the dark niche behind the arched pillar where Garrett had once shown her the entrance to the secret tunnel. Hiding there, she knelt beside the frightened boy.

"Edward," she said quietly, "We must be very brave—like your daddy . . ."

"He nodded, his eyes round and earnest.

"Is your mother OK?" she asked anxiously.

He nodded.

"Have they done anything—locked her in her room—said anything?"

He shook his head.

"Good," sighed Ellen with relief. "Then we still have time. Go find her. Bring her here quickly. Don't talk to anyone else. Don't tell anyone else. This is very important—do you understand?"

"Yes, ma'am," he said, then looked at her anxiously. "Are we in trouble?"

"Not yet," she said, patting his soft cheek. "We'll be OK. But go quickly now." And with a glance to see that the hall was clear, she sped him away down its dark length, praying he would succeed in his errand and return safely. As his little form disappeared around a corner, Ellen sat down upon the floor of the dark niche and grasped the iron ring in the stone door of the tunnel, pulling at it with all her strength. It did not budge. Exasperated, she flipped open her knife, wedging its blade in the crack around the stone, grinding the blade dull against the sand and grit that held the stone fast.

Daylight was fading outside; she knew that by the angle of its rays in her dungeon cell moments ago. The guard would be bringing her bread and cup of water soon. There was no way to know exactly when, but he would find her cell empty, and the alarm would be sounded. If Alice and Edward were not hid with her by then, they would likely be detained; Leticia would not chance losing them also. And if Alice were taken, all would be lost.

Fiercely then, she pulled against the stone, straining every muscle as she braced her feet against the wall on either side of it, and wrenched the ring one way and then another. She was almost at strength's end when at last she heard a faint rasping sound, and the stone slid out a hair's breadth. Wiping her brow, she scraped its edges again with her knife and, with a last herculean effort, pulled and pulled until the stone slid out and the opening beyond was clear . . . not a moment too soon.

As Ellen leaned back, breathing heavily, and felt in the bottom of her satchel for the flashlight, she heard footsteps in the corridor. They came nearer. They stopped near the stone arch that shadowed her hiding place, and Ellen held her breath.

"Ms. Ellen?" a small voice queried, and Ellen breathed out in a burst of relief as she quickly reached out to grasp the small hand and pull Edward and the startled Alice into the dark alcove with her.

"Ellen . . . what—" whispered Alice in surprise, but Ellen silenced her with a quick "Hush!" and squeeze of her arm as other footsteps were heard in the corridor: the guard with Ellen's evening meal. He passed them and stomped away down the cellar steps.

"Quick, Edward," said Ellen, "Scoot in here." She pointed to the tunnel's dark mouth. "Go quickly—we will be behind you . . . There is an opening at the other end," she explained to Alice's worried look. "I'll explain everything as we go, but we must leave quickly."

The sound of the dungeon door banging open echoed in the corridor, and a shout rang out as the guard discovered her missing and sounded the alarm. Ellen and Alice huddled close in the dark as the soldier ranted through the cellars, searching each dark corner, before his pounding footsteps echoed away up the corridor.

"Quickly now," hissed Ellen. "They will form a search party and return soon and we must be far from here." She shoved Alice into the tunnel's small opening and crawled in behind her while all was momentarily quiet in the corridor. She knew it would not be quiet there for long, and she strained to pull the stone back into place behind her as she had seen Garrett do once before. Then, flipping on the flashlight, she handed it to Alice, who took it gingerly, and shone it out ahead of Edward as they crawled forward.

Reaching the far end of the tunnel where the well-like shaft rose to the flat stone on its curbing above, Ellen flipped off the light and stood a moment, listening. All was deathly quiet in the tunnel. The stone walls apparently deadened all sound from within and without; and for one brief moment, Ellen considered hiding there, but then dismissed the idea when she imagined being trapped like a rabbit in its burrow. No, they would await the fast falling cover of darkness and then make their escape.

"Ellen, what is going on?" asked Alice in a small frightened voice.

"Has Garrett told you anything . . . ?" asked Ellen.

"He said to be careful, to stay close to you—do as you tell us to."

"Well," said Ellen, "Leticia wants you dead."

Alice gasped.

"And Edward and me too, if she can manage it."

"But she can't . . . ," protested Alice. "How could she? When Garrett and David return . . ."

"She does not mean for them to," Ellen interrupted. "She has spies—traitors—planted among their men. Remmel and Hotchkiss lead the raiding band. She's planned it all, and she's planned it well."

"But why?" protested Alice. She had always disliked and distrusted Leticia, but such cruel intrigue was hard to attribute to one she had lived beside daily.

"Greed, Alice. Greed and power. That's all I know, and now I must ride to warn David and Garrett of what I have learned. But first, I will see you and Edward to someplace safe."

"My father's?" suggested Alice.

Ellen shook her head in the dark. "No, Leticia will suspect that, and pursuit would be close upon us. But I know of a place: the turret attic of the Garrison Keep tower. I think you will be safest where she least suspects you: right under her very nose." She paused. "Do you agree?"

"Yes," said Alice quickly. "Yes, we will hide there."

"Good," said Ellen, relieved. "Now let's see if I can move this stone." Wedging her fingers into the stone crevasses that formed a sort of ladder in the wall, she clambered up and shoved against the stone lid with her shoulder. It was heavy; and it moved slowly, inch by inch, as she pushed it aside and the dark night sky appeared above.

This time, there was no thicket of plums to hide the tunnel's opening, but a thorny clump of gorse bush instead. Ellen pulled herself up and sprawled among them, reaching down to take Edward under the arms as Alice lifted him up to her, and then grasping Alice's wrists as she too scrambled up out of the dark pit. After carefully pushing the stone back into place, they smoothed it over with dirt and dry leaves before sliding away under the cover of the Hawthorne hedges.

"Take Edward with you," whispered Ellen when they were some distance from the torch-lit windows of the Keep. "Follow the garden hedge east to the woods."

"What are you going to do?" asked Alice.

"Go to the stables and get my horse. I'll meet you two behind the sheepfolds."

"What if you are caught?"

Ellen hesitated. "Go to the river. Follow it to the shoals, and go west. Find the gypsy camp and ask for a man named Grimmel. He will aid you."

Alice nodded, and they both prayed desperately that things would not come to such ends as they hugged and parted quickly. Waiting until Alice and Edward were some distance away, Ellen crawled through the tall grass under the practice yard wall, thankful for the dark cloak and the pitch black of the night. The waxing quarter moon would not arise until much later, and the starlight was little more than noble comfort gleaming above the canopy of the trees.

The stalls of the stable were empty, their usual occupants far away somewhere to the north in service of their masters, and all was terribly quiet as Ellen slid through the outer door of the roan mare's stall. Grabbing the bridle from its peg, she quickly led the mare out into the night with only the reins flung over her neck. Once some distance away and assured that none had seen her, she bridled the mare and quickly led her behind the paddock fences and around to the sheepfold where Alice and Edward awaited, crouching in the shadow of the wall where it bordered the woods.

Away, they fled deep under the forest's sheltering cover until Ellen dared stop long enough to lift Alice up onto the roan's back and hand Edward up to her. Then with Ellen leading the mare, they travelled more quickly and soon had passed around the fields of the Garrison Keep holding to their bordering tree lines and coming up behind the stables.

Ellen could not know how much time had passed, but she did not doubt that word of her escape had long since reached whatever guard remained at the Garrison, and she dare not let herself or Alice and Edward be seen by any within those walls. Now she stood for a long time in perplexed study. She must find a way past all watchful eyes, breach the security of a fortress long held impermeable, and not only get in—but back out again—without being detected.

She wondered how many of the garrison remained within and hoped the number was few as she formed her plan.

"Alice," she said, "do you see that small door, the one next the scullery?"

Alice nodded.

"There is a sort of sunken place near it where the soldiers cut and stack wood for their cooking fires. Take Edward and hide there. Do not move from there until I reach you."

Without a word, Alice led Edward by a circuitous path up under the Keep wall and to the place Ellen had directed, while Ellen led the horse some distance back into the wood and tied her firmly to a tree. From there, she ran to the stable and, relieved to find it empty and quiet, she knelt in the thick straw of a stall and lit a match. She watched it flare as she lowered it, with a guilty twinge of heart, down onto the dry bedding. "I can't believe I am burning my own stable," she thought sardonically.

The straw caught quickly, and the smoke rolled thick as flames leaped up and licked outward. Out into the darkness, Ellen leaped, running away under the trees toward the Keep and Alice's hiding place as shouts rang out from the walls above and men dashed out of the doors and along the stable path, shadows and light dancing eerily over the open green and flinging weird silhouettes high up on the grey stone walls. The night was alive with shouts and men running and the roaring crackle of the blaze, and all pandemonium reigned.

If any had been watching, they might have seen three figures appear out of nowhere and silently file through the small scullery door, but none were watching toward the Keep, and the smoke and heat of the flames made it difficult to see into the dark.

The halls and corridors, so familiar to Ellen, were quickly navigated and without mischance they at last mounted the stairs to the attic. Alice watched intrigued as Ellen stacked boxes on a trunk against the tower wall, leaped up on them, and quickly slid several boards of the ceiling aside. "Up here, Edward," she whispered, and she lifted the boy up over her head, shoving him into the dark space beyond.

"Now you." She beckoned to Alice who grasped the edges of the opening as Ellen made a saddle for her foot and heaved her up. Pulling herself up when Alice was clear, Ellen crouched on the floor for a moment to catch her breath, while Edward crawled into his mother's lap and huddled there in the embrace of her protecting arms. He looked so small and so frightened, Ellen thought, and he had been so brave.

"Edward," she said, glancing at Alice. "Your father and your uncle used to play here when they were little boys. This is their secret place, and only they know about it. "Look," she said, reaching into the pocket of the cloak and pulling out the small bronze horse. "This was your father's. He left it here once. Will you keep it for him?" She asked, holding it out to him; and he smiled and took it eagerly, clutching it with both hands.

"Thank you," said Ellen, smiling at him. "Now you must not move, and you must be very quiet until your daddy comes for you." She placed her hand on Alice's arm. "Of all the soldiers, trust only Derrick. If you find yourself in need, he would aid you. I will tell him where you are as well as Garrett and Lord David. Now I must go before my magic wears off and the soldiers return. Tell me, when is the fourth watch?"

"Between four and five in the morning," replied Alice. "Why?"

"Because that is when our hope will be betrayed. I must reach Garrett and David before then. Do you know where they are?"

"Only to the north, beyond the band of hills. Follow the river and cross it when it bends wide to the east. You will see the moorlands rising upon the horizon when you come out of the trees. They will likely camp in the shelter of the trees below them . . . It is a long way."

"Then pray that I reach them in time," Ellen said as she slid to the opening and lowered herself down. Alice's face appeared above her for a moment as she slid the boards back into place.

"Ellen," she said.

"Yes?"

"Thank you."

With only a nod and quick smile, Ellen jumped down from the stack of crates and hurried away through the still silent halls. She pulled the cape well over her face and clutched it around her as she walked unnoticed past a group of soot-blackened men, who stood in animated conversation near the scullery door. Like a phantom, she slipped away into the dark; and no one much heeded the distant sound of galloping hooves as she spurred the mare over the fields, checking her pace only in the thick of the river woods where the night was most dark and still and the paths most easily lost.

UNDER THE SWORD

The night and the winding paths seemed to go on forever; and Ellen, fighting fatigue as she pushed the mare to what pace the ground would allow, was at once relieved and dismayed when the thin quarter moon rose at last and gave her the aid of its light. The hours were slipping past her, and she had no idea how much further she had to ride. She wondered if she could find the encampment at all . . . the right encampment . . . and who she could trust to take her to David and Garrett if she did find it. Should she just ride in sounding the alarm? she wondered. Or would that only trigger worse events? She shook her head tiredly. None of this was as cut-and-dried as it sounded in the history books.

Realizing that the river was bending away to the east and had been for some distance without her noticing, she wondered if she had already followed it too long as she turned the mare to the west. Moonlight flashed like diamonds in the splashes and ripples of its surface as the mare waded across and scrambled up the far bank and into the woods.

All was just as Alice had described when at last they broke from the forest's deep gloom and rode out onto a rolling grassy plain that rose gently to the high moorland above. Now in the open and unhindered by vine and tree, Ellen set the mare forward at a gallop, feeling the horse's tired muscles tighten with the strain, her ribs heaving under Ellen's knees. The tall thick grass swept up before her, and up, under, and away in a dreamlike fantasy of speed, the whole world opening before them as if it were not they who were moving at all but the earth beneath their feet that sped to meet them and fled away behind. Ellen wondered if she had fallen asleep and were dreaming this whole wild night ride. Maybe she was really still back in the dungeon, she thought, and she might have believed it if her aching body did not tell her differently. Then a band of trees loomed across her path, a wide band of forest below the moors, and she drew rein at their border.

Alice had told her that David would likely be camped somewhere within the shelter of these woods. The camp should be somewhere here; but finding where might be a real trick, Ellen thought, scanning the expanse of deep shadows before her. With a shrug, she kneed the mare forward: she would look for firelight and trust to providence. So far, she told herself, providence had yet to fail her.

But even those positive thoughts were growing weak and thin from overuse when, pushing the tired mare to the humble crest of a brushy knoll, Ellen looked down to scan the woodland glades below and with great relief and delight, saw the glowing embers of campfires scattered across the low sheltered ground before her. Dark figures slumbered upon the ground beneath the trees: horses stood drowsing on picket ropes, and all were swathed in the cool damp of the morning's small hours.

Now what? thought Ellen but was not required to answer the question before the voice of a sentry demanded her to halt and identify. With exuberant relief, Ellen recognized the voice of Derrick, the only soldier she knew she could trust, and she made a mental checkmark on the notepad of providence as she dismounted quickly and called to him in hushed tones.

"Derrick," she said, seeking out his shadowy figure from among the trees. "It's me. It's Ellen."

"Lady Ellen!" he gasped in recognition. "But why are you here?"

"There is no time to explain," she said quickly. "There is treachery afoot and danger near. What watch is this?"

He glanced up at the stars and the moon. "The third, my Lady—but nigh on to the next."

"Then we must act quickly, Derrick," she said as she tied the mare's reins to a sapling. "Please, take me to Lord Garrett's tent."

With a quick nod, Derrick led off through the thicket, down the side of the knoll, and into camp. As silently as cat's paws, they passed among the sleeping men to the door of a tent where Derrick stopped. "This is his, my Lady."

"Good," she whispered. "Now go quickly and awaken Lord David . . ."

"But, my Lady!" he protested.

"On pain of your life, man," she hissed, grabbing him by the shoulder. "Do it and bring him here! Your commander also, if you deem him loyal and trustworthy. Then go saddle their horses."

Derrick stood undecided for a moment, but something in her face made him loath to argue; and to her relief, he hurried away to do her bidding. Turning quickly, then, she lifted the tent flap and slipped inside. There, wrapped in a heavy cloak, Garrett lay asleep upon the ground; and without thought, Ellen knelt beside him and placed her hand upon his shoulder.

"Garrett," she whispered. "Wake up!" And in one instant, she felt his fist close upon her shirt front, yanking her down as his dagger flashed to her throat. "Don't!" she choked as she felt its cruel point under her chin. "Garrett, wake up. It's me—Ellen," she gasped.

As the sleep faded from his mind, he loosened his hold on her and sat up, slipping the dagger back to its sheath as Ellen sat back heavily upon the ground, shaken. "Remind me never to do that again," she mumbled.

"Ellen," he said with some consternation, lifting her to her feet, "What are you doing here? Where is Alice?" A brief fear flickered across his face.

"She and Edward are in the turret of the Garrison Keep tower. I hid them there," she replied. And quickly, she recounted her imprisonment and their flight. "But I had to leave them there," she said miserably. "I had to warn you."

Looking into her tired, earnest face, he held her close for a moment, steadying her. "Warn me of what?" he said softly.

The tent flap stirred then, and Ellen quickly pulled away as David, Derrick, and David's captain of the guard stepped into the small space.

"What is this, brother?" asked David in surprise at the sight of Ellen, and Ellen was glad to see that he was armed. He buckled the coat of mail hanging loose upon his shoulders as she spoke, telling them all she had overheard of Leticia's plans, of the traitors within their camp and the signal in the fourth watch.

"She would have us dead in our sleep, brother," growled Garrett as he shrugged into his armor and buckled on his sword.

"Aye, but not now," David replied, his face a hard mask of will and determination. "Lady Ellen, once more I owe all to your bravery," he said with a bow "and I have that within my power to reward you well. Garrett, see her clear of the field, and then come to me. Derrick, Shawn," he turned to his captains, "canvas the camp. Awaken only those men born in the service of our house, but ward them to lie still as if they yet dreamt, with their swords at the ready. Saddle our horses ere you build up the fires. We will await the signal, but the surprise shall not be ours."

They left to do his bidding, and the brothers clasped hands in parting before David ducked through the tent door and out into a night now active with clandestine activity. Garrett grabbed up his thick leather gauntlets and helmet as Ellen quickly latched the metal clasps of his armor. Garrett smiled wryly, shaking his head. "It's time you took some thought for yourself," he said, taking her hand. "You must not be here when all of this happens." And he led her out into the night, past the wakeful sleepers to the edge of the camp.

"Where is your horse?" he asked.

"Just up there." She pointed to the knoll above them.

"Then go quickly. I know you will not ride far even if I ordered you to, but do not tarry too near." And to her surprise, he pulled her close and held her for just one lingering moment.

"When last you did that, you were saying good-bye," she murmured.

"I do not mean to tell you good-bye," he replied. "Now find your horse and stay out of trouble. I will ride with you again on the morrow." And he pushed her away.

Ellen found the mare standing tied to the sapling with one foot cocked in slumber. She gathered up the reins and took one last look at the fire-lit camp before turning to lead the horse away into the woods. She stood for a time in indecision just at the base of the knoll, unsure of where she was going or how far she would walk. It was from there that she heard the cry of the sentry and the ringing clang of swords on shields from across the glade near at hand. Struggling up astride the mare, she turned the horse's head away from the rising sound of the conflict—the shouting of the soldiers and drumming of hooves—and unwittingly spurred her mount straight into the onrushing band of horsemen under Remmel's command.

The mare reared and turned as the charge bore down upon them. A sword was raised over them and Ellen moved—for once without consideration—ducked under the sword and rolled from the roan's back. The stroke that followed was meant to slay, but struck only a glancing blow as the mare lunged and leaped over her fallen rider, foiling the enemy's attack.

Ellen fell—and fell—and fell . . . It seemed a terribly long time before she felt the ground beneath her, solid and damp and smelling richly of moss and leaf mold. The sounds of the skirmish swam around her in a grey fog. The shouting, the cries of fury and of pain, the ring of sword on shield, the neighing of the horses . . . all became distant and dreamlike until they all faded and silence cloaked her as closely as the darkness; and she slept in a peace deeper than that of weariness.

Then something soft nuzzled her cheek. She felt its warm sweet breath on her neck. It tickled. Struggling upward through a thick heaviness of slow thought and dull pain, Ellen opened her eyes.

HOME AGAIN

The soft warmth of the summer night, alive only with the chirping of crickets and soughing of a light breeze in the branches above, held all in quiet slumber as a thin quarter moon rode high above. No sounds of horses. No noise of battle. As wakefulness slowly returned and conscious thought with it, Ellen pushed herself up from the damp earth and sat dizzily, her hand to her aching head.

"I need a helmet," she grumbled to no one in particular and looked around her quickly at the sound of a horse's snort and impatient stirrings. *What of the battle?* she thought, suddenly recalling the events of the night. She must have been out cold for hours, and now it was all over. It seemed terribly quiet and with a lump of fear rising in her throat she wondered if perhaps they were all dead and she alone remained.

Staggering to her feet, she turned to the horse that had been nuzzling at her back. But it was not the roan mare standing there as she had expected; instead, there stood the black filly, saddled and bridled, a stirrup hanging at the end of a broken leather. Numbly, Ellen reached out a hand to stroke the sleek neck: it was warm and real. The moonlight shone on the trunk of the felled tree nearby, and everything was terribly as it should be—terribly, disconcertingly, all back in place.

Ellen rubbed her hand over her face, wincing as she touched the bruise at her temple. *Maybe—maybe it had all been just a dream*, she thought wearily and, gathering the filly's trailing reins, began walking slowly up through the woods toward the Garrison Keep. Coming out onto the paved lane just outside the entrance gates, Ellen was too tired just then to notice the neatly trimmed hedge, the park-like woods all cleared of brushy undergrowth, the terrace walls in tidy order spanning the gardens, and lawns all tended and clipped and shorn. It was not until she walked into the stable yard that she stopped short and stared in bewildered amazement at the scene the moonlight and a glowing watch lamp over the stable entry revealed.

No sagging roof timbers, no fallen palings and crumbling masonry: all was in order and in perfect repair for all its obvious antiquity. Down through the stable run, Ellen led the mare, gazing at all around her and wondering bemusedly if somehow she were in the wrong place. But there was the filly's stall, her hay and feed already in the manger, the brushes and tack all in place in the tack room, and all impossibly neat and clean in a stable that was more like a showplace than the decrepit artifact Ellen knew it should be.

"Maybe burning it down did us all a world of good," mumbled Ellen as she turned with a shrug and walked the path to the kitchen door. All was dark and quiet within. Ellen flipped on the light with a motion born of habit, looking around carefully as if expecting to find all here changed as well. "Maybe even a surprise party," she chided herself, but she found all exactly as she had left it instead . . . dirty dishes still in the sink.

Dropping the satchel upon the table and laying the cloak over a chair, Ellen stood for a moment in the center of the room, gazing at the normality of all around her; adjusting her mind to it gradually. The clock on the wall chimed one. She had been riding home from the kirk, Ellen remembered, to find the drawing on the table in the Great Hall and read from the books to know what had happened, what had changed or not changed. Now she walked slowly to the library and took down the heavy volume, carrying it to her room, where she dropped it upon the bed and went to pour up a hot bath.

Feeling finally, deliciously, warm and clean, she curled up among the soft blankets and pillows and opened the pages to the Coltstone family history. The portraits winked out at her like old friends in the soft light from the bedside lamp, and she traced her fingers over the familiar features of David, bold and golden and handsome as ever, and Garrett, darker, with strong earnest eye. There was a lady that Ellen did not know, pictured juxtaposed to David on the page. "Beatrice of Huntington," Ellen read and smiled. "Second wife of Lord David, Baron of Coltstone." And with a growing feeling of warmth and pleasure, Ellen began to read of a family she loved well and whose happiness and success gave her only joy.

Leticia had deserted her husband, Ellen read, and—in fleeing to her father's house—had met with a grave accident: caught in the skirmish of some local civil strife and accidentally struck down.

"Accidentally!" smirked Ellen. "Nice accident, David!"

Lord David had remarried a year later to a daughter of the lord of Huntington. She bore him two daughters: Ellenor Marie and Elizabeth Annise. Apparently, both David and Beatrice had lived well and happily together and died peacefully of old age.

Lord Garrett had married Alice in the month and year that Ellen knew. They had four sons, two of whom followed after their father as architects, one becoming a merchant mariner and the eldest, the heir and baron of Coltstone.

"Lord Garrett," the book read, "began his career as an architect early, designing and building first the great Coltstone manor house at Briarwick, before building . . ." (and the book listed five or six other sites built on commission for other nobles and royalty.) "At first funded by Lord David through the family estate, Lord Garrett later acquired greater land holdings through the income from a fleet of merchant ships . . ."

As the words began to blur on the page, Ellen closed her eyes and fell asleep. She dreamed of sailing ships and knights in shining armor and of Edward playing upon the castle green.

It was midmorning when she awoke to the sound of a mower and of clippers at work on the hedge outside her window. Stretching and yawning, she pulled the drapes aside and quickly dropped them back as Darvin walked past the window with two young workmen to whom he was giving direction. Perplexed, Ellen wondered when she had hired gardeners and with whose money. She shrugged as she pulled on her linen shirt and riding skirt and boots and went to fix breakfast.

The day was full of wonders as she explored her world anew. She might have decided that she was trespassing in someone else's home had it not been for the papers still on the table in the Great Hall, the stack of paper bills still on the dresser in her uncle's room, family pictures and books in the study, and the envelope of tax documents still on the table beside her bed. Otherwise, the castle from cellar to attic was in impossibly good order, clean and neat and furnished with the meticulous taste of a museum curator. Ellen surmised that the articles in the Keep were original to the fourteenth century, though who had seen to their preservation and who had supervised the house cleaning she could only guess.

Old Mr. Darvin was some help in solving the mysteries as, later that morning, he paused in his work to visit with her as she walked about the grounds.

"Mornin', miss," he'd called. "I brought your mail up from the post. Left it on the back stoop"

"Thank you," she answered, trying not to look too perplexed.

"Darvin," she asked, "who fixed the roof?"

He looked up to the corner turret, following her gaze. "Didn't know there was aught amiss there . . . ," he muttered. "But if it needs summat, Lord Garrett will see to it."

"Lord Garrett?" she said, surprised by the name.

"Aye, miss," Darvin answered, giving her an odd look. "He's back at the manor house as of yesterday . . ."

Ellen tried to nod knowingly. "Does he, then . . ." She paused, unsure how to ask what she wanted to know. "I mean. A place like this must demand a great deal of maintenance . . ." She gazed at the ivy-grown grey walls, the lead-glass windows in the high casement with heavy wooden shutters sturdy on their iron hinge pins, all in perfect repair. "And these gardens . . ." She glanced around them. "Who?" she began to ask, but Darvin chuckled smugly.

"Oh, that would be the baron, sees to all that. Did old Mr. Sidney not tell ye?"

"No," she said doubtfully. "It must have slipped his mind."

"Well, now. Seems odd to some folk, but when Lord Garrett's father sold the Keep to your great-aunt, it was agreed that the Coltstone family would see to its repairs so long as it remained in your family and was never to be sold to aught other."

"I see," said Ellen, "and the housekeeping?"

"Once a month, miss," Darvin replied, wiping his face with his handkerchief. "Crew from the manor."

"And when will that happen again?"

Darvin squinted one eye in study, counted on his fingers, and then smiled triumphantly. "Friday next," he said, and Ellen nodded. "I'll be working in the orchard tomorrow," he went on, and Ellen smiled to think how she hadn't known that she had an orchard until just now. "Young Grimmel's to help me with the mowing. Peaches about to ripen."

"Grimmel!" said Ellen. "Ebenezer's son?" she guessed.

"Oh no, miss. Ebenezer's his uncle, runs a shop in the village. Jimmy's dad is foreman over the farm east of the river. Their family has been gamekeepers for the Coltstones for generations back."

"Ah," said Ellen thoughtfully, intrigued at how all the pieces now fell into place. Now the only odd piece here seemed to be her. Gamekeepers, gardeners, housekeepers, and a new Lord Garrett, Baron of Coltstone . . . in the manor up on the hill. *That would be nice to see,* thought Ellen as she walked back to the Keep and pulled on ice pack out of the freezer. But not today.

Instead, she pulled out the phone book, thumbed through it, and decided to make one phone call before she took a nap.

"Hello, Coltstone Tours. May I help you?" said the voice on the other end.

"I saw your number in the book," said Ellen. "I wondered, are you operated by the Parks Service?"

"No, ma'am," the voice replied. "The castle is privately owned and only opened for the public three months of the summer while the family travels abroad."

"Oh," said Ellen, and she politely asked for tour hours and information before she hung up.

Still owned by the family, Ellen mused as she lay down and closed her eyes. And they travel abroad. *Wonder if they go to America?* she thought. *That would be an odd twist.*

Over toast and tea the next morning, Ellen watched Darvin and a tall young man that she assumed was Jimmy Grimmel working in an orchard that spread across the grass, which once had been the pasture near the stable and decided that she would saddle the filly and explore. She wanted to see the Coltstone Keep, and though she felt some trepidation in doing so, she wanted to see the manor house on the hill that pictured so grandly in the history text. She was beginning to feel that it might be time to bow out of all of this gracefully, forget the job at Kingston College, and go on home to Texas.

What it would be like, she wondered, *teaching these histories now?* When the students questioned, would she forget and answer, "Well, when I was there . . ." or "What I saw was," or "No, it really wasn't like that at all—the book has it wrong here . . ."? She shook her head in silent amusement. Would she be like old Dr. Abbott of her undergraduate days who trembled and cried when he spoke of the castle at Versailles or like her professor of ancient histories who had claimed to be Julius Caesar reincarnate?

"It was cold . . . We had SOS for breakfast, and I wore a purple T-shirt . . . ," he always said when he lectured about Caesar crossing the Rubicon. Crazy. They would think her crazy. She would have a secret she could never share with anyone and be thought insane. *Better go home,* she told herself as she rode out from the stable, waving at Darvin and young Grimmel as she passed. *Better go home and forget about the whole thing.*

Passing the Coltstone Keep and its verdant grounds, a road wound away toward the river woods, and Ellen followed it, wondering as she did so if she were trespassing or whether her presence here would be welcomed. The road left the trees and skirted the hill below the grassy rise to the manor house that stood in the place where once she had visited a tumble of ruins, and Ellen drew rein and gazed in awe at the scene before her.

"Oh, Garrett," she breathed, "you truly built magnificently!" The square towers rose high with crenelated tops above the steeply peaked slate roofs. The walls between curved artfully with the contour of the hill, and every stone and every facing of every arched Gothic window was chiseled and formed with patterns of angelic detail. The effect was stunningly beautiful.

From the structure high above, Ellen's gaze was drawn to the figures upon the green below the towering walls. A man astride a tall grey stallion was working a hawk—or a falcon (Ellen could tell little about it from her vantage)—while a young boy stood watching nearby. The scene was enchanting, like a window into the past, and Ellen sat her horse and watched for a time. She hoped to pass unnoticed and was just reining the filly to leave, when the stallion whinnied; and to her dismay, the man and the boy looked her way.

She thought still that she ought to leave, but hesitated as the man handed the hawk down to the boy, turned his horse's head, and rode toward her.

He had all the appearance of the baron of the estate as he drew rein near her and bowed slightly in the saddle. "Good morning, miss," he said. "I do not believe we have met."

"No," replied Ellen "We've not. I am Ellen Lancaster, Sidney Lancaster's niece . . ."

"Ah, yes, so I thought you might be." he said "I am Garrett Coltstone—and your neighbor."

Ellen nodded as she looked at him and hoped she was not staring. He had the stature of the Coltstones, but his hair was blond and very curly and closely cut, and his eyes were a striking blue.

"I am sorry to hear of the passing of your uncle," he was saying. "I enjoyed his friendship."

"Did you?" said Ellen.

"I am sad to have missed his funeral. I was away . . . for the month . . . business on the Continent."

"Really," Ellen replied distractedly and wondered if she sounded idiotic as she thought to herself that a month ago, he was really nowhere at all. "You do not look like him," she said without intending to say it out loud.

"What?" he asked, frowning slightly.

"Oh, I'm sorry. It's . . . nothing," she said disconcertedly. *It was starting already*, she thought. *He would think her crazy, and he would be right if she didn't get better at this.*

"Oh," he said smiling. "I misunderstood." It was then that she changed her mind and decided that there was something remarkably familiar about his eyes, not the shape of them exactly, but the look within them that reminded her of his ancestor.

"You have been here before," he said, more statement than question as he pulled off his leather gloves and flicked at a smudge on the sleeve of his white cotton shirt.

"Yes," she said, looking up at the tall castle above them. "But it was different then . . ."

"Different?" he queried, and again, she felt that she had painted herself into a corner. She was going to *have* to get better at this, she told herself.

"Yes, less—complete . . . ," she said with a wry smile. "Perhaps because you were not here yet. You complete the picture quite well."

He lifted one eyebrow amusedly; and Ellen, feeling like a silly schoolgirl, made murmurs that perhaps she should now be going.

"Please," he rejoined, "there is no need to leave so soon. If you would like to see more of the old place, you can ride with me to the stable, tie your horse in the paddock, and I will show you around a bit. I should like to become better acquainted with Sidney Lancaster's niece."

Ellen gazed up at the tall towers and elegant windows then looked back at him. "I think I would like that."

"Then you are welcome," he said, kneeing his horse around beside the filly and guiding her along the road that skirted the hill to an elaborate and immaculate stable as grand and as impressive as ever the mansion itself was. As they rode, they spoke some of the history and architecture of the place, of its builder, and his plans and designs.

Ellen stood in the stable courtyard and gazed at the magnificent garden and park that surrounded them, with a feeling of awe. "If only he could see this now," she said, and this new Garrett only smiled and motioned for her to lead the filly within the stable following his tall grey. She tied her horse in a box stall over a manger of hay, loosening the girth, before she closed the gate. Her companion stood leaning upon the top railing, watching the horse eat as he pulled off his riding gloves.

"Your uncle always told me that you enjoyed riding," he said.

"Uncle Sidney . . . told you about me?" she laughed.

"Yes . . . when I asked. You see"—he gave her a sidelong glance—"since I was a boy of ten, I had always wondered if there was a girl by the name of Ellen Lancaster somewhere in West Texas . . . and if I would one day meet her . . ."

Ellen tensed, watching his face intently, but he continued to watch the black filly and did not look at her.

"Why?" she whispered, feeling goose bumps prickle.

"Well, you see, there is a legend in our family," he said evenly, pulling his gloves between his fingers absently. "A story held secret in closest confidence among a very few of each generation." He paused thoughtfully. "It was written by the first Lord Garrett of Coltstone in the year 1449, and it tells of a young woman who appeared in the woods above the kirk. She was thought a witch, at first, but then proven otherwise, saving the life of the eldest son, exposing the treachery of one within the household, and saving all from the traitorous hands of her hired assassins. This person was thought to have come to them not from a far place but from a far distant time. She knew of the most inexplicable things and told the strangest stories and—in the end—disappeared. It is a very odd tale, written in detail by the hand of Lord Garrett himself and witnessed to by his wife, Alice, his mother, and his brother."

Ellen stood transfixed, hardly daring to breath; but the young man did not look at her, only rubbed his chin thoughtfully as he continued.

"With the writing of it went a command that it be read and known and passed down—along with certain articles—by each generation.

And so it was done, at first, no doubt, out of respect and in honor of the great man who had commanded it. Later, out of tradition and with some amusement at such an outlandish tale. But still, it was read and the tradition kept, until at last, the time of its fruition drew near. It was then read with great curiosity and speculation."

"My father read it to my sister, Lenore, and me, when I was ten. For twenty-four years now, I have watched for events to unfold. Most surprisingly, when I was fourteen, an elderly woman named Eunice Lancaster visited in Briarwick. My father spoke with her at church that Sunday. She expressed great interests in the old Garrison Keep, which was vacant and in some disrepair at that time. She said that she wished to rent it. My father sold it to her instead, much to the surprise of the villagers, on the agreement that it be willed to her nephew, Sidney Lancaster, and sold to none other."

Taking a deep breath, he straightened and turned toward her, leaning casually against the wood palings. "Does this sound like utter madness to you?"

"A divine madness, perhaps," she said, laughing nervously. "But actually, you are making more sense than you can guess."

"Good," he replied with some relief and a knowing smile. "Your uncle used to show me photos of you, in an old album." (Ellen thought of the one she had shown Garrett—her Garrett—and felt a cold shiver run up her spine.)

"I have long felt as though I knew you well," this Garrett was saying, "from those photos and the things he told me about you."

"Not too well, I hope," Ellen replied, and he favored her with a measuring gaze.

"Lord Garrett," he said, "wrote in great detail of the events within his time, but of other things less clearly."

"Such as?"

"Such as . . . when he is told of the possible fate of our family, if his brother should die, and then afterward is told of his own travel through time, at the date of his execution . . . That is all a bit sketchy, clear enough, but lacks the color and life of his other writings, being told third hand as it were . . . I should like to know more of that. Questions—I would like answered . . ."

Ellen nodded. "And I will tell you all of that one day. I would like for you to know of that. But not today. These things are more than legend to me," she said quietly.

“Come, then,” he said amicably, offering his arm. “There are things perhaps you will like to see.” And he led her out of the stable, through its carriage courtyard, and into the wide expanse of park and garden that encompassed the once-barren hillside. Up a brick path that wound pleasantly from shade to sunshine and back again, they were nearing the wide verandas that curved like arched and pillared curtains across the back walls of the house when they entered a tree-shaded cloister, paved circular around a mirror pool.

It seemed an enchanted place, still and quiet and close amid all the space and grandeur roundabout. The waters of the pool were unmoving as if not even the summer breezes were admitted here without sanction, and they reflected with mirror perfection the stone image that admired its clear depth. Ellen blanched, dropping her hand from Garrett’s arm and he watched with concern as she walked forward alone.

The stone image seemed almost alive, so lifelike were its features: a woman, seated upon the curbing of the pool, leaning to look into its depths with her hands upon its brim. Ellen knew her. The dress was the one she’d worn on the night of the feast—her hair braided like a crown. The face . . . Ellen touched the cold stone cheek, and her fingers were shaking. The face was her own. She looked into the pool and saw the two images reflected there: the living and the dead. This was her tomb, she realized. This was her memorial.

Shuddering, she stumbled back, and Garrett was there with an arm to steady here.

“Are you all right?” he asked, concerned.

“Yes,” she replied shakily, pulling herself together.

“I’m sorry. I should have warned you, I suppose.”

“No, it’s OK. Silly of me, really. It shouldn’t bother me so much . . . I’m just a little tired.” She rubbed her forehead and winced.

Noticing the greenish bruise under the stray wispy curls at her temple, he brushed the hair back with his fingers. “What’s this?”

“Oh, I fell off a horse day before yesterday.”

“Fell?”

“Or thrown,” she laughed self-consciously, “or got whacked by a broadsword, if you’d believe that.”

“I would,” he grinned.

“Yes, well, I should never have left my helmet in Texas . . . terrible headache,” she sighed. “And now I really think I had best go home.”

She looked up at him apologetically. “I have seen enough ghosts for today . . . Perhaps you could show me around the place another time—if you wouldn’t mind.”

“It will be my pleasure,” he said with a slight bow. “You might come tomorrow afternoon—have tea with us.”

She nodded gratefully.

“Good,” he said. “Now shall I drive you home?” he asked, again offering his arm.

“Oh no,” she said. “I can manage. The ride will do me good. Give me time to think.”

In the stable courtyard, he gave her a leg up onto the filly and backed away. He seemed all golden in the sunlight, standing there as Ellen thanked him and bid farewell.

“You know,” she said, “you really are much more like him than you appear.”

His look was questioning.

“The Lord Garrett I knew was an honorable man. You seem to me much like him.” She paused for a moment, weighing her thoughts. “I think it is important for you to know that he was true in his love for Alice and their son—always—in two different lifetimes. His heirs need never doubt his loyalty or his faithfulness to her,” she said evenly, and Garrett smiled.

“Thank you,” he said. “I had thought it so, but it is good to hear it said by you.”

With a wave, she turned the filly and trotted her away down the curving road. He watched her retreating figure out of sight before he turned and walked back to the house.

“Who was that, Uncle?” asked the boy of twelve who met him at the door of the veranda.

“An old friend,” he said tousling the boy’s hair. “You’ll meet her tomorrow, I hope.”

A LETTER FROM THE PAST

Ellen's phone rang early the next morning, and Ellen leaned on the counter, listening in amazement as Professor Lowell spoke loudly and excitedly over the connection. The members of his department had received her research notes and reviewed them. He wondered if there were really such documents and where she had found them and he wanted to know if she was certain of their authenticity.

Thinking of the pile of parchment papers on the table in the Great Hall, Ellen grimaced to think of the stack of research she'd left somewhere in a past century, but she was able to assure him anyway of the documents' origin and authenticity.

"We found the parchments in the attic of the Garrison Keep," she said. "They were written by the baron Lord Garrett of Coltstone who lived in the fifteenth century.

"Wonderful! Lovely!" he said, and he would like to drop in one day next week to see them, perform some tests on the ink and paper, perhaps bring them back to Kingston to be placed in the archives . . . And he had some papers for her to sign for the administration and payroll departments.

"For who?" she asked.

"Administration . . . payroll. Typical hiring stuff, you know?"

"No, I did not know."

"But of course!" he shouted over the wire jovially. "That was all decided two days ago. I thought they had sent you notice."

Ellen eyed the stack of mail Darvin had brought in: a week's worth unopened upon the table. It really hadn't seemed important.

"I'll need you down here for staff meetings in mid-August. Term begins September 9."

"Yes, sir," she replied, feeling that things were moving extremely fast for her and everything that had been so difficult was now disturbingly simple.

"Good, then! I will see you next week. Thursday?"

"Yes, that will be fine," she replied. "But, Dr. Lowell, the documents, in all fairness, belong to the Coltstone estate. I do not want them removed from here."

"Oh," he said, somewhat disappointedly. "Well, then, that will be fine. Still, I shall wish to view them, and perhaps you could bring them with you for the staff to view in September?"

It was all agreed and arranged before Ellen hung up the phone.

So that was it, she said to herself as she walked outside to inspect her orchard; she had a job with a good income, a castle (taxes paid and damage repaired), and a good neighbor, it seemed. Now all she needed was a good dog and her horse, and all would be peachy keen. It seemed too simple. Then thinking back over the last month, she decided it really hadn't been simple at all.

She almost decided to wear her Sunday dress to tea at the baron's that afternoon, assuming that she would be meeting his wife, after all, and would want to make a good impression; but then she decided not to and belted on her faithful old brown riding skirt instead. "Just be yourself," she admonished her reflection in mirror. "It's always stood you on good ground before."

At fifteen to four, she drove the old coup up the road to the Coltstone Manor and parked on the verge of the circle drive before its impressive entry. A butler opened the door at her knock, a young boy beaming at her from behind him.

"You must be Ms. Ellen!" he piped up before she or the butler could speak.

"His Lordship is busy at the moment," the butler said as he stepped aside and motioned her in. "But . . .

"But I'm not! And I am to show you the house," the boy broke in excitedly, "until he sends for us."

With a querulous look at the butler, who nodded acquiescence gravely, Ellen put herself in the charge of the bright-eyed diminutive tour guide, who whisked her away exuberantly from room to room, upstairs, and down until every niche of the castle was inspected. They talked a lot about horses, of knights, and of armor and of battles. He was very impressed that she had a sword and knew how to use it.

"Really?" he asked, wide-eyed.

"Really!" She laughed. "But not very well."

"Still, could you show me?"

She was saved the embarrassment by the butler who had found them at last and motioned for them to follow him.

"Great!" said the boy. "I'm hungry." And he offered her his arm importantly as they walked down the long halls, down the spiraling stairs, to a vast library where the windows opened onto a sunlit veranda.

"Ms. Ellen Lancaster, my lord," the butler announced as they entered, and Garrett Coltstone turned with a pleasant smile to greet her as she was led forward on the arm of her beaming escort.

"I am sorry to have been detained," he apologized. "Trust to young Gregory here to lose you among the masonry." He gave the boy's shoulder a tweak and sent him to sit at a table nearby where the china was arranged for tea.

"I trust you have rested well and are some recovered?" he inquired.

"Yes, thank you," she replied.

"Good." He gave a nod to the butler as he led her to the table. "I thought you might wish to look at this while things are being brought in." He said and, pushing several dishes aside, set a very yellowed and brittle manuscript before her.

Scanning the first page quickly, she glanced up to find him leaning back comfortably in his chair, watching her.

"This is it, then?" she asked, fingering the pages carefully. "The story that was written and passed down through your family?"

"The same," he said, "and the original, though I have had copies made. Go ahead, read it . . . out loud if you like. Gregory and I like to hear it."

And so she did, pausing here and there at some point of remembrance and trying her best not to add to or amend things as she read them. This was her story from Garrett's point of view, and that was new and unique to her.

The tea was served, and she set the manuscript aside as a waiting man poured and the dishes were passed. Eyeing the fourth chair yet empty, Ellen asked, "Shall we wait?"

"For what?" asked Garrett, looking up.

"For your wife," she replied matter-of-factly, "if she would like to join us."

Garrett and the boy looked at each other, and the boy laughed as if at some private joke.

"What?" she asked with some consternation.

"Uncle Garrett's not married," laughed the boy mischievously. "Not yet."

"You're not?" she asked, surprised.

"No," he said, joining in the merriment at her expense. "Not yet.'"

"Oh, I'm sorry! I assumed . . . I thought Gregory was your son," she declaimed.

"My sister's oldest," he replied. "Spends most of his summer holiday here if I let him . . . And I hope you are truly not that sorry."

"I have not had time to decide that," she replied with much deprecation. "Do you say grace?" she asked quickly to cover her embarrassment.

"Aye. But not over tea. It's a snack, not a meal."

"Thank you," she said. "I've never been sure of that."

She sipped her tea, munched a sandwich, and read on at their request. The manuscript ended with an account of the battle on the border, which Ellen was glad to know more of, and the vain search to find her. In closing, the author commanded and implored the reading of the legend by each generation and the manuscript to be passed down faithfully. "That when the time is full, all things shall be in place . . ."

"And thou," it read, "of that far generation, if thou shouldn't meet this one, and she be truly returned to you, it be to thy gain and our great loss. Honor her well, and if thou must needs prove her true, ask only where the ancient dagger lies. There also lies my gift and my tribute to her."

Ellen's brow creased in thought as she read the last sentences again silently. She heard Garrett's cup click in his saucer as he watched her, and Gregory leaned forward with anticipation.

"So what does it mean?" Garrett asked when she looked up, laying the manuscript carefully aside.

"Do you know of a jewel necklace?" she asked thoughtfully. "And an emerald-and-ruby tiara?"

"Yes," he answered with a shrug. "My sister keeps them."

Ellen was silent in thought for a moment. Garrett had placed the knife and the jewelry into the secret niche in the cellars. Could it be that he had later removed the jewels and never told another of that hiding place?

"That must be it!" she exclaimed excitedly, to Garrett's surprise. "Do you know the treasury room in the cellar of the Coltstone Keep?"

"Yes, of course," he replied.

"You've seen it?"

"Often."

"And do you know of a stone—removable—with a space behind it?"

He shook his head. "No."

"Of course not," she laughed. "He never mentioned it in his writing, and I wondered why. But of course he would not have anyone knowing of it . . . too much hinged on the things he had secured there." Ellen's eyes sparkled in appreciation. "Uncle," exclaimed Gregory. "Can we go look . . . now?"

"Certainly," he replied, bringing his chair forward with a thump and tossing his napkin onto the table. "If the lady so wishes."

With a nod, Ellen arose, and they walked quickly outside. Ellen tossed the keys to Garrett as she opened the passenger door and Gregory piled into the backseat.

The halls of the Coltstone Keep were quiet as Garrett unlocked the doors and flipped on the light. The last tour had ended over an hour before. Glancing around her as they walked through the terribly familiar halls and passages, Ellen felt gratified to see so little changed and only necessary amenities added to modernize. Down past the kitchen and scullery, Garrett led them, flipping on the recessed electric lighting as they went. Down the long corridor, they passed the dungeon steps and went down into the store room cellar beyond.

Although the food and flour storage bins were empty and the great wine casks untapped, Ellen was glad to see all as it had been on her last visit there and no piles of rotting boards, no dirt, and no decay. "You keep things well," she commented to Garrett's back.

"Only as they should be," he rejoined, turning the massive key in the iron lock on the wooden door of the treasury. It swung easily on its heavy hinges, and Garrett stooped to light a lantern that sat on the floor just inside. Hanging it from a hook in the wall, he looked at her expectantly.

"So where do we look?" he asked at last.

"Three stones over from the arch," Ellen said, touching the stone with her hand. "But it is too heavy for me."

"All right, then," said Garrett, eyeing the close seaming of the stones doubtfully. "If you insist . . ." But he was not disappointed as the stone slid forward easily to reveal the dark opening behind.

As Gregory watched excitedly, Garrett turned to Ellen and motioned silently for her to step forward while he lifted the lantern from its hook and held it high for its light to shine within. There, much as Ellen had expected, was the elongated bundle of the dagger next to the little wooden jewel chest that had once been Lady Eleanor's. Beside these lay a scroll of parchment tied and sealed; and all rested on a large, flat, ornately carved wooden box that was bound in gold bands and latched tightly shut.

Carefully, she removed each item, handed the scroll and jewel case to Gregory—who beamed proudly—and held the heavy wooden box herself as Garrett placed the dagger upon it, rehung the lantern, and stooped to lift the stone back into place.

Then, feeling like children at Christmas or maybe just a bit more like tomb robbers, they blew out the lantern, closed and locked the door behind them, and hurried up into the light above with their treasures in their hands. Without a word, Garrett led them back down the hall and into the room of the scribes, where a rustic chandelier overhead set all the room aglow and the rays of the lowering sun angled through the narrow windows and onto the stone flagging.

Placing the items down in a row upon the scribe's ink-stained table, they gazed at them in silence for a moment, and Ellen felt—for all the world—that the room was alive with those whose faces she could yet see so clearly in her mind's eye.

Carefully handling the long bundle in its wrapping, Garrett peeled back the crumbly leather, and Ellen watched his face as he touched the finely wrought dagger appreciatively.

"It was Garrett's grandfather's," she replied to his inquiring glance. "Garrett stole it off his father's corpse." Gregory's eyes were big as saucers as he looked at the blade upon the table.

"This," said Garrett, picking up the parchment scroll and examining its writing and wax seal, "is meant for you." And he handed it across to Ellen. Reading the label written in Garrett's scripted hand, she sat down in a chair at the table and carefully broke the seal.

The paper was stiff and brittle, and she unrolled it carefully as she read. It was a letter written to her in the month after she had disappeared.

Dearest Lady Ellen, (it read)

After the battle we searched for you among the living, until we found you not, and then we searched among the dead. Having found you with neither, I write this now with grief of heart, knowing that you are lost to us forever.

I can only find hope in the belief that somehow, even as you came to us, you are now returned to that far place in time from whence you came, and that should the strength of my lineage succeed through the centuries and hold true to the command I have given, you will one day read this.

Know, dear Lady, that I hold thy memory in highest honor, as does my Lady Alice, who does never grudge it you, as it is through your bravery and watchful care that we are blessed in our great happiness together.

Some tokens of my esteem I leave to you. As once before I gave them to you, I pray they be yours again, and may the years and the memories of this time be a kindness to you.

Always in Faithful Memory
Lord Garrett, Baron of Coltstone.

Ellen's hand shook ever so slightly as she read the words through once again before leaving the curling parchment upon the table and leaning back thoughtfully in her chair. Gradually, she became aware of Garrett watching her.

"May I keep this?" she asked quietly.

"Of course," he replied. "It is meant for you." And he looked at her in surprise as she pushed the letter across to him.

"You should read it," she said simply. "It is, in some ways, written to you also."

And as he read the letter, she touched the golden inlay of the jewel case lightly with her fingers, her thoughts far away.

"Will you open it?" Garrett asked, drawing her mind back to the present when he had read the letter and laid it aside.

Gregory leaned on the table eagerly. "How can we? I don't see a key."

"Oh, there's a key," replied Ellen. "It is here." And she showed him the small hidden drawer where the silver key still lay. Slipping it behind the pin, she heard the latch click and lifted the lid as Gregory leaned far over to see inside.

On top was a small lumpy something wrapped in the rotted shreds of a red silk cloth. The threads fell away as Ellen lifted it out a set it upon the table: the small bronze horse she had given to Edward.

"The horse?!" cried Gregory, "from the crusader!"

"Yes," smiled Ellen and, pulling the shreds of old cloth out of the box, found a small leather pouch beneath them. Opening the drawstring, she tipped the bag into her palm and out tumbled the emerald ring that Garrett had once placed upon her hand.

"Oh!" she gasped, gazing at its sparkling brightness and held it up for them to see.

"So this is the ring," said Garrett. She handed it to him, and he held it to the light appreciatively as Ellen turned to open the odd, flat wooden box.

"My notes!" she cried excitedly when she had lifted the lid. Indeed, there within, all carefully tied and bound, though stained and darkened by time, was the stack of parchment papers she had written so diligently in that other time.

Laying the ring beside the bronze horse on the table, Garrett studied the papers as Ellen carefully lifted first one and then another from the stack.

"These are the things you wrote?" he asked in amazement.

"Oh yes! And oh, bless the foresight! They could not have appeared at a more opportune time. Professor Lowell will be here next week to study and review the notes Garrett made for me while he was here. Now with these, the collection is complete and sound for research. I can write books for the rest of my career based on these . . ." Her excitement set her face aglow as she leaned over the table, and Garrett smiled.

"You will take the job at Kingston's, then?"

"Yes," she said happily. "With these . . . I cannot think of any reason why I should not.

"Good!" he said "Then we will be neighbors . . . and I shall be glad of that."

"I hope so," said Ellen absently as she looked at the horse and the ring beside the jewel box. The horse's shadow pranced long across the table, "I suppose that you should keep these . . . they really belong to your family," she said.

"No," said Garrett adamantly. "They are gifts to you, and you should have them." And taking her hand in his, he slid the ring onto the ring finger of her left hand.

Choosing to ignore the suggestion of his action, Ellen thanked him; and together, the three of them carried the treasured antiquities out to her car, where Garrett placed them in the backseat with Gregory, before he drove them back to the Coltstone manor.

Before its doors, Garrett and his nephew got out of the car as Ellen walked around to take the driver's seat.

"I hope," he said as he held the door for her, "that you will visit again soon."

Gazing up at him, Ellen sighed and leaned her elbow on the doorframe. "You know, Lord Garrett," she said, "I have fallen in love with the same man—twice—in one month and in two different centuries." She smiled wanly. "My heart is just a little bit tired."

"And I," he said, "have waited twenty-four years to meet you. I can wait a little longer . . . for your heart. I was actually only thinking about a picnic by the river."

Ellen laughed. "You do beat all."

"Yes," he replied. "I should hope so. Would you like to ride with us on the morrow?" he suggested, glancing at the enthusiastic Gregory.

"On the morrow," Ellen murmured. "Tomorrow is Sunday . . ."

"Ah, you're right! Then we shall see you at the church?"

"Yes, of course."

"Good. Then we'll save a place for you in our pew."

The pew Lord Garrett and Gregory chose to save her a place in that Sunday was none other than the one directly under the gaze of one particular statue beside a very old crypt. As she sat beside this golden-haired Lord Garrett and listened to the priest's liturgies and the voice of the organ rising high in the arching columns above the choir, Ellen could not resist a furtive glance at the alcove so near. The dates engraved on the tomb were 1421 through 1493, and the visage of the statue was of a man older than she had known, time worn, with eyes of patience and wisdom.

As the tall young man beside her placed a strong hand on his nephew's knee to still his swinging feet, Ellen smiled. *Oh, Garrett,* she thought, *if you could only see this . . . I wish . . .* But she stopped herself short, almost believing that a flicker of a smile had passed over the stone features. No, she decided, it was best not to wish unwarily . . . not here . . . not so near.

Later, as they walked among the gravestones and paused a moment beside Uncle Sidney's grave, Ellen turned to Garrett and smiled.

"You know, I'm going to take you up on your proposal," she said.

"Proposal?" he asked with a grin.

"Yes, the one about a picnic by the river and . . . whatever else you have to suggest."

A year later, when Professor Lancaster of the Garrison Keep stood before the altar to take solemn vows with Lord Garrett, Baron of Coltstone, all those who witnessed were smiling. Only a few noticed the bouquet of flowers that lay at the feet of the old stone statue in the alcove of the Baron of Coltstone's crypt. And there the rose light from the windows played the mischief, and warmed the stones, and made them seem almost . . . alive.

Wild Mountain Thyme
(A Ballad)
Oh, the summer time has come, and the trees are sweetly blooming,
And the wild mountain thyme grows around the blooming heather.
Will ye go, lassie, go?
And we'll all go together.
To pull wild mountain thyme all around the blooming heather.
Will ye go, lassie, go?

I will build my love a tower down by yon clear crystal fountain.
And I'll fill every bower with the flowers of the mountain.
Will ye go, lassie, go?
And we'll all go together.
To pull wild mountain thyme all around the blooming heather.
Will ye go, lassie, go?

If my true love, she were gone, I would surely find another
To pull wild mountain thyme all around the blooming heather.
Will ye go, lassie, go?
And we'll all go together.
To pull wild mountain thyme all around the blooming heather.
Will ye go, lassie, go?

I would range through the wood, and the deep glens so dreary
And return with the spoils to the arms of my deary,
Will ye go, lassie, go?
And we'll all go together,
To pull wild mountain thyme all around the blooming heather.
Will ye go lassie, go?